BLOOD SAPPHIRE'S REVENGE

DR. BRUCE FARMER

ISBN-13: 979-8-9854343-0-9

Layout by: epigraph
Library of Congress Control Number: 2021925669
Cover Photo: Sheldon Sabbatini
Published in Portland, Oregon
Printed in the United States of America

For those who have borne the trauma of neglect, abuse and violation and struggled to make sense of it all, this book is dedicated to you. May it affirm your life and give meaning to your suffering. You are not alone.

—Dr. Bruce Farmer
Portland, Oregon
January 2022

Solitary trees, if they grow at all, grow strong: and a boy deprived of a father's care often develops, if he escape the perils of youth, an independence and a vigour of thought which may restore in after life the heavy loss of early days.

—Winston Churchill
The River War: An Account of the Reconquest of the Sudan, 1899,
p.21

1

—————

The Yemeni dust burst into a cloud as the black helicopter appeared. The blades hovered as the sniper slung the McMillan TAC .50-caliber rifle over her shoulder. Haddy felt the wind in her face and flipped the bird to pilot Moshe Zur, who laughed and deftly pulled back the stick and swung the silent helicopter into the night. Staff Sergeant Haddy Abrams's spotter, Sergeant Shira Alian, turned to Haddy, asking,

"What'd he say?"

Haddy replied in a low-pitched sultry growl, "Random bullshit about my eyes."

The hardened veterans distributed the ordinance between them: this included 175 pounds of food, water, rifles, ammunition, grenades, and binoculars to name a few, and they set off without a word. Their target? Al Qaeda mastermind Anisur Salam.

The splintered stones gleamed in the moonlight as the soldiers avoided the treacherous ravines heading south. Two and a half hours later, dawn arrived promptly at 5:29 a.m. with a tinge of tangerine orange sun backlighting a dinosaur spine of rock. They slithered on their bellies a quarter mile beneath the ridge to avoid detection. A rock dislodged and skittered into the ravine below, leaving a trail of noisy reverberations. Shira touched Haddy's shoulder.

"What's going on?" she whispered suspiciously.

"Got a lot on my mind," Haddy replied, but said to herself, "This may be my last op."

"Get your head out of your ass, hotshot," said Shira. "Don't fuck this up."

After holding the torn body, her friend's daughter, shattered by the jihadi's mayhem, Haddy steeled herself and countered, "I'll crush Salam like a cockroach," but sighed within, "What would Mom think if she could hear me? What would those tender hands do? Would her tears tear me apart?"

Haddy checked the GPS; 15 32' N, 48 31' E. They had arrived. She took off the ruck and tucked strands of glistening black hair under the camo hat. The sniper wiped the olive-green grease paint from her eye and inched forward on her elbows to peek over the ridge.

Shira did the same and both looked down through hand-held thermal binoculars. Forty-odd huts lay across a valley thirteen hundred yards away. Arranged in two tiers on the opposite ridge, they fronted a dirt track, coming from the south. The road weaved its way through the village like a backwards "S" and disappeared north into the mountains. A lone house lay above the others. "Chief's house," Haddy commented in her no-nonsense voice, "but the wedding is in the second hut as you enter the village. That's where Salam will be the best man. When he enters the backyard, greets the bride and bridegroom, I'll introduce him to his seventy virgins in Paradise. A little luck wouldn't hurt, either."

"Firing two thousand rounds a week? That's not luck," said Shira.

"God, chance, or the devil; I'm here to make sure Anisur and whatever is on the other side have a face to face today," answered Haddy. "What's the range from here to the backyard?"

Shira lightened playfully and said, "Guess." Adding to herself, "I've got to do something to get the prima donna out of her funk."

Haddy sighed and gave her head a shake. "One thousand, three hundred, and thirty-five yards. What's the wager?"

"A fifth of tequila for you and a case of beer for me; same as always," said Shira. "I say thirteen hundred and forty, and so would the King."

"One thousand, three hundred, and forty-five," replied Haddy. "Keep Elvis out of this."

Shira countered, "Okay, bubble ass, you say forty-five? I say fifty."

"Fifty-five is my final," replied Haddy.

Shira looked through the range finder. It read *1,351*. She flashed a perfect set of teeth and said, "Fifty-one. Don't mess with the best."

"We're even," said Haddy and belly-crawled down the steep slope. She set traps with trip wires and alarms one hundred yards out, warning if the enemy looked for them. Silently, with no wasted motion, she returned and secured their blind side.

Shira hung netting over the small shrub to start the hide. She wove a ceiling of twigs and branches over their "nest," until their sniper position became a bump in the arid landscape. Haddy laid out the mat as Shira lifted the McMillan TAC 50-

caliber A1-R2 rifle from its case, remarking, "This is a heavy motherfucker." Built of fiberglass, set to Haddy's exact specifications, with a smaller handgrip and lighter pull on the trigger, the weapon consisted of two parts. Haddy examined the stock and gun barrel, and both were free of dust and grit. Using the hex screws, she fastened on the barrel and tightened them with the torque wrench to a precise 6.64 ft-lb – 7.10 ft-lb. The sniper screwed on the suppressor to dampen the sound. When it was fully assembled, she held a 30-lb, 6.0-ft cannon. Haddy put on the front bipod and slammed home the five-round box magazine. The manufacturers offered the R-2 variant with its built-in hydraulic recoil system, and Haddy chose it.

Built like a cheetah at 5' 9" tall, weighing precisely 119.80 lbs, Haddy got comfortable behind the weapon and thought, "Another night stretched out with Ori Daniels would have been very nice. What a fucking animal."

The morning Muslim call to prayer began and cut short Haddy's musings. She placed her eye to the telescopic sight. The hypnotic singsong squawked like a crow from the distant loudspeakers, and the holy words floated upwards on drafts of warm air. Haddy growled, "That is the worst fucking sound in the world."

Shira lowered her voice and sang, "You ain't nothing but a hound dog, been snooping 'round the door ..."

Haddy rolled her eyes and said, "What's with you and the American South?"

Shira sighed, "Rhythm and pain, sweetie, rhythm and pain."

"That'd be a sight, getting the Iman hooting and hollering like Elvis," said Haddy sarcastically.

Shira laughed softly and replied, "Shib needs some dancing. Anyway, we're five and half hours away from the big moment. It would help."

THE SUN ROSE SILENTLY on oiled rails. By 10 a.m., Haddy had finished the first of her regulation six liters of water. A fly buzzed past, and buzzards circled above in lazy circles. She flicked her tongue through the gap in her front teeth and commented, "Noontime temperature will climb to one hundred Fahrenheit," and paused. "Shira, how many missions have we been on?"

"After six years?" replied Shira. "I don't know, like fifteen per year? Why?"

"Just thinking," said Haddy. Two burka-clad women had thrown garbage into the road. Through the telescopic sight, Haddy counted the rings on each finger and said, "Tell me about Zohn Chait."

"You want to get jealous?" said Shira. "You know that black bodycon dress?"

"Slinky twist with the front cut out, six-inch hem?" replied Haddy.

"I put on deep purple lipstick, black eyeliner, and the yellow gold necklace," said Shira. "I went up to the Royal Beach lounge and sipped on a gin and tonic. Mr. Zohn Chait, big millionaire and all and me, made eye contact. He sauntered over and zeroed in on my ..."

"Boobs," deadpanned Haddy.

"Partner, if you got 'em, use 'em. We went to his mansion," and pursing her lips, Shira slid her tongue in and out and said, "I had him howling like a drunken wolf. I'd have you over, but your mojo is ice cold. I'm concerned."

Haddy said sarcastically, "Life is good, don't you know?" "Life has been good," she assured herself, as the joy of learning Jeet Kune Do as a six-year-old and then punching bully Joel Lowenstein in the face came to mind.

Shira pressed, "I saw Nietzsche's *Thus Spake Zarathustra* on the kitchen counter. That's a fucking vortex."

Haddy's tone sharpened. "*The madman jumped into their midst and pierced them with his eyes. 'Whither is God?' he cried; 'I will tell you. We have killed him—you and I.'* Partner, I fucking killed God."

Shira took a deep breath and said, "It's a metaphor. You can't kill God," but to herself she thought, "Will she never let up? Haddy swills this philosophy crap like cheap booze."

"I had a God moment after my Bat Mitzvah," said Haddy, "a vision and everything, but after my rape, I killed him."

"Partner, you dress this up in fancy talk, but it's just bad-mouth depression. You have dark circles under those big black eyes, you're up all hours of the night and you've been a royal pain in the ass. Go see a shrink. Get drunk and under the sheets with Chief Sergeant Ori Daniels, whatever works," declared Shira.

"It's more than that and you know it," said Haddy. "It's Nietzsche and Kierkegaard and Camus rolled up in one."

"Camus's coffee cup?" replied Shira.

"Yeah," said Haddy. "You either want to drink your coffee or kill yourself. I'm tired of the brew," and Haddy's letter in her back pocket confirmed it. She had wrestled with suicide from childhood, and as the years rushed by, Haddy couldn't let go of the question, "Who was I before I was broken? Why am I this way? The rape ... Oh fuck that, it's in the past, but my birthday is twenty-six days from now, when Father was murdered. I will *not* face that mind-numbing pain *one* more time. In eight days, I have two weeks' leave. I will commit seppuku on my own time and get this meaningless hell over with." To her partner, Haddy said, "But hey, why go to a doc when I got you?" Then she swung her scope up the hill. "Range the chief's house for me."

Shira checked the laser finder. "Two thousand, six hundred, and sixty-seven yards, a bit over a mile and half. If

you made that, it'd be an Israel Defense Force record."
Suddenly the soldiers saw two three-man patrols exit the
chief's back door.

Haddy chewed on her lip and sighed, "Dammit, things were
going so well."

"With Salam coming? I'm surprised there aren't more."

Haddy opened her communication link with Army Military
Intelligence. "You see this?" The drone floated serenely above
at twelve miles. Its cameras could zoom in and read the print
on a milk carton.

The "secret squirrel," buried beneath bunkers in Tel Aviv,
examined the monitor and replied, "Roger that."

By 11:30 a.m., the heat boiled up in waves from below. Shira
looked at the vultures in the brassy sky. "Those birds give me
the creeps, but I see something worse."

Haddy kept her eyes glued to the village. "What now?"

"Clouds."

"That wasn't in the forecast." A fly droned, and a scorpion
scampered across the front of their sniper nest as Haddy pulled
out her Meals Ready to Eat, or MRE.

Shira sang Mahalia Jackson softly,

"Precious Lord, take my hand

Lead me on, let me stand

I'm tired, I'm weak, I'm lone

Through the storm, through the night ..."

"That's a contradiction," remarked Haddy. "You bust my
butt because I talk truth, and here you are singing about God
and giving Zohn Chait a blow job."

"Back off, nihilist," said Shira. "I was a sinner Druze, now
I'm a sinner Christian. And God loves me."

"Fuck you," said Haddy, as she opened two sealed packages
of couscous and a chicken potato casserole and ate hungrily.
"Like clockwork, I eat and gotta poo," said Haddy, and loosened
her belt, rolled on her side, and pulled down her pants. She

had a Winnie-the-Pooh tattoo on her right butt cheek and knew what was coming. She affixed the bag.

Shira deadpanned, "You got Pooh on your butt."

"Don't you ever get tired of that? Did Zohn see *your* tattoo?"

"I made sure of it," said Shira.

At 11:45 a.m., Haddy keyed her comm link. "Range to target is one thousand, three hundred, and fifty-one yards, winds southerly at five miles per hour, and patrols are six hundred yards out."

"Roger that," came back the reply. "Proceed."

"Copy that," said Haddy.

Shira gnawed on the inside of her mouth. It wasn't the haji patrols or clouds or wind that worried her, but Haddy's confession of the coffee cup. She said, "Promise me you'll talk with a shrink or a rabbi about your darkness and that existentialist shit."

"Shira," said Haddy, "we have a fight between two heavyweight champions. In one corner, Nietzsche. You 'kill' God through *dead* faith, embrace the Will to Power, and become the Ubermensch. Across the ring broods the lonely Dane, Kierkegaard. You leap into the Almighty's hands from a plane without a parachute and hope he catches you. It's one or the other. I'm betting on Nietzsche. If I'm God, I can kill myself. No problem, checkmate." Shira said nothing but thought, "I don't want you to die. Can't you get that? It would kill me and your family. Dammit, Haddy, there are times when I feel terrible and want to off myself, but that would be a *big* sin." Haddy continued, "Fuck all the philosophy, something's not right down there. We've got a big party with four card tables and three women. Where's the stage, food, and drink?" Haddy swung the scope south and continued, "We'll know soon. I see dust."

A small caravan of SUVs snaked towards the tiny village of Shib. In minutes, three black Suburbans hit the brakes in front of the second hut. Four men with checkerboard kaffiyehs stepped out with Kalashnikovs, automatic weapons. Two faced the open desert while the others entered the house. They soon reappeared, and an old man followed, who talked with a passenger in the second car. Suddenly, he opened the door, and Anisur Salam dashed inside the house. As if on cue, villagers left their homes with gifts and food and children in tow. A stage was thrown together in the backyard with wooden pallets. More card tables, banners, delicacies, and wine were set up along with a band.

"There's your party," said Shira. "We'll have our moment when he steps out back."

Haddy's muscles tightened like a cobra ready to strike.

The wedding commenced, but Salam stayed inside. Haddy muttered, "Come on, you motherfucker. Show yourself." An imam appeared and vows were exchanged. The bride and bridegroom danced, and the terrorist celebrated from inside the open door. The next moment, he confounded the soldiers when he came out front and leaped into the second SUV.

"Fucking A," muttered Haddy.

"Wait," said Shira, "he's not turning around." In a cloud of dust, the caravan shot forward, sped through the village, and slid to a stop at the chief's house.

"Luck," declared Haddy and adjusted the rifle's telescopic reticle while inwardly rejoicing, *Thank you, God. Thank you, thank you, thank you.* She noted the 2-inch Picatinny rail allowed for placement of a precision-guided firearm system. The computer measured the speed of downfield crosswinds among thirty other variables and acquired the target, calculated necessary corrections, and guaranteed a dead shot. She lined up the sights on the chieftain's back door. "What's the distance?" she asked eagerly.

"Two thousand, six hundred, and sixty-four yards," replied Shira.

Salam entered the backyard, encircled by a wall, but the

soldiers saw inside from their vantage point. A green-and-red-checkered tablecloth lay over a single table with two chairs. A carafe with water and glasses were present, along with plates of appetizers. A servant appeared with small cups of coffee. Rather than take a seat, Salam stood and sipped his drink, ever wary and scanning the hills.

Command said, "Suggest standing down. You're beyond range." But Haddy wasn't listening. The firing system had locked on to the terrorist.

"Shooter up," said Haddy.

Shira replied calmly, "I didn't hear them either. Spotter up! Target at twelve o'clock."

Salam stood tall. Haddy examined the chest, which measured 36 inches high by 18 inches wide, but from 2,664 yards the bullet would inscribe an arc like a basketball lobbed from the opposite hoop. As it came down on the net, Salam's chest would shrink to an 18- by 18-inch square. Haddy took a deep breath and exhaled slowly, took another and exhaled slower through pursed lips. She became deadly quiet. Haddy had trained her heart to slow down to fifty beats per minute. She felt each pulse in her fingertips. No movement. No tremor. *Ice.* Haddy let the crosshairs hover like seagulls over Salam's chest. His white ankle-length *thawab* shone bright in the sun.

"Send it!" came Shira's command.

Haddy's tummy melted into the earth. It was her ground zero, and nothing could disturb her. She tightened her grip like squeezing a baseball, to apply equal pressure to the rifle and trigger action and prevent a microscopic jerk. She watched Salam eat and laugh, knowing he knew nothing of the silent judge, jury, and executioner hidden under a rock on a ridge so far, far away.

"*Ka-boom!*" The AAA Cyclops suppressor reduced the blast from an earsplitting 182 to 151 decibels, yet still louder than a jackhammer's paltry 100 decibels. A dust cloud blew up in front of the hide, and bugs, beetles, and lizards scattered. Sniper and spotter counted the seconds and saw a puff nick the wall above and behind the terrorist. The round fell harmlessly to the ground.

"Dammit to hell," said Haddy, but made a split-second decision. "Shira, turn off the firearm control and switch to manual override."

Shira shook her head slowly. "You sure, Wonder Woman?"

"Do it."

Shira inhaled and rattled off the data quickly, "Range two-six-six-four yards, wind five miles per hour, direction south by southwest, our present elevation four-nine-nine-zero feet, line of sight angle twelve-point-six-seven degrees, temp one-o-five Fahrenheit. Bullet will drop two hundred and thirteen feet. Wind and spin will push it south twenty-three feet. Flight time four-point-two-three seconds. We're close to the equator firing east to west, so scratch the Coriolis effect of Earth's rotation. Not to rush, but the patrols heard the shot."

In the distance, shouts erupted, and the jihadis instinctively ran towards the ridge. "I've got time," Haddy said to herself and tightened her jaw, sniffed the air, and glanced at the clouds. The wind would change direction three times during the bullet's flight. She checked the sheets fluttering on the clotheslines strung across the second hut's roof. She observed the tinfoil ribbons, which flickered on the hut on the second row, above and behind the second house. Finally, she noted the heat waves boiling up from the corrugated metal roofs near the chief's mansion. Haddy adjusted the scope and went inward. As she exhaled, she imagined her breath flowing out and filling the valley. Her soul substance surrounded Anisur Salam and wrapped its lethal fingers around his heart. Haddy saw herself riding the 2.5-inch Hornady copper-jacketed bullet as it galloped across the sky like a silver-winged thoroughbred, straight into his left ventricle.

"Shooter up," she said.

"Send it," replied Shira.

Haddy squeezed the trigger. The round exploded from the barrel with another *"Kaboom,"* and the soldiers counted, "One thousand one, one thousand two, one thousand three, one thousand four ..." Haddy watched Anisur Salam stop eating, sensing something amiss. He looked at the circling vultures. Haddy said to herself, "Don't move, you motherfucker. Feel the force of fifteen-hundred-foot pounds of energy slam into your fucking heart."

Salam's mouth dropped open, his hands flew up, and his knees buckled in the perfect synchrony of sudden death. The white *thawab* blossomed red. The force lifted him off his feet and blew him back into the wall like a fastball.

"I cannot fucking believe it!" said a shocked Shira.

Haddy closed her eyes, stirred by the intense arousal of battle. Her breath paused and she clenched in orgasm.

The military intelligence officer from Command said, "Congratulations, Staff Sergeant; that's the longest kill in IDF history. Be advised, six fighters are approaching."

"Copy that. Call Zur," said Haddy and examined the chief's backyard through the telescopic sights. Bodyguards crouched with binoculars fervently searched the hills. They shot their weapons to alert the patrols to the catastrophe. The jihadis below began firing up the ridge, still uncertain as to the exact location of the sniper nest. The chief ran inside, as the bodyguards gathered other fighters and jumped into the gleaming Suburbans. The engines roared to life.

"I'll take the hajis," said Shira. Haddy turned on the firearm computer. She put her crosshairs on the first SUV racing through the village. As it came into the open, she locked on the driver and squeezed the trigger. His head exploded, and the car slammed into a hut. The second Suburban shot past the first and drove towards the ridge. Haddy took a bead on the man behind the wheel and fired. The car rolled to a stop on the open plain.

Six enemies clambered up the ridge, having zeroed in on the sniper nest. Their rounds zipped and zinged and ricocheted off rocks surrounding the hide. Shira took aim with her Tavor 7 assault weapon and killed two in quick succession. The other fighters scrambled behind boulders. The third SUV drove across the open valley, bouncing up and over mounds and trenches. Haddy fired into its hood. The car veered off, and she put a round into the front tire. The car stopped. Haddy aimed and squeezed off the shot with deadly effect. A sudden whine got the soldier's attention.

"*Incoming!*" Shira shouted. The mortar shell exploded twenty-five yards to their two o'clock. Showers of rock, earth, and debris fell upon the nest like hail.

"The chief has a mortar," said Haddy and radioed Command. Calmly, she stated, "We're heading to the rendezvous site."

Israeli Command replied instantly, "Roger that. Zur's on the way."

"Copy that," said Haddy.

"A jihadi has a phone," said Shira. "Calling in strikes." The telltale high-pitched whine appeared from above, and both soldiers shouted simultaneously, "*Incoming!*" and rolled into fetal positions. The round slammed fifteen yards to their ten o'clock. The blast stunned them. Bits of schist and slate rained down from the air. Shira grabbed her partner and sprinted, as a third mortar round found their nest. The blast shot a clod of earth into Shira's back. She fell and Haddy wrenched her to her feet. The dust cleared, and the jihadis entered the one-hundred-yard perimeter. Grenades exploded and patrols lay dead. The battle buddies didn't stop to watch, but dashed along the top of the ridge to their escape route, a zigzagging goat path down into the steep ravine. The remaining enemy loosed his

AK-47 at the fleeing soldiers. Just as Haddy and Shira ran down the path, the high-pitched whine of a mortar whistled over their heads and hit the tiny trail. The ridge disappeared into a landslide of tumbling rock, dust, and smoke.

Haddy shouted to Shira, "Cover me!" She turned and raced back up the ridge in a crouch, while Shira fired her assault weapon. Haddy pulled the pin on the M26 Fragmentation grenade and tossed it over. When the dust cleared, they found him dead. Haddy keyed Command and said, "Our southeast route's gone. We'll have to meet Zur in the valley."

Warrant officer Zur spoke through the static with rough-hewn nerve, "How long before you reach it?"

"Five minutes," said Haddy. "And there's a storm coming." The soldiers looked up and saw dark clouds. The ridge they must descend fell away sharply. They would run down the treacherous slope, strewn with rock and bramble and knurly shrub. Like downhill slalom racers bouncing from gate to gate, the soldiers dove forward, their boots grabbing the dirt like icy snow. They leapt back and forth, dodging obstacles, aware the fighters of Shib awaited them below. Haddy stopped and pulled out her binoculars, her breaths coming in ragged gasps; three pickups full of the enemy had joined the fray. "What's our ammo like?"

"Hundred rounds," said Shira.

"Make each shot count."

The terrain was flat, marked with small trenches and mounds etched from erosion. It extended a thousand yards before climbing to Shib. A few sparse bushes dotted the area, but no boulders of any size were present. They were desperately exposed, but Shira ran forward, lay in a small trench, and fired at the approaching throng. Haddy sought cover and fired with cold precision.

The villagers fanned out and used ditches for concealment. They came at a steady pace, and Haddy saw a .50-caliber machine gun in the back of a pickup truck bouncing towards them. The truck advanced, turned, and the combatant unloaded a torrent of rounds into their position, shredding their trench in pieces and filling the air with sizzling lead hornets. The battle below seemed to unleash the rain-laden clouds above, and the water fell hard.

Haddy sensed the end coming. Their ammo was low, they were soaked to the skin, and the jihadis pressed forward. The soldiers heard the terrible whine of another incoming mortar. It exploded ten yards from their position, thumped the earth, and covered their bodies with flying debris. Haddy shouted, "Where's that fucking Zur!?"

Six spinning blades appeared from the steep ridge behind them. The Boeing AH-6 Little Bird, nicknamed the "Killer Egg", dove towards them like a falcon from the skies. At the last second, the blades leveled, and the Little Bird screamed past the soldiers. Haddy watched as Moshe Zur triggered the side-mounted miniguns. The six-barreled rotary guns fired six-thousand rounds per minute. They darkened the air with lead, decimated the enemy, and pulverized the .50-caliber gun. Zur's Killer Egg approached Shib and unleashed one of four AGM-114 Hellfire missiles at the chief's house, which blew up in flames and dust. The attack helicopter soared up, wheeled, and came back into the valley for a second run, unleashing four-teen Hydra 70 rockets. It came to a sudden halt next to the soldiers. The sisters dove in the open side hatch. Shouting over the storm and engine noise, Zur yelled, "Buckle up!" and the Killer Egg shot skyward like a missile climbing at an impossible rate of 32 feet per second.

Out the bay door, Haddy caught a trail of wispy white smoke from the village. "Stinger!" she shouted. Zur climbed up the ridge, as the Raytheon Systems FIM-92 Stinger sought the helicopter's turbo shaft power plant. Flying at a terrifying 2,460 feet per second, it delivered a 6.6-lb high-explosive fragmentation warhead into the engine. Zur had climbed five hundred yards above the ridge, when he tilted the Little Bird sideways and plunged straight into the canyon below. The Stinger missed the helicopter by a few inches and flew up, but the heat seeker curved around and attacked. Zur put the helicopter in a spiral twist. Haddy's face tightened in determination, as the river rock in the narrow canyon got bigger.

Shira hollered, *"Jesus! Save us."* At the last second, Zur pulled up, and the helicopter's skids scraped the rocks on the dry riverbed. The missile zoomed past and exploded on the canyon floor.

Haddy shouted, "Luck, God, devil or fate, I don't fucking care, but what a rush!"

2

Day 1
The "Fortress," Hidden in the Caucasus Mountains, Five
Miles North of Dombay, Russia
Monday, September 18
Thirteen-hundred hours

The man known as "X" closed his leaden lids and wondered if he was blessed or cursed? He reclined in a dark Italian leather chair on a raised dais of beaten gold. Alternately lost between Bella Bartok's eerie Solo for Violin #117 and his dead sister Rahil's predawn appearance, he sat still. "I am a genius. A prophet cursed with photographic recall. I remember each triumph, struggle, and treachery. Every detail, smile, and deception, every fear and failure lying on the surface, like frail jellyfish washed ashore. I am the richest oligarch in Ukraine, yet to what end? What does it amount to, as long as Rahil floats like a specter above her Kiev Baikove gravestone uttering vengeful rants and raves?"

Eyes bleary from her tortuous cries, X glanced at the tarot cards arranged on the elegant Louis XIV end table. His deep-set amethyst eyes fixed on the Judgement card, where the archangel blew his trumpet from heaven and a man, woman, and child rose from graves. After Rahil had left, X reshuffled the deck and picked the Judgement card again. He wiped the perspiration from his brow and turned to his African gray parrot, Kitten, and asked rhetorically, "What say you, Kitten?"

"FUCKKKK! Let's go on the merry-go-round," it said clearly.

"Exactly," replied the oligarch. The parrot had an endless bevy of intelligent, often lewd one-liners: "Nice pussy, pussy, pussy," "She's got big tits," "I want a piece of that," etc., etc. The all-black English mastiff, Smert, barked for attention. Atop a French antique end table sat an open skull dipped in gold and a humidor. Master Trang had done an exquisite job in capturing the scream of the victim before the blade fell. The mouth and teeth were caught in wide openmouthed terror. The skull overflowed with precisely cut 2-inch squares of Kobe beef. X pulled up the sleeve of his silver sharkskin jacket and tossed his pet a tasty morsel. Smert swallowed it whole. X peered over his aquiline nose and took another. He examined the jaw and thought of the days past when he laughed and sang in the choir as a boy and opened his mouth just as wide.

X put the tarot cards and a rare first edition Monopoly game away. He opened the humidor and peeked inside. Seeing nothing suspicious, he picked a hand-rolled Cuban, licked it carefully, and rolled it around his mouth. X lit the stick with a wooden match, aware of the precise temperature and hydro-carbon mix of the fire, not like those butane imitations. He tasted the excellent smoke and intoned, "Blessed are the hungry, they will be filled," in a low-pitched trill. X tucked his yellow silk tie inside his shirt and kissed the mastiff's massive snout. "Smert, you are a good doggie," and he nibbled on the dog's lip, continuing, "You like that, don't you?" Kitten waddled over to Smert, perched on the mastiff's head, and announced, "FUCKKKK! I want a piece of that." X puffed deeply from the cigar to settle his nerves. He glanced at the 60-inch plasma screen to his right and with photographic recall captured the stock market data from Hong Kong. X observed the large mask of the goddess Kali, hanging next to the screen. "In a short time, I'll call upon you," he said to the goddess of death.

The newly remodeled Palace Room, occupying the upper story of a twelfth-century monastery, had a new floor of gold-inlaid walnut parquet, polished to a dazzling shine. It glittered as dozens of candles flickered, sending and reflecting their light from gilt-edged mirrors. In the near corner stood a small art studio, a table with brushes and paints. His latest work, a miniature self-portrait inspired by sixteenth-century Dutch masters, lay drying.

Using his cane, X stepped down slowly. He cursed the effects of age, which bedeviled his joints. Sixty-five years earlier, he won gold in epee fencing in Paris, and boxed, and test-flew fighter jets. X limped to his rare orchids, next to the paints and brushes, and spritzed a light mist on their tendrils. "Grow, my little lovelies. So tender. Grow," he said sweetly.

As he headed for the French doors leading to the garden terrace, the billionaire paused in front of the roaring fireplace. He beheld his newest acquisition, the priceless *Last Judgment* by Fra Angelico. The Renaissance master had painted a monstrous black demon gobbling up terrified sinners as they plunged into hell. Straightening his tie, he said, "Rahil, my darling sister, you died so young from that hideous leukemia. Now you rise in the night with revelations. Do not fear, I will do your bidding." He crossed himself in Orthodox fashion. With index, middle finger, and thumb together, X touched his fore-head, his chest, and then his right shoulder, finishing with the left. For good measure, he quoted Eumenides in the original

Greek, "*Hear the hymn of hell, O'er the victim sounding, —Chant of frenzy, chant of ill, Sense and will confounding! Round the soul entwining. Without lute or lyre—Soul in madness pining, Wasting as with fire!*"

X continued to the French doors fronting the garden terrace. He tapped his cane on a hidden door guarded by a pair of floor lamps, fashioned by Trang, their shades from traitors' skins. The door gave access to his live-in private secretary, Miss Fusako Kitashirakawa.

Fierce and strong, armed with emerald-green eyes, Fusako had begun a Kyokushin kata an hour earlier. At first, each movement proceeded at a deliberate leisurely pace, but soon increased in speed, until her steps and wings blurred like racing light. Drenched in sweat, the tattooed woman showered, not in steamy water, but glacial mountain runoff. After her father died in yakuza warfare, Fusako remained the sole blood relation of her grandfather, Gorou Kitashirakawa. He was her *kumicho* and the aging giant of the Yamaguchi-gumi, the largest yakuza clan in Japan. Should Gorou offer her the sacred rice wine sake, Fusako would ascend to the top of power. She would be *oyabun*, the family head and *kumicho*, the ruler in the rigidly all-male hierarchical organization. Gorou had said, "My daughter, for such you are, I received a call from an insider to X. A rare opportunity presents itself. Though it will pain you, go and submit to this chieftain and learn all you can about his music boxes."

Fusako wrapped herself in a translucent kimono. The garment revealed her skin, covered by a dense blend of intricate, multicolored tattoos, the handiwork of Huriiyoshi III, Japan's most famous tattooist. Designs encircled her ankles and enveloped her body, save for her hands and wrists, neck, and face. The artwork took a year. Patiently, the master craftsman used the electric needle and created a masterpiece of golden koi, bursting suns, cobras, lizards, and dragons. They entwined each other like naked lovers. A cobra rose from her pelvis in a coil and stared out, tongue flicking and ready to strike, between pendulous breasts.

Fusako heard the tap, opened the door, and bowed slightly. She stood even to the tall and stately figure of X. His combed silver-gray hair, suit, and tie highlighted a handsome and regal presence. His ever-restless eyes, which darted about like swallows seeking nests, were disconcerting. Fusako helped X don his leopard coat and opened the glassed doors to a garden of flowing fountains, rare plants, and raised vegetable beds. Two and a half miles distant lay Mt. Dombay-Ulgen, where skiers and snowboarders spent their days and climbers braved the soaring Mt. Mussa-Achitara.

The September wind struck them like a bracing tonic. Fusako dutifully checked the fountain, a replica of Napoleon's Josephine in Baden-Baden, the limestone walls, and the portholes for hidden electronic bugs and announced, "All clear."

X ambled his way along the wall and surveyed the surrounding dense forest and commented, "The mine fields are finished?"

"The ridge from the Teberda river is secure," said Fusako.

The oligarch continued, "And the cones?"

Fusako pointed at the trees where wicker baskets overflowed with pinecones and said, "The forest is clean."

"Cameras?" he asked.

"Spread throughout the trees," replied Fusako.

X peered through a telescope at the tiny village of Dombay, five miles south of the castle, and said, "Little ants running back and forth. And the vegetables?" Fusako gave him a trowel, and X dug for insects disguised as electronic listening devices. He found a shiny beetle. Fusako plucked off the wings and placed the remains in his hand. X quoted Psalm 23, verse 4, "'Though I walk through the valley of death I will fear no evil,' but my enemies will fear, for I have determined to lay waste to Jerusalem. Women will be raped, people will starve, and I will see them eat their young." After more digging, they found eleven insects blown in from distant lands by wind. X spread out his hands and intoned, "I will follow my fellow Jew, Lazar Kaganovich, the mass murderer of my countrymen under Stalin, and unleash anarchy on the earth."

Fusako replied, "Should I call Vladimir P.?"

"Harvest the kale and the winter cabbage first," said X.

"He liked your tip on the RussOil-European oil merger," commented Fusako.

X waved her off and said, "He always likes my tips. What about Anisur Salam? He's coming today?"

Fusako replied, "Everything is ready."

"His blessing cements our heroin and sex-slave trading routes through the Gulf of Oman. We netted $110,821,634.08 last year, but will double that with Anisur Salam. Did you send money to the Kiev Orphanage Home yesterday?" Fusako nodded. "Screen the girls," continued X. "Some deserve college education and positions in Eastern Machine Systems." Fusako led X back to his chair inside. He turned and addressed her. "You've been here a week. Are you happy? Do you like your room? Is the food to your taste? Are you sleeping well?"

She replied, "I'm content."

X answered, "Should I bring some women here, or do you want to go out? Karpov will fly you to Odessa."

"Appreciated," she said.

"You're welcome. I had a mother once. She took me to the park and pushed me on the swings. I thought I could fly," said X.

Fusako's cell phone buzzed. She announced, "Ivan Juric, the Enforcer."

"A brutal Croatian dog," replied X. "I found him, but my brother Semion, the 'Rat,' made him ours." X let the cigar smoke curl around his face. "I both love and loathe his psychopathy. Put him on speaker."

"X," came the nicotine-stained voice. "Major Lebed stole the plutonium from the Plutonium Palace in Mayak, Russia and is en route over Kazakhstan. I'm meeting him at the Army Munitions Group airport."

"Excellent, my son. You've been gone far too long. How's my Sakharov syndicate?"

"I have a trophy for Master Trang," said Ivan.

"Come to the Fortress," replied X. "Meet Fusako and congratulate your sister Jaca on finding her. Anisur Salam is arriving today to finalize our business agreement."

"The other reason I called," said Ivan. "Salam is attending a wedding in Yemen. He'll arrive tomorrow." The line disconnected.

X's thorny eyebrows drew together. "I don't like it."

Fusako switched subjects. "We caught a traitor yesterday."

The oligarch stared at Angelico's *Last Judgment*. "The intruder's below? Do you want to watch?" Fusako nodded. X took the Kali mask and descended to the dungeon. On the steps, he paused. "What a burden to do what must be done, but I must show mercy." Fusako placed her eye on the scanner. The locks on the steel door clicked open. The pair entered an autopsy suite. "I designed it for the master," continued X. "With pale-green ceramic tile, stainless-steel table, and new equipment. Nothing can be done for the stench of decaying flesh and formaldehyde except a perfumed scarf. Trang also requested a dermatome used by plastic surgeons for skin grafting."

A naked man whose wrists were shackled hung from a hook in the ceiling. His ankles were tied to an iron ring on the floor. His mouth was gagged. Fusako watched him writhe, as Trang entered. He hummed a garbled tune and approached the kimono-clad beauty to admire her tattoos. "Enemies cut out his tongue before I rescued him," X explained.

Trang, a short, seemingly frail, wispy-haired man, turned on the hose, climbed up a step ladder, and washed the victim's skin. He shaved the trespasser carefully, then slathered a slurry of Dead Sea mud, filled with organic salts, over the body and left.

Suddenly, X unbuttoned his shirt and bared his chest. He showed Fusako an intricate red, black, and gold tattoo in the shape of a skull from his neck to his rib cage. "Someday, Trang will fashion a lamp, like those by your door, from this," he said, and touched Fusako's cobra and quoted Exodus 21 verses 23–25 in Hebrew, then English, "'And if any mischief follow, then thou shalt give life for life, eye for eye, tooth for tooth, hand for hand, foot for foot, burning for burning, wound for wound, stripe for stripe.'" X turned to Fusako and said. "Do you like the taste of human flesh?"

"No," said Fusako, stunned.

"Trang saves me the best parts. I share them with Smert."

Ten minutes elapsed. Trang reentered and switched on the hose, adjusted the temperature, and sponged off the trespasser. He turned on the dermatome and placed the whirring blades near his ear. He applied a few drops of sewing oil to the slicing razors, and the machine quieted. The master began, oblivious to the incoherent cries of the traitor.

X put on the Kali mask and in a high, shrill voice quoted Leviticus 3:3: "'And he shall present of the sacrifice of peace-offerings an offering made by fire unto the LORD.'" He made the sign of the cross and asked Fusako, "Do you play Monopoly? It's my only vice. I have every edition beginning with the Landlord's Game in 1903. An attempt to show the evils of the monopolists and tax theory. I think you'll enjoy it. Master Trang does."

The pair returned to the Palace Room, and Fusako begged off an introduction to the board game. The heir apparent of the Yamaguchi-gumi clan immediately got in her shower and scrubbed herself vigorously. X, a detestable gaijin, had touched her. She must be cleansed of his pollution and defilement, of the *kegare*. Cleansed, Fusako opened a small safe and removed an untraceable burner phone. She sent an encrypted text to Grandfather Gorou: "X is bloody shit, but I will do your will. Let me know when I may strike."

3
_____

Day 2
**Duplex of Staff Sergeant Haddy Abrams and Sergeant Shira
Alian**
Tuesday, September 19
Zero-eight-hundred hours

Haddy and Shira returned to base, accepting the congratulations of the officers and platoon, and were sent home. Nevertheless, Haddy fired 250 rounds and went to the Mixed Martial Arts Academy in Tel Aviv. She spent two instead of her usual three hours, working on her Jeet Kune Do and Krav Maga. When she returned to the duplex, Shira had ordered Chinese and started the online war game Bullet Force.

"You feeling okay?" asked Shira, observing her partner pad about nude. "Hey, babe, I've said it before, but it bears repeating: that's a strange habit."

"Can't take a joke?" said Haddy.

Shira replied, "I'm sore from the war you started. You getting in on some Bullet Force?"

"It's tequila time, in my room, alone."

"I haven't forgotten our talk," said Shira.

"Didn't doubt it for a moment," countered Haddy.

Shira said, "I'm worried."

"I'm sure you are," said Haddy and grabbed the Herradura and locked her bedroom door.

She poured a shot and sipped on her favorite beverage as her hand fell between her thighs. She rubbed and writhed, while pinching and twisting her nipples with the other hand. Haddy worked herself to the cliff of release and then backed off, until she could stand it no longer, gasping as the corkscrew from deep within worked its magic. Spent, she lit a Lucky Strike and inhaled deeply. "That feels so damn good," she said to herself. Haddy's eyes closed again. "There was that one time on the mountain when my eyes caught that climber. Gold, amber eyes hidden in a bushy beard. I'll never forget them. But he was in one party and I in another, and we had to move on. What would have happened had I turned back and touched his shoulder? Would he have been the one? Did I miss my chance? How I miss being loved, really loved."

4

Day 2
The Fortress, Five Miles North of Dombay, Russia
Tuesday, September 19
Zero-eight-hundred hours

X rose early. He watered the orchids, anticipating Salam's arrival. He walked his garden rounds and delighted in the overflowing baskets of pinecones. Kitten perched on Smert and waddled down between the mastiff's paws, saying, "Give me a kiss, give me a kiss." In his chair, X fingered a cigar as the Wall Street numbers sped across the screen like Lamborghini race cars. He said to Fusako, "Call Shin Lui in Hong Kong and buy one hundred thousand shares of Thirty-seven Capital Inc. Have him sell tomorrow. We'll net $31,803,040.01. Pass the tip to Vladimir and our man in Manhattan." He puffed. "Tell CEO Cremini of Teekay Oil to start production on the oil tankers discussed in our last meeting. Call Sukhoi President Tamarov to sell twenty Su-Fifty-Seven jets to North Korea."

Fusako's phone buzzed. She took the call and said, "Mr. Salam, you're on speaker with X."

"Anisur?" replied X cheerfully. "We await your arrival with high expectations."

The voice answered coldly, "This is Wasim Salam, brother of Anisur and bearer of bad news. An Israeli sniper murdered my most esteemed brother noon yesterday in the village of Shib in Yemen. She escaped by helicopter." X grew livid. His lower lip trembled. He crushed the cigar in his hand.

Kitten squawked, "Bombs! Lower the lifeboats, we're dead in the water."

X glowered at the bird. "My deepest condolences. I'll fix it." The call ended, and he said to Fusako, "Call the Enforcer." Ivan Juric came on the line, and X said in a tone laced with venom, "A Jew dog, a slavering cur, struck down Anisur Salam. Find and kill her." He hissed, "Be quick about it, and make her death bloody."

IVAN RECLINED in his gaudy Baroque-style red-and-gold suite on the second floor of Club Ibiza on Arcadia beach in Odessa. Finding the sniper would take time, but he nursed a worry closer to home. How to tell X about the scientists working on his rockets? As Ivan broke down the heavy semiautomatic .44 Magnum, he grappled with the loss of Professors Andreyev and Zohar from X's nuclear program. As he understood it, one required a nuclear physicist to design and fit the bomb inside the missile, and a software engineer versed in nuclear laser technology to trigger the device properly. Andreyev had performed the first and Zohar the second, but Andreyev had vodka poisoning, and

Zohar quit in disgust. The schedule mandated a man-portable device by December 13, chosen by X to commemorate the opening of the Neuengamme concentration camp in Germany in 1938. Finding qualified replacements bordered on the impossible, but Ivan had other concerns as well. The rebellious escort, Brianna Ivanova, his most gifted man-trap, had forgotten her place, and must be brought to heel; while the second, his Greek Adonis Pavlos Doukas, had turned traitor, working under the table for rival Dumka Sovann in Dnipro, Ukraine.

Swallowing two shots of vodka, Ivan slapped the gun together. The sniper was blood sport and thrilled him; he thought of a sharpened pole. As the stake forced its way through the anus, it would gut its way up to her chest. He would film the torture for X. Ivan opened his phone to *"Contacts—Israel."* He scrolled to a name and sent a text: "Looking for Anisur Salam's killer. Provide name, date, and place of birth, etc., etc. $100,000 dollars."

Dinner was served, and Ivan ate his fill and felt the itch. He descended to his private booth on the first floor and studied the dancers, looking for a slim, lithe newcomer. He saw a perfect body and signaled to his trusted bodyguards, Stanislov and Yegor, to fetch the attractive teen. She had long auburn tresses and pert breasts.

The anxious girl entered the booth and put on a gymnastic show, while the bodyguards formed a 500-pound wall of muscle outside the curtain. Rules against touching didn't apply, and Ivan pulled the fresh figure on his lap. The girl swayed like a willow, exposing her neck. Ivan smelled her and licked her skin; it tasted like an ice cream cone. The "ding" of an incoming text tugged him away. *"Have information. Meet at Bat Yam Bistro, corner booth. Derech Ben Gurion 73. 1930 hours. Thursday, 21 Sept."*

Delighted with the news, Ivan smoked a joint with the dancer and unbelted his pants. He shed his jacket but kept the pistol in the shoulder holster. The teen kneeled to blow, but two iron hands spun her around. Ivan placed his hand between her shoulder blades and shoved her on her elbows, while gripping her hips like a vise. He spit on his fingers and rubbed her ass, found her, and pushed inside. He listened in pleasure to her gasp and muffled cry. Ivan slapped her butt, his hand like a switch on a horse. Holding her hips, he thrust in and out as his eyes rolled into his head. Just before his climax, Ivan returned to a poignant memory when his older brother had climbed into bed with him. The sharp pain, the same wild-eyed cries, the same thrusting and tearing. His mind looped back to that episode in fury, as it did every time before coming. Holding the image, Ivan climaxed and allowed himself a drenching, satisfying grunt. He stayed inside for a time. The memory faded, and he pushed the girl away. On cue, Stanislov reached inside with a washcloth. The torn teen cleaned Ivan off as he dialed Anatoly Karpov, his pilot, and said, "We leave for Tel Aviv in an hour." Clicking off, he turned to the dancer. "You enjoy fucking? You like jokes?" The dancer nodded tearfully, biting her lip to control the pain. "The man asks the doctor where they're going. And the doctor says, 'The morgue.' The man replies, 'But I'm not dead.' The doctor says, 'We haven't arrived yet.'" Juric guffawed and slapped his thigh. "Stanislov will escort you home. You're mine now and under my protection." The girl, who looked all of seventeen, straightened. Her lips tightened and her face grew taut. Against all Ivan considered holy, she grabbed his face and kissed him hard.

She said with a furious coldness, "No, you are mine, and I own you, and you will never do that again without my fucking permission." She walked out of the booth, leaving Ivan stunned and quietly amused.

5

Day 3
Second Floor, Corner of Jefferson and Henry Streets,
Manhattan, New York
Wednesday, September 20
Zero-four-hundred hours

New York Police Detective Liam "Wolf" James stared through the scope. He wanted a Camel but swore after ten hard and glorious years in the Rangers, he would chew gum. A retired master sergeant could do no less, he reasoned, but chuckled; that was bullshit. He could do anything he damned well pleased, but just for the pleasure of spiting himself said, "No."

Wolf kept his eyes on the six-story redbrick apartment building across the busy street. The night stars twinkled, while a cacophonous mix of horns, cars, motorcycles, bus engines, and drunk restaurant patrons floated up to the second-floor hideout. Inside, the air conditioner kept the room cool. Such a contrast after silent Afghan deserts, waiting for a Taliban fighter to appear and plant a roadside bomb. Wolf would wait with his MKII Mod 0 semiautomatic sniper rifle, carried by Ranger marksmen. He relished the memory; that .308 round carried a lethal punch. Wolf turned his mind back to the game at hand. A tipster had revealed that drug lord and cop killer Ricky Jam had set up shop in the apartment building across the way.

Jam was smart, rarely showing his face. His underlings moved in and did a brisk business in one place and were gone within the week. A search warrant meant nothing to Wolf. Drugs were not his concern. To nail this bastard for killing Officer Kansas, one had to wait, watch, and grab him if he showed his face. Wolf discussed this with Lieutenant Kelson of the Ninth Precinct and his partner, Detective Second Grade Maria Valenzuela.

The lieutenant, a grizzled hard case after eighteen years on the force, had said, "Detective James, I know this is personal for all of us, but collar the creep, don't kill him. I want to see him do the perp walk." The lieutenant warned Maria, a deceptively petite Latina, "Officer Valenzuela, you're second grade. This punk here," and he looked at Wolf, "is a newbie third grade. I don't care what he did overseas; you are senior. Taser the bastard if he won't listen, and bring Jam in alive."

Wolf and Maria set up in the office building across the way, and in the wee hours of the morning, Wolf sipped on a Styrofoam cup of stale coffee. The room was dark. Maria was out, and Wolf kept watch as the seconds ticked away, until he lost patience. He stood to his 6' 4" height and removed the rust-red gingham shirt and chino mountaineering pants. Wolf shook out his bulky pectorals, extended his fingers towards the ceiling, and rolled his head around. He pulled himself up an imaginary rope for sixty seconds and then placed his palms on the floor to stretch taut hamstrings. Wolf knocked off jump-ups, lunges, crunches, and push-ups, until he collapsed in a sweat. He went to the bathroom and lathered a washcloth and rubbed himself down. He redressed and buffed the brown leather tennis shoes. Unlike his fellow detectives, Wolf didn't favor the tailored suits and ties of the detective squad, preferring to "stay loose," as he called it. Examining the building again, Wolf traced the fire escape next to the Shanghai Cosco & Kawasaki Company, and finished the coffee. He would be there when the creep arrived. Then Wolf's thoughts returned to the Christmas bash nine months earlier, an event which had changed his life. The precinct had gotten the word about the mandatory Brock Christmas party. Lawrence Brock chaired the New York City Police Commission, and his word moved mountains. Wolf's mountain moved.

6

Day 4
Second Floor at the Corner of Jefferson and Henry Streets,
Manhattan, New York
Thursday, September 21
Zero-four-hundred hours

Nothing eventful happened as Wolf and Maria waited for Ricky Jam, apart from teen drug runners moving in and out of the building. As dawn approached, the detective listened to jazz trumpeter Chet Baker and thought back to the Christmas bash. He remembered his hope that someone, perhaps Brock himself, would kick-start the investigation into his family's fiery death.

Lawrence Brock's 400-acre plot of manicured lawns and forest along the stately Hudson River lay covered in snow. Wolf had arrived in his black Tacoma 4 by 4 at precisely eighteen hundred hours. The night was crispy and cold, the way he liked it. The valet parked, while a butler dressed in a Revolutionary war costume opened the massive door. An attractive woman with an easy smile asked for his coat. Dressed in a rental tuxedo, Wolf hit a wall of warm, pine-scented air and live music. He put a finger in the starched collar and stretched his neck. Wolf abhorred social gatherings, able to "blend" in polite conversation only so long, say thirty seconds. The inane chitchat drove him batty. Like a rifle, he aimed at a target, as in, "What's the point?" and would note, "You say New York taxis are wrong, as in overpriced, smelly, the drivers are difficult to understand, and the threat of violence is a factor. Then take the subway, or bus, or walk, but for God's sake stop whining and get out of my face." He wasn't solitary either, escaping into a cave; he enjoyed mountaineering with a friend or two, or sketching delicate nudes in his Bronx apartment.

The party seemed massive. An expansive room; a 30-foot-tall fir decked with red-and-green ornaments and tiny lights sparkled. A crackling fire and one hundred of New York's wealthiest and most politically connected people mingled. A four-piece jazz ensemble filled the room with oozing gold. The guests were clotted in small groups, talking, holding drinks, and plucking hors d'oeuvres off trays. Wolf's first thought was, "How long is long enough? I need to leave without being rude," but he remembered his family and continued, "Shut up and see what gives."

Wolf threaded past the throng of wealth to the bar, with its own mirror, and asked for four fingers of Maker's Mark bourbon, neat. He kept his eyes on the reflective glass and observed on the sly. He knew, once he faced the crowd, an unseen invitation would ripple throughout the room. Wolf studied the knots of glitz and glam in the mirror. He ignored the dazzling women and assessed potential spots of trouble and ran scenarios in neutralizing those threats. Where were the other entrances and exits, and where to hide for an active shooter? Satisfied that nothing was imminent, Wolf kept his head down, finished the glass, and ordered another. He ran a few fingers through a tangle of wavy cocoa-colored hair and scratched his freshly trimmed beard. Wolf caught the master of the house, Lawrence Brock, gesticulating to a group of cognoscente. His homework on the Brock investments bull revealed three sons: two in investments, and a third back from Afghanistan in a box. His only daughter, twin to the dead soldier, was a striking, smart, and flashy New York socialite. Kathryn Brock's philanthropic endeavors, revolving door of posh bad boys, and outlandish parties kept daddy's PR firm busy. She lived hard and fast and could do no wrong. Wolf resolved to avoid her. His discomfort eased by the alcohol, the detective decided to mingle and make his way to the bull. He straightened, turned, and came face to face with a tipsy female. Wrapped in a skin-tight Coco Chanel one-shoulder leopard-print blouse, with classic white slacks and glittering red stilettos, she held an uncertain martini. A pair of delicious red-ribbon lips announced in a high-pitched educated slur, "Bru... tal."

Wolf's eyes narrowed. He said, "Excuse me?"

The woman stepped closer. "As in gor... geous. I'm Kathryn Brock."

"Congratulations," replied Wolf.

"The party just got interesting," said Kathryn.

Wolf asked, "How many of those have you had?"

"I hold a PhD in positive—" she reached out and steadied herself against his shoulder "—psychology from the Claremont Graduate University. I went to Bryn Mawr and am way drunk and your name ...?"

"Detective James. Ninth Precinct."

"Where's your badge?" demanded the socialite. Wolf flashed the gold shield,

and Kathryn grabbed his hand, drawling, "Come ... with ... me," and tugged him past amused faces to an outside porch overlooking the Hudson River. She faced him with a hand on his tuxedo's lapel and said, "Let's talk."

Snow carpeted the vast lawns, and Wolf wished for nothing more than to dive into the waters and swim away. He said, "Lady, you're standing too close." Wolf couldn't fail to catch the cleavage, toned abs, layered blond hair, and luminous wide brown eyes.

"No," Kathryn said firmly. "I'm happy right here ... and I know ... what I'm doing. I'm a psychologist. God." The socialite took a sip of the drink and drawled, "Those eyes, like the Amber Room in ... Catherine's ... palace ... in St. Petersburg." She hiccupped. "Are you like a ... lumberjack from Oregon?" Wolf counted the seconds. "I read pain for a living, Detective, and you ... well, you carry a lot. My office... is in Manhattan." She swayed backwards like a palm tree and fell over. Wolf caught her. The Bryn Mawr graduate clung to his arms and climbed to her feet. She pulled his head down and kissed him.

"Dammit!" Wolf exclaimed and wiped his mouth.

Kathryn pressed on. "I could drink ... whatever that cologne is ..." and her eyes narrowed. "Did you kiss me, Detective?" and hiccupped.

Wolf thought of Murphy's *"Laws of Combat Rule 31—'If the enemy is in range, so are you,'"* and pried her away. "Let's move inside," he urged. But the socialite touched the bulge under the tux.

"A gun? I detest violence. When we're married, you'll do something else." Kathryn groaned and her hands flew to her mouth. "I'm going to vomit."

Wolf swung her to the railing as her father, Lawrence Brock, came outside. "You the Ranger?" he said gruffly.

"Yes, sir."

In a droll tone, he said, "I see you have things in hand."

"I'm sorry for your loss, Mr. Brock," Wolf said, as he ignored the retching.

"Coming from you, that means something. Take her upstairs but use the side entrance." Wolf slung Kathryn over his shoulder like a sack of cement and ascended the stairs two steps at a time. At the top, Kathryn pointed from her perch and mumbled, "The last door. *God.* You are so ... fucking strong. Did you buy those muscles?"

Wolf lay her on the bed. "You can take it from here."

Tightening her fingers on the tux, Kathryn said, "No. Stay."

"Another time."

"Wait, then. Hand me that ... pad and pen ... on my bureau." Kathryn scribbled a number and pressed the paper in his palm. "Call me."

Wolf found Mr. Brock below. "Katy's a handful," he said. "But I'm impressed. Most men don't come out. Detective James, a word?" Lawrence Brock led Wolf downstairs into a smoking room and offered Wolf a cigar and Maker's Mark Cask Strength.

Wolf declined the smoke but raised an eyebrow when offered the drink. "How did you know this is my favorite?"

"You've been a police officer for three years, have an excellent case closure rate with no hint of taking bribes," announced the titan. "Your family immigrated from Ukraine to 'Little Ukraine' here in the East Village. You were eight, got back from school to see your family's shop in flames with them inside. You lied about your age, left high school early, signed an Option Forty, and enlisted with the Seventy-Fifth Ranger Regiment. After years in the Middle East, First Sergeant Alpha Company, Second Battalion, you retired as a master sergeant and came back home as a NYPD detective. You are a man on a mission, Detective; call it revenge. You want your family's killers. I can help, but I trade for a living." Wolf cocked an eyebrow up as Mr. Brock said, "I'm looking for a son-in-law."

7

Day 4
Bat Yam Bistro, Bat Yam, a Town South of Tel Aviv, Israel
Thursday, September 21
Nineteen-thirty hours

Colonel Nathan Yevhim, senior Israeli intelligence officer, tapped the Formica table with nervous fingers and waited. He kept a guarded eye on the door. Not naked flesh, or crushing debt, but the back rooms of the Riviera card games thrilled him, but that required money. He kept his duckbill cap pulled down low over a pair of wraparound sunglasses and pulled up the collar of his gray windbreaker. Nathan sipped his coffee in silence. The bell tinkled as someone entered the shop. He inhaled sharply, recognizing instantly the dark sunglasses, flattened nose, mangled ears, and bare bullet-shaped head.

The man approached the colonel's corner table, sat down,

and with a menacing rasp came right to the point. "You have the information?" asked Ivan Juric.

Nathan had pored over Haddy Abrams's files. He said, "An elite spec-ops Israeli sniper named Staff Sergeant Haddy Abrams, code name the Queen of Hearts, killed your golden boy from two thousand, six hundred, and sixty-four yards and set an Israel Defense Force record for long-distance shots."

Ivan sat back, struck by the magnitude of the achievement. He didn't like it but nodded grudgingly. Nathan slid a piece of paper across the table with the number of a Swiss bank account. Ivan opened his phone, entered his username and password, and pressed "send." Nathan kept his eyes on the malign presence, while waiting for the confirmation on his phone. It dinged, and he smiled briefly as $100,000 entered his account. Ivan nodded and began to get up, when Nathan raised a staying hand. "We're not done. There's more." He saw the eyes tighten and a facial tic curl back the Enforcer's lip, and continued. "You and I met twenty-six years ago in Jerusalem, remember? Over drinks, you mentioned an interest in one Aaron BenMenashe and missing photos. At the time, you offered $100,000 for actionable intelligence." Nathan caught an imperceptible dilation of Ivan's pupils, a sign of interest.

Ivan Juric reigned in the cold shivers racing up and down his spine. He took out a Gauloises and lit the harsh Turkish tobacco. He inhaled deeply to calm himself as the name *Aaron BenMenashe* pounded within him. Aaron BenMenashe, the London *Guardian* investigative reporter, was his worst nightmare: the only person to track down X and discover his true identity. BenMenashe broke into the Eastern Machine Systems secret archives in London. Ivan caught him on a hidden camera, photographing hundreds of Jewish emigres' files, who had fled from Odessa to Tel Aviv in the 1980s. X had put together a company called the Ukrainian Israel Travel Agency

(UITA), which "helped" these hapless victims. He robbed them of their children, savings, and belongings. When X learned what BenMenashe had done, he had Ivan fire a Stinger missile into a bloated Airbus of Ukrainian International Airlines Flight 114 out of Gatwick International Airport. It killed everyone aboard. Ivan then ransacked the reporter's apartment and came up empty-handed. X never forgot—he never forgot anything—and blamed Ivan.

"Aaron BenMenashe, missing photos and $500,000," Nathan replied slowly. "Do we have a 'yes'?" Ivan nodded. Nathan continued. "The name Aaron BenMenashe was an alias, created to let him investigate Eastern Machine Systems as a London *Guardian* reporter. His real name was Joseph Abrams, the father of Staff Sergeant Haddy Abrams, your shooter." Ivan Juric drew in a sharp breath and lit another cigarette. Nathan paused to sip his coffee before proceeding. "While BenMenashe worked in Odessa, he fell in love with a woman we know only as Sasha, or Sasha BenMenashe. She gave birth to your sniper, and not at the University Hospital of Brooklyn, as records indicate. The Mossad agent running the op, after learning of Joseph's death, traveled to Odessa and informed Sasha. He helped her come to the US with forged documents." Nathan motioned for Ivan to let him have a Gauloises. The intelligence officer had the tic-faced demon on a barbed hook and relished the moment. Nathan blew out the smoke. "Sasha Abrams joined the dead husband's father, David Abrams, in Southampton, who's now eighty-one and lives at Fifty-Five Linden Lane, Southampton, New York. Ms. Sasha Abrams lives in Apartment Six, 140 Perry Street in Manhattan."

Ivan grappled with the enormity of the Mossad's nefarious plan to take down X. "I have the sniper. Now I have her mother and grandfather. They have the film," he said to himself. To the Colonel he said, "Do the Abrams have the film?"

"I don't know."

Ivan transferred $500,000 to Nathan's account. "You'll get another $500,000 when you bring me the film and Sasha's birth name and family. Have fun on the Riviera."

8

Day 4
Duplex of Staff Sergeant Haddy Abrams and Sergeant Shira
Alian
Thursday, September 21
Twenty-hundred hours

Haddy lay down on her bed, downed a double of tequila, smoked, and opened her personal journal. The time to remember had come and she read, "I turned twelve and did my Bat Mitzvah. The rabbi called me before the congregation. I recited the first blessing, read the week's Torah portion in Hebrew and English, and closed with the final blessing. Mother gave me eighteen dollars times one hundred, since the Hebrew word for 'life' is 'chai,' and equals eighteen. She gave me Shabbat candlesticks to light the way for Shabbat. Grandfather David gave me a gold necklace with matching pearl earrings. I'm happy."

Haddy flipped the page and continued, "Mom is clairvoyant. She's a dreamer and saw her first angel at three. Neighbors come over for sittings. She told me she can *see* into people. Maybe that's why she sent me to this doctor of psychology, since I'm reading about Nietzsche's madman.

"'Do you want to kill yourself?' he asked.

"'Sometimes.'

"'Can you tell me about it?'

"'I want to take Zarathustra's knife and get bloody.'

"'Have you tried to kill yourself?'

"'No, but I think about it a lot. Life seems pointless and painful.'" Haddy remembered he wanted to start some medicine called an "antidepressant," but she refused.

"'I hear you are very good at karate,' he said.

"'Jeet Kune Do, by Bruce Lee, and Krav Maga.'

"'Tell me about it.'

"'When I hit my opponents, the anger goes out, instead of in.'"

An entry a month later lay highlighted in red. "I woke up last night with this sudden craving for God, like I would die if I didn't see Him that moment. A Presence filled the room. I shook all over and couldn't breathe. Suddenly, my hands started dripping fire. My fingers took hold of a bayonet brighter than a lightsaber. As fast as it happened, it disappeared. I ran into Mom's room and told her.

"Mom started crying. 'It's started,' she said. 'I'm happy and terrified for you.'

I asked her what she meant.

"'You have my gift," she replied. "I told you I *see* things, and I saw your destiny. I told you I met your father in Odessa where he worked for the London Guardian. You were about to be born. He left the airport to join me, but you came early. As you were crowning, I felt a sharp stab in my side and shrieked. The jet had burst into flames with one hundred thirty-seven people aboard, including your father. He died as you were born.' Sasha paused and wiped away her tears. 'Haddy, you will kill the man who killed your father on your birthday.' I was speechless."

Haddy put away the journal, sobered. She picked up the *tanto* knife, wrapped in a cloth and used by samurai wives to kill themselves after their husbands had committed seppuku. The ceremonial linen fell away, and the blade, seven inches long with a 6-inch wood handle, shone like a razor. God willing, she would end her torment and prove her mother wrong. "I'm not a clairvoyant. I don't have her gift. I will be long gone before my birthday. Someone else will avenge my father."

9

Day 4
Ben Gurion International Airport, Tel Aviv, Israel
Thursday, September 21
Twenty-one-hundred hours

I van raced north to the Ben Gurion International Airport. A drizzle wetted the pavement, and he braked the roadster to stay in control. He phoned Mikael Sokolov, president of the Army Munitions Group, and snarled, "I don't want excuses. Get Andreyev and Zohar back," and hung up.

Ivan climbed the small staircase into the black Citation X jet. In a gold circle on the tailfin were the letters *EMS, Inc.* Relishing a night with his new teen squeeze at Club Ibiza, he ordered, "Get this thing in the air, Karpov. We'll spend the night in Odessa. Tomorrow, we go to the Fortress." Ivan went to the wet bar and demanded angrily, "We have billions, and you can't find a woman to serve vodka?" An hour later and a pint down, Ivan steadied himself and phoned X. Fusako answered and Ivan said, "Put me on the phone with X."

The secretary replied quietly, "You're on speaker. Go ahead."

"X," breathed Ivan, "are you sitting down?"

"Go on," said the oligarch.

"Aaron BenMenashe," whispered Ivan. The line went cold and silent. Ivan could hear X breathing and the parrot spouting nonsense in the background.

Tremulous, the voice said, "Go on."

Ivan repeated Nathan's account word for word. A long silence ensued when suddenly a piercing cry shouted, "The wheel of Karma has turned! My nemesis had a daughter! She kills the righteous Anisur Salam! Now she and her family are mine! We'll enshrine their skulls over the fireplace! You have earned redemption, my son, and a big bonus!" X shrieked again. "Three auspicious signs: stealing the Mayak plutonium; Rahil's appearance with a new X3 launch date to honor her death, October thirteenth at sixteen hundred hours; and now, the Ben Menashe revelation!" X calmed down. "You have other news?"

"Professor Andreyev is in the hospital. Professor Zohar quit."

The line disconnected. Ivan, the brutal Enforcer of the Sakarovkh, froze, captured by X's madness. He knew Hitler's general staff considered the Führer a maniac but tolerated his tantrums while in power. Was this the same? A tyrant seeing ghosts? Changing the launch date on the whim of a spectral presence? Ivan did a quick calculation. December to October lopped off sixty-two days; not enough time to finish the rockets. Ivan finished his vodka and muttered, "But the real problem with changing the date? Not enough time to kill X."

10

Day 5
Second Floor at the Corner of Jefferson and Henry Streets,
Manhattan, New York
Friday, September 22
Zero-four-hundred hours

K athryn Brock had called Wolf repeatedly, and he finally relented. Now he stared at the apartment building and thought of her, troubled. Once they started dating, a real affection took hold in the warrior for her urbane and dazzling sophistication. With the world at her fingertips, Kathryn was well-spoken and knew the art of conversation. She idolized Julia Child and prepared an all-French cuisine for their first dinner at her 16 Dutch apartment in Central Park. They met three more times before Wolf played tennis at Kathryn's private Manhattan club. No match for her practiced skill, he still gave a good account of himself. They had fun, but Kathryn learned he sketched. Intrigued, she insisted on going to Wolf's Bronx two-bedroom apartment to see his work.

"Prepare yourself," he warned her. "This is the Bronx, not Central Park." Kathryn had entered the small apartment curious as a cat. Her eyes widened when Wolf pointed out the grass mat, sleeping bag, and flaxseed pillow in the corner. "We've got your backpacks, boots, crampons, ice axes, and other mountaineering equipment on this wall, books of criminal law and Russian literature over there and over here," nodding at the kitchen counter. "Coffee beans, grinder, French press, and five different bourbons." But Kathryn's jaw slackened as she gazed on the farther wall. Wolf said, "That's an original Russian icon of St. Joshua, the Warrior Prince. Next to it is a Russian Orthodox triptych called the Desis, or 'supplication,' with Jesus flanked by St. John the Baptist and the Theotokos the God-bearer."

"You're serious?" Kathryn exclaimed, disbelieving.

"I haven't been to church since the Rangers," said Wolf. "I was adopted by a well-to-do Ukrainian couple who placed me in the St. George Academy. I attended every service at St. George's Ukrainian Catholic Church. I have a thing for icons."

"You're Catholic?"

"Not a good one," replied Wolf. "I haven't taken Mass in years."

Kathryn stared at the icon. "You really believe in this?"

"The icon is a window into sacred mysteries," said Wolf. "Like a prism, it refracts eternal light into a visible rainbow. You *see* the *unseen*. St. Joshua was a warrior prince. A conqueror who carried water for Moses. When I venerate him, I gain courage and humility."

"I'm at a loss," Kathryn stammered. "I'm a scientist. How can you touch what can't be measured?" Then she walked into the small adjoining bedroom and paled at the charcoal nudes on sketch pads. "My God, you are one surprise after another.

Why are you a policeman? These are exquisite. The faces ... the lips reveal such tenderness. They hurt and weep and I hurt. I want to cry." Wolf asked if she wanted water. "Pour me some bourbon. I should learn to like that stuff. It's corn, right? When did you start drawing?"

"Nine years ago," said Wolf.

"What happened back then?" asked Kathryn, as she took a sip of the fiery liquid and made a face. "Burning! But let me guess. Pain and art, art and pain, pain and heart, heart and pain: Wolf, you met a woman and fell in love." With drink in hand, Kathryn opened a portfolio. "I know I'll find her."

Wolf took her hand away. "Enough."

Kathryn put down the glass. "Do you still talk to her?" thinking, "He's still in love, anyone can see that, but I'd have his children in a moment. Could I satisfy him? Does he want kids?"

Wolf's tone darkened. "She's dead. I buried her last year."

"Oh God, I'm so sorry," said Kathryn. To herself, she said, *Fantastic*, so loud she thought Wolf could hear her, but to Wolf she continued, "Tell me all about it. I do this for a living."

Wolf had poured himself a bourbon and sat down against the wall, while Kathryn pulled a chair close. "I had returned from Mosul," said Wolf. "Me and two buddies decided to climb Mt. Rainier outside of Seattle. We left camp at midnight, summited, and during descent passed another group of climbers just as dawn broke. A sunbeam fell on the face of a young woman. Our eyes connected, and I knew instantly she was my mate and knew that she knew. I should have turned back and got her number, but regretfully, I moved on. I couldn't get her out of my mind, didn't want to really, so I started drawing her. I tried to find her, but after nine years decided to move on. I burned three portfolios full of sketches and buried her ashes a week before your dad's Christmas bash. I have three remaining drawings. When I return to Odessa, I'll scatter them on the Black Sea."

"You never met her?" said Kathryn, astonished and baffled. "You've looked all those years?" Kathryn threw herself on Wolf and kissed him. "You poor, poor thing."

Three months later, Kathryn asked Wolf to marry her "with conditions." He weighed the decision with his usual gravity before accepting. Kathryn made their bedroom antics torrid affairs. Yet, only three nights ago, before Lord Ricky Jam and the surveillance had started, Wolf had lain by her side unable to sleep, riven by a troubled conscience. Why couldn't he tell Kathryn that when he made love to her, he saw the girl on Mt. Rainier? For a windless calm had rested on the mountain. Wolf had opened his climbing jacket and remembered his beard wasn't trimmed. This woman, whom he dubbed his "Snow Queen," had a long braid of black hair. Her eyebrows were thick, bushy, and straight. She had light olive skin, like his. Around her neck hung the Star of David. Her cheeks and chin were stone; her nose was straight. When she saw him, she stopped. Her hand took off her reflectors, and her lips parted. Wolf never forgot her eyes, luminous, dark, and shiny. Her lips were almost fat, not sensuous, but like earth and dirt and grit. She had the bearing of a queen, dominant, sure, and unwavering. She was night and light, and as their gazes locked, his heart cracked and Wolf fell inside. How could he tell Kathryn he was still in love with this woman? To be so close to the wedding yet have such lava within? Wolf rolled on top of his bride-to-be and loved her fiercely to wipe away, if only for an instant, the Snow Queen.

It didn't last. Wolf slipped out of bed and picked up his worn and tattered prayer book. He went to the living room, fell to his knees, and though he had the book, his hands didn't open it; he knew it by heart. Why was he with Kathryn if he loved a dream? Guilt began when he chose to bed Kathryn. He crossed the line with God. He knew it. His biting conscience demanded the books be balanced.

Kathryn was beautiful. Wine and bourbon, music and dancing in her apartment, and then she unbuttoned her blouse. Her breath, hot on his lips, and practiced fingers moved between his marbled thighs. She had unbuckled his belt and let the pants fall away and taken him like a woman possessed. Wolf held her hair, drowning in chocolate and bloodred roses. His loins clenched in release. He shared that most intimate instant of sublime death; a joining that sent his soul to heaven but lay outside God's blessing. He had committed adultery. His Snow Queen was dead, but he couldn't escape his transgression by an unseen finger in the sands. Did God understand? Wolf's hands formed powerful fists, and he slowly beat his chest three times, repeating, "Be merciful to me, O God, a sinner."

Kathryn came up behind him, put her hands on his head, and said gently, "Wolf, darling, what is it? Why are you so disturbed?"

"Nothing, sweetheart. Just thinking of our wedding."

"Just three weeks away," she said.

11

Brianna Ivanova heard two quick raps on her seventy-fourth-floor apartment in Moscow's Neva Towers. She peered out the peephole and relaxed when she saw her bodyguard. Brianna took the silent elevator to the streets of the ancient city. Her guard escorted her past the drunk to a gleaming Mercedes limousine. He examined the driver's identification before putting his charge in the back seat. Brianna laid her head against the cushion, thinking of the next twenty-four hours. The slender gazelle would entertain a Russian industrialist and his wife. And plan a harrowing escape.

The client had contacted her. A transfer of $168,000 to her Swiss account meant they would each die and live again in the practiced arms of Miss Sable & Diamonds, Moscow's top escort. Like most in the top one-half percent of Russian society, the billionaire belonged to the Platinum Girls Gentlemen's Club. Brianna was worth every penny. Educated at the prestigious Lomonosov Moscow State University, with a degree in Russian literature and minor in Shakespearean drama, she spoke fluent Japanese, maintained confidence, and was expert in the Japanese art of *shibari*, rope bondage.

As the limo absorbed the bumps, Brianna opened her laptop with tremulous hands. There would be no turning back once she purchased the tickets, one for herself and one for Ulyana, her five-year-old daughter. She pressed "accept" and watched the confirmation code appear. Brianna rechecked her Swiss account, which contained a cool $18,492,355.24 in savings. In thirty-six hours, they would flee to Tokyo and escape Ivan Juric, the fearsome Enforcer of the Sakharov crime syndicate. Brianna would leave her small circle of girlfriends, formed in her senior year at university. They had met to read Nabokov, and from them, Brianna found her one faithful friend and lover, Lada.

A favorite word in Brianna's lexicon was "idiot," and like an *idiot* she had succumbed to the lying charmer, Ivan, who, dressed in Saville Row pinstripes, rubbed elbows with everyone at Platinum Girls. She chose to ignore what her expert eyes had told her: that while he could spin wonderful stories, underneath lay an unconscionable hardness. Ivan had offered the breathtaking beauty an opportunity to be the honey in his "honey trap," assuring her there would be no violence. Brianna abhorred blood, the mere sight and smell of which caused her to faint. One time, while helping Lada with her dying puppy, Brianna lost it all and retched. But Ivan understood, he said. Only the finest Russian hotels with epicurean foods, for she had a sensitive stomach, and scents would do. He would get her in and out. Brianna had seduced the Russian four-star general and earned $100,000 for her trouble. In the beginning, this work came in spurts, and Brianna relaxed and warmed to the wiles of Ivan. Was it greed, she wondered, that had clouded her judgment? She had never been "pimped." She was, in many ways, a misfit, a highly intelligent, adventurous vixen who required absolute control.

But her tight inner circle had cautioned her. "Back away," they said. "We hear rumors."

Finally, she told Ivan, "No more."

The charmer betrayed his outward calm with a tic that tugged on his upper lip.

Dull, flat, and utterly cold, he replied, "You're mine, Miss Ivanova. You belong to the Sakharov, and no one leaves our club." Then came Madrid, three weeks earlier.

The featured speaker at the European Automotive Industry yearly forum was the president of ZZK Motors, Inc., a glamorous car manufacturer in Italy. Talks between ZZK and Eastern Machine Systems had reached an impasse. Ivan told Brianna the contract required only the president's signature, and with her wiles, she could get it done.

After a sterling address to the conference, the dashing man entered the hotel elevator. Brianna squeezed between the doors and stumbled. The Italian caught her, transfixed by the clinging black dress, perfect red lips, diamond choker, and cleavage. Like a flirty coquette, Brianna fluttered her eyelashes and placed her hand inside her bra to adjust her chest. She broke into a shy smile and asked for an apology, her breath heavy with alcohol. They ended up in his bedroom. Brianna slipped an MDA-laced chaser in his champagne and worked her magic. She mounted the man, and while fucking him, set a contract and pen before him and wooed him to sign. As she kept him on the verge of climaxing, he agreed, but just then, the magnate suffered a not uncommon reaction to the psychostimulant. "I hear my wife!" he shouted. Panicked, he pushed Brianna off. Ivan's goons burst in and forced him to sign.

Brianna threw the sheets over her head. She heard the president scratch out his name and wrestle free. Brianna saw him dive for his pistol in the nightstand. The magnate fell dead from four slugs, one of which took off the back of his head. The elegant gazelle fainted. When she awoke, blood and goopy gray matter lay splattered across the suite. Brianna retched, lost her urine, and shit the bed. In horror, she watched Ivan's thugs stuff the body in a foot locker. Before she could dash into the shower, Ivan's henchman ordered her to clean up the room.

Brianna returned to her sparkling clean Moscow suite, disgusted and ashamed. But she wouldn't be cowed. She could be hard as nails and let her ingenuity have its way.

The Mercedes rolled to a stop. The bodyguard escorted Brianna, wrapped in her sable full-length coat, to a side entrance. A butler led her to an elegantly stained mahogany door on the third floor. She entered and selected romantic jazz, appetizers, vodka, and champagne. Brianna chose a shimmering red satin dress, whose hem floated above her crotch. She wore a black garter belt, designer black fishnet stockings, and stilettos. Brianna's lips were full and luscious. She leaned into the mirror and applied the burgundy-colored pencil along the vermillion border, where white skin turned red. Brianna worked patiently to perfection. She glossed her lips dark raspberry and kissed a tissue to remove the excess lipstick. She applied a light powder over flawless skin and stood back and admired her symmetry, two halves of a perfect pomegranate.

The billionaire knocked and entered, and Brianna tossed back her long tresses with natural highlights. She thrust out her chest and approached the industrialist like a leopard in heat. She let him inhale her perfume and spoke in soft, sultry tones, saying, "I've been waiting." After food and drink, she patted the bed and purred like a kitten. "Relax and talk. I want to hear every word, leave nothing out. Tell me your darkest desires. How do you want to fuck me?" The industrialist discussed his marital problems, political intrigues, and company politics. Brianna matched the timbre of her tone to his pain. She whispered lewd passions until his manhood stood tall like a fir. She touched the tip and smiled seductively. Parting her lips, Brianna said, "You want me," and slipped off the bed. She stood and twirled around and then, bending over, Brianna winked at the man from between her thighs. "Hey. What are you looking at?" she teased, "Look me in the eyes if you can." Brianna let her eyes twinkle. "Wait," and walked behind the curtain. Appearing as a nurse (his request) in white garter belt and stockings, silky nipple-less bra, and cap, Brianna danced with the grace of a ballerina. Then the medical examination began, ending as she blindfolded and tied him down. Brianna worked her magic patiently, keeping her client in ecstasy. When he came, he groaned and growled for a full minute.

After dinner, they played on his game console and bowled on his private lane. Brianna did him twice more. In the morning, he said, "Are you ready for Anastasia?" Brianna showed him the ropes, the gag, paddles, whips, and handcuffs. He smiled. "True Russian stamina. Come again next week, and if you don't mind me asking, would you allow me to spank your delicious bottom?"

Brianna's teeth gleamed. "I need to know you more, but yes, if you're very good." As he left, she sniffed two pinches of high-grade cocaine and made ready for the glamorous wife.

Twelve hours later, the bodyguard met Brianna, and the Mercedes took her home. She tucked her earnings inside her floor safe in her walk-through closet and envisioned a yacht in Tokyo Bay.

12

Day 5
Duplex of Staff Sergeant Haddy Abrams and Sergeant Shira Alian
Friday, September 22
Zero-five-hundred hours

Haddy and Shira mustered from their beds at 5 a.m., arriving at PT thirty minutes later. Haddy took the platoon around the quarter-mile track performing "earthworm crawlers," consisting of standing at attention and then running one's fingers down the legs and feet, out on the track, until stretched out full length while not touching the stomach. Then, using the toes and keeping the legs straight, one came back, standing at attention. Haddy had the soldiers sprint a lap forwards, then backwards, and then side to side, left and right. Finally, the group died with bear crawls. The partners went to mess hall, ate, and went to the range. Shira remonstrated, "What are you trying to do? Kill everyone? What happened to push-ups, sit-ups, and jogging?"

"Boring," said Haddy, while admiring her new McMillian .50-caliber rifle. "Let's sight this in and warm up the barrel."

"What are your plans this afternoon?" asked Shira suspiciously.

"After MMA?" said Haddy. "Going to the Lacoste Bar and Grill in Tel Aviv."

"What about me?" replied Shira.

Haddy rolled her eyes and said, "I know your game. 'Suicide watch.'"

"Until you see a shrink?" said Shira. "Yeah, so fuck you."

The battle buddies ordered appetizers. Shira drank from a pitcher of beer, while Haddy swallowed tequila. As the music played, they relaxed. Shira said, "Tell me. What's on your mind?"

"I was thinking back when I turned fourteen and the rape," replied Haddy. "You know I was quite the looker."

"Nothing's changed," said Shira.

Haddy continued, "Mom had talked with that sportswear company. They carried a line of hot bikinis. The president called me in and watched me spin and brought in a photographer. They liked me; bold, cut face, strong clean lines, and nice figure. I was fighting a lot, and Mom named me her 'Cheetah girl.'" Haddy swallowed a shot, and her tone darkened. "I was raped by four men. I don't know how I got away. The police found me and called Sasha. I didn't want to go to the hospital but felt too weak to refuse. They did an exam and took samples. It was humiliating. Mom cried and cried. She took me to Grandpa David's, where I stayed in bed for a week. During that time, I kept asking myself, 'What did I do to deserve this?' I remember feeling filthy and worthless, like a pool of black pitch. Sasha never left my side. When I could walk, I went to the dining room. Grandpa loved the artist Marc Chagall, a

Russian Jew. He had a rare lithograph entitled *White Crucifixion*, on the wall. I grew up with those scenes of persecution, pogroms, and the Holocaust as a child. The painter had a fascination with Jesus, the false Messiah crucified. Chagall rendered him with a peaceful face, as Nazis rampaged and pillaged around him. I stood the longest time staring at him. Suddenly, I couldn't take it anymore. I exploded in rage and screamed, 'You did this! You fucking fucked me' I punched my fist in the air. 'I kill you.'"

They returned to the apartment in silence.

"You have to let it go," said Shira, shaking her head. "Why do this to yourself?"

"I saw life at its ugliest and faced it," said Haddy. "It made me the warrior I am today. I'm immune to threat. Nothing an enemy can do gets close. That's why I get cold in the heat of action. All my fear got swallowed up. That's why I have no pity. And why I can get wild and fuck all night. I just don't care. That's why I don't want to talk to rabbis or therapists. I've been places they can't dream of. I'm filled with a fucking sense of meaninglessness; a despair I can taste. I live the absurd and laugh because I survived. Sasha was never the same after that. And why didn't my grandfather do more? I've learned that David was a member of the Irgun, the Israeli kill squads before the Mossad. He could have made some calls."

"I am so frightened for you, partner," said Shira, shaken. To herself, she thought, "Don't make me call the lieutenant and report you. Don't make me, Haddy, but God help me, I'll do it."

"I can't give up my suffering," said Haddy. "Without this constant anxiety, I have no rudder. My pain is part of me. Take it away and I go away. It's called 'angst,' and I need it like the air I breathe."

13

Day 5
The Fortress
Friday, September 22
Seventeen-hundred hours

The elevator whisked open, and the Enforcer stepped into the new Palace Room. He held a bowling ball bag, and his heart skipped a beat. A stunning full-chested female in a transparent light green kimono, covered in a tapestry of rich tattoos, greeted him with a nod. Ivan looked into the emerald-green eyes of a killer and smiled, like to like. Fusako ran expert hands over his body. Satisfied he carried no weapons, she took the bag and placed it at X's feet. Ivan followed her movements with feral fascination; precise, balanced with one eye on him at all times.

"FUCKKK, she's got big tits," commented Kitten, perched on top of the black mastiff, who emitted a low growl. Ivan glanced at the glowering face of the dog. "Try it, Smert," he said to himself. "I'll break your neck and stuff the parrot down your throat." He turned his attention to the fireplace and the laughable painting of a monstrous black goblin eating people falling into hell, before observing the Louis XIV furniture, burning candles, and dazzling crystal chandelier. The scent of jasmine incense filled the room.

X fed Smert a cube of beef from a gold skull and addressed Ivan cheerfully. "Welcome, my son. You recognize the skull?"

Ivan looked closer and smiled. "Vlasta Korovich from the *American Dream?*"

"Twenty-seven years ago," exclaimed X. "The same yacht where I threw the orgy."

"And Aaron BenMenashe showed up," said Ivan.

"You haven't forgotten, and I won't forget Korovich screaming," X answered and let his eyes roam about the room. "We took his skin and made a lamp. It's at Fusako's door, but I've been rude. Ivan, meet my new assistant, Fusako Kitashirakawa, from Tokyo, Japan. Fusako, my Enforcer, Mr. Ivan Juric." Fusako gave a stiff nod and served each man a shot of ice-cold vodka from a new bottle. X waited until Fusako sipped the liquid. Seeing no ill effects, he raised the glass in toast. "To Joseph Abrams and his filthy daughter and to the recovery of the photos. Have you learned the identity of her mother's family?"

"No," said Ivan, "but soon." Fusako poured another shot.

X toasted, "To Rahil and my missiles. Did Andreyev recover? Is Zohar back?"

"Not yet," replied Ivan.

X's handsome face purpled. In a fit of ire, he threw the shot glass into the fire, he snapped, "I don't tolerate weeds in my garden," and sunk his forehead against a closed fist. "Ivan, tell me about the Americans. How far along are they?"

"Their man-portable rocket carries a warhead equivalent of two hundred tons of TNT," said Ivan. "Professor Danilenko developed a plutonium detonation trigger that makes it more powerful. Orders are coming in for the X3, but losing sixty days with Rahil's new date, coupled with Andreyev and Zohar gone, bodes ill. I urge you to reconsider the launch date."

X trembled in rage. A dribble of saliva fell on his chin. "Andreyev and Zohar are traitors," he exclaimed. "You don't like the new date, do you, Mr. Juric? You think me mad; that I've lost my mind listening to a dead girl? But I require only four missiles to plunge Jerusalem into chaos. Clients will see their destructive power and will wait in line gladly. Find replacements for Andreyev and Zohar at once."

Ivan felt a series of electric tics shoot down his face. His lip curled back painfully. He took out his smartphone, thinking, "Fucking, fucking lunatic. I'll kill him and take the woman." To X, he announced, "I have four physicists and five software designers on file. Still, finding the right pair to step into Andreyev's and Zohar's shoes? Difficult, if not ..."

"No! Mr. Juric," shouted X. "Not impossible! That's what I pay you for: the impossible! Remember, I rescued you from the gutter! I redeemed your shit life! I'm a father to you and expect miracles! Nine names and you can't find two?" X put on the Kali mask and shouted, "Kali! Give us two or we die!"

Ivan's spine chilled as he pulled up his notes and said, "We have Yuri Kharitov, head of the Explosion Laboratory at the Institute of Chemical Physics, Kazan, Russia. He's suffocating under crushing debt, but closely watched by the FSB."

X interrupted, "I thought you were on medicine for that tic."

"I, uh," Ivan stammered. "The side effects are worse than the drugs."

"Fix it. You look like a gargoyle. Anyway, I know Yuri Kharitov. He's brilliant and designs *both* software and bombs. But he would prove difficult."

"There's François LeCompte, PhD, in Beirut."

"I don't know him." Ivan detailed the remaining two physicists, and like Yuri Kharitov, both were closely guarded by their respective governments.

"There are five nuclear detonation software experts, but only two worth the effort. Young Professor Helmut Gott at Johannes Gutenberg University of Mainz. He likes fast women and faster cars. And Professor Stefan Danilenko. He splits his time between the Odessa National Polytechnic Institute and the Lawrence Livermore National Laboratory in Livermore Labs, California. He collaborates with their High Energy Applications Facility. He's a widower, in poor health, and raising his adopted cousin."

"Her name?" asked X.

"Raisa Danilenko, eighteen, in high school," said Ivan.

"If Danilenko was in Odessa," replied X, "I'd grab the girl and take him. Where is he now?"

"At the Cleveland Clinic for a knee replacement."

"Put a man on him and this girl Raisa," replied X. "Tell me about the Frenchman."

"François LeCompte works in Beirut," reported Ivan. "He's in league with the Iranians, but there's trouble. The mullahs want him in Iran, but LeCompte wants Professor Gott to join his team. The mullahs don't like Gott. Professor LeCompte has threatened to quit."

"Is he jihadi?" said X. "He could work anywhere in the world. Why the Iranians?"

"The French government put a moratorium on further research in man-portable rockets," replied Ivan. "The professor needs plutonium. The Iranians obliged. The professor likes Beirut and the ocean; he's a long-distance swimmer. He hates politics and religion, no porn, drugs, or debt. Dates occasionally but lives in his lab."

X took his cane and hobbled to his orchids. He wet the

plants down with the mister, while Kitten hopped off the mastiff. "Who is our best hooker?"

"For men? Brianna Ivanova, and Pavlos Doukas for women." Fusako brought up the escort's web page, Sableand-Diamonds.com, on the plasma screen. The oligarch took one look and exclaimed, "An absolute fox. Get her."

"After our last job, Miss Ivanova got bloodied and lost her nerve," said Ivan. "She sent back my bonus and won't answer emails."

"Family?" said X.

"A five-year-old daughter," replied Ivan.

X said, "Pay this traitorous whore a visit. Hold the child here in the Fortress. Galina, the new housekeeper, can take care of her." He lit a cigar before plunging ahead. "Hire Herr Gott immediately, promise him the moon, but get him. Drive a wedge between our young Frenchman and the mullahs."

"And if we can't get Gott?" asked Ivan.

"Get Danilenko," said X. He closed the subject and switched gears. "Who's in the bag?"

"Michael Bianchi from Sicily. A crime boss dipping his hand in the till."

X waved him off. "Take him to Trang and examine the lamps before you leave. They're works of art."

14

Day 6
Ben Shemen Forest, Israel
Saturday, September 23
Thirteen-hundred hours

After another grueling workout, morning report, and practice shooting, Haddy received the lieutenant's permission for the afternoon off. She drank her standard four shots of espresso and steaming cream, then donned compression tights and a long-sleeved Lycra-polyester T-shirt. In her day pack, Haddy tossed in a breathable Gore-Tex parka and Stephen Turnbull's *The Samurai: A Military History.* She wrestled into the lime-green motorcycle jacket and grimaced, as the helmet scraped her cheekbones and ears. Haddy petted Shira's Mickey Mouse on the way outside and swung a leg over her midnight-blue Yamaha YZF-R1 crotch rocket.

A light mist filled the air, as the in-line four cylinder ignited and pitched into a 200-horsepower scream. Haddy popped a wheelie, swerved onto the main road and accelerated to 120 mph. She slowed for the first curve, leaned, and touched her knee to the center yellow stripe. Haddy maintained her balance and did not let the rubber tires lose their precarious grip on the asphalt. She pushed the roaring buzz saw into a series of hair-raising hairpins, leaning to the left and right and fading into the thrill of dancing on a knife's edge. When Haddy hit the straightaway, she pushed the engine to the red line. The front wheel lifted off the ground as the bike howled to 175 mph before a series of high-pitched screaming downshifts into the Ben Shemen Forest parking lot. Haddy parked in the farthest corner, tucked the helmet and jacket beneath the crackling machine, and checked the straps on her day pack. She sucked water from a small tube attached to the pack's hydration system and dashed off.

A sky burdened with gray clouds greeted the runner, as Haddy dashed up the trail and leaped abruptly off into the forest. She forged a path up the ridge. Tight muscles burned like the motorcycle engine as she dodged rocks, bushes, and downfall. Haddy climbed higher until she noticed a game trail and decided to follow it. She slipped in among the trees, darting left and right, throwing low-lying branches over her head, despairing this would lead to anything. But Haddy continued until she dived beneath some scraggly trees and suddenly entered a small meadow ringed by thick pines. The fluffy clouds broke open, letting the sun peek through. Sparkling rays reflected off a crystal-clear pool fed by a small, bubbling spring. Jays flitted among the trees, squawking in short bursts as tiny wavelets lapped against the water's edges.

"Perfect," said Haddy, and wasting no time, stripped naked and slid beneath the water. With her head just above the surface, she bobbled off the sandy bottom and let the spring tickle her toes. She couldn't resist water, hot or cold, but because of her low body fat, the threat of hypothermia kept her alert. She judged the mountain pool at 51 degrees Fahrenheit, ten degrees above the North Korean winter seas. Haddy figured she had ten minutes before succumbing to uncontrollable shivering. Even so, the cold water cooled her roiling emotions. As the seconds ticked by, she floated, alone and empty in the water like a dark moon. Haddy knew her loneliness had no solution, but why was her soul so tuned to this central fact of human existence? There were hundreds of psychic radio stations, but hers had but one.

Haddy toweled off and made a fire, warmed herself, smoked Luckies, and opened Turnbull. Her fingers ran along the words, which described the ritual act of seppuku. An eighteenth-century picture captured the samurai warrior plunging the *wakizashi* short sword into the left side of his abdomen, pulling the blade to the right to sever the abdominal aorta. His second stood behind him to his left, ready to lop off his head, should he waver. If the samurai displayed unusual courage and honor, he took the blade out and plunged it again from the abdomen up to his sternum. Finally, for those rare few with a remaining pulse, they took out the blade and thrust it deep into their necks. Virtue was obedience. Much honor. Much glory. No shame. All shame gone. Samurai wives, however, wrapped a rope around their knees and used a knife called a *tanto* and made a single cut across the carotid artery in their necks. When they collapsed, their enemies found the thighs closed. They, too, had seconds, individuals chosen by their lords to deliver the singing whisper of the blade and decapitate the victim. Haddy had no seconds.

The sniper returned to the apartment, content she had found the ideal place to end her torment.

15

**Second Floor at the Corner of Jefferson and Henry Streets,
Manhattan, New York
Sunday, September 24
Zero-nine-hundred hours**

Wolf observed an uptick of drug runners in and out of the bunker-like door of the apartment building. He told Detectives Goodman and Zellner, nicknamed "G" and "Z," to hang tight in Iguazu's restaurant next door, saying, "Jam will show today." Wolf opened a fresh package of beef jerky sprinkled with sea salt and black pepper. He rechecked his Sig Sauer P320 M17 sidearm and Marine favorite, a 15.75-inch KA-BAR knife, with a 10-inch blade. He kneaded the scars on his chest, presents from insurgents in Iraq. Wolf had earned two Purple Hearts, among other medals of valor. He repeated Rule 85 from *Murphy's Laws of Combat*, "*A Purple Heart just proves that you were smart enough to think of a plan, stupid enough to try it, and lucky enough to survive."*

A rap on the door got Wolf's attention. He checked the monitor. Detective Maria Valenzuela stood outside in a sharp black pin-striped suit with two deli coffees and a brown bag.

She slipped past as he opened the door. "Drink this," she said. "Plus, here's some protein bars."

"Jam's posted a watcher on the roof," said Wolf. "The H&K is zeroed."

Maria observed the Heckler & Koch G28 scoped semiautomatic rifle. "Detective James, this is against regulations. But it's a sweet weapon." She took the rifle and sighted along the apartment rooftop. "Yeah, I see the watcher." Maria paused. "You still on Captain Greening to reopen your family's cold case? I thought you had an in with Brock himself."

"Something's holding the captain back," said Wolf.

Maria kept her eye on the apartment building and said, "Quite the story about Miss Brock and her proposal. 'Stay on the force, pursue law, but put away the gore and guns.' You'd need to be reassigned." Wolf grunted, but Maria hadn't finished jerking around the former master sergeant. She took out a *New York Times* art review section, saying, "I checked out your nudes at the Bleecker Street Gallery."

Wolf put down his coffee, opened and then shut his mouth. After the surprise wore off, he said, "What? How did you find out?" Maria handed him the article. Wolf's face reddened as he read and exclaimed, "How in the hell!? I mean the squad—no, I take that back, the entire precinct will roast me alive."

"Rich girl, high society, and racy sketches," Maria replied, happy to see Wolf blush. "You're a celebrity. Just stay away from guns and gore, and you'll be fine." Her demeanor changed, and she said, "I think our man just arrived. Here's the SUV."

Wolf's pulse quickened as the car slid to a stop across the street. "Have backup block both ends and clear the street," he said. "G and Z can approach on the sidewalk and do the same. I'll dip out the fire escape. You take the Heckler & Koch and watch my six."

Maria looked at Wolf, startled, saying, "And what?"

"Wait for my signal," replied Wolf.

"My God, like *'One, if by land, and two, if by sea'*?" asked Maria. But Wolf had run out. He slid down the fire escape and left the alley running. The curbside doors of the shiny SUV had opened when he turned the corner. Three men, like New York Giants linebackers, stepped out, along with Lord Ricky Jam, hands free, looking like a well-fed cat in a full-length black leather coat. The bodyguards carried bullpup-style submachine guns. Wolf recognized them as FN P90s, which fired nine hundred rounds per minute. Each bodyguard wore regulation sunglasses, headscarves, black T-shirts, and coats.

Wolf crossed the street and opened his cognac bomber jacket. G and Z had run behind the parked cars from the other direction. Wolf felt the pedestrian noise fade. Mothers whisked away children, and diners disappeared beneath tables. Wolf moved forward with one simple rule: project force. The air crackled in tension as a sun-glassed linebacker stepped between the detective and his master.

Jam saw Wolf and laughed. "A surprise visit, Detective? Where's your gun? I hope you have one, you're going to need it."

"Jam, you are under arrest for murder. Put down your weapons."

Ricky Jam's voice chilled. "I heard about you, Detective Wolf James. You're one hard motherfucker, but don't make me spill your blood."

Jam waited.

Wolf didn't move.

Jam gave an imperceptible nod to his man on the roof, when the report of Wolf's Heckler & Koch semiautomatic rifle came from the second-story window across the street. Before Jam's sniper fell to the pavement, Wolf's M17 leaped into his hands. The guards ripped out their P90s as Wolf drilled single rounds into the foreheads of the two closest bodyguards. The Heckler & Koch boomed again, and the .308 round struck the temple of the third guard. All three linebackers toppled to the sidewalk as the drug lord fled inside the building, coattails trailing in the wind. Maria hustled across the asphalt. Wolf exclaimed, "G and Z, get up on the roof and sweep from above. Maria, follow me."

Wolf and Maria cleared the first and second floors. Wolf bounded up the stairwell to the third and poked his head out. Jam's .357 Magnum shredded the door casing around him. Wolf waited a second, poked out again, and saw the cop killer step out the window at the far end onto the fire-escape landing. Wolf gripped the M17 with both hands and sprinted down the hall, blasting. The twenty-one-round magazine let the former Ranger maintain a steady fire as the glass and windowpanes around the fire escape shattered and splintered. Wolf flattened himself in a doorway as he saw Jam's Smith & Wesson eight-shot revolver come out over the sill and fire blindly into the hallway, until the chamber emptied. Wolf dashed forward, jamming in a fresh clip before the other hit the floor. He leaped through the window and caught Jam in the act of reloading. Wolf stuck the hot barrel of his pistol against Jam's head and said, "You're dead."

Jam let the pistol fall to the metal grating and raised his hands. Suddenly, one of Jam's drug runners below started shooting at Wolf. The fire escape pinged with bullets, until police dropped the teenager. Jam slammed a giant fist into Wolf's gut, which doubled over the detective, but Wolf got his hands up to protect his face as Jam unleashed a series of punishing blows. Wolf staggered back and would have plunged to the street below, save for the railing. Then he came back and moved inside Jam's arms, hitting the big man with a flurry of his own wicked left and right uppercuts. Jam pulled a knife and stabbed. Wolf grabbed Jam's wrist but slipped on blood, lost his footing, and fell. Jam took his chance. He planted both feet over the fallen detective, stretched out his knife, and made ready a killing blow. Wolf grabbed his razor-sharp KA-BAR from below. Jam unleashed his strike, but froze as Wolf's 10-inch blade pierced his rectum. The former Ranger jammed the 1095 Cro-Van steel up inside with both hands. Jam's eyes and mouth widened in a paralyzed gasp. The big man nose-dived to the pavement below.

Maria crashed out the window to find her junior partner covered in blood. Shaking her head in admiration, she said sarcastically, "I thought Miss Brock said, 'No guns or gore'?"

Wolf wiped his face on his sleeve and looked at the lifeless figure of Jam below. "Damn, that was close."

"That fight earned you a mandatory review, and the Brocks will shit their collective pants and not be happy. Tangling with titans is tough business, partner."

16

Day 7
Modi'inn-Maccabim-Re'ut Army Base
Sunday, September 24
Zero-seven-thirty hours

Haddy and Shira settled back for morning report, both unaware of the drama unfolding in the commanding officer's office, which explained why the lieutenant appeared flustered. Prime Minister Benjamin Netanyahu waited within. After the order of dismissal, the lieutenant asked sniper and spotter to step inside. The soldiers froze at the sight of the prime minister, snapped to attention, and saluted. He announced, "On September 18, seven days ago, Al Qaeda leader Anisur Salam met his fate at the hands of Staff Sergeant Haddy Abrams and Sergeant Shira Alian, by a bullet fired from two thousand, six hundred, and sixty-four yards. They brought havoc to the terrorist stronghold in Shib, Yemen, and escaped under massive fire. This is the longest shot recorded in the Israel Defense Force history. Their feat represents the finest of Israeli courage and training. The Thirty-Third Caracal Battalion and our special operations units stand honored." He shook their hands and gave each a letter of commendation. "Thank you for your brave service to our nation." Taking a stunned Haddy aside, he said, "Congratulations, Staff Sergeant Abrams. I'm recommending you for Officer Candidate School."

Haddy's dark eyes widened. "Sir?"

"You're taking two weeks' leave starting tomorrow. See me when you get back."

"Thank you, sir," Haddy stammered, as Shira snapped a photo on her phone.

The battle buddies left the building stunned. Shira wheeled and took Haddy's shoulders and addressed her partner proudly. "You are the Queen of Hearts, General Haddy Abrams, the world is at your fingertips."

Haddy appeared grim. "I feel nothing."

"Dammit, partner," said Shira, "don't do this to yourself. Hey, I found you a special rabbi. He is a philosopher and psychologist in Tel Aviv. I called him, he'll see you tomorrow."

Haddy flushed an angry red. She shoved Shira backwards and spit, "Fuck you, Shira, and fuck off. I don't want your fucking help." The veins in her neck bulged as she lost it. "Get the fuck out of my face!"

Shira flared and said, "You want me to call the lieutenant? Because I'll do it. Your head is so far up your ass, you can't see. You just got a letter of commendation. Me, your family, and your unit love you."

Haddy's rage boiled over. She slapped Shira. "Leave me the fuck alone!"

Shira lashed out with a right cross and leveled Haddy, putting her down in the dirt. "You fool," she said. "You are just itching to die. Most likely you've been up in the Ben Shemen and have yourself a grave site. Well, I'm washing my hands of you. Just make sure you do it right. No mistakes. None of that halfway shit. I'm not taking care of some drooling idiot *fool* the rest of my life. Swallow the gun and pull the trigger. I'm through with your fucking Camus and coffee cups, Nietzsche and shit angst." Shira gave her head a final shake of disgust. "I hope God kicks your butt to hell and back."

HADDY ENTERED THE APARTMENT LATE. Expecting silence, she tossed her clothes on the sofa, and heard muffled sobs from Shira's room. Haddy put her ear to her best friend's door, riven with guilt for hitting her. Maybe she should go to this rabbi? But wouldn't it delay the inevitable?

Haddy was ready to apologize when she heard Shira wail, "Jesus, dear God, save my Haddy. Save her, save her. Father, you are the God of the impossible. Do it. I know you can."

Fuck you and fuck your God, Shira, Haddy shouted to herself. She showered, and after toweling off lay down, lit a Lucky Strike, and stared at the ceiling before saying, "I wanted a father, but maybe the whole fucking world wants a father, like a little girl wants her dad to pick her up. A protector, provider, and guardian rolled into one. What a fucking fairy tale." Haddy reread her terse suicide letter, *"Mother, Grandfather Abrams and Grandfather Danilenko, cousin Raisa and sister in blood Shira: I have wrestled with an unspeakable torment, my father's murder at my birth. I will not face this pain again. Life lost its meaning a long time ago. I have decided to end this charade on my own terms. Staff Sergeant Haddy Abigail Abrams."*

It was 10 p.m. Haddy set the alarm for zero four thirty hours, time enough to fix a quad-breve, toast a bagel, slather it with cream cheese, and slip away before Shira got up. The sun would chase away the night at zero six zero seven hours tomorrow, and she wanted to be at the pool when its rays struck the water.

Haddy returned to her most cherished memory on Mt. Rainier. "What is it about a face," Haddy asked herself, "that stops you for a lifetime?" It was chiseled, like a hammer had struck a mighty blow to Gibraltar and a chunk of granite fell off. She had read about amber eyes, but never seen any. They changed colors in the morning's light. Their eyes had connected, and her belly fell. She would never see him again ...

They climbed Mt. Rainier, and then her group filed down the mountain, melting under the hot July sun. The climbers passed a blue ice-filled moraine and dared each other to jump in. Without hesitation, Haddy stripped to her panties and bra and dived into the icy water. She almost passed out from the shock. Her eyes opened as she lay submerged under the frozen slush. She could see sunlight piercing the surface from above. The water sparkled like diamonds, and Haddy stayed down as long as her lungs would allow. The stillness became a solitude, which she never forgot. In another life, she would have stayed submerged, holding the man with the amber eyes.

17

Day 8
Ben Shemen Forest, Israel
Monday, September 25
Zero-four-thirty hours

Haddy lit a Lucky Strike and tossed back her high-test coffee. She tugged on her polyester garb and day pack. Donning the motorcycle jacket, she wrestled on the helmet as quietly as possible, petted Mickey Mouse, and left without looking back.

Rain and wind buffeted the midnight-blue racing machine as Haddy made a dash to the mailbox. She dropped in the suicide note to Shira along with the others to her family. Haddy punched the accelerator and screamed down the road, around the curves, down the straightaway until she arrived at the Ben Shemen Forest parking lot in record time. She glanced at her watch: zero four fifty-five hours. First light arrived in sixty-seven minutes. Haddy parked and tucked the jacket and helmet under the sizzling machine. She put the keys in the jacket and with a lingering gaze at the motorcycle, turned and ran off.

With flashlight in hand, Haddy found her mark, a cut left in a tree, and jumped off the trail. She busted up the steep rocky ridge. Haddy saw the broken branch she'd left Saturday. She followed the game trail and found her rain-soaked meadow. The dense ring of pines buffered the direct rain from sweeping the area clean, but gusts of wind swirled, and bent some trees close to breaking. Tiny wavelets on the pool were whipped into a froth. The spring bubbled as it had, unconcerned by the maelstrom. The clouds raced past like puffs of fog.

Unfurling the ceremonial red mat used for hari-kari, Haddy arranged it at the edge of the water. She settled down cross-legged, lit a cigarette, and swallowed a double of tequila. *Here it ends*, she said to herself. *My pain stops. So be it.* Haddy took the rope from the pack, wrapped it around her thighs, and tied it off. Then, she got on her knees and faced the pond as wet mist drizzled down her face. She placed the razor-sharp edge on her neck.

Haddy called upon the frozen solitude of the Mt. Rainier glacial moraine. The amber- eyed mountaineer was absent. She breathed in and exhaled slowly. On the third exhale, her grip tightened when suddenly, a burst of wind cracked a tree. It crashed into the water. The shock knocked the blade loose from Haddy's hand, and she tumbled over. "Fucking A," she exclaimed. "That is fucking weird." Haddy untied her legs, brushed off her pants, and shook her head in disbelief. Her fingers touched the neck and tasted blood. So close, but for a gust of wind.

Haddy kneeled and retied the rope. In spite of the wind and waving trees, she relaxed and repeated the steps. Moraine lake, inhale ... exhale ... Her fingers tightened. Down came the blade when a branch broke behind her like a gunshot. The sound hurtled Haddy headfirst into the pond. The knife splashed in the pool. With her face beneath the water, she swallowed a mouthful. Haddy pushed up with both hands to get air, choking and coughing. She spluttered like a fire hydrant. When she got to her knees, Haddy untied the rope and turned, angry and fearful, not knowing who or what it might be.

Standing like a Grecian sculpture, a twelve-pronged Persian fallow buck deer stood stock-still across the windy pond. The beast stared at her with an unblinking gaze. He was so close, Haddy saw her reflection in its two round glassy eyes. The animal lowered his mouth to the water and drank as rainwater dripped off his hide. The antlers swung back to their lofty height on a wide, wizened neck. His ears twitched, and suddenly, the buck bounded away, leaving a trail of crashes through the trees and wind and rain in its wake.

The same gleaming sword, which she had held in her twelve-year-old hands, appeared. It burned like a lightsaber, but now it ran itself through her chest. Haddy's breath stopped. The pain split her apart. Her hands tried to wrench out the blazing unseen rapier. Haddy collapsed face down on the grass as a darkening presence fell on the meadow. Quivering, trembling, shaking, unable to move, Haddy came face to face with pure ... *dread*, a terrible, earthshaking *dread*. She lay frozen in a paralyzing all-encompassing fear that had no bottom. In a barely audible voice, Haddy said, "*What do you want?*"

Instantly, as in a vision, Haddy saw herself on the edge of a moonlit desert canyon. Far below, a river sparkled like an emerald snake. She looked behind her, and the desert, still hot from the day's furnace, burned. Her bone marrow began to vibrate, and a voice asked gently, "*What do you want?*"

Haddy looked into the canyon below, dizzy. Her heart thumped wildly. She said, "To know ... why ... you killed my father when I was born."

Silence, deeper than silence, ensued until Haddy tasted the reply: "Then *leap*."

As she peered into the chasm below, Haddy's heart pounded so hard her chest hurt. What was it, a mile below? Did it matter? Like a high diver, Haddy took a deep gulp of desert air and launched herself forward. She hurtled headfirst and fell like a stone as the river reached up with cold fingers to receive her. Haddy shut her eyes ... and awoke with her nose buried in the grass. She checked the time and gasped: three hours had elapsed.

Endless calm enveloped her. Haddy's soul floated like a feather on the surface of a mirrored lake tucked away in alpine forests. Untethered and weightless, it danced on the water. Her mind raced to the sea. Haddy saw herself as a castaway, clinging to a salt-sodden timber on a lifetime of endlessly restless waves, now washed ashore on a desert island. Her face and fingers sank into the warm sand. The briny salt smelled fresh and clean. The sound of breakers crashed behind her. Haddy summoned the courage to speak to what she didn't understand. "I'm leaving the Army. I want to study philosophy at Columbia and help Mom, and I want to be loved and treasured. Let him have amber eyes."

HADDY FLEW home in the midnight-blue racer, diving and darting along the slick curves of the road, her world an upside-down welter of peace and strange fear. She couldn't guess at how the question would be answered, but knew she had been heard. Her reenlistment came up on her birthday, and she would muster out, return to Manhattan, and start a new life.

As the in-line four zoomed past the now empty mailbox, Haddy cringed. She had put Shira through torment. Haddy turned off the engine and coasted to the front door. She peeked inside. Shira was on her knees with her elbows on the couch, wailing.

Haddy coughed. Shira spun around like a top. Her big brown eyes widened, and she leaped on Haddy like a panther. She wrapped her arms around her and gave her a big bear hug and covered her face in kisses. "You stupid bitch. You put me through hell. I should deck you, put your ass back on the floor, but I'm so glad to see you."

"I'm so sorry," exclaimed Haddy, bursting into tears.

Patting the couch, Shira swallowed and said, "Tell me what happened." Haddy removed the lime-green jacket. Shira saw the torn shirt and livid cut along her neck. "Oh, dear Jesus," she exclaimed.

Haddy retraced the events in detail. "The tree breaking the first time was weird, but when I stared into those buck's eyes, I knew beyond knowing. I collapsed and shook and heard. I opened my eyes three hours later."

"Do you feel okay?"

"I'm exhausted and famished. And yeah, I'm okay. And I'm leaving the Army. Going back to Manhattan, helping Mom with the gallery, studying philosophy. I don't care what the prime minister wants. I'm out."

Shira brightened up. "Ori Daniels called this morning. He wants to take you dancing tonight. Eat and rest, you'll be fine."

"I would like that," said Haddy.

Haddy fell asleep immediately and awoke hours later to a hot bath laced with the sensual woody fragrance of Marc Jacobs Decadence perfume.

Shira came in. "I want you to soak. Try something new and shave, like all over; you understand?"

Haddy went to her room. Shira had laid out Haddy's red-and-black-striped dress. Next to the dress were stylish black sandals.

Shira arrived. "Put on that glossy bloodred lipstick you

have, the one with the sparkles." When the knock came on the front door, Shira flung it open. "Can I help you?" she said to Ori.

"Hi, Sergeant, is Haddy in?"

"Hell no. She's gone, but I'm here and all alone."

Haddy came up. "Come in, Ori. It's good to see you."

Ori produced a bouquet of red roses from behind his back. "You look fantastic."

Shira fanned herself. "You two get out of here and don't come back. I need my rest."

A delightful Mediterranean breeze blew into the Lacoste Bar and Grill, as Ori and Haddy entered the trendy establishment. The music throbbed and the atmosphere shimmered. Haddy felt surrounded by youth and tantalizing aromas.

Ori ordered a growler of HaDubim IPA, lentils with spinach and lemon, and grilled calamari. They found a table next to the dance floor. Ori took a big gulp of the tasty beer, while Haddy downed a pint without coming up for air. The soldiers hit the floor in full hip-grinding mode. Loosened by a newfound joy, Haddy danced with abandon. On a slow beat, her lips searched for Ori's. The Sayeret Matkal spec-ops chief sergeant pulled her closer.

Just then the front doors opened, and the ocean breeze wafted in a salty coolness with aromas off the street. The music stopped. A glass clinked. Haddy looked up to see a youngster in a coat with a box strapped to his forehead. It was a GoPro camera, used by sportsters to capture live action. She glanced at Ori; they sensed before they knew.

"Allahu Akbar!" the boy shouted at a fevered pitch. Haddy felt Ori wrap his arms around her. But then he was flayed apart, as the bomb exploded. The compression wave lifted Haddy off the ground like a rag doll and flung her into a brick wall and utter darkness.

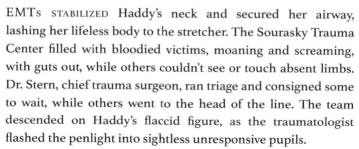

EMTs STABILIZED Haddy's neck and secured her airway, lashing her lifeless body to the stretcher. The Sourasky Trauma Center filled with bloodied victims, moaning and screaming, with guts out, while others couldn't see or touch absent limbs. Dr. Stern, chief trauma surgeon, ran triage and consigned some to wait, while others went to the head of the line. The team descended on Haddy's flaccid figure, as the traumatologist flashed the penlight into sightless unresponsive pupils.

"Find neurosurgery," he barked. "Who's on call?"

"Dr. Rammoth," said the ER nurse. Dr. Stern performed a head exam using the acronym HEENT: head, eyes, ears, nose, and throat. He noted fresh blood in her left ear and announced, "Left cranial fracture." He moved over Haddy's body with a stethoscope and deft fingers, probing for fractures, bruises, and bleeding. "Face, neck, and shoulder are shredded. Call maxillofacial and reconstructive surgery and orthopedics. Prepare for a craniotomy."

The anesthesiologist stood by with the endotracheal tube. She adjusted the ventilator settings, as the resident surgeon found Haddy's femoral vein in the groin. He plunged in a large bore needle, withdrew blood, and gave it to the lab technician to assess her electrolytes and blood count. The anesthesiologist looked at Dr. Stern for the go-ahead. She saw the nod, and the resident injected one milliliter of the curare-like Pavulon, developed from what Amazon tribes used for centuries to induce paralysis in their victims. The blood zipped into Haddy's heart and lungs; in nanoseconds, she stopped breathing. The anesthesiologist threaded the endotracheal tube into her trachea and attached it to the respirator. It huffed and puffed, inflating Haddy's lungs with oxygen and removing waste gases moments later. The ER door burst open.

Dr. Rammoth, the neurosurgeon, a weary man cloaked in a white coat, came in. "Dr. Stern, what've we got?"

The trauma surgeon replied in a cold, crisp professional tone, "Left side intracranial bleed. Pupils fixed and dilated." Dr. Rammoth's surgical assistant shaved off Haddy's hair and splashed the scalp with purple antiseptic, placing sterile drapes. Taking a scalpel, Dr. Rammoth made a half-moon-shaped incision above Haddy's left ear. He took a hand-operated drill and bored a hole through the cranial bone. A geyser of pent blood poured out from blood vessels in the brain. He screwed in a titanium bolt to allow further drainage and attached a pressure sensor.

Drs. Miriam Adina, chief of maxillofacial and reconstructive surgery and Dr. Amberg, the orthopedic surgeon, arrived, came in, and examined Haddy. "Poor girl," they said in unison. "Take her to Trauma Room Three."

The surgeons prepped and scrubbed and entered the operating suite as Haddy arrived. "You know the drill, folks," said Dr. Adina. "One gram of cephalexin per liter of saline, irrigate the hell out of those wounds, and get X-rays. Get the metal out and start the marathon."

18

A glassy dawn gleamed throughout Moscow. Brianna dreamed of a wealthy Asian telling her to apply Hoppes gun-cleaning solution to her lady's Ruger LC9 pistol. Her eyes burst open to the distinctive scent of the gun oil. Brianna's pulse exploded from first to fourth gear in a second. She checked her daughter Ulyana, who lay asleep beside her. Brianna wrapped her slender fingers around the slim semiautomatic pistol, always on the bedside table. She quietly racked the slide, flicked the safety off, and swung a pair of shapely legs to the floor. In haste, Brianna threw on her robe. She passed through the spacious closet, lined with furs and clothing and countless shoes, to the other side. With her weapon grasped firmly in both hands, Brianna entered the darkened living room and saw a figure sitting on the couch. The living room lamp clicked on. Brianna's face paled. The beautiful woman felt the blood pool to her feet.

"You haven't returned my emails," said Ivan Juric, rasping. Brianna's spine went cold. She tried to control the panic, which tightened its fingers around her throat. Should she run? Brianna kept the three-dot sight of the semiautomatic on the man's face. With one hand, she flipped on the overhead lights, which winked from a curvy track above.

"Ivan," she muttered breathlessly.

Ivan lit a cigarette and patted the couch. "Sit beside me. Let's chat and let me admire your new breasts." Ivan's henchman appeared from the closet. He reached around from behind her and grabbed the pistol. He tore off her robe and bra and pushed her to the couch.

"I did nothing wrong," cried Brianna. "I ... I just can't work for you anymore."

Ivan put his arm around her. "Your enhancements remind me of those sixteen-inch guns on American destroyers. You should be pleased." Brianna watched as a vicious tic tore back his lip. Terrified, she began to breathe heavily, and before she could stop herself, vomited, urinated, and shit.

Ivan bounded off the couch, wet a towel, and cleaned off his suit. "You fucking whore!" Turning to Stanislov, he ordered, "Clean her up," and barked to Yegor, "Get her bastard daughter."

Brianna fought like a wildcat as the burly thug threw her on the floor and wiped her ass. Ulyana's scream fueled her terror. The child kicked and flailed about under the tree-trunk arm of Yegor. "Ivan! Not Ulyana," she pleaded. "Please, please, please, I beg of you."

"You don't disrespect me, ever," Ivan raged. He slammed a pocket-sized gold skull on top of a leather folder on the coffee table. "This man must sign a contract with Army Munitions Group and move to Odessa. Yegor will take you to the jet. You're going to Beirut."

Brianna wrapped her arms around his knees. Wailing, she said, "Ivan, let Ulyana stay. Let her stay, please."

Ivan barked at her like a junkyard dog. "Get your filthy hands off me. Ulyana stays with me. You'll get her back when you're finished." He threw her aside. "Open the floor safe." Brianna crawled into the closet as Ulyana's shrieks faded down the hallway. She spun the dial, and Yegor cleaned out her earnings. Brianna's brain raced. She made a mad dash to the door, but Ivan grabbed her ankle and tripped her. He slammed an iron hand between her shoulder blades and tore off her panties. Brianna heard his belt buckle open, the pants come down, and felt a throbbing rod push against her asshole.

"No, Ivan!" Brianna screamed. "I won't be able to walk!"

Ivan kept his knees straddled over Brianna. He leaned down and rubbed her shoulders. With his mouth next to her ear, he said, "Never break someone's heart. They only have one. Break their bones instead, all two hundred and six." He stood and straightened his tie. "Get up!" Brianna peeled herself off the floor. Ivan slapped her in the face. Brianna lost her balance and crashed backwards. "Stop wasting my time. Get ready," he ordered.

BRIANNA THREW TOGETHER A QUICK WARDROBE. Hours later, she stumbled out of the limousine, ill from head to toe. The driver pulled out two suitcases and a vanity bag. Brianna had thrown on a full-length fur coat over a loose cotton-knit burgundy sweater. With distressed jeans and ballet flats, she waded through the Moscow International Airport, tugging the luggage on rollers while holding back tears of rage, shame, and a distilled black hate. Brianna focused on placing one foot in front of the other as she walked in a daze across the cold tarmac.

She made her way to the black jet, whose staircase lay open and waiting. Brianna had put up her hair in a hasty knot and only dimly recalled covering her swollen and bruised cheek with powder. She kept her sunglasses on. Her cinnamon eyes had lost their luster amid tear-soaked red rims and bloodshot whites. Brianna pulled up the fur around her head and moved slowly to the plane.

The flight attendant, Irena Yaroslava, helped her aboard and said nothing, but got her seated and returned with tissues, ice packs, aspirin, and vodka.

Brianna curled up, bringing her knees to her chest. Could she disappear? Alone? What could she do? Kill herself and leave Ulyana to those wolves? Call the police? Find and shoot Ivan Juric? *Yes, God yes.* She would put the barrel on his forehead and pull the trigger, but where could she find this human pile of shit? For all she knew, he was in the airport lounge swizzling vodka, watching her get aboard. Brianna's fists pounded the seat cushions as she visualized tying him down, taking a butcher's knife, and hacking him into pieces. She fed each into the kitchen disposal, listening to the fresh flesh being ground into garbage.

Brianna felt the stewardess touch her on the shoulder. Irena held four aspirin and iced vodka and urged her to drink. The escort put her head in her hands. "I'm a rat in a maze," she said to herself. "I can't climb out. I can't turn around. I'm afraid and hate myself for underestimating that jackal."

Irena returned and refilled her glass and left. The vodka burned, but felt good, and Brianna wanted to get off the jet and drink herself into oblivion; maybe the nightmare would end. She looked at her palms and saw blood. There was blood also on her razor-sharp fingernails. She tasted blood and realized she had chewed the insides of her mouth. Brianna had watched documentaries which showed wolves and saber-toothed cats caught in tar pits. Each time they moved, they sank deeper, until they disappeared beneath the slime. "Who will save me and Ulyana!?" she screamed within. "*Ulyana is everything. I will fight for her to my dying breath.*" Brianna applied the ice to her cheek. She lit a cigarette and let the nicotine cut through the fog. Irena appeared again with steaming hot Russian tea, patted her shoulder, and left.

The slim leather briefcase lay in the seat beside her. Brianna touched it, sipped the tea, and tossed her hair back. She shook off her fear and panic. "Start fucking thinking." As her nerves settled, she said, "You have allies, you just don't know who they are. Now get yourself out of this. You've done it before, and you can fucking do it again."

Brianna's fingers tapped on the dark leather briefcase. Her jaw tightened as she considered the nameless face in the file. No doubt a CEO essential to Eastern Machine Systems. Heavy and overweight, a drinker who stank with entitlement and self-importance. Old and shriveled, it did not matter. "I'll fuck you up, down, front, and back until your dick falls off and force you to sign your life away. Once you're in my mouth, you will beg me to sign." Would her services be required tonight? Brianna would take him to bed with an icy vengeance and fuck him until the deed was done.

Opening the briefcase, Brianna removed the typewritten note.

"Subject must sign employment agreement with Army Munitions Group in Odessa, Ukraine."

"Subject is Professor François LeCompte, PhD, a graduate of the Ecole Polytechnique at eleven, with a PhD in nuclear energy, University Bordeaux Center of Nuclear Studies at fourteen. He is the youngest winner of the Niels Bohr Prize in Astrophysics, Stockholm, Sweden, *Multi-dimensionality and the*

Many Worlds Hypothesis of Quantum Uncertainties. Current head of the Lebanese University Nuclear Physics Program. Born: September 10, 1997. Resides in Apartment 2D, The Residence 649, Beirut, Lebanon. Professor LeCompte swims daily, plays billiards, and reads widely. He frequents two bars of note: The Blue Note Jazz bar and the Iris Beirut rooftop restaurant and bar. No debt, drug use, or porn. Never married, no children; and infrequent dater."

Brianna straightened up. She had never seduced a genius. "Interesting. Wonder what he looks like?"

The next page contained a 10- by 12-inch color-enhanced photo.

In spite of herself, Brianna's breath caught; he was certainly easy on the eyes. In the photo, her prey was clad in a lab coat. The photographer had surprised him in his lab and makeshift office.

François LeCompte reminded Brianna of a California surfer. He had a slender oval face, and his sun-washed hair fell over his shoulders. He held a coffee cup in one hand, while adjusting a knob on some piece of scientific equipment. Though it sprouted wires, pipes, and tubes and lay covered in radiation-warning stickers, he evinced no concern whatsoever. A cigarette dangled from a lip which Brianna studied with expert eyes. Kissable. Very kissable. But Brianna leaned closer to get a better look at the eyes. They possessed an ethereal, almost otherworldly quality. Vivid electric blue, they sparkled with intelligence. With a hand on her chest, Brianna knew with him there would be no pushing. She must call on all her feminine guile and play her cards like a Las Vegas gambler. But he was a man, wasn't he?

Brianna examined the rest of the picture. He wore a T-shirt, but she couldn't make out the face or writing across it; slim-fit jeans and boat shoes completed his ensemble. Nice ass, definitely fit. She thought she recognized the Three Stooges on the coffee mug.

Brianna placed the file and photo away, sipped her vodka, and nursed her cheek. She twirled her hair, asking herself how she should dress. "The beige satin Givenchy shirt with a burnt sienna merino U-cut sweater. Clean. I'll go with the black leather pants, red alligator belt, and casual sandals, a gold necklace with my ruby pendant nestling in my cleavage and gold earrings. A light powder to cover this bruise (but not too much), a touch of rouge to highlight my cheeks, and ruby lipstick. Musk perfume behind my ears and neck and the slender gold Patek watch with rubies." She wondered about her hair. "I'll pin it up. Take my camera. When things warm up, I'll let things down."

The wheels touched the tarmac. A Syndicate man met the airplane and ferried Brianna to the Le Royal Beirut Hotel, penthouse suite. The day was bright and balmy. Brianna lay down, swallowed a Xanax, and sipped on vodka. On the bed lay a note, "Be ready tomorrow."

19

Day 9
University of Beirut, Lebanon
Tuesday, September 26
Zero-five-hundred hours

François LeCompte left his apartment at 5 a.m. He touched his Galadriel, the photo of Cate Blanchett who portrayed the Elven princess in one of the films based on Tolkien's *Lord of the Rings*, before jumping in his cherry-red Audi R8. François hit the accelerator, and instead of thirty-nine minutes of normal driving, he cut that in half. He drove like a maniac along the M51 to the White Beach south of Batroun. "Galadriel, oh Galadriel, you are my muse. Let me find wisdom today and may love find my heart open." He did not think of himself as a dangerous driver, but had no patience for other cars, road signs, or pedestrians. He pointed the roadster straight forward and drove in helter-skelter fashion. Today, unlike most days, he struggled with anxiety; he would argue with the Iranian and have it out. As he raced north, François thought of the one woman he had known, his "Black Swan," full of beauty, grace, and a deep intelligence from Cambridge, and wished for her. "If you were with me, I'd have the answer."

François pulled up at the pristine and deserted sands of the beach. "I love with all my heart my studies, and if this disagreement is not resolved, I will go elsewhere to find enriched plutonium. But that would mean unacceptable delays."

A soft warm breeze touched his skin, and François tugged on the red silicone cap and adjusted his goggles. He started the stopwatch and let his bathrobe slide to his feet to begin his regular swim. Depending on the pressures of the day, François swam through the sea with powerful strokes for either ten or fifteen miles. Today it would be ten. This meant seventy-three minutes north to Selaata, where he did a 180-degree turn and returned to the White Beach. The solitude focused his mind. Perhaps if he had not locked himself away in his lab, his Cambridge Black Swan would still be his.

François cut through the water and considered his appointment with the Iranian emissary to Ali Khamenei, supreme leader of the Islamic Republic of Iran. What options did they have but to answer either "yes" or "no" to his request for Professor Helmut Gott? The dispute was an irritant. It took him away from the lab and his time to meditate on the mysteries of plutonium. He had left the prestigious IN2P2 Institute for Advanced Nuclear Studies in Paris, due to the imbecility of the French government. The minister of finance had pulled his research funds in favor of "sexier" investigations into global warming. François had thrown up his hands in disgust and flown to a conference of nuclear physicists in Beirut. He listened to Professor Helmut Gott speak on his advances in third-generation laser trigger software for fission devices. In addition, enjoying it all like chocolate icing on French pastry, he spoke with Professor Stefan Danilenko, the collaborator with the Lawrence Livermore Labs High Explosives Applications Facility, "HEAF," in California. To Danilenko alone went the prize of having designed the first third- generation software.

During break time, François met Dr. John Clattering, PhD, director of the Los Alamos National Laboratories in Santa Fe, New Mexico. Dr. Clattering had said, "Professor LeCompte? Join us tonight over cocktails. Meet my associate Mr. Richard Vauntnon." But didn't they know New Mexico didn't have beaches? Then the beautiful face of a young Lebanese woman captured François's attention. Standing at her side was a tall Arab with an immaculately trimmed beard and white *thawab* which flowed to the floor like cream.

He bowed and said in a mellifluous tone, "Professor LeCompte? *As-salamu alaykum*, peace be upon you. Allow me to introduce Miss Sehresh Khoury, my able assistant. I am Abd al Hakim. The Iranian government understands your dilemma and will fund your research. Stay here at Lebanese University. We will provide your plutonium." François had glanced out the windows at the glittering sea and saw the easy access to the ocean waves.

Blind to the ways of religion and politics, François declared, "I require my Audi R8, Spencer Marston billiards table, and a Legacy Audio Wavelet DAC Preamp Crossover sound system. And solitude above all."

"You shall have them," said the emissary. "My able assistant, Miss Khoury, will help you."

François remembered her dazzling cognac eyes, but they had faded as his need for the genius of Helmut Gott grew. At the unheard-of age of sixteen, François broke the barrier on the minimum baseball-sized sphere of enriched uranium for fission explosions, reducing it to the size of a Ping-Pong ball. He then increased its explosive powers by three. The French government secretly tested the device in the ocean and confirmed François's breakthrough. His small handheld missile, in the hands of one soldier, could fly farther and faster and level ten city blocks of cement and steel. For himself, François cared little about the military applications and did not hate the emissary, but he was close to another scientific discovery. He pressed Abd al Hakim for the gifted software engineer, but received the same tedious answer, "The council hasn't decided." François abhorred lying and sensed the emissary lied.

François drove to the university and locked the office door. For two months, he had stayed inside. Today, as he did every day, he ate his usual minced prime beef, egg yolk, herbs, spices, and anchovy filets, along with double shots of French espresso. He lit a pungent Gitanes cigarette, whose unadulterated Turkish tobacco sharpened his brain and curdled his blood. François turned on Frederic Chopin's Piano Concerto No. 1 in E minor, Op. 11 and sidled up to the billiards table.

François took the black-lacquered cue stick and racked the balls into their customary triangle. He chalked the tip and with deft precision struck the white cue ball against the cushion behind the rack. The ball caromed exactly between two balls. The transmitted force sent the first ball of the rack, the yellow "1", forward. It banked off two cushions before dropping into the side pocket. François didn't stop, but sank each ball. He left the white cue in position to continue onto the second rack. He rehearsed his arguments to an imaginary Mr. Hakim. "Men like Danilenko and Gott make detonations more potent. Their 'firing pins' detonate the ultra-high explosive faster and with more precision. The inward blast, or 'shock wave,' sends the core from 'subcritical' to a 'super-critical' explosion."

Later that day, François returned to the table. He sipped on his favorite drink, absinthe, the "Green Goddess" of van Gogh fame, while cutting the rack apart. He had a straight run of 129 balls when he heard the knock. His pulse increased; he steadied his nerves, put on his sports coat, and waited.

Abd al Hakim flowed in. Putting his hands together, he bowed. "*As-salamu alaykum*, peace be upon you, esteemed professor."

François nodded and kept his hands on the billiards table. "Thank you, emissary," he replied coldly. "Now. No more dissimulation. Yes or no. Will you hire Helmut Gott?" François observed the emissary's eyebrows narrowing and face tightening.

"The supreme leader believes your genius can further the revolution by joining our eminent laser physicist Professor Ebrahim in our Iranian research facility in Natanz."

François's blue eyes sharpened. He took three short puffs on the Turkish tobacco. "This is fatuous nonsense. Ebrahim is an aging fossil, and you know I won't live in Iran. You've been stalling. You and your exalted leader are liars."

The Iranian paled. "You impugn the supreme leader?"

But François's calm demeanor broke. He raised his voice. "I quote your Quran. Beware, I inform you regarding the greatest of the mortal sins: associating anything with Allah, disobeying parents, and *lying!*" The Iranian emissary turned various shades of white and red, but François saw daggers. His lips tightened. He lay hold of the white cue ball and tossed it into the air. "I think you should leave, emissary, before you lose your lying teeth." Abd al Hakim's eyes widened in fright. He rushed out the door as the ball landed squarely between his shoulder blades with a resounding "thwack." "Good riddance and don't come back!" shouted François.

François checked the time: 5:44 p.m. The Iris Beirut rooftop bar and café opened in sixteen minutes. François frequented the Iris enough they reserved him a table in the corner from six to seven p.m. It afforded an unimpeded view of the ocean, but how he wished for his Black Swan.

20

Brianna sipped vodka after resting. Ivan called and said, "He's at the Iris Beirut. Don't fuck this up. I'll be watching." The line disconnected, and Brianna steeled herself, colder by the second. She must do the devil's bidding, though aware Ivan would likely kill her and sell Ulyana when this was over. Outfoxing him would be the Mt. Everest of deception. Could she do it?

Arriving at the club with her Nikon slung over her shoulder, Brianna spied François at a small table in the distant corner. He had a light scruffy beard, and thick sandy hair fell over his shoulders. Her mark gazed over the ocean at the fading horizon. Brianna ignored the receptionist and the stares from men and women who were sure a model or movie star was in their midst, and approached François on the prowl. She glided to the railing, faltered, and bumped his shoulder. François whipped up his head in irritation.

"Pardon, monsieur," said Brianna weakly. She watched François's frown turn to an expression of shock.

He held his breath, mouth parted. "Mademoiselle," he said and got up. François put his arm around her slender waist and helped Brianna to his chair. He pulled another to the table. She observed François gazing at her ruby. Then his eyes went to her lips, before breaking free and looking into a dazzling pair of shimmering cinnamon eyes.

Brianna placed the camera on the table. "I'm sorry," she said. "My deepest apologies, monsieur. I'm so embarrassed. I wanted one more picture of the fading sun and pushed myself too far." Keeping her eyes alert to his reaction, Brianna recognized the stare. She nodded at his water. "Can I have a drink?"

"Exactment," he replied hastily. "I'm a fool, an imbecile," and signaled for the waiter, who brought a glass and carafe.

Brianna sipped. In a silky-smooth modulated tone, she said, "I'll feel better in a moment," and looked around. "I'll be gone before your date arrives."

"You needn't go," said François, and turned towards the setting sun. He took the napkin and patted his forehead. *"Sacrebleu.* Oh, Galadriel, you are full of mischief."

Brianna had underestimated François's uncommonly good looks. She whispered to herself, *"Sacrebleu* yourself." François remained fixated on the darkening waters and remained quiet. Brianna tapped François on his shoulder and extended a hand. "I'm Brianna Ivanova."

When he faced her in the candlelight, Brianna's heart skipped a beat. He wiped his palm on his jeans and took her hand. "François LeCompte."

"Ooo la la!" Brianna said to herself. "I'm going to enjoy this." François would fall fast and far, and if she must seduce him,

she would savor every bite. "Three times a day with this piece of chocolate?" and laughed to herself. Brianna nodded at his drink. "Is that good?"

François was in a quiet reverie. "Very," he said. "Would you like one?" Brianna nodded, and François ordered another but came back to her face. Where other women might be embarrassed, Brianna rose to the occasion. She took the cigarette from his fingers, and François said, "Those will kill you."

Brianna placed her elbows on the table and let the ruby shine. She inhaled deeply, raised an eyebrow, and blew out the smoke. "I'm Russian and more deadly." François opened his pack and placed a fresh Gitanes between her lips. "You look at me and say nothing," said Brianna. "Should I be alarmed?"

"You tell me," he replied with a twinkle in his eye. "From your voice I detect both innocence and hardness; a practiced guile, perhaps? What have I, a besotted male, done to deserve the honor of such a beauty?" Stunned, Brianna wondered if he had seen through her façade. Fortunately, the drink arrived, and Brianna took a sip. "It's called the Green Beast," said François, "made from absinthe."

"Very tasty. I assure you this moment was not arranged, except perhaps by fate. Do you believe in fate, François?" François retreated into silence. A little nervous, Brianna read his T-shirt. It was a picture of Monty Python's *Holy Grail* with the quote, *"Bridge keeper: What ... is the air speed velocity of an unladen swallow?"* Brianna giggled. "So, what is the velocity of an unladen swallow?" she asked playfully.

François's eyes cleared. "Making a calculation."

"A calculation?"

"From general relativity." François spoke briefly of gravitational fields and spacetime warping. "Because I have mass, when I walk, I bend the planets around me like the sun, but infinitesimally smaller. I ran a calculation on how much you bend them when you move."

"Probably more than I want," Brianna replied. A sly smile crossed her face. "How do I move?"

"Like a gazelle," he replied. "Your hair is sable fur, chocolate with tints of gold. Is it natural?" François spoke without effort or guile.

Brianna let it down and shook it out. "It's me. Would you like to touch?"

He ran the strands through his fingers and then lifted her chin and touched Brianna's cheek. "A bruise," he said simply.

Brianna's eyelashes fell. "Apart from my camera, I spent the day with an attorney. My husband Sergei's wealthy, but he's abusive when he drinks. I married money and power. What more do you want? But you must be a physicist to speak like you do."

"Head of nuclear physics at the university, and you?"

"I have a degree in Russian literature from Lomonosov, with a minor in Shakespeare. And before you ask, my favorites are Nabokov and *Macbeth*." The Green Goddess lubricated an easy discourse. Brianna sensed their chemistry deepen and scored points with a joke. "An Englishman, Frenchman, and Russian are in an art gallery observing a painting of Adam and Eve in the Garden of Eden.

"'Look at their reservation and calm,' says the Englishman, 'they are clearly English.'

"'Yet, so beautifully naked; they are French,' counters the Frenchman.

"The Russian shakes his head. 'No clothes, no bed, no roof over their heads with only one apple? And this is paradise? They are Russian.'"

François laughed and commented, "Brilliant, so will you teach after the divorce?"

"Do I look like a teacher?" Brianna chuckled. "No, monsieur Professor, I need answers."

"Would you like to eat?"

"I'm famished." Dinner arrived with a bottle of Chablis.

François pulled out his smartphone and tapped on the Universal Splitter App icon. He explained the principle of quantum uncertainties. "Your question sends a photon into a splitter, where the light particle may stay in this universe or pass into another. Essentially a 'yes,' or 'no.' What is your question?"

The band had arrived, and Brianna snapped her fingers with the rhythm in the balmy air. She placed slender fingers on François's forearm, saying, "Should I fall in love?" Her shoulders moved with the beat. She removed the sweater and unbuttoned the blouse to her navel. Brianna bit the lower half of her lip as if waiting for the answer. Before François could hit "send," she said, "Wait. I have another question. Should I fall in love with," and touched his cheek. "With you?" Brianna laughed, took his hand, and led him to the dance floor. Like a genie released from a bottle, she danced gaily. François responded, and she drew him closer, kissed his neck, and whispered, "I'm very attracted to you" and parted her mouth. But the lips never touched. François steered the surprised woman back to their table, glancing at the hulk of Stanislov, two tables away.

Brianna's body shivered, as the morning memory of Ivan returned. "You recognize him?" asked François.

"No," but François cupped his palm against Brianna's cheek.

"I think you're lying," he said. "*See how she leans her cheek upon her hand! O, that I were a glove upon that hand, That I might touch that cheek!*"

Brianna's eyes swelled. Tears came unbidden. "You quote *Romeo and Juliet*? You're my Romeo?"

François turned. His eyebrows lowered as he stared at the brute. "Is that your husband's watchdog? Should I have a word?"

Fear ran down her spine, and Brianna quoted *King Lear*, "'*Come not between the dragon and his wrath*,'" adding, "Your gallantry will get you killed."

The ocean breeze picked up. François said, "I once knew a gifted clown who entertained a tyrant. Halfway through the performance, he pulled out a gun from baggy pants. He pointed it at the children and the despot and pulled the trigger. A bouquet of flowers popped out, and everyone laughed. He did this the first two days. In the finale, he pulled out a real gun and shot the dictator dead. The moral? Jokesters often have the last laugh, Miss Ivanova."

"You're my madman, poet, and protector?" said Brianna and squeezed his hand. She tossed back her hair and said fetchingly, "Would you escort me to my room?" François turned towards the sea in silence, as though in a trance. "François?" asked Brianna.

He slowly turned back and took her hands. "What do you want, Brianna? Why are you here?"

Brianna pulled her chair next to his. She grabbed his face and kissed him hard, her tongue tasting him thoroughly, as her passion flowed into his mouth. François gasped and pulled her in, hotter than a torch. Brianna felt an atom bomb explode inside her and the ground shake. She took his hands and placed them on her chest. "Can't a woman want a night with Prince Charming?" François took her lips and made them his own, pushing his tongue deep inside. Brianna broke the connection, gasping, not unlike the night when she conceived Ulyana with her Spanish prince. Her heart pumping wildly, Brianna's mind raced. "Idiot. You seduce *him*, not the other way around." Panting, she said, "I'm at the Le Royal. Come with me."

François leaned back and lit a Gitanes. "You take me for a fool?"

"*What?*"

"Miss Ivanova. What sane man wouldn't want to lose himself in your arms? But sex is easy; it takes no skill, like smoking this cigarette. But I see abuse and fear and distress beneath your dazzle. You've been terrorized and stalked by thugs. You want to escape and die orgasm's 'little death.' For those few precious moments, to leave Earth like Icarus and touch the sun. But in the morning, you will fly away. I, however, will be changed forever. I don't do one-night stands."

Brianna tried to hide her panic. Had she failed? Then the startling thought that François might free her from Ivan's treachery arose, that this Frenchman might be her answer. Brianna had to have him, for reasons she didn't understand herself. "François," she implored. "Let our love be the phoenix tonight and burst into flames. In the morning, we will sift through the ashes and see who walks away. Or perhaps it's the start of something new?"

21

Day 10
Trauma ICU, Sourasky Hospital, Tel Aviv, Israel
Wednesday, September 27
Zero-six-hundred hours

Haddy opened her eyes. A fluorescent tube glowed over a washbasin. Myriad machines, cramped together, winked in green lights in maniacal automated precision. She recognized the hazy numbness of morphine. Her eyelids fluttered. She twitched, and her muscles, frozen from inactivity, recoiled in pain. Haddy's head throbbed, as if beaten by a hammer. Her ears were drowned in a high-pitched roar. She opened her jaws to relieve the pressure, causing more distress. She shivered; damn, she was cold. Haddy swallowed, but her throat was dry sand. Her efforts spiked an increase in heart rate, which triggered an alarm in the nursing station. She heard a curtain open and a nurse bustle in. At the same time, Haddy noticed a flaming boy dance across the room, holding a shining music box. She tried to swat it away, but her right hand wouldn't move. "Why is that?" she wondered. "And I see cold, like deep blue sky."

The nurse notified the resident physician, adjusted the temperature, and returned with heated blankets. She wiped with a small, soaked sponge on a stick around Haddy's mouth. The nurse checked the drip-rates on the plastic intravenous bags, as Haddy thought, "They look like dead men hanging from stainless steel poles."

The resident bent over his patient. "Hello, Staff Sergeant, how are you?" When she didn't respond, he recognized the loss of hearing. He shined his penlight in her eyes to check pupil responsiveness, and Haddy turned away in discomfort. The resident checked the head bolt and intracranial pressure and for the record asked, "Can you hear me?" He could see she was trying to listen. "How's your pain? On a scale of zero to ten, what is it?"

His patient muttered, "Get the fuck away from me."

The resident ignored her. "Open your mouth," and opened his mouth to help her understand. When she didn't, he pried the tongue blade between her teeth. Diving and dipping his head to catch a look at her throat, the doctor saw reddened raw tissues from the previous endotracheal tube. Haddy gagged. Her left hand worked, and she grabbed his wrist and threw it back. The resident, unperturbed, commanded, "Smile for me," making a clown face. "Can you do that?"

"You are a fucking jerk," mouthed Haddy. The doctor ignored the insult and placed his index and middle fingers in her palms, continuing, "Squeeze my fingers." Getting no response, he squeezed with his own and repeated, "Squeeze my fingers." Haddy nodded and tightened. Her left hand worked; the right did not. Finally, the resident took the polished steel end of his reflex hammer and ran it up the soles of her feet to test primal reflexes.

"Goddammit, you motherfucker. Get out of here," came the shout. With no desire to enrage her further, the resident left in a hurry.

"Am I paralyzed?" Haddy asked herself. Her face widened in fear, and the movement tugged on the bandages. She touched herself with her left hand. "My face. What happened to my face?" she said in mounting horror.

The nurse returned and injected four milligrams of morphine into the IV. As Haddy drifted off, she watched a fiery boy and dazzling box dance across an iridescent Tahitian sunset.

22

Day 10
Fighting Ninth Precinct, Manhattan, New York
Wednesday, September 27
Zero-seven-thirty hours

Monday, Wolf went straight from the precinct to his Bronx apartment on a mandatory thirty-day review. He avoided Kathryn. They talked that evening by phone. She said, "Why aren't you here with me?"

"I need some quiet time," said Wolf.

"What happened?"

"Big-time violence," Wolf replied. "No doubt you'll see it on the news."

Kathryn shuddered and said, "Wolf, I buried my brother. I will not bury you."

The following day, Holly Rawlins, Captain Greening's secretary, called with a terse message, "He wants to see you tomorrow."

Wolf arrived at the precinct and received sober congratulations. Street cameras had captured the fight scene from street to fire escape. They showed Jam's preemptive strike and Maria and Wolf's justified response. Nevertheless, the detective strode inside the squad room, wondering about what Captain Greening wanted. The chatter died down. Wolf's partner, Maria, stood next to his tiny cubicle, holding the *Times* art review of his charcoal sketches. Helium-filled party balloons were tied to his chair, and he saw the *Playboy* and *Penthouse* centerfolds pinned to the walls. Someone had written, "You supply the crayons, I'll come without the clothes," and "Paint me, Wolfie, paint me," on the photos.

"Fucking motherfuckers," said Wolf and looked around to see the squad laughing. Maria arched her eyebrow and smiled.

Lieutenant Kelson entered and surveyed Wolf's cubicle. "As if I didn't have enough problems," he said. "First it's Jam, and now this. Couldn't you find something less public? Like Play-Doh?"

"It's the fucking reporter," said Wolf.

"Boo-hoo for you," said the lieutenant. "Captain wants you upstairs."

"No idea?" asked Wolf.

The lieutenant shook his head and said, "None, but whatever it is, you earned it."

Wolf rode to the top floor of the redesigned "Fighting Ninth" precinct headquarters. He poked his head into the captain's outer office. Holly looked up from her work and blushed. She waved the *Times*. Wolf put up his hand and stopped her. "Holly. Not a good time."

She tossed her hair back, flashed him a lascivious smile, and pointed with her pencil. "Inside, van Gogh," she said. "He's waiting."

Wolf knocked and heard a powerful voice call out, "Come

in." Wolf came to attention before Captain Greening, whose buzz-cut silver hair highlighted a tight square face and fireplug body. The *New York Times, Wall Street Journal,* and *New York Post* lay on his desk with fresh coffee and a burning cigarette. A sign reading "NO SMOKING BY ORDER OF THE FIRE MARSHALL" hung behind him. The captain didn't smile but addressed his young star in a smoke-stained rasp. "Coffee?"

"No thanks, Captain," said Wolf.

Captain Greening folded his hands on the desktop. "This meeting has nothing to do with Ricky Jam or your antics. The police commissioner recommended you for a special assignment."

"Say again, Captain?" Wolf said, startled.

Captain Greening took a puff on his Marlboro. "The commissioner received a request from the bureau chief of the International Criminal Investigative Training Assistance Program in Kiev, Ukraine." The captain leaned back in his chair, warming to the subject. "After the 2014 Maidan revolution, the Ukrainian government declared the level of corruption in the Ukraine National Police irremediable. The new deputy of internal affairs, Eva Zebreze, fired the entire force. Can you imagine firing an entire police force?" He shook his head in disbelief. "Mrs. Zebreze gave the job to a veteran captain, Artem Troyem, a former soldier and no-nonsense guy who doesn't take bribes. A tough bastard. Troyem asked Eva for help. American police departments send him specialists to train recruits. It's our turn, and the commissioner wants us to send you. I don't know how he knew you were born in Odessa, but his timing couldn't be better."

"Odessa for thirty days?" asked Wolf, thinking about his wedding.

"Three months," replied Captain Greening. "You fly out Friday. Congratulations, Wolf. The commissioner asked for you personally and wants you there pronto. It's good publicity for the Ninth and a feather in your cap. Not to mention deflecting heat from the Jam investigation. Just stay out of trouble."

"What about my family's death?" Wolf asked. "Can I open that cold case?"

"You'll be gone, but it'll be here when you get back," replied the captain.

"So that's a 'yes'?" said Wolf.

"I signed the paperwork," the captain said.

"Thank you, Captain," replied Wolf.

Wolf rushed downstairs, wanting to get a look at the case files. He left a message for Kathryn, went to his cubicle, popped the balloons, and cleaned up the pictures.

"You look better," Maria said. "What happened?"

Wolf smiled like Blackbeard himself and said, "Come with me." They descended into the bowels of the building to find Sergeant Brennan sitting behind thousands of boxes locked securely behind a wire cage. The sergeant pushed the log sheet towards them, watched them sign under a 24-7 surveillance camera, and then clicked the lock open.

The sergeant's eyes sharpened when he saw the name, and he remarked, "The James case? I remember it, 1994. Dad, mom, and little girl? Captain Greening was a young star on the rise."

The pair found an aisle marked "J-K." Wolf ran his finger along the boxes, until he came to four cases marked "James. Boyko P., Zoriana Q., Matvi D. Case #478882-94."

Wolf and Maria carried them to a scarred wooden desk, lit by crackling fluorescent tubes. They untied the strings and lifted the lids.

Maria said, "Captain Greening did the initial investigation. How much do you recall?"

Wolf pawed through the dusty papers. "Nothing, except the pain. I came home from school. My dad owned a shop in Little

Ukraine with a small upstairs apartment. I heard ambulance and fire truck sirens around the corner. I turned onto Seventh Street and saw the store in flames. My dad, mom, and sister were caught upstairs. I remember caskets and a graveside service. They sent me to the East Village Orphanage Home. Two years and many fights later, a rich Ukrainian businessman adopted me."

Maria found the murder book and photos. "Look at this," she said in a hushed tone. A boy in tears, framed by huge flames across the street, stood enclosed by the arms of a police officer.

Wolf shuddered as the memory unleashed a jolt of pain. "I've never seen this photo before," he said.

Maria's hand flew to her mouth. "And this?" she said hesitantly. Maria handed Wolf another photo. His gut sickened. Three skulls, two adult and one child-sized, sat next to each other, dipped in gold. "What in the hell are we dealing with?" said Maria.

Wolf's chest tightened in fury. He knew his father was tough as nails. Standing behind the counter when the thugs walked in, Wolf remembered the flashing guns and demands for money for "protection." He was a boy. He had no idea of the monster they represented, but when he saw the flames of the shop, he knew he would return and exact revenge someday. Wolf ran his fingers through his hair and jabbed his finger against the gold skull photograph. "Who are they? Is this why Detective Greening dropped the case? And how convenient I've been reassigned to Odessa when I need to be in Manhattan."

"Way over my pay grade, partner," said Maria. "This is mob stuff. Maybe we should let the Major Crimes division take a look?"

"Maria," said Wolf. "I've waited twenty-four years for this moment. I've followed orders all my life, and many were bad orders. I knew they were bad, but I did my job. And now? My instinct is all red flags. I don't fucking care if it's Greening, the commissioner, or Lawrence Brock himself, I will hunt them down."

"Just keep me in the loop," she replied.

Wolf's phone rang. "Darling," said Kathryn. "Come to the apartment. Let's make up."

"Okay, honey," said Wolf, thinking, *She knows something.*

WHEN WOLF SMELLED the Julia Child's Lasagne a la Francaise and saw the twelve-year-old Elijah Craig 133-barrel proof, he knew Kathryn had celebration on her mind.

Wolf accepted the bourbon gladly, saying, "What's the occasion?"

"Just some scuttlebutt you came out of Captain Greening's office charged up," replied Kathryn. "And don't ask, I have my sources."

Wolf decided to eat. After dinner, he announced, "The food was delicious, but I do have big news."

"Oh?" replied Kathryn innocently. "I knew something was going on."

"I've been reassigned," said Wolf.

"Thank God," exclaimed Kathryn. "It's about time. Shall we toast?"

"Did your father have a hand in this?" asked Wolf suspiciously.

Kathryn played coy as she nestled against him and replied, "Maybe, and maybe not."

Wolf said, "Captain Greening got a call from the commissioner. I'm going to Odessa, Ukraine, to help train police officers."

Kathryn's face slackened. Breathless, she exclaimed, *"What? When?"*

"Saturday," replied Wolf.

Kathryn shook her head and slowly mouthed the words, "That's not possible."

"True story," said Wolf. "Some police captain in Odessa put out the word he needs help and spoke to Greening."

"What about our wedding?" asked Kathryn, incredulous. "I've already sent out the invitations."

Wolf replied, "We can postpone, or move the venue to Odessa."

"I'm going to be sick," said Kathryn, and excused herself and lay down. An hour later, she came back into the living area, shaken. She poured herself some wine and sat down. "This is terrible."

"You don't know the half of it," said Wolf.

"There's more?" she asked.

"Katy," replied Wolf, "when you asked for my hand in marriage, you had conditions."

"I remember, but you seem to forget," said Kathryn.

"Captain Greening reopened my family's case. I looked through the case files and saw something horrible. I haven't said much about the war, but maybe I should. Once, in Mosul, our unit got word of Abu Khalaf's hideout, Al Qaeda's number two in Iraq. Our squads from the Second Ranger battalion approached silently over seven rooftops on graphite ladders. I dropped over the twelve-foot wall and placed an explosive charge on the door. The platoon sergeant gave the order to breach. I rushed into the living room, ran down the hall, and found a man and woman asleep. I ordered them to raise their hands, but the man put his hand in his robe. I shot him. The woman reached inside his garment, and I shot her. Snipers shot Abu Khalaf as he fled." Wolf paused. His eyes tightened and tone darkened. "Katy, I was a soldier, now I'm a detective. Perhaps the day will come when I can 'put away the gore and guns,' as you say, but I will always be a warrior. My job is finding those who brutally murdered my family. I will put them away behind bars, or if they choose, in the ground like Ricky Jam, but you can't have me without that."

23

François lounged like a contented bull on the spacious balcony overlooking the glassy Mediterranean. He smoked and sang to the seagulls as they danced in the ocean air.

Brianna slipped her shapely legs from under the satin sheets. Her eyes drank in the bright sun glinting off the calm seas. She put on a robe and came to his side, aching with undisguised passion. The escort rubbed his nose with her own and said, "After last night, I'm on fire."

"And our union sparked a revelation," said François with a faraway look. "A problem with quantum tunneling has bedeviled me for months, but suddenly, the solution came in a flash."

He pinched his thumb and forefinger together and said, "I'm this close to a Nobel Prize."

Brianna opened her robe. "I told you last night I have a ten o'clock meeting with my attorney," she said. "So don't tease me and waste time."

François and Brianna walked into the Benhazi Law Offices, which occupied the upper floor of a ten-story complex. The pair entered a spacious room with ancient Middle Eastern and Phoenician artifacts. An Ibex head stared across Persian rugs, and Brianna spoke with a gleaming receptionist, who ushered her into an inner sanctum and closed the door.

Inside with the attorney, Brianna looked out the window at the ocean, cold and sullen.

Ali Benhazi asked, "Does he suspect?"

Brianna replied bitterly, "No."

"You're not having doubts, are you?" said the ever-observant attorney.

"Let's move on," said Brianna, sickened by her own betrayal. "Is 'Uncle' Sokolov ready?"

François was flipping through travel magazines when Brianna left the office in tears and disappeared down the elevator. François got up to catch her when the attorney beckoned him inside his office. "Allow me to introduce myself," he said. "I am Ali Benhazi, Brianna Ivanova's attorney. Brianna and I had a painful talk. She called you her friend and appears, shall we say, quite taken by you. I learned, however, her husband, Sergei, is refusing to sign the divorce decree. Miss Ivanova is in distress. Comfort her. Provide emotional support. It will help a great deal." François nodded in assent when Ali Benhazi added, "She said you are head of nuclear physics at the university? Did you know her uncle works with nuclear physicists?"

François found Brianna on the sidewalk, pacing back and forth, smoking and hidden behind designer sunglasses. "Let's go for a ride," he said, and drove to the White Beach. Brianna's death grip on the door signaled he should slow down.

The pair kicked through the surf, and Brianna described her months with Sergei. Two evenings ago, he drank too much and hit her. "I left and came here. In the afternoon, I got my camera and took pictures to get my mind off things. When I came to the Iris Beirut, I felt exhausted, but had to get a last shot of the fading sun. Today, I discovered Sergei will make things difficult. I'm at a loss and don't know what to do." Brianna looked up at the gleaming white sands and said, "What a beautiful beach. Thank you for bringing me here." François described his early morning swims, and Brianna continued, "Ten to fifteen miles? That explains your physique."

"Let's visit the bakery down the road," said François.

He roared down the highway, and Brianna raised her voice. "Must you drive like a maniac?" she said.

François knitted his eyebrows and wagged his finger, saying, "You agree these drivers are imbeciles?"

"Please keep your eyes on the road," replied Brianna.

At the bakery, the pair ate chocolate croissants and drank boiled coffee. François left, saying, "I'll be back in a few minutes," and returned with a bucket of red roses.

Brianna's heart melted. "They are beautiful," she said. "Will I see you tonight?"

François replied, "I phoned your hotel earlier and made some arrangements. Your luggage awaits you in my apartment. We can be together."

Brianna leaned over and kissed him. "I would like that," she said. "What are we waiting for?"

François kept the speed down to a snail-paced 80 mph.

As they neared Beirut, Brianna's phone rang. "Let me speak to the professor," said Ali Benhazi.

Brianna gave François the phone and said, "It's my attorney."

"Put it on speaker," François replied.

"Professor LeCompte?" said Ali Benhazi. "I learned just minutes ago the Lebanese University hired Prime Minister Saad Hariri's personal lawyer to file suit against you for breach of contract."

"Ridiculous," said François.

"I agree," replied the attorney. "But we must act, or you'll rot in jail. Let me make some calls. Where are you?"

"Close," said François. "Five minutes away."

"Come to the office at once," said Ali Benhazi.

THE LOVERS TOOK the elevator up, and now it was Brianna who thumbed through a French *Vogue* in the reception room. François sat behind the closed door.

"You quit?" said Ali Benhazi, astonished.

"I threatened for months," replied François.

"Professor," said the attorney. "You don't threaten the Iranians. The prime minister received a personal call from the supreme leader. You will be ordered to pack your things and move to Iran in one week, or face jail. And don't think of escape; your passport's been revoked. Come to my office tomorrow. I'll make some calls and know more."

François couldn't believe it. "I'm a prisoner?" he said.

"Not if I can help it," replied Ali Benhazi.

François came out thoughtfully, glanced at Brianna, and said, "Let's stop at the university." In minutes, they entered his office. Brianna warmed to the wet bar, sound system, and billiards table. François turned on Chopin and asked, "Do you play?"

"A bit," and she smiled as the white cue struck the nine ball, which bounced off two banks into a side pocket. "Remind me to never play you for money."

"How about clothing?" asked François.

Brianna put her arms around his waist. "How about now?" she said.

François turned up the sound, removed a device from his jacket, and swept the room. The tiny box stayed red, but flashed green under the light over the pool table and desk in his office. Shaking his head, François opened his safe. He filled a box with notebooks, money, and important papers. He placed an unusual ring on his finger and extended his hand to Brianna to shake. An electric buzz zipped up her arm and neck and down her spine.

She flew into a purple rage. "Idiot! Idiot!" she yelled and pummeled him with her fists.

"A hand buzzer, a joke," François said, laughing.

Brianna huffed, "Idiot," but hid a smile behind her hand. Dripping with sexiness, she continued, "Darling man. *Lover.* Do I have your attention?" François nodded. "Good, for punishment you shall learn Dogberry's soliloquy in *Much Ado About Nothing*, Act Two, Scene Four, as to why," Brianna raised her voice, "you are an 'ass.' Humor me or risk reprisal."

"Like what?"

"How about that buzzer up your ass while you sleep?"

"Then we shall get along just fine," said François. François locked his office door, and they went to the car. After a sweep with the device, he drove off.

"What did Mr. Benhazi say that made you run to your office and clean out the safe?" said Brianna.

"I'm in danger," replied François. "I offended people far worse than Sergei and must flee Beirut. You are welcome to stay in my apartment, but I wounded my benefactors' pride. You are no longer safe with me, and besides, you can't leave because of your legal issues."

Brianna said, "My uncle can help."

"Nonsense," replied François.

"Mikael Sokolov works with nuclear physicists," said Brianna. "He's president of Army Munitions Group."

"Never heard of it."

"I'll call him," said Brianna and hit speed dial.

"No," François said forcefully.

"Yes," said Brianna, matching François's tone. François tried grabbing the phone. Brianna held the phone out the window, took his wrist, and fought him off. "Don't you dare, you brute. I'll bite you."

"I'll spank you," he said.

Her phone rang, and she put the call on speaker. A receptionist said smartly, "Army Munitions Group. How may I help you?"

"I'm calling for President Sokolov?" Brianna said calmly. "Tell him his niece Brianna Ivanova is on the line." She stuck out her tongue and middle finger at François.

He banged his head against the steering wheel and said, "Women. Impossible."

"Uncle Mikael?" Brianna said lightly. "This is your niece, Brianna. How are you? How's little Petrov? So big? I have a favor. I found a wonderful man, a nuclear physicist who needs your advice. Could you speak with him? His name is Professor François LeCompte." Brianna made an ugly face and thrust the phone at François with another middle finger extended.

"Hello?" said François. "This is Professor LeCompte."

"The Ecole Polytechnique François LeCompte, PhD?" the voice gushed. "My God! Such an honor. How can I help you?"

François softened. "I'm having some difficulty," he said, "and your niece—" he stuck out his tongue at Brianna "—has the preposterous idea you can help me. I'm stuck in Beirut with some legal issues."

The voice grew serious. Mr. Sokolov said, "How fortuitous, your call. We are in desperate need of a nuclear physicist and would pay dearly, anything in fact, for someone like you to join our team. Send me the name of your attorney." The line went dead, and François handed Brianna the cell phone. He folded his arms and admitted nothing.

IN HIS APARTMENT, Brianna disappeared and began unpacking. François stepped out on the veranda and closed the sliding door. He dialed a number on a burner phone from a dog-eared business card. It went to voice mail, and he said, "This is Professor François LeCompte with an urgent request to speak with Dr. John Clattering or his associate, Mr. Richard Vauntnon, at Los Alamos."

François sat watching the gulls, sipping espresso, and chain-smoking when the cell buzzed. "Dr. François LeCompte?" came the voice. "This is Richard Vauntnon."

"Thank you for calling promptly," said François.

The Los Alamos man laughed. "Let me guess," he said. "This is not about a job."

"No," replied François and continued, "May I assume you are more than a scientist?"

"You can trust me, Professor," replied Richard Vauntnon. He paused a moment before saying, "Are those pesky Iranians double-dealing?"

François described the events since his argument with the supreme leader's emissary, including meeting Brianna Ivanova and her attorney. "I need advice," said François.

"Text me a photo of the woman," replied Mr. Vauntnon. "I'll get back to you within the hour."

François opened the sliding glass door and stepped inside the apartment. Brianna met him in a crotchless lace teddy, holding a paddle. Her lips parted and she said, "So you want to spank me?"

"I'm waiting for an important phone call, my love," said François. "It will have to wait."

"You are impossible!" said Brianna.

"You have no idea," replied François.

24

Day 10
Beirut, Lebanon
Wednesday, September 27
Sixteen-hundred hours

François stayed on the veranda while sipping absinthe. Expecting Richard Vauntnon, he was caught off guard by Ali Benhazi's call. "Professor LeCompte, it's a miracle," gushed the attorney. "Miss Ivanova's uncle has power. You have been granted a temporary visa to Odessa, Ukraine. I took the liberty to mention Brianna's situation. He made a call, and Sergei just faxed a signed divorce decree. She's free. Say 'thank you' to Miss Ivanova."

The line disconnected, and François knew Brianna was not who she seemed. Far too beautiful, classy, and schooled in bed to have "stumbled" upon him. The chance a Black Swan had fallen into his arms, after his fight with the emissary, was slim to none. Were the Iranians behind this? Was it all an act?

The man from Los Alamos called. Richard Vauntnon said, "Are you sitting down, Professor LeCompte? Buckle up. The Iranians are bad, but this is worse, like evil empire stuff. I hope to God you're not in love with Miss Mata Hari."

"The Dutch exotic dancer?" replied François, as his stomach soured. His gut confirmed what he didn't want to believe.

"Spy extraordinaire," said Mr. Vauntnon. "Miss Ivanova is none other than Sable and Diamonds, the highest-paid escort in Moscow and known to work for the Sakharov crime syndicate."

François groaned and said, "Let me tell you about Ali Benhazi's phone call." He described the recent conversation.

"Professor LeCompte, rumors in the intel community are swirling around this Army Munitions Group in Odessa, that they are manufacturing nuclear weapons. It's a subsidiary of the worldwide weapons conglomerate Eastern Machine Systems, Inc., a spinoff of the former USSR Production Union Southern-Building Plant, which built the Soviets their weapons. President Sokolov hired Miss Ivanova to seduce you. This situation is dangerous. I have local assets who can get you out."

François said gravely, "A serpent in my garden? But humor me, Mr. Vauntnon. Without enriched plutonium, the Army Munitions Group is powerless."

"A few days ago, four men stole twelve containers of enriched plutonium from the Plutonium Palace in Mayak, Russia. We believe the culprit is the Army Munitions Group."

"Who's their lead scientist?" said François.

"Professor Smernen Andreyev," replied Mr. Vauntnon.

François started pacing. He had seriously underestimated Mr. Sokolov. He said, "He's a brilliant researcher, working with my shrink-wrapped plutonium design."

"Zohar is writing the detonation software," replied Mr. Vauntnon.

François's heart began racing. He chewed on his lower lip. "How far along are they?" he asked.

"Professor, why the questions?" said Mr. Vauntnon. "Ever watch an insect in a Venus flytrap? You are the fly."

"Tell me more about Miss Ivanova," insisted François.

"Apart from globe-trotting, gems and furs and tricks at seven grand a pop?" said Richard. "After her website was pulled, our contacts confirmed her five-year-old daughter disappeared."

"Wouldn't you like to know what Army Munitions Group is doing?" asked François, intrigued. "What they are planning?"

"Before the ink dries on your contract with Mr. Sokolov," said Mr. Vauntnon, "Miss Ivanova will be on a jet back to Moscow, painting her toenails and laughing all the way to the bank. This is their modus operandi. When you get back to your hotel, she will be gone, a rat back into its hole. And may I remind you? You are not James Bond. If Mr. Sokolov gets a whiff of your duplicity, you will be fish food on the bottom of the Black Sea."

Like a conspirator, François said, "And if I choose to be a Trojan horse?"

"A wild and reckless course, Professor LeCompte," replied Richard Vauntnon. "But you have my number. Don't hesitate to use it."

François pondered his dilemma. He knew what Mr. Vauntnon did not, that he had looked into Brianna's eyes at the Iris bar and rolled the dice. He couldn't guess at the dark whirl-winds swirling around her, but knew, against herself, she had given herself to him, and their lovemaking at the Le Royal Beirut confirmed it. He had chosen her. "God help me," François told himself, "Brianna is my Black Swan. Of beauty, only Bardot surpasses her. Of wit, Nabokov, and there is an unmistakable steel in her soul. Perhaps I will perish as I tie my fate to hers, but I cannot live without her."

Brianna came out from the bedroom in a playful mood, dressed in a black satin nightgown. "How long will you tease me?"

"I talked with Mr. Benhazi. Your uncle made some calls. I'm leaving for Odessa Friday, with Saturday lunch. Sergei signed your papers. You're free. If you choose, you can come with me. Would you like that?"

Brianna lowered her gaze, and her lip trembled. She nodded as tears filled her eyes. "You have no idea."

François smiled and lowered his voice. "Now get your paddle, but you must do exactly as I say before I release you from prison."

"Prison?"

"You have handcuffs? I'm putting you in jail."

25

Day II
Trauma ICU, Sourasky Hospital, Tel Aviv, Israel
Thursday, September 28
Zero-six-thirty hours

L ike a spaceship, the hospital room lay packed with computer screens and monitors, their tiny clicks and incessant beeping having grown louder. The smell of chlorinated disinfectants seemed to accentuate a lonely window closed with levered drapes. The pressure in her brain, like a balloon ready to pop, had subsided. The clanging in her ears had lessened. Haddy realized the nightmare was real. *What happened?* The memory lay at the edge of consciousness, and Haddy realized her right hand wouldn't move. She thought fearfully, "I can shoot a pistol, five rounds into a bullseye at a hundred yards, but ...?" and shuddered. "I'm paralyzed. I'll be in rehab for months, maybe years."

Her left hand worked and trembled as it touched the gauze

covering her face. Haddy's fingers traveled down to the edge of her mouth. It lay in a pool of saliva. "A bomb. A head injury," she remembered suddenly. "I have a head injury." Haddy couldn't help but see herself after multiple reconstructive surgeries, making small talk with other wounded vets. She held a cane while dragging a foot. "Fuck me, fuck me, fuck me." Then, the awful irony struck her: "I tried to kill myself but couldn't, now I want to die and can't." Haddy became aware of a soft furry animal propped against her ear. It was Pooh Bear, her father's single gift given to her mother before her birth. Sasha must have brought it from home, but where was she? Haddy started weeping.

At zero seven hundred hours, the curtains opened with a whoosh. With the shift change, a flood of medical students, interns, residents, and doctors filed in. Haddy, not entirely deaf, dimly heard the same questions repeated over and over again. She wanted to retreat. Her most primal fear was claustrophobia, experienced when she got stuck in a tiny cave as a child. Now the fear returned. She was in the cave. Abrupt commands like "Follow my fingers" came as penlights flashed in her eyes. She gagged as tongue blades poked the back of her throat. Cold stethoscopes touched her breasts. Students argued with each other, saying, "Do you have the CDC antibiotic guidelines for blast trauma?" Other white-coated technicians checked the wire leads stuck to her chest. A nurse tugged on her urinary catheter, which stung. As the circus of medical professionals left, Haddy exhaled.

She signaled the nurse, who said, "Hey, pretty girl. You have gorgeous black eyes. How are you?"

"I can barely hear you, but do they all have to come in at once?" said Haddy, hoping she was understood.

The nurse wrote on a whiteboard and shrugged. "*Modern medicine*, Staff Sergeant. Hang in there."

"You see this flaming boy holding a music box?" said Haddy and pointed.

The nurse scribbled. "You're having hallucinations. What is your pain? From zero to ten?"

Haddy pointed at "9," and mouthed, "I'm ... drooling. Can't move foot or fingers."

The nurse replied with an all-knowing smile. "The doctor is coming." As though on cue, Dr. Rammoth strode in, his face a tired cascade of skin folds. Hidden within the sags were a pair of intense, light-brown eyes, and he reminded Haddy of a sad basset hound. He shot questions at the nurse, and Haddy heard her reply, "The patient has trouble hearing. Nine pain, right-sided paralysis, and hallucinations."

Dr. Rammoth removed his penlight. "Good morning, Staff Sergeant Abrams. Is that Winnie-the-Pooh?"

Haddy's left hand grabbed Dr. Rammoth's wrist with surprising quickness. "Get that light the fuck away from me. Where am I?"

"Sourasky Trauma ICU," he wrote on the whiteboard, and "Be patient." Dr. Rammoth dangled his fingers in front of her eyes and said, "Follow my fingers," and moved them from her upper right to her upper left, down lower left and back lower right, forming a square. "Now smile. Squeeze my hands. Push your wrists up and down. Push your toe up. Now push the foot down." Haddy's head whirled with the commands. Then a sharp needle poked her left toe. "Feel that?" came the question.

Lightning fast, Haddy slapped him. "Get the fuck away from me, you motherfucking son of a bitch!"

"I'll take that as a yes," said Dr. Rammoth and stepped back. He asked the relatives in. Haddy's heart lifted as she watched Sasha, Shira, and David Abrams file in. Dr. Rammoth started talking. Haddy gleaned what she could, catching the dialogue as it swept past her like a rider on a fast horse. "I'm Dr.

Rammoth, Haddy's neurosurgeon. She's not in a good mood.
I'd be careful."

"It takes a brain surgeon to figure that out?" Shira said
dryly. "Hell, I'm not getting paid enough."

Dr. Rammoth ignored the jibe and said, "The left side
of Haddy's head took the brunt of the blast trauma and
caused internal bleeding. It turned off the lights in the left
side motor cortex; like having a stroke. When it shuts
down, on the right side, our seat of art and sense of time-
lessness and intuition express themselves. Don't be
surprised if she imagines things, 'sees' temperature, or
'feels' color. She has a temporary hearing loss. Any questions?" The neurosurgeon waited a prescribed second and
announced, "Good, I'll be back tomorrow. Relay concerns
to the nurse."

But the aged David Abrams blocked Dr. Rammoth's hasty
exit and said, "She'll recover?"

"Brain trauma is unpredictable. The paralysis we see might
reverse within the week or never. A conservative guess would
be a year before she's back to normal. She's out of the Army for
sure and will have her dose of PTSD," announced the neurosurgeon.

"Flashbacks?" said Sasha.

"My granddaughter is one tough son of a bitch," David said.
"She has nine lives."

"Mr. Abrams," replied Dr. Rammoth sagely. "She *had* nine
lives."

As soon as he left, the maxillofacial resident walked in with
supplies. "Dressing change, you folks need to step out."

"No," said Haddy, and motioned for the one closest to come
near. She observed her mother's beautiful tear-streaked face
and long blonde tresses, which looked like windblown wheat
drenched in dew. Nothing could dim her aquamarine eyes, but
the mother opened her purse and put away her Jewish prayer

book. Tears swelling, she clasped Haddy's face and kissed her face and bandages.

"Oh, my precious, precious darling," Sasha gushed.

Haddy watched her mother's lips and said, "Speak louder. Good to see you, Mom. Thanks for Dad's bear."

Shira came up and kneaded lifeless fingers. Taking her cue from Sasha, she spoke directly to Haddy and said, "Hey, partner. Damn, you got hit hard. Take courage, you're harder."

"I remember the blast," said Haddy and teared up. "I'm frightened. I see you as the color red, and I cry all the time."

Shira took Haddy's hand and placed it on her chest. "You see red? Then feel this. It's called anger. So fucking hot it burns." Her lip quivered. "Get better. Bank your revenge. We'll hunt them down one by one or all at once, whatever it takes."

David took her hand. With iron in his voice, he said, "I know people, Granddaughter. Trust me, we will find them."

Sasha approached Haddy again. She lowered her eyes and sighed. She said, "I've thought about this long and hard; not knowing if I should ..."

"Louder, Mom," said Haddy.

"I need to tell you the dream I had before your birth. I've been afraid for so long, but it's time. Tomorrow, when you're more awake."

"A dream?" said Haddy. "No. Now."

Sasha hesitated. "I saw your birth. You came out as a golden dagger covered in sapphires, dripping blood." Seeing Haddy's confusion, Sasha hastily drew the picture on the whiteboard and continued, "You understand?" She pointed at Haddy and said, "You are the dagger."

Before Haddy could respond, a pair of tight-lipped men in pedestrian clothes entered the room. She saw them flash their credentials and corral the group into a bunch. Haddy heard dimly, "... Shin Bet, counterintelligence. Tell us about your other relatives."

"There are two more," replied Sasha. "Haddy's grandfather Stefan Danilenko and his daughter Raisa, really his cousin, will arrive tomorrow."

"You'll receive new identities and secure quarters," said the first agent. "Talk to no one outside your immediate family." To Shira, he said, "Sergeant Alian, this is a security matter. Say nothing about the staff sergeant. Do not converse with her family. You can no longer visit."

"So this wasn't a random bombing?" said Shira.

The second agent stepped in. "That's enough, Sergeant," he said. "You're dismissed."

Haddy's family filed out, and the physician gave her an IV injection. "Morphine?" said Haddy. He nodded and began the arduous task of soaking the blood-stained and serum-encrusted layers of gauze on her face. The physician used a solution of warm saline and diluted hydrogen peroxide, which bubbled away the bloody goo. He cut and peeled away the wrappings. The last layer was the most difficult as ninety-nine tiny nylon sutures were stuck in the gauze fibers. Using tweezers, he teased away scabs to prevent infection. Haddy winced and howled from time to time.

Dr. Adina, chief of plastic surgery, waltzed in, put on a mask and pair of magnifying loops, and said to the resident, "How are we doing?" as she minutely examined the wounds.

"Magnificent work, Dr. Adina," he replied.

Dr. Adina turned to Haddy. "Staff Sergeant," she said. "You are a lucky woman."

"Why?" said Haddy.

"We'll talk tomorrow."

Haddy lapsed into morphine dreamland and shivered. The hurricane of emotions raised the specter that a fearful reckoning stood close by. She looked at the crude drawing made by Sasha and said, "I'm a fucking bloody dagger?" and slept.

26

Day 12
Trauma ICU, Sourasky Hospital, Tel Aviv, Israel
Friday, September 29
Zero-seven-hundred hours

Haddy drifted in and out of consciousness Thursday. Her head stopped pounding, and her hearing improved, but she wrestled with shame and guilt. What was it she had done to deserve this?

The nurse removed the urinary catheter and large intravenous lines from her groin. Shortly after one am Friday, Haddy inched her good leg over the bed and pulled the right leg over. "I'm getting out of here," she told herself. Alarms sounded outside, and a flood of staff arrived and got her back to bed. A nurse entered with morphine. "No," said Haddy. "I need my mind back."

"Only a doctor makes that decision," replied the nurse calmly. "Let's wait until tomorrow, shall we?"

Haddy raised her voice. "I hear the wind and trees cracking, and I'm seeing a giant buck deer and a flaming boy! No more!"

The nurse called for backup, and Nurse Shevchenko took command, with thirty years of experience across continents and conflicts. "What's this nonsense?" she said gruffly, "no pain medicine?"

"Fuck you," said Haddy.

"Let's reduce the dose, shall we?" the charge nurse replied with a tone which said, "Case closed."

"Get the doctor in here," Haddy demanded.

In minutes, the in-house resident stood at the bedside. "You really want the narcotics stopped? You'll hurt like hell."

"I need my mind back," declared Haddy.

"As you wish," replied the resident. "Ring your buzzer if the pain becomes unbearable."

In hours, Haddy's face burned and screamed from the stings of swarming fire ants. She gritted her teeth as her thoughts sharpened. The white-hot lightsaber in her chest had cooled, but remained as a dull, boring ache. She remembered jumping over a cliff and ... praying ... and washing ashore and being at peace. Then Shira, a bath, and the lipstick and Ori Daniels and ... nothing.

At the zero-seven-hundred-hour shift change, the nurse said, "You stopped cold turkey? Unbelievable."

"Tell me about my surgery," said Haddy. She willed her right hand to move, but it lay there.

The nurse said, "Two teams of surgeons times fourteen hours."

"What happened to my face?" asked Haddy.

The nurse politely punted to Dr. Adina, "Your plastic surgeon can answer best."

Dr. Rammoth entered, shaking his head. "You have the highest pain tolerance I've ever seen," he said in awe, and performed his exam with lightning speed.

"I don't see people as colors any longer," said Haddy.

"Your left side is waking up," he replied. "And faster than I expected, but the brain is full of surprises. Sometimes it takes months, others a day; you never know."

A few hours later, Haddy's family returned. Raisa, a cute blonde high school senior, dashed forward. "Cousin Haddy!" she said excitedly. Haddy moved uncomfortably as Raisa kissed her cheeks, hugged Pooh Bear, and touched the titanium bolt. "Definitely a cool Frankenstein vibe. Punk all the way. With the bandages, you're the mummy."

"I haven't seen it yet," said Haddy. "When do you start medical school?"

Stefan Danilenko stepped in and said, "Next year and not a day too soon for my 'Wild Card,' as I call her. The boys drive me insane."

Haddy turned to Raisa. "'Wild Card'?" she said. "You are practicing safe sex? You have friends watching your six?"

Raisa bent down and whispered in Haddy's ear, "I love to *party*."

"I've been there, but listen to your father," said Haddy. Addressing Stefan, she said, "Hi, Professor. What's with the crutches?"

"Knee replacement at the Cleveland Clinic," Stefan answered. "When I heard about your misfortune, I stopped rehab and came immediately."

Haddy and the foursome chitchatted until the nurse opened the curtains. "Out, all of you, your fifteen minutes are up."

Haddy signaled Sasha to come closer. "Mom, since waking up, I have seen a boy on fire holding a glittering music box. Do you know what that means?"

Sasha brushed strands of blonde hair from her face and paused, troubled. She said slowly, "David owned a fancy music box, but got rid of it."

Dr. Adina arrived. With the resident assisting, she removed the dressings. The surgeon observed Haddy's pain as the saline and peroxide bubbled away the accumulated crusts of blood and scabs and remarked with grim admiration, "You are one tough woman, Staff Sergeant. When I'm in trouble, I want you by my side."

"I ... I need to see my face," said Haddy.

Dr. Adina shook her head. "It's too early. You were not burned, but the left side of your face was flayed apart by the metal fragments. Wait a few more days, until I remove the sutures."

"I can't rest not knowing," said Haddy. "I need to see what that motherfucking jihadi did."

The surgeon gave a tiny shrug and directed the nurse to place a mirror on the bed tray. She motioned for the resident to step outside. The nurse closed the curtains.

The room lay quiet, apart from the machines. Haddy's heart beat wildly, erratically and suddenly, her rape flashed in front of her. Was this the beginning of the flashbacks Dr. Rammoth mentioned? "But I'm Haddy Abrams and will not be ruled by fear," she said to herself. She had turned away from the mirror. Haddy took a deep breath and looked.

It was gruesome. A titanium bolt stuck out like a small tree from a scalp shorn of hair and painted in purple antiseptic. Wires curled up to an overhead monitor. The left side of her forehead, ear, and cheek lay crisscrossed in a drunken maze of cuts and lacerations, and tiny nylon sutures were like railroad ties. Horribly swollen, her features distorted, her face was a mass of red and purple and blue and black bruises. Slowly, Haddy traced the outlines of her lips and noticed a facial droop and drool. When she smiled, only half of her face responded. Arctic cold shivered down her spine and out into her limbs. Haddy did not recognize this monster. She grabbed her stomach and retched, filled with despair, and awash with waves of shame and hopelessness. A vindictive cry burst from her lips as she cursed the gentle voice, heard clearly in the Ben Shemen Forest. "*You* are blacker than bloody shit and worse than any Satan." Haddy threw the mirror across the room. It shattered into shards. She wailed, "Who the fuck am I? What have I become?"

~

THE SHIN BET agents arrived after the resident had redressed Haddy's face. She lay glum, her eyes dull and mood sour. Agent Gavot took charge and described the carnage of the bomb, the eighteen dead, twelve on life support, and others maimed for life.

Haddy eyed them bitterly and said, "I get it, pure evil. I was at the wrong place at the wrong time."

"Not quite," said the agent. "The jihadi had a camera on his forehead. He aimed at you, Staff Sergeant. Some sick son of a bitch wanted to watch *you* get blown up."

"Then we know the culprit," replied Haddy. "The Anisur Salam Al Qaeda network."

"We have agents talking to informants," said Agent Gavot. "Combing our networks for any hint it might be them or Salam's family, but nothing points to the terrorist. We don't know who is responsible. Which is why we're putting you into our witness protection program tomorrow. Dr. Rammoth will remove the bolt in the operating room. We will announce a press release saying you died on the table."

Cold fingers of fear crawled up Haddy's spine as the agents left. "Who would send a boy to kill me, and film it?"

Late in the night, Haddy fell asleep, exhausted not from the unremitting pain, but nerves on edge. She awoke in a dream, walking in a hall of mirrors. She had no face or name. A trumpet blared, *"Allahu Akbar,"* and men raped her. She fell into a sea filled with thousands of dead men staring at her with fish eyes. A hand offered her a fish head to join the dead. Haddy's eyes popped open, her heart racing, panting. The sheets were soaked in sweat. "That was fucking horrible," she said. "Fuck witness protection. I will find a way out of this and run for my life."

27

Day 12
JFK International Airport, New York City
Friday, September 29
Twelve-thirty hours

Kathryn leaned against Wolf while JFK airport security checked his weapons and luggage. A special crate for his icon and a separate portfolio of remaining Snow Queen sketches lay close at hand. Kathryn hadn't recovered from her painful evening. Her father's call to the police commissioner had backfired badly. Wolf's war revelations and vendetta against his family's killers shook her. Couldn't he let it go? She longed to see inside the secret portfolio, yearning to see the beauty who had bewitched her fiancé. "What kind of man searches nine years for a dream?" she wondered, and shivered. "The same man who brutally kills a man and wife in bed. And where has he buried all those he killed? Will he bury me and my father as well?" Kathryn touched the drawings and broke free of her dark musings. "Wolf, can't I take a little peek?" she said. "Why not let me see her once? Don't you understand?"

Wolf politely ignored Kathryn, making sure the crate was handled properly. "I phoned this Captain Troyem last night. I told him you arrive in Odessa on the thirteenth. We'll get married the next day and honeymoon in Istanbul." She flashed a sexy smile and whispered, "I found the coolest glass dildo ..." and spread her hands. "Like this long," and giggled.

Wolf raised an eyebrow. "And?"

Kathryn kissed him. She licked his ear and said, "Add a little imagination ... You'll figure it out."

Wolf traveled light and swung into his chair near the bulkhead behind the first-class compartment. He noticed a man in a loose green jacket glance his way and bury his face in a newspaper. Once in the air, Wolf walked past him to the bathroom. The man wore cargo pants and sneakers and looked suspicious. Rather than return to his seat, Wolf went to the first-class galley. He pulled the stewardess aside. After showing his badge and credentials, he asked her to check on the passenger in seat 17A. Wolf returned to his seat, and minutes later, the attendant pressed a piece of paper in his hand. "He's signed in as Boryslav Kolisnyk, One Eighty-Four Clarkson Avenue, Number Five C, Brooklyn, New York."

Wolf called the Sixty-Seventh Precinct and asked for Detective Hoylan, who took the information and phoned him back shortly. "Detective James. Kolisnyk has priors for burglary, fraud, and bunko with connections to the Ukrainian mob." Wolf thanked him and settled back. So he had a tail, or was it more?

Wolf slept on and off through the night. The Airbus 330 droned like a giant locust, and at 5:15 a.m. local time, the plane landed. He ambled into the Istanbul International Airport for his connecting flight in two hours. The sun gleamed hot in the rising dawn. Wolf stopped at a shop. He leafed through a *Gun Digest* magazine and glanced in the overhead mirror. He saw Kolisnyk receive a folded newspaper from another in passing. "Gun," thought Wolf and looked up and down the terminal. He didn't see airport security and headed to the restroom. Wolf double-checked the stalls, which were vacant, and waited behind the metal door. Kolisnyk entered, holding a suppressed semiautomatic handgun. Wolf grabbed the barrel, cupped the grip, twisted, and yanked the gun from his hand, hearing the satisfying snap of the bones in the man's trigger finger. He punched the killer twice in the face, and then punched him in the throat. Kolisnyk fell, gagging, and Wolf shot him in the head with his own gun.

Kolisnyk's lifeless eyes stared up as blood oozed from the ears. Wolf rifled through his pockets and removed his wallet. He propped the assassin in a toilet stall, locked the door from the inside, and climbed out. Wolf cleaned his hands and face, ran his fingers through his hair, and left. At a coffee stand, he found two photographs in the wallet. A photostat of the three gold skulls from the murder book and another of him and Kathryn leaving the 16 Dutch Apartments. Scrawled on the back were "$10,000" and the pirate sign of skull and cross-bones. Wolf clenched his jaw and lay the photos down. "Come and get me, you motherfuckers," he seethed.

The jet touched down in Odessa a short time later. A fresh Black Sea breeze with partly cloudy skies brought back a host of memories as Wolf entered the thronging concourse. Among the hundreds of travelers, he saw a short, tough, mustached man holding a *New York Times* and scanning the passengers. Their eyes connected in recognition. Wolf warmed to the crisp dark brown suit and polished black Italian loafers. The man extended a hand. "Welcome home, Detective James," he said smartly. "I'm Captain Troyem of the Odessa Police Force. Let's get your luggage." After passing through customs, Wolf joined the captain at baggage claim.

Uniformed officers held his gun cases. With admiration, Captain Troyem said, "A Heckler & Koch G Twenty-Eight sniper rifle, Sig Sauer M Seventeen, and KA-BAR? You come prepared. I was the demolitions expert in the One Hundred Third Guards Airborne in Afghanistan. I'll introduce you to my closest friend and now famous Professor Danilenko, the squad sniper." Another officer set Wolf's luggage, portfolio of sketches, and the small crate containing the icon on a luggage cart and wheeled them to the captain's curbside SUV.

As the driver pulled out, Wolf buckled up in the back seat along with the captain, who placed the current *New York Times* on his lap and said, "Open to page three. It's an interesting article." Wolf opened the paper and stared at his NYPD graduation picture. The accompanying headline read, *"NYPD's Fighting Ninth, Odessa, Ukraine, Join Forces. Odessa, Ukraine's Police Chief Artem Troyem found what he needed and more when he went to Captain Vincent Greening of Manhattan's Ninth Precinct."* The article described the cooperation between the city of New York and the Ukrainian government and was continued on page 16. As Wolf turned the page, he tensed in disbelief. The same photograph of him as an eight-year-old boy stared back at him. A blue-clad officer restrained him, while his family's shop and home were engulfed in flames. The article spoke of Wolf's Ukrainian roots, his stint in the Rangers, and now a detective coming home to help Odessa law enforcement and the lauded Captain Troyem. "Good publicity at least, for you and me," said the captain.

Wolf rubbed his beard and gave his head a shake. Pointing to page 16, he said, "I saw this picture only yesterday." Then he showed Captain Troyem the photos lifted from the assassin's wallet. "This one is me and my fiancée. These three skulls are an exact copy of one buried in the belly of Manhattan's Ninth Precinct."

Captain Troyem examined them. "$10,000 with the skull and crossbones? You are marked, Detective James, like your unfortunate family. Only sworn enemies of the Sakharov syndicate earn the skull. They are the most feared mob in Europe and the Eastern seaboard of the United States. Now I understand the *New York Times* article. The Sakharov let you know they know who and where you are."

"I shouldn't be here," said Wolf. "My enemies are in New York."

"The Sakharov?" declared Captain Troyem. "I have news for you, Detective James. The syndicate is headquartered in Odessa and run by Semion Rolovich, the 'Rat.' I know him. We've met. He operates out of Club Ibiza. The dragon you seek is here, Detective." The SUV had arrived at the II Decameron Apartments, an ultramodern group of beautifully designed buildings in the heart of the city. Wolf gazed upward at the multistory complexes. "You're in the penthouse suite," continued the captain.

"Kind of spendy."

"You'll need protection. My niece Oksana runs this place with eyes in the back of her head. She's our first line of defense."

As they entered the spacious atrium, Wolf slapped his forehead. "I forgot to phone Katy." He called, and it went to voice mail. "This is Kathryn Brock, PhD. Author of *The Art of Compromise: Keep Your Marriage Alive*" ... blah, blah ... "Please leave a message."

Wolf followed Captain Troyem to the reception desk, where they were greeted by an attractive young woman with thick auburn hair and smooth olive skin. She blushed when she saw Wolf and placed a hand over her mouth to hide the smile. "Detective James, a pleasure to meet you," she said. "I've placed you in Penthouse Suite One. Here's the key code. You have complementary vodka in the refrigerator."

"Niece," said Captain Troyem. "Let's remove Detective James from the computer and create an alias. Say, 'Mr. Bill McKenny, a computer engineer from Albany, New York.'"

Oksana made a notation. "Mr. McKenny," she said. "We host an informal party in the lounge with live music every evening. Any questions?"

"None. Thanks," said Wolf.

"If you need anything, don't hesitate to ..." said Oksana as she wiggled the phone with a sexy smile "... call any time." Captain Troyem smiled ruefully.

Wolf turned to him. The lines around his eyes relaxed. He said knowingly, "First line of defense?"

"In more ways than one," said the captain, and left.

Wolf turned to Oksana. "Where is Club Ibiza?" he asked.

28

Day 12
Hotel de Paris, Odessa, Ukraine
Friday, September 29
Twenty-three-hundred hours

They flew from Beirut, Lebanon, to Odessa, Ukraine. After getting into bed for the evening, Brianna's dark thoughts engulfed her, as she was overcome by François's passion and her inner torment. Normally she would tie up her mark and suspend him in ecstasy until he agreed to sign whatever Ivan wanted. But now? Brianna held François in a dreamy pool of desire and possibility. "François is an inspired lover," she thought. "A genius and thinker who can save me and my daughter. I need to wrap my heart around him and woo him, not betray him, but how? Can we be a family? Would he take Ulyana as his own? Does he want children? Do I? But if François signs Ivan's contract, Stanislov will knock and fly me home. What then? And would I have the courage to call

François and confess all?" "I gave you to Ivan Juric," she heard herself say. "The Enforcer of the Sakarovkh syndicate." Brianna stopped. "Idiot. François would despise me. He'd hunt me down and shoot me."

Brianna awoke early the following morning. François would meet with Michael Sokolov for lunch. The hotel suite, draped in burgundy curtains with a fire crackling in a wrought iron hearth, set the stage for romance. Brianna removed the oiled purple ropes she'd put in her luggage. As François slept, the escort slipped expert knots around François's wrist and ankles. She tied him down, kissed him out of a peaceful slumber, and whispered, "I have a surprise."

François opened his eyes. He tested the restraints and said, "Those are tight."

"I don't want you moving." Brianna placed a blindfold over his eyes and began with kisses. She worked her way down his neck and chest, lingering on his tummy before diving between his thighs. Brianna did not hurry. "When you return after the meeting," she said, "there's more." Then she took him in her mouth and pushed him inside, pausing every so often to say, "A new contract and a new life."

François squealed, "You want me to sign it?"

"Promise," she said. François arched his back higher and higher, nearly tearing the ropes. She stuffed his mouth with a silk handkerchief to quiet his cries and watched his pelvis twist in agony.

"Brianna," came the muffled cry, "Stop. I will sign. I promise." Brianna swallowed him deep, filled with betrayal. François exploded and collapsed.

Brianna untied the ropes. She held François tightly and said to herself, "Ulyana, I've done my part. François, forgive me."

François let his fingers comb Brianna's sable hair. He

sniffed her perfume and said, "I love you. And I have a question."

"Yes, my love," she breathed, fearful of what the day might bring.

"What is your daughter's name?" Brianna gasped. Her body tensed and froze. She tried to wrench away from François, but he held her close. "What is your daughter's name?" came the question again, and Brianna wrestled free. Holding her stomach, Brianna ran into the bathroom and turned on the shower, hoping she could drown herself and find deliverance from this hell. *How did François know? Who told him?* she asked herself. Brianna berated herself for vastly underestimating François; he wasn't a genius in word only, but in deed. No one except Ivan knew about Ulyana. Should François mention anything to Ivan about his suspicions, she and Ulyana and François would die. Brianna couldn't let that happen.

She stepped out of the shower as the chauffeur knocked on the front door. Wrapped in a bath towel, she caught François, wanting to say, "Don't go." He held her gaze and said, "Will I find you when I return?"

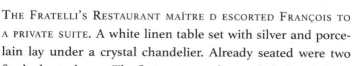

THE FRATELLI'S RESTAURANT MAÎTRE D ESCORTED FRANÇOIS TO A PRIVATE SUITE. A white linen table set with silver and porcelain lay under a crystal chandelier. Already seated were two finely dressed men. The first got up and extended a hand. "Professor LeCompte? I'm Mikael Sokolov, president of Army Munitions Group. May I introduce the general manager and vice president of our parent company, Eastern Machine Systems, Mr. Ivan Juric?"

"A great honor, indeed," said Ivan. François took one look at Mr. Juric and sensed the threat, as if a foe had pulled a knife. François nodded politely and took his seat.

"Thank you for joining us, Professor," gushed Mr. Sokolov and launched into a history of his company. Ivan placed his hand on Mr. Sokolov's arm.

"Professor LeCompte," he said. "Due to the classified nature of our subject, we require a nondisclosure agreement." Ivan opened his briefcase and set a pen and contract on the linen. François read it carefully and signed it. The contract disappeared into the leather folder. "Don't be offended, but I must search you for any wires and remove your phone's SIM card," continued Ivan. François shrugged as Ivan worked quickly and efficiently.

Satisfied François didn't harbor electronic devices, Ivan nodded to Mikael Sokolov, who leaned forward. "Army Munitions Group has developed a man-portable nuclear device."

"You have *plutonium*?" said François.

President Sokolov nodded. "Yes, but our lead scientist fell ill."

"Who designs your detonation software?"

"You've heard of Professor Helmut Gott from Mainz, Germany?" replied Sokolov. "He accepted our offer to join us and starts tomorrow. Professor Andreyev was our nuclear physicist and has prepared the nuclear cores, but we must be ready to launch by the thirteenth of October at sixteen hundred hours."

"The missiles must also come with a 'command' switch, controlled by a single person," interjected Ivan Juric.

François frowned. "Nuclear devices are constructed from thousands of parts from around the world and subject to the sequential grading protocols. They are not part of networks controlled by an individual. This is standard operating procedure. The idea of an 'override' switch, controlled by one person, is nonsense."

"Under normal circumstances, yes," said Sokolov. "But Eastern Machine Systems started this process thirty years ago and before that as Southern under the Soviets. They build every wire, board, and piece of metal and plastic used in the X3, and write the code. Hence, our missiles are 'in network,' controlled from one central location."

François narrowed his eyes as his nerves shivered. "One man, one button?" he said to himself fearfully. "Even the Iranians can't match this sorcery." "How far along are you?" asked François.

"Ready for sphere placement," replied Sokolov

"What size?" said François.

"Racquetball. When could you start?" said Sokolov.

Acting every bit like James Bond, François announced, "Tomorrow, but I will reduce the spheres to Ping-Pong-ball size."

Both men were astonished. "You can do this?" they exclaimed.

"With Helmut Gott, my device has three times the explosive power of Professor Andreyev's, which is why the LeCompte rocket flies farther and faster than any designed."

Sokolov laughed out loud as Ivan said, "We will toast and sign the necessary papers, but please excuse me a moment." Ivan stepped into the restroom, checked the stalls to make sure no one was present, and phoned Brianna. "Pack. Stanislov will take you to the jet," and rejoined his guests. He ordered champagne and pulled out the Army Munitions Group contract.

François read it closely but raised a cautionary finger. "A good start, but lacking key ingredients," he said. "It must stipulate I exercise absolute control over the production schedule and the personnel on this Building Thirteen, Floor Seven. I require four times my current salary with full amenities and benefits." Sokolov grew solemn and set the champagne aside. Ivan sat back and lit a cigarette. François continued, "A $20 million signing bonus plus five percent on each missile sold, plus an additional five percent for each successful detonation.

The money transferred to my private account immediately upon signing."

Sokolov went white. "That's extortion," he said.

"The LeCompte rocket will sell for a minimum $100 million," replied François, unconcerned. "If the terms aren't acceptable, find someone else." Sokolov sweat and mopped his brow. Disfiguring facial tics ignited on Ivan's face. Then, François leaned forward like a conspirator. "President Sokolov? I also have a secret of my own. I'm in love with your niece Miss Ivanova and will ask for her hand in marriage this afternoon. I've come to depend on her. Without Brianna, I cannot complete the project. As a token of your good will, I'm asking for a betrothal gift. Nonnegotiable, you understand. Deposit $5 million into her account today." François slid numbers for a new Swiss bank account in Brianna's name to the stunned conspirators.

Ivan Juric turned pale green. He rose to his feet. "Please excuse me one more time." Ivan hurried to the restroom and called Stanislov. The sound of a jet whooshing through the air was the backdrop to horrified screaming. Stanislov said, "A few more minutes over the sea. Her head's out the door."

"Stop! Let me talk to her!" yelled Ivan.

Ivan heard Stanislov shout, "Shut up, whore! Mr. Juric has something to say." Ivan held the phone at arm's length as Brianna cursed. "You fucking, fucking, fucking bastard pig!"

"You done?" said Ivan. "Now listen. The Frenchman is in love with you and wants to marry you. Keep him fucking happy until I say otherwise. Say nothing, or I will send you Ulyana in pieces." Ivan returned to the dining table and said to François, "Eastern Machine Systems leases two penthouse suites at the Two Decameron apartment complex in downtown Odessa. You may thrill your new bride with the finest accommodations in the city. Now, allow President Sokolov to buy you the finest billiards table money can buy. Go with him and then join your betrothed."

A hot afternoon sun beat down as François returned to the hotel. Loud sobs echoed throughout the suite. He opened the bedroom door. A half-empty fifth of vodka and vial of Xanax lay open. Brianna lay under the sheets with her head under a pillow. "Go away! Leave me alone!" she shouted.

François observed the dark welts and torn skin on Brianna's wrists and ankles and forced back a red-faced roar of rage. He walked to the famous Potemkin Steps and smoked. After cooling down, he returned to the suite, and Brianna met him in a stunning negligee with diamond choker. Forcing a tear-streaked smile, she said, "Do you like?" He put his finger to her lips and took out his "bug" detector. He swept the suite, finding three expertly planted listening devices.

François enclosed her in his arms. "Very much," he said. "Now put some clothes on, we're going for a walk." Outside, François took Brianna's face between his hands and continued, "Listen carefully. I love you."

Brianna began bawling. "You have no idea what I've done, what an evil person I am."

François held her until she calmed down and said, "I start tomorrow in Building Thirteen at the Army Munitions Group. You must return to Beirut and wrap up my affairs. The Two Decameron Penthouse Suite Number Two is our new home. Can you tell me anything?" Brianna lowered her eyelashes and shook her head in fright. François continued, "Where is Ulyana?"

"I don't know, but how did you know about her?"

"I can't say right now, but be patient. We'll find her."

Exasperated, Brianna blurted out, "Are you sure you want me? I betrayed you. My job was to deliver you to Ivan Juric, the most cruel and malicious sociopath on the planet."

"Yes. I forgive you. It's forgotten. Done. Past."

Brianna sobbed afresh. "François," she said. "You realize if Ivan learns I told you, he will kill us all?" François nodded. "Then, there's one more thing I have to say. I'm grateful for everything. You saved my life and Ulyana's, but I don't *love*, love you. You understand? I can't. It's too soon and I need time to sort things out. Can you be patient with a traitor?"

"What wouldn't I do, if I were in your shoes?" replied François. "What wouldn't any mother do?"

29

Day 13
Trauma ICU, Sourasky Hospital, Tel Aviv, Israel
Saturday, September 30
Zero-eight-hundred hours

L ike fresh buds in a spring shower, Haddy's right side woke up. She grasped a carafe of water with her right hand and wiggled her toes. Both sides of her mouth smiled. "Fucking A, I'm back," she declared.

The Shin Bet agents arrived with Haddy's family. After congratulations for her returning health, Agent Gavot described the witness protection program. "Dr. Rammoth will remove the bolt tonight, and Haddy will 'die' on the table. We'll arrange a short press release." He paused and looked each in the eye before continuing. "Until we know the culprit, you will leave Israel with your new passports and personal bodyguards. Do not return home immediately. This malevolent power may want to hurt you. Do not discuss Haddy or attempt to contact her. She may contact you on these burner phones with a prearranged code, 'Horizon Vacation Resorts.'"

Raisa objected and said, "I can't go back to school? What about volleyball? I'm the star striker. The team depends on me, and the big game is next Friday."

"We want you to disappear," said the agent. "Your lives may be endangered. Tell the school it's a family emergency. Have them send your assignments by secure email." Agent Gavot turned to Stefan. "Professor Danilenko, you have two phones?"

Stefan held them out. "The white one is an iPhone I use to check regular email," he said, "and speak to Raisa. The Boeing Black is an ultra-secure phone for the High Explosives Applications Facility in Livermore, California."

"Professor Danilenko, turn off the iPhone," said the agent. "We'll make sure Haddy has your Boeing Black number."

Turning to Raisa, Agent Gavot said, "And you?" Raisa removed her "Hot Pink" Smartphone from her purse. "Turn it off," he said and gave her a burner. "Use this. If Haddy contacts you, it will be on this phone. If Stefan contacts you, it will ..."

"On the trashy black phone with no screen?" said Raisa. "I get it, but really? Are you saying I can't play volleyball? You realize our inter-city match with Kiev is two weeks away on Friday? I'm sitting for my premed exams Thursday. I'm supposed to put my life on hold for two weeks?"

The agent sighed. "Raisa, work with us. A high-profile volleyball tournament is too exposed."

Raisa's face flushed red. She tightened her fists and turned to Haddy for support. "I don't think I can do it. We're vying for number one in the country."

"You're asking Frankenstein?" said Haddy.

"You are my hero, the toughest woman I know."

"Then there's your answer," said Haddy. "Be tough."

Agent Gavot turned to David and Sasha Abrams. "The

same restrictions apply to you," and he gave them similar black burners. "Now collect your belongings and say goodbye."

Haddy looked at each, her chest tight and full of dread. "None of you has said anything about the letter I mailed."

Only Raisa replied, her face still red from anger. "I read it and tore it up. It's not you." She bent over and kissed Haddy. "Sorry for all the drama. I'll miss the bolt. I'll give up the game, but I can't make any promises after that—unless of course we are in real danger."

"I appreciate it; now watch yourself," Haddy said. "Kick ass against Kiev."

The other three shrugged their shoulders. "We haven't been home. We left the moment we heard about the bombing. What letter?"

Stefan hobbled up, his knee still in a cast. "You remember the Barrett fifty-caliber sniper rifle I bought after your father died?"

"The American cannon?" said Haddy.

"It's yours. When you find these fuckers, use it."

David came up, gripped her hand. "Take care, and when you're better, kill the bastards."

Sasha's aquamarine eyes swelled. "I think I know about the letter. I don't know the meaning of your flaming boy, but the music box? I asked David about it. He still has it."

As they left, Haddy wondered if she would see them again after this new turn: declared "dead." In thirteen days, she would "celebrate" her twenty-seventh birthday. Could she do it? Did she have the strength? Haddy knew that courage was more than firing a weapon. It consisted of saying "yes" to another day. A tiny, tiny *yes*, to fulfill a destiny she could only dimly see through the mist. "Yes. I'm torn up beyond recognition, can barely walk, and am full of strange fears and flashbacks, but yes, I can say 'yes' to one more hour ... one 'yes' at a time."

Dr. Rammoth removed the bolt Saturday evening. He filled

the hole with an experimental mesh plug, which assisted bone growth. In the stillness of the operating room, a phone rang. The caller asked for an update on Staff Sergeant Abrams. The nurse, with Agent Gavot at her side, said, "The staff sergeant died on the table from a massive intracranial bleed. Who is this?"

Colonel Nathan Yevhim clicked off, set down his wine, and sent a text: "Staff sergeant dead in the OR." He took solace in the announcement but, aware of Shin Bet tricks, the colonel posed as a physician and called the hospital pharmacy. "Any new med orders for a patient in the hospital's secure ward?" he asked.

"Jael Benjamin," replied the pharmacist. The colonel informed Ivan.

"Check it out," replied the Enforcer.

30

Day 14
Penthouse Suite One, Two Decameron Apartment Complex,
Downtown Odessa, Ukraine
Sunday, October 1
Zero-nine-hundred hours

W olf had surveyed the modern penthouse, which put a king-sized bed covered with black satin sheets at one end. The satin shone in the sunlight as light pierced overhead glass inserts, while floor-to-ceiling windows ran along the wall. The black leather couches, kitchen area, and tiled walk-in shower brought a smile to the detective. Kathryn would love this.

After hanging his clothes in the armoire, he placed the icon of St. Joshua on the bedroom wall. On a small table underneath, he set up a triptych. He lit a candle, crossed himself, and prayed, "O, my most holy lady Theotokos, through thy holy and all-powerful prayers, banish from me, thy lowly and

wretched servant, despondency, forgetfulness, folly, careless-
ness, and all filthy, evil, and blasphemous thoughts from my
wretched heart and darkened mind. Holy Saint Joshua, my
Warrior Prince, pray unto God for me, the speedy helper and
intercessor for my soul. Complete the healing of my heart as I
lay to rest my Snow Queen. Open my soul in holy matrimony
to Kathryn. Amen."

Wolf took out the three remaining sketches and set them on
the dining table. His finger traced the charcoaled features with
a wistful sigh for something precious lost forever. He gazed into
her eyes, and fire ignited inside him, but he couldn't live his life
chasing a dream.

Captain Troyem came Sunday afternoon. Wolf welcomed
him and poured ice-cold vodka. The police chief declared, "To
your health and success in the city of your birth. Where were
you born?"

"The apartments on Osypova and Velyka Arnauts'ka
Streets. Fourth floor, Number Three," replied Wolf.

"*I know it!*" declared the captain. "Do you remember my
friend, Professor Danilenko? He lives on the second floor of the
same apartment."

"I was four," said Wolf. "Did he have a daughter named
Sasha?"

Captain Troyem shook his head in wonder and said, "What
a small world." Wolf uncorked a Maker's Mark fifth and filled
his tumbler while the captain sipped on vodka and took in the
expansive views of the city and the Black Sea. He walked past
the dining table, homed in on the icon, and picked up the small
Orthodox prayer book. "You're Orthodox?" he asked incred-
ulously.

"Saint Joshua and I have a thing," replied Wolf. "The Prayer
Book has prayers used by the ancient church."

The captain examined the icon closer. "Priceless," he said
reverently. "Is this Andrey Rublev?" Wolf nodded, and the

captain gushed, "The saint looks at you with eyes aflame. I will tell Oksana to keep a sharp eye out. Thieves go after these. But Detective James ...?"

"Wolf."

"Something has come up, which might interest you," the captain continued. "I received an anonymous tip a few weeks ago about a half ton of Afghan heroin arriving in Odessa by tanker. The Rat himself will oversee the operation. He arrives at four a.m., and I will set a trap."

Wolf's teeth set on edge at the mention of that name. His eyebrows narrowed into an angry glare. He set down the bourbon, leaning forward, and said, "I'm in."

"I thought as much," said the captain. "But there's a caveat. The freighter Novarsk docks Friday, October thirteenth. I've heard from your fiancée. The day is off-limits."

Wolf buried his head in his hands and said, "Dammit to hell. I meet Kathryn at nine a.m., which means I'm off shift at seven. But, if Rat shows at four, we could do it. Who's team lead?"

"You're the most qualified," said the captain.

Wolf's eyes flashed as he shook the captain's hand and said, "Thanks."

"I'll inform Oksana," beamed the captain. "We'll meet here every day at zero nine hundred hours," and lifted the shot glass one last time. "To your good health and a successful mission." He walked to the dining table and paused at the sketches. "These are exceptional," he declared. "Who did these?"

Wolf downed another shot of bourbon, sat back, and reflected on this strange turn of events. "It's serendipitous, don't you agree?" he remarked. "How often does a man have a chance for personal payback?"

The captain wasn't listening. "Wolf?" he said. "Who did these drawings?"

"I did."

"Who modeled?" the captain asked.

"I call her my Snow Queen," replied Wolf. "I saw her once." Wolf described the moment on Mt. Rainier. "We parted and I started drawing. I searched for nine years and gave up. I destroyed most of the sketches, except these three. Next week, I'll scatter the ashes on the Black Sea, close to home."

The captain bent over and studied the drawings in detail. His eyes widened as he straightened and said, "Unless your Snow Queen has a doppelgänger, I know this woman," and dug out a photo from his wallet. "I told you Stefan Danilenko and I served in the war?"

Wolf was getting antsy. "To the point?" he said impatiently.

"I snapped this photo two years ago at our family reunion," said Captain Troyem. The photo showed signs of wear, yet on a grassy field in front of a long table filled with food stood a large group. "Here's Stefan," he pointed. "To his left is his daughter Sasha, your babysitter, and down front is Raisa. This one? To his right is his granddaughter, Staff Sergeant Haddy Abrams, identical to your model." Wolf sighed, thinking of Rat, and took the wallet photo reluctantly. "The reason you can't find her," continued the captain, "is she's a black ops sniper in the Israel Defense Force."

Wolf compared the woman to his drawings. He never got dizzy, but now his head whirled. He fell on the floor, staring blankly at the ceiling.

The captain put up a hand and said, "She might not be the one."

"The daughter of Sasha who lived two floors up from us?" said Wolf. "How is that possible?" Suddenly, Wolf came alive as he saw comets colliding in the night. He bounded to his feet and roared, "That's her! Dammit, that's her! Call Professor Danilenko."

"Stefan returns my calls no matter where he is in the world, but not lately," replied the captain.

"But what about the blonde?" asked Wolf.

"The volleyball star? Raisa's in school," the captain said and wrote down the contact information. "I doubt if she's home, but she lives in the same apartment. If you reach her, tell her to have Stefan call me."

"And Haddy?" said Wolf.

"Her mother and grandfather live in New York and own and manage an arts gallery in Manhattan," replied the captain. "It's called Abrams' Fine Arts on West Broadway."

"I showed her my sketches," said Wolf, astonished. "Sasha is Haddy's mother? Why didn't she say anything?"

The captain left, and Wolf dialed Stefan and Raisa, without an answer. He left voicemails. Using his NYPD connections, he tracked down David Abrams in Southampton and Sasha Abrams in Apartment 6, 140 Perry Street, Manhattan, but neither answered. He left more voicemails and then spoke to the assistant manager of Abrams' Fine Arts, asking him to have Sasha call the moment she got his message. Wolf then caught a cab and went to the apartment where he had been born. He saw the handwritten sign, "Danilenko," above the buzzer for the second-story apartment. He rang and rang and finally turned back.

That evening, Wolf lay beneath the black satin sheets and stared at the stars through the skylight. The room was cool, and the drowsy warmth of an evening of bourbon gladdened his belly. First Rat and now his Snow Queen! Wolf saw in his mind's eye Haddy standing on a lone balcony from a centuries-old hotel, overlooking the famed waters of Lake Como in Italy, the land of love. She stood draped in a delicate nightgown. Wolf's pulse quickened as he came into the quiet room and beckoned the olive-skinned beauty to lie next to him. His pelvis stirred as Haddy's black hair flowed across his face. Wolf felt her breath upon him and inhaled her strong feminine scent. He stared into her infinite eyes. He had drawn her lips for years and knew every crease and curve; how voluptuous they were. Wolf's eyelids closed. He wished for nothing more than to taste the kiss and feel her burn. Haddy's muscles rippled as she rose on her elbow and kissed him. Like bourbon, her soul tingled in his stomach and dived deeper. He removed her nightgown. Haddy lay back as Wolf placed his ear on her chest and listened to her heart throb with excitement. She stopped being a Snow Queen.

"Surprise me, Wolf," she told him, "with wicked delights. The stars are out, the moon hovers over the mist, and the Italian waters beckon."

Wolf wasn't dreaming and stopped short. He let the amorous thoughts fall away like sand through his fingers. His mind turned to Kathryn and guilt. Wolf shrank at the idea of telling his fiancée the truth. How and when could he tell her? Tonight? Wolf wondered if Kathryn would strike back in rage, the jilted lover, thrown over for someone else. He didn't think so, but Lawrence Brock was vindictive. Another call to his friend the police commissioner, and his tenure as a detective would be over. Done. "Maybe that's why I never confessed my darkest secrets to Kathryn?" he wondered. Wolf's erection hadn't faded, and his imaginary hands roved over the silken skin of Haddy's chest, down her belly, and onto her thighs. "I'm glad I didn't tell Kathryn about you, Haddy. She might think we cooked this up to hurt her." But Wolf hadn't found Haddy yet, and a terrible fear with bony fingers strangled his throat. When he did find her, would Haddy reject him? She'd say, "Who are you?" or "I'm married." Wolf forced himself to shake off the dreadful thought.

Wolf turned on the bedside lamp and stared at St. Joshua. "I need you bad, God. One moment I'm joy, the next fear. What kind of cosmic chess game are you playing? Is this an inside straight or divine disappointment? Is Haddy mine, or will she say, 'No'?"

31

Day 14
Secure Room beneath Sourasky Hospital
Sunday, October 1
Zero-five-hundred hours

I n a secret ward below the Sourasky Hospital, Haddy's recovery began. The machines and monitors, incessant energy, and frantic pace of the ICU were gone. When she awoke, Pooh Bear lay next to a single lamp. The illumination in the quiet room cast shadows on the floor, and she felt haunted. She whipped her head around. Was there a threat? The room remained silent.

Haddy shook it off and put down the bedside railing. She stood for the first time, weak and wobbly. Dr. Rammoth told her that general anesthesia set back the body's metabolism two weeks. Like "pulling the plug on Manhattan," it took time for the billions of neurons to recover. Haddy gripped the IV pole, reached the bathroom, and looked in the mirror. She was a mummy with a nasogastric feeding tube taped to her nose.

Haddy observed the toilet, the weight scale, and step-in shower. She filled the washbasin with water, poured in peroxide, and started taking off the bandages. Skipping the laborious soaking of each layer, Haddy plunged her face into the sink. A suture removal kit lay in the cabinet. With scissors, she cut away the wet mass of bubbling and fizzing cotton. She daubed her face and appraised the result. The swelling had diminished, but ghastly yellow, black, and purple skin remained. The Frankenstein bolt was gone, while a peach fuzz of hair had sprouted. She saw the mesh plug and remembered Dr. Rammoth's warning, "Don't push it, you may black out." Not content with that sage advice, Haddy put her index finger on the plug and pushed. A wave of dizziness and nausea hit her stomach. She collapsed on the toilet. "Okay, I believe you, but I don't like it," she said. Haddy smeared antibiotic ointment on her wounds and checked her weight. She was down 10 pounds. Angry and disconsolate, Haddy yanked out the feeding tube and the IV in her forearm. Blood flowed from the site, and she applied pressure and a Band-Aid. She left the pole behind.

Haddy tottered back to the bed. Standing as erect as possible, she grasped the railing with both hands, and tightened her body. She placed her feet straight ahead, brought her shoulder blades and head back, and tucked in her chin. Then Haddy tightened her pelvis and squeezed her bottom and abdominal muscles. Maintaining the arch in her low back, she pushed her hips out. Her butt lowered to the floor. She reversed the motion and congratulated herself on her first squat since the blast. Haddy ignored the cool breeze on her bare backside, a gift from the hospital gown, which fluttered open. Haddy grabbed both butt cheeks and squeezed. "At least you survived," she said.

Haddy continued the exercise until her thighs burned. She

gobbled down the cheese, peanut butter, and crackers, and cleaned out the cranberry and orange juice. Haddy had resumed the squats when Agent Gavot came in with two fresh coffees. He caught the full bare ass flying in the breeze. The cups spilled on the floor, and the flustered Shin Bet counterintelligence agent tossed a passport on her bed and left hurriedly. "Can't take a joke?" quipped Haddy and examined her new identity. She raised an eyebrow in approval. "Jael Benjamin? Cool."

The nurse arrived and bustled in with characteristic professionalism. She helped Haddy into a T-shirt and pajamas and said, "We will find you lunch. You like juice?"

"I need breakfast and two lunches and a mid-afternoon snack and two dinners," replied Haddy.

Agent Gavot knocked, poked his head inside with fresh coffees, and said, "You decent?"

Haddy ignored him. "I need more than a passport," she said. "I want a black wool cap for my head, casual clothing, fitness garments, compression tights, and T-shirts, all black. Cross-trail running shoes, a powerful laptop computer, a Glock Nineteen with a suppressor, cartridges, and ear protectors, and an Ontario MK Three Navy Knife." He nodded as she continued, "Someone is trying to kill me. Remember?"

The physical therapist entered, as the agent left with Haddy's list. Exuding tons of *positive mental attitude*, he said enthusiastically, "Hey there, how are you?"

"I'm an eleven on your fucking pain scale," said Haddy.

"I'm your rehabilitation specialist," he replied. "We can do an evaluation and start tomorrow."

"You've got foam rollers?" said Haddy. "You're an expert in 'proprioceptive neuromuscular facilitated stretching'? Start now, with another session this afternoon."

The therapist smiled. He folded his arms across a broad muscled chest, forearms flexing with bulging biceps, and said,

"Wonder Woman, eh? With a fresh head wound. I don't want to fight Dr. Rammoth, but I'll see what I can do." In minutes, Haddy lay on her back. The therapist had one hand on her hip, while he took her heel with the other and raised her leg. "Keep that knee straight," he said. "Now push your heel against my hand for seven seconds *hard* ... now relax." As she did, the therapist raised Haddy's leg farther, ratcheting the thigh to her chest.

"God dammit, you'll rip my hamstrings," Haddy screamed. He worked each muscle group and added lunges, pelvic tilts, and a few push-ups.

"I'll be back in four hours," he said as lunch arrived.

Swallowing the last of her coffee, Haddy lay back just in time for Dr. Adina and her assistant to enter. "How's Wonder Woman?" said the plastic surgeon. "I talked with the physical therapist."

"What's going on?" asked Haddy.

"Sutures out," said Dr. Adina.

"How long will this take?"

"Why? You going out to dinner?" replied Dr. Adina. "Someone I know? Stop whining." The surgeon donned her mask and loupes, and with stainless steel tray and lamps and equipment close at hand, painstakingly snipped and removed ninety-nine sutures. She painted the skin with a sticky resin, then put on dozens of tiny butterfly bandages over each cut. "Staff Sergeant?" she said. "These strips keep the edges together and minimize scars. Water is your enemy. It causes the skin to swell, which opens the wounds. If you ruin my Picasso, I'll be very unhappy. Sweat is water. Balance your workouts by keeping the skin as dry as possible. Apply my magic healing cream to your face, and wipe off that glum look. If you're good, no one will know in twelve months."

"Twelve months?" said Haddy.

"One year," declared Dr. Adina. "Remember, scars improve

with time." The surgeon took off her gown and gloves and continued, "We're not done. I have a surprise. Now, close your eyes." Dr. Adina lifted a blonde wig from a box. "Okay, look."

Haddy groaned. "Blonde? I *hate* blondes."

"You mean Staff Sergeant Haddy Abrams hates blondes," said Dr. Adina. She snapped her fingers and continued, "But wait, you're Jael Benjamin, and Jael loves golden yellow with highlights."

Haddy examined herself in the mirror. "I'm a bimbo," she said.

Dr. Adina teased the strands across her face and said, "We're not done yet," and placed a pair of mirrored aviators on Haddy. "No one will recognize you. That's the point." Dr. Adina left with a smile. "Be good," she said. "Be patient. You'll get better and be able to swing your hips and dazzle some young man with those magnificent eyes in no time."

Haddy lay back, her face and body a mass of pain. She started to relax when the psychotraumatologist arrived. He launched into the benefits of mindfulness meditation and the effects of blast trauma, including nightmares, flashbacks, disturbing memories, and mood disorders. "You may find yourself angry, irritable, and depressed. Have you experienced any of these before?"

"Yeah, Doc," said Haddy. "I can be a royal bitch."

"Avoid loud sounds, and don't bump your head," he reminded her.

"Do you know what I do and how stupid that sounds?" said Haddy.

"Don't shoot the messenger, Staff Sergeant," he replied. "You'll heal. Just give yourself time."

Haddy worried her fingernail. "I'm having nightmares and panic and feel like I'm a ghost or something. I'm not sure who I am. Is that weird?"

"Staff Sergeant, your brain got scrambled, like eggs," said

the specialist. "Be prepared for ghosts, vivid past traumas, visions, and voices. We have medicines, but as your brain heals, you'll find ways of facing them. When you see them, embrace them and integrate them into your new self. You'll not only survive, but be stronger and wiser. Time, Staff Sergeant. Remember: time. Give yourself time, and this will become an unpleasant memory. I'll be back tomorrow."

Haddy collapsed. "'Time,'" he said, and "'Be good,'" remarked Dr. Adina, but they weren't running for their lives. Where was her center in this storm? Haddy asked herself, and concluded, "*Run, hide, and heal.* Get word to Shira, and get back into this fight when you are ready." Haddy fell asleep at once.

Later, Agent Gavot knocked on her door. There was no reply. He found Haddy snoring. The agent covered her with a blanket and left a leather satchel full of clothes, a gun case, and a laptop on the floor before leaving.

32

Day 14
Sailing aboard the Yacht *American Dream*, The Black Sea
Sunday, October 1
Thirteen-hundred hours

Bodyguards assisted X, bundled up in his leopard-skin coat, aboard the twin-engine jet helicopter. Snow flurries swirled about the helipad, and crystals glinted softly against the rays of sun poking through the swollen overcast. Fusako and Trang followed in coats and fur-lined hats. The pilot, Anatoly Karpov, assisted by the flight attendant, Irena Yaroslava, powered up the blades, and off they went, snaking through the forested Teberda river valley. Once clear of the mountains, Karpov veered west for the Black Sea. X lay deep in thought, hardly seeing the landscape below. His sleep was troubled. Rahil had come unbidden, weeping for justice, but worse, he learned Haddy Abrams had not perished. He had also learned his personal assistant, Fusako, was not who she seemed.

X held the cigar and saw it quivering. He knew moving the missile launch from December to October jeopardized the program. He took a pull from his hip flask of vodka and puffed the tobacco to quell a mounting dismay. Perhaps he should hit the "reset" button back to December? But the risk of offending his dead sister weighed upon him. Then a darker thought struck him. Perhaps Rahil was a deception of the highest order? Maybe he had read the signs the wrong way? Kali was mischief as well as dread. Maybe it was a divine joke and he merely a pawn in the hands of forces beyond him?

X looked at Trang. He could trust the mute, but Fusako? His Japanese assistant wore an immaculate sea-green woolen overcoat and coffee-colored designer boots. Her eyes were serene in servitude, but his spies told him Miss Kitashirakawa was a yakuza assassin and next in line to ascend to *kumicho*, head of the Yamaguchi-gumi clan. X had called Gorou Kitashirakawa, the *kumicho* himself, and said, "You think I wouldn't discover the truth about your granddaughter?"

"Fusako is many things, X," Gorou replied carefully. "But she's been sent to protect you. You are not the only one who wants the green jade box."

The helicopter passed over the lower Caucasus Mountains, snow glinting off the peaks in the overhead sun, and swept over the ocean. X saw his 300-foot long, five-tier yacht *American Dream* in the distance. The gleaming white vessel was moored off Kiev in the sapphire waters of the Dnieper River but had traversed the Black Sea to this rendezvous site.

Once the helicopter landed, X went to the bridge and ordered everyone out. This was the reason he was here. He needed respite from the confines of the Palace. The yacht let his mind expand. After a pleasant day and fine dining, he would be refreshed and renewed. He also had a surprise for

Fusako. X took the bridge and settled in to sail over the vast blue waters. He meditated on his new world following the fall of Jerusalem, but a foreboding shadowed his vision like a dark cloud. The staff sergeant had survived the blast, and Shin Bet had faked her death at surgery. She lived and threatened all.

FUSAKO TROD softly on the thick rugs in the stateroom below. She placed her thick woolen coat on a luxurious bed and went to examine the other rooms. Entering through the first door, she let her eyes adjust to the black walls and purple fluorescent light. Rows of gold skulls sat next to each other on shelves behind glass cabinets. Similar to the Palace Room, each lay in wide-mouthed terror. On the floor were tattooed-skin lamps. Fusako touched herself where X had touched her and shuddered. Instinct warned her he wanted Trang to make her into a lamp.

Fusako passed into the next room of soft rose hues. She examined paintings and intricately carved ivories, and photos of a younger X. Covering one wall were music boxes of extraordinary craftsmanship. This must be what Grandfather Gorou meant. The first box appeared to be Russian, of the same quality of the Faberge eggs shining in diamonds, rubies, and white porcelain. She saw others from Japan and Bavaria and England and on and on. A scroll lay underneath and read: *"Therefore this is what the sovereign lord says: I swear with uplifted hand that the nations around you will also suffer scorn."*

X entered the room. "My music boxes?" he said. "Mysterious, aren't they? Most have secret compartments. I'm still looking for a French one, built in 1786, with a secret compartment underneath a Star of David. It was commissioned by Louis XIV for a Jewish mistress but disappeared after the French Revolution. I have a drawing from reports, seen here." X paused and directed Fusako to another drawing. "This one, I drew this from memory. It's a box from the Ming dynasty. Last year, I went to a secret atoll in the South China Sea on a China Houbei Class Type Twenty-Two missile boat. I met a Chinese researcher who developed something far more deadly than hydrogen bombs. He buried a container with his deadly pestilence on the mainland and hid the location in the Ming dynasty box. I returned in a week with the payment he demanded, but he was dead, and the box stolen. Only one other man knows of this box, which contains directions to a bioweapon to extort nations for untold wealth and power." Fusako remained silent. X continued, "I prepared a treat for you. She's waiting in the other room."

33

Day 14
**The Nirvana Bar and Gambling Hall Bar and Grill, Eastern
Shore of the Azoz Sea
Sunday, October 1
Zero-thirty hours**

Arc lamps cast filmy cones of light on the Army
Munitions Group private runway. Tonight, Major
Nicolai Lebed would learn who had gotten him
thrown into a Siberian prison.

Nicolai boarded the Cessna Caravan 208B EX and hit the
ignition. The triple prop burst into a blur. He taxied, and thrust
the throttles forward. The powerful little plane jumped off the
tarmac into the night. In minutes, the Caravan flung itself over
the Black Sea. Two hours later, the eastern shore of the Azov
Sea appeared. Following land markings, Nicolai steered the
plane up the coastline, until the neon red-and-purple lights of

the Nirvana Bar appeared below like a tiny gem. He said, "Comrades. A pile of shit with Christmas ornaments."

Nicolai dropped the plane a half mile distant from the gambling joint on a dirt-farm track. The three others fanned out, using bushes as cover. They came up behind the bar and settled in for the wait.

The Nirvana Bar closed at 3 a.m. The strippers and kitchen staff left from the rear door. Wrapped in a trench coat, a platinum blonde stood out against the cool night air and lit a cigarette. She walked hastily across the lot to a sedan resting under a single lamp. Nicolai's pulse quickened. It was her, the woman of his terrible dreams. He gave the nod, and Spetsnaz Senior Sergeant Grigor crept behind the unsuspecting woman. For a big man, he moved with surprising speed and stealth. He clapped his gorilla-sized hand over her mouth and with the other pressed a 6-inch razor against her neck. Nicolai grunted in satisfaction as Grigor said, "If you open your mouth, I'll open your throat." The spetsnaz soldier pulled the dancer into the bushes. Flashlight beams illuminated a white face, devoid of color and filled with terror. Her eyes couldn't open any larger. Her breaths came in tiny gasps.

Nicolai leaned over. "Remember me? Take a good look. I'm the man who won big on roulette, and you gave me drug-laced vodka. The table spilled and there was war?"

The platinum hair bounced up and down in fright. "Don't, don't ..." she cried.

"Who's inside?" asked Nicolai. The dancer spilled out the information. Nicolai had former FSB Captain Dimitri "Loverboy" Popov zip-tie her ankles and wrists and tape her mouth shut.

Grigor and former First Sergeant "Tiny" Talgat from the Seventy-Eighth Kazakhstan Tank Regiment pulled on masks and snuck to the back side of the building. Garbage cans and a small dumpster lay next to a metal door. Grigor sprayed paint over the video cameras, while Nicolai and Loverboy went to the front and banged on the entrance. A bouncer opened the door a crack, and Nicolai shot him, as Loverboy tossed in a flash-bang grenade. Nicolai rushed in and drilled two blinded bouncers. Loverboy ran to the back and opened the rear entrance. The team cleared the building in seconds and went to the office door. Talgat triggered a Kalashnikov and sawed the door in two.

Two men lay huddled in the corner, cringing in fear. Grigor dragged the platinum blonde inside and ripped off the tape. The dancer identified the owner and manager. Nicolai shoved a knife up the owner's nostril and showed him a photo of Ivan Juric. "You know him?" he asked.

"Yesssss," came the scream.

"He arranged my capture?"

"Yesssss."

"And the others?"

"Yesssss." Nicolai grunted in satisfaction and shoved the blade inside the nose to the hilt. He turned to the stricken manager. "Anything to add?" The man wet his legs and couldn't speak. "Open the safe," Nicolai ordered. "I want the cash in two bags." Turning to the platinum blonde, he said, "Ivan Juric will discover what happened here and come after you." The manager finished shoveling cash into bags, and Grigor shot him. Nicolai thrust a bag of cash into the dancer's hands. "You speak English?"

"A little," she said.

"Then run like hell," declared Nicolai. "Go to America and change your name, but before you do, give me some of your red-star pasties for my girlfriend."

34

Day 15
Secure Recovery Room
Monday, October 2

Haddy wrestled with demons and dark visions through the night. She arose at 4:57 a.m., fatigued and restless. Her body had stiffened into painful exhausted cords. She moved her fingers and made fists, curled her toes, and drew her knees up to her chest before rolling on her side and placing her feet on the floor. She got her bearings and walked stiffly to the bathroom. Haddy peed and weighed herself, and approved of the 2-pound weight gain. She examined a face of rainbow reds, yellows, blues, and purples and noted the diminished swelling. Haddy ran her fingertips over the tiny butterfly bandages. They were unwanted trespassers, and she wished them gone. Disconsolate, Haddy ate cheese and crackers. She found the leather satchel and gun case, then picked up the computer and took it to bed.

Frazzled by the persistent vision of the dancing boy, Haddy typed "boy in flames," "flaming boys," and "Roman statues" in the search engine. After wading through a flood of porn, she found an article entitled *Eros's Flame: Images of Sexy Boys in Roman Ideal Sculpture by Elizabeth Martman. Memoirs of the American Academy in Rome. (2002), pp. 249–271.* Her pulse quickened, and she searched the archives of sculptures with interest. Haddy examined the London Museum of Art and Antiquities and the National Roman Museum with no success. Not giving up, she entered "music boxes." After viewing sites with dozens of photos, she narrowed her music box search to the eighteenth century, but couldn't decide if it was Swiss, Spanish, Italian, or French.

Breakfast arrived at 7 a.m., and Haddy ate like a horse. As her energy improved, she started planning an escape. She dumped the satchel on the bed. Sports bras and panties, black and dark gray high-waist, ankle-length tights, and sweatpants, T-shirts, and hoodies were lumped together. The gun case held her Glock with three fifteen-round magazines and two boxes of 9mm rounds. Haddy hefted the semiautomatic. She screwed in the suppressor, broke into a solid, balanced bent-knee stance, and popped the pistol forward. She kept the barrel level with the floor and focused on the front sight. The gun trembled. Haddy tossed it on the bed, disgusted.

Knowing her PT session would begin shortly, Haddy tugged on the black tights, sports bra, and polyester T-shirt. She applied Dr. Adina's cream to her wounds and brushed her teeth.

The door opened, and Agent Gavot stepped in. "Get your things," he announced urgently. "We're leaving." He gave her a newer passport. "You have a new identity."

Haddy's mind raced in hurried confusion. "What?" she said and looked at the passport. "Abilene Kirsch? What about Jael Benjamin?"

"We're wasting time," said the agent.

"What the fuck is going on?" Haddy said angrily, as she tossed the clothes, wig, Pooh Bear, bullets, and gauze into the satchel with the computer. She ditched the gun case and fed a round into the Glock. Haddy pulled a black hoodie over her head and held the weapon inside an appendix holster, while picking up the satchel in her other hand.

Agent Gavot poked his head out, looked both ways, and moved to the exit of the hallway. Halfway down, Haddy heard steps behind her. She turned and caught sight of a male nurse entering her hospital room. She turned and looked at Agent Gavot, who had one hand on the exit door, when running steps caused her to look back. Haddy freed the Glock from the pouch as the nurse raised a pistol. She aimed and froze. The counter-intelligence agent fired behind her. His Beretta .22 automatic weapon exploded twice and punched two tiny holes in the assassin's forehead, as a round from the killer's gun laid a furrow in Haddy's scalp. She reeled and hit the ground while the blast of the agent's pistol triggered a sudden headache. Blood spurted and flowed down her face and eye.

Agent Gavot grabbed Haddy's hand. "Can you walk?" Dazed from the wound, Haddy merely nodded. "Let's go," he said. They fled down the stairs to an underground parking garage. A nondescript beige sedan sat against the curb, idling. Agent Gavot flung open the passenger door. Haddy dove in, and the car squealed away. She opened the satchel and fished around for gauze. Haddy ripped open the package of 4" x 4"s and pressed them to her scalp. Heart pounding, she lay in the back seat to staunch the bleeding. Taking peeks, Haddy saw they were traveling on Route 40, the main north-south route dividing Israel in half. The car sped two and a half hours south under overcast skies. They passed into the Sinai Desert thirty minutes south of the small city of Mitzpe Ramon.

The car came to the front entrance of a camouflaged special

operations base amid the desert wastelands. The duty soldier, after phone calls and checking Haddy and the driver, waved them inside. The sedan drove straight to the small hospital tent. Her black sports hoodie, tights, and shoes were stained with blood. The medic injected stinging, numbing medicine into the skin and closed the wound with a running suture. He slapped twenty pain pills in her hand and gave her clean fatigues. "You're good to go," he said. "Welcome to Mitzpe Ramon spec-ops."

Escorted by her driver and another fellow soldier, Haddy arrived at the commanders' office wrapped in fresh bandages. Though her head and body ached, the desert smell and familiar memories brought hope. First Lieutenant Gabriel and Chief Sergeant Yosef Adelman stood to one side, as Haddy came to attention before Major Rudin. On the wall behind him hung the Sayeret Matkal special operations motto, *"Who Dares, Wins."* Major Rudin, base commanding officer, said, "At ease, Miss ...?" He glanced at her papers and continued, "Abilene Kirsch? How are you?"

"Angry," said Haddy.

Major Rudin acknowledged the driver with a nod, who identified himself as Shin Bet. "Miss Kirsch, welcome to Mitzpe Ramon special operations. Any questions?"

"How long will I be here?" said Haddy.

He looked over the papers and gave a tiny shrug. "Until Shin Bet says you can go."

"Yes, sir. Thank you, sir," said Haddy.

The major turned to Chief Sergeant Yosef Adelman. "Chief, escort Miss Kirsch to her bunk."

"Sir," replied the chief smartly. He took Haddy on a small tour of the base, including the medic station, showers, gym, and mess hall. "Mitzpe Ramon quarters sixteen men, one platoon. You're in Tent Four, private quarters. Mess is open twenty-four seven. Questions?"

"None, thanks," said Haddy. She locked the door, threw her leather satchel on the floor, and lay down on the bunk. The room came with a small fan, which whirred in the corner. Haddy got up and readjusted the cool wind on her face. Her head throbbed, but her questions throbbed louder. Someone knew her. "Jael Benjamin" had lasted forty-eight hours. If they found her so quickly, what of her family? "And me," she asked herself. "Am I safe? If Salam's family is not behind this, someone who knew him wants me dead, but why?"

Haddy worked on this puzzle but avoided the larger issue: *she had frozen*. Her finger should have pulled the trigger, but didn't. "I have never done that," she said soberly. A sense of foreboding gripped her. How could she follow the Talmudic statement, *"If someone comes to kill you, rise up and kill them first"* if she hadn't the courage to fire? But was it a hellish lack of courage, or something from a darker abyss she did not understand? Then Haddy recalled a Churchill quote: *"If you're going through hell, keep going,"* and rephrased it, "If you're passing through an abyss, darker than hell itself, keep going." She took a calming breath and in an imaginary discussion with Albert Camus said, "I want the coffee. I can put one foot in front of the other, shower, shit, and eat. I can say 'yes' in a thousand ways, and it takes fucking courage to say 'yes.' And with 'yes,' there's hope, and where there is hope, there's light. And then, I'll hunt down the bastards who did this and kill them all."

Haddy drifted to sleep. When she arose, she knew, "ghosts" or not, she wasn't safe and must find out who was after her. She padded to the showers, mindful of Dr. Adina's warning to not wet the tiny butterfly bandages, some not more than an eighth of an inch wide. She patted the skin dry and applied lotion. Haddy kept the scalp dry as well. She donned the standard-issue fatigues, sports bra, short-sleeve T-shirt, and a tight watch cap, in lieu of the wig in the satchel. She stretched and grimaced as the muscles resisted in pain. With head throbbing, she headed for dinner, determined to get back her edge.

Word of her arrival had spread among the operators. She stepped into the mess hall to complete silence and stiffened at the stolen glances from the rough-hewn lot. Her normal "I don't fucking care" attitude lay in the ash heap. Her resolve weakened, and the temptation to set down the tray and go back to her bunk grew. Yet Haddy went back to basics. She tightened her pelvis and washboard abs, squared off her shoulders, pulled her head up, and tucked her chin in. Haddy heaped her plate full of chicken, rice, and beans. When she turned for a table, each Matkal warrior stood in honor. Chief Adelman took her tray, and a table became available. He joined her, and they ate in silence. Something inside her wanted to blurt out that she was lost and in a panic, but she said, "Chief, where do you practice knife throwing?"

The chief had a brow of iron, strong nose, and tight-cropped graying hair. "First rule, Miss Kirsch. First names only. Call me Yosef."

The familiarity lowered Haddy's guard, and she relaxed a bit. "Yosef, where do you throw the fucking knives around here?"

He cocked an eyebrow and pointed. "Two trees on the south perimeter next to the picnic table."

35

Haddy knew she should sleep, but the night dragged on, broken by nightmares, restlessness, and fear of the unseen menace. The spec-ops base must be the safest spot on the Earth, yet her firm inner voice said, "Head south. Cross the Red Sea into Egypt and disappear." Meanwhile, whether she was asleep or not, the boy danced on the fringes of her conscious mind, and the image of his box had sharpened.

"Fuck it," said Haddy, and opened her laptop and picked up where she ended in the eighteenth century. She found museums, art dealers, and private collections, filled with music boxes from that time period. Haddy decided to check out art galleries and caught a break.

Unique to dealers, the RB Triconnia Art Gallery in Rome kept sales records back to the 1970s. In their search bar, Haddy entered, "18th century jeweled music box," and a surprising 147 images popped up. The box she saw was unique, comprised of silver and porcelain with a Star of David on top. Heart beating faster, she typed in "silver" and added "porcelain," and the field narrowed to eleven. She tried "Jewish." Haddy gasped. Her music box! *The Shema. Original one-of-a-kind Louis XIV 1786. Gift for a Jewish courtesan. Mozart's Requiem."* The vision was real, and its greater mystery lay in Rome. She copied the title and description and put the paper in her pocket.

Haddy dressed and went to the mess hall. She stuffed herself with high-calorie foods and plenty of coffee and marched to the perimeter fence. She walked south and found the trees and picnic table as Yosef had described. Haddy took a felt-tip marker and drew bull's-eyes on each tree trunk 5 feet from the ground. The outer ring measured 6 inches in diameter, the middle ring 4, and the center 2 inches. Taking a deep breath and collecting herself, Haddy took the knife and tossed it underhand at the tree. Her first throw missed. "What the hoary fuck was that?" she said. She walked across the sand, retrieved the blade, and paused, gripped by an eerie sense someone or something was behind her. Haddy knew there wasn't, but the compulsion to look overcame her good sense. She whipped her head around and saw nothing. "Dammit!" she said. "You're a fool. Get rid of your fucking ghosts." Haddy tossed the knife again, and this time, it hit the outer ring. She turned and threw it at the opposite tree: another outer ring. Haddy worked herself into a rhythm, varying the distance between herself and the target from 5 up to 12 feet away. Whack! Whack! went the knife as the point drew closer to the center. Haddy drank some water and drew a devil's face over the bull's-eyes with the mouth at center. "Eat this, you mother-fucker," she said and threw the blade, shouting, *"Eat it!"* The sun burned hot. Haddy kept her face dry with frequent pats with a handkerchief. She paused again for water and a granola bar, then flipped the knife over and practiced overhead throws until her stomach growled.

Haddy went inside for coffee. She rested for ten minutes and made a beeline to the kitchen. She found the cook and asked for medium-sized paper bags and string. He went down an aisle and returned with a fresh package of 250 bags and a ball of cotton string.

Haddy walked into the black rubber-floored gym. Bare-chested soldiers grunted, groaned, spotted for each other, and lifted weights. A mat for fights and wrestling lay off to the side, and Yosef and Sergeant First Class David Olahem worked on Krav Maga skills. The banter ceased, and curious heads followed the newcomer. Haddy opened a utility closet and removed a stepladder, which she positioned beneath an over-head steel girder. She climbed up and tossed the ball of twine over. She threw a loop in the string and made some adjust-ments until a 15-foot length of twine dangled from the girder to the floor. Haddy inflated the paper bag. She poked a tiny hole in the end and threaded the string through it. Finally, she puffed up the bag as tight as possible and wrapped a rubber band around the opening to form a noose. Now Haddy adjusted the balloon 5 feet off the ground. She stood back and admired her work. When she was in top form, her skills included striking a paper bag with a knife hand, fast enough to cut the paper. Her last practice session seemed ages ago. Haddy loosened up, cracked her neck, and focused on Bruce Lee fighting principles. "'Simplicity,'" she said. "Just one jab can stop punches, kicks, and throws. 'Directness,'" she continued. "The shortest distance between two points is a straight line; don't pull back punches." Haddy took the marker and drew a smiley face on the target. Then she slowed her breath, steadied her feet, focused her chi, and "saw" her hand cut the paper.

Haddy punched and expelled a short, high-pitched burst of air. The fist struck the bag with a harmless *whap*. She switched hands and sent punch after punch into the paper balloon with bird screams.

Yosef and David stood off with arms folded across their chests. As Haddy worked out, she caught them admiring her physique and overheard David say, "Do you think she'll pop it?"

Yosef replied in admiration, "Damn right."

"Bet?"

"Ten dollars," replied Yosef.

"When?" asked David.

"Today's Tuesday, I say Sunday," answered Yosef.

"Twenty dollars she does it Saturday," challenged David.

"You're on," said Yosef. From the corner of her eye, Haddy watched the two conspirators fan out and talk with the other operators. Some stood up and watched her, while a few walked closer to observe her style. They nodded and rejoined Yosef and David.

Haddy knew the bets were in. "Damned Matkal," she thought. "I'll fuck all of you and get it done Friday." Then she overheard David ask Yosef, "What kind of bird is it? Hawk or eagle?"

"Eagle," replied Yosef.

Haddy concealed a smile and thought, "Fucking Matkal, you either love them or hate them, but always fear them."

After another break, Haddy returned to the gym and began her splits. She stretched one leg out front and the other out back and lowered her pelvis to the mat. Her groin hovered an uncomfortable 6 inches from the surface. Haddy worked on splits with legs extended out to each side, with the same result. She rested on a weight bench and wiped her face as Yosef came over and referred to the bag trick, saying, "That's some mean shit if you can pull it off."

Haddy lay down on the mat and said, "You like that?" She tossed her leg straight up. "If you want to grab my ass, come help. Hamstrings first."

Yosef knelt beside her. "Is it safe to touch you?" he asked.

"Fuck you," said Haddy and raised her eyebrow. "Maybe I want your hands all over me. Here's your chance." Yosef anchored her hip with his left hand as the physical therapist had done earlier. As he pushed up her leg with his right hand, Haddy winced.

"Mind some advice?" asked Yosef. Haddy studied his face.

"Maybe," she said.

Yosef reached over and touched her neck where the *tanto* blade had left a red scar. "Looks like your knife slipped," he said. "Want to talk?"

Haddy said, "Maybe," and thought to herself, "Nothing you can do about the neck. You did it, you wear it, get over it."

Yosef left after stretching her out. Drained, Haddy went to the mess hall, ate, rested, and returned to the gym. She squeezed out a paltry fifty crunches, yelling, "Push yourself." She barely got thirty push-ups, saying, "Tighten that butt, tighten those abs. Do one more." Haddy knocked off fifty lunges, fifty squats, and a two-minute wall sit followed by pull-ups, bench presses, and leg extensions, all the while shouting at herself to do more.

It was late afternoon when Haddy decided to pay a visit to the indoor shooting range. She left the barracks with gun case in hand. Four Lockheed Martin F-35 Lightning II fighter jets screamed over the desert and vanished like smoke. In their wakes, a crescendo of sonic booms followed. The shock sent Haddy back to the Lacoste Bar and an exploding Ori Daniels. The pressure wave flung her into the wall, and she blacked out.

Haddy opened her eyes in the medic's tent with Yosef standing by the stretcher. Her heart pounded and head whirled. "God, that was fucking terrible," she said.

The medic administered antianxiety medication, and Yosef leaned over. "Trauma does that. I'll escort you to your quarters."

"I can manage," said Haddy.

"I'll walk by your side anyway, hard ass," he said. "Lie down and rest. Come to dinner, then go straight to bed. Trust me, I know."

36

The mess hall was deserted when Haddy ate breakfast. She kept her eyes peeled for any jets as she walked to the indoor firing range. She took a lane, plugged her ears, and put on earmuffs. Haddy screwed on the suppressor, got in her stance, and breathed out. She fired three rounds in quick succession. Electric shocks like ice picks stabbed her brain, and dizziness blossomed inside like a warhead. She lost her balance and hit the floor.

The range master escorted Haddy to the medic. Yosef leaned against the wall with his arms crossed, wearing a bemused expression. "Miss Kirsch," said the medic, "you suffered massive head trauma. You realize there's a burr hole in your skull? Can you not back off?" The medic scratched his chin and gauged his patient. Two black eyes stared at him like large bore pistols. "However, in case you decide differently, here are packs of injectable ketorolac for pain, and sumatriptan for headaches. When you're in trouble, plunge them into your arm or thigh."

"Time for lunch," said Yosef. "Perhaps you can eat and return to quarters for the afternoon without another incident."

"Or what?" said Haddy.

"Or I'll lose my bet you can," replied Yosef. "The first lieutenant and first sergeant say you can't."

After lunch, Haddy fell on her bunk. Flashbacks to the Lacoste Bar and Grill, mixed with the vivid rape memories, were paralyzing. She had seized in the Sourasky underground hallway, escaping by a hair's breadth. Her thoughts turned to Yosef, and she yearned to be held.

On Thursday, Haddy wore the wig tied in a ponytail and let the blonde hair bounce behind her. She went to breakfast and spent an hour honing her knife skills, until the steel stuck in the center ring. Back in the gym, Haddy planted her right foot firmly on the floor and suddenly pointed the left toe at the ceiling. Then, like a cat, she fell to the mat on both hands and made a wide sweep with her foot. She worked tirelessly, took a break, and returned for calisthenics. In the early afternoon, Haddy approached Yosef and said, "Join me in some sparring?"

"A bit early, isn't it?" he replied.

"I'm scared, but need to get back in the game," said Haddy. They each donned leather- padded masks and boxing gloves. "Here are the rules," she continued. "I can hit your face, but you can't return the favor, at least for now. Maybe tomorrow or Saturday."

Haddy fired a flurry of punches. Yosef tucked his head behind a wall of raised elbows, absorbing the blows easily. Then he swung a looping overhand right hook, avoiding Haddy's head, but landing squarely on her neck. Haddy reeled, dropped her guard, and felt Yosef's straight left to her chest. He moved in for the kill, but Haddy gut-punched him. Then, holding his left shoulder with her right glove, she slammed her left elbow into his jaw and kneed him in the groin. Yosef tumbled to the mat. Using a jujitsu move, Haddy fell on her bottom and pulled Yosef's arm between her thighs. She torqued his arm backwards, threatening to dislocate the shoulder and elbow joints. Yosef tapped out.

Haddy sat on the bench, spent. Her head throbbed and whirled. She fought back the dizziness and nausea and lay down. Yosef joined her and gave her an electrolyte drink. "Help me to my quarters," she said. "I need injections. I overdid it."

Yosef walked by Haddy and said, "We got a circular last week from command of a record shot. An IDF sniper killed the number two Al Qaeda at two thousand, six hundred, and sixty-four yards. I did some checking. A Staff Sergeant Haddy Abrams died in the Lacoste bomb explosion along with Chief Sergeant Ori Daniels. Ori told me about this sniper. A JKD Krav Maga black belt who beat him at the MMA academy in Tel Aviv. Ori and I were friends. Had he lived, he would have proposed marriage to this warrior."

The thought of Ori made Haddy feel guilty. She hadn't jumped in harm's way, paid respect to Ori's family, or sat shiva to help them grieve. "What do you want?" she asked.

"If I'm not mistaken, you're Staff Sergeant Haddy Abrams, here under witness protection. There's fire in your belly, Staff Sergeant. You and me and the men want payback."

"I want that, too, but—" said Haddy and pointed to her neck. "The red line was a *tanto* blade. At the last instant, I was stopped by a twelve-pronged buck deer, and don't ask, it was weird. A few hours later, I got blown up." Haddy looked at Yosef. "Now I have PTSD, can't shoot without blacking out, and am afraid of my own shadow, not to mention a persistent dream. I know I'm in danger. Helping me is not a good career move, Chief."

"What are you thinking?" said Yosef.

"To find Ori's killer," replied Haddy, "I need a new passport and some cash plus a ride. Whoever did this found me after two days of witness protection, and they'll find me here." Yosef rubbed his forehead slowly, deep in thought. Haddy looked him in the eyes. "Yosef, *'Who dares, wins,'* remember?"

37

Nothing could dissuade Wolf from his single-minded obsession to track down Haddy, but "What happened to the family?" he asked himself repeatedly. Where were the Abrams and the Danilenkos? He left voice mails and peppered Maria with requests to check out 140 Perry Street. She confirmed Sasha Abrams's absence since September 25. The Southampton Police detectives visited the David Abrams estate, and the housekeeper stated he had left suddenly on the twenty-sixth. Wolf called Odessa National Polytechnic University and learned Professor Danilenko was out of the country. Raisa's high school principal stated she had left due to a family emergency.

Kathryn noted a change in his tone. "Wolf, darling," she said. "You seem distant. Are you seeing someone?"

"Got a lot on my mind, honey," replied Wolf. "Nothing to worry about."

During Friday's mid-morning break, the captain took Wolf aside and said, "Our prodigals have returned."

"The Danilenkos?" said Wolf.

"Stefan is meeting with the board of trustees of the university, but something is amiss. He called me on his secure phone. He has a bodyguard. I arranged for us to gather here at seven p.m."

STEFAN PULLED HIS COAT CLOSER, as the fall brought with it chills and mild gusts off the nearby Black Sea. He required a cane following his operation and hobbled to the Decameron elevator with the agent bringing up the rear. "Do not mention your cousin Haddy or Israel or anything," he warned Raisa.

"At least we're getting out," replied Raisa. "This place is nice. Who is Bill McKinney?"

"No clue, but he has been asking about Haddy," said Stefan.

"Haddy's our secret," replied Raisa and zipped her lips together and tossed away an imaginary key. "And Dad," she continued, "don't forget this Sunday."

Stefan mopped his brow and nodded. As the playoff between her high school and their opposition drew near, Raisa's pent-up frustration had blown a gasket. "I know I said I wouldn't play tonight," she said. "But if our team wins, my friends and I always celebrate."

"Bad idea," replied Stefan. "Haddy wouldn't like it, and my heart doesn't like it." When stress mounted, the angina made him weak and breathless. A heavy pressure, as if an elephant had decided to sit on his chest for a cushion, would strike suddenly. Stefan fingered the nitroglycerin tablets in his pocket. When he felt the pressure, he placed two little tablets under his tongue and sat or lay down. They restored oxygen to his starving heart muscle, or so his cardiologist had told him. He also rehearsed the doctor's instructions. "'Breathe in, hold, exhale, and rest, each for four seconds.'"

"We meet at Club Ibiza on Sunday afternoons," Raisa pressed. "Yana picks me up at five and brings me home by eight. I'm with my friends, Dad; it's totally cool."

"What about our bodyguard?" said Stefan.

"He stays with you. You're the important one, not me."

Stefan wiped his forehead again. "You'll be the death of me," he said and stopped arguing. It was a lost cause. He knocked on the door of Suite 1, as the agent stayed by the elevator. Raisa had squeezed into a pair of distressed skinny jeans and pink volleyball shirt. She wore pink lipstick, and her hair fell gracefully around a heart-shaped face.

Wolf and Captain Troyem opened the door in tandem. Smiles abounded and introductions with hugs and pecks on the cheeks were exchanged, while both men observed the man at the elevator. Raisa blushed and said to herself, "Mr. McKinney is gorgeous. I need a pic. My friends will die."

Wolf took his guests on a tour, avoiding the sketches. The captain poured vodka for a toast and exclaimed, "To your good health." Wolf asked Raisa what she would like to drink.

"Vodka tonic," she said and blushed again. "God, I'm so embarrassed, you're really cute."

"Good to know," said Wolf. He smiled at Raisa's resemblance to Haddy and opened the refrigerator. "Here's the vodka, there's the tonic. Go for it, young lady."

"What are you having?" asked Raisa.

"Barrel-strength Maker's bourbon."

"Neat? No ice? Can I try some?"

"Strong stuff," said Wolf. "It's okay with me if it's okay with your father."

Raisa tried and liked it. "He doesn't care, but I'm a light-weight. Dad and the captain can go through a fifth like water. I'll add an ice cube."

Wolf set out hors d'oeuvres, and the banter was light. Raisa talked to Wolf in typical mile-a-minute fashion about volley-ball, school, and plans for medical school. Wolf watched her pour a second drink.

The captain said, "Enough about the weather. Stefan, where have you and Raisa been? Tell us about the bodyguard."

Stefan launched into the story of his Cleveland Clinic surgery and subsequent trip to the HEAF at the Lawrence Livermore Labs. "I needed time off and wanted to visit the American Southwest and sent for Raisa."

"I hiked to the bottom of the Grand Canyon," Raisa interjected.

"The Americans insisted on the guard," said Stefan. "The project I'm working on is top secret."

Captain Troyem's bullshit meter was off the charts. It was all too neat and tidy, but he sat back, temporarily mollified. "Huh," he said. "Well, Wolf has a remarkable story I want you to hear."

Wolf recounted his tale of climbing Mt. Rainier, saying, "The morning light broke over the mountain. A sunbeam fell on this woman. Our eyes connected, and I fell in love."

Raisa swooned and brushed away a tear. "That's so roman-tic. It breaks my heart. What happened?"

The captain raised his finger in the air like a circus emcee and announced, "Bill has a surprise. Follow me to the dining table."

Wolf overheard Stefan tell Raisa, "No more. You've had too much."

The group saw the sketches, and Wolf watched Stefan. His

brow tightened and mouth opened as he examined the drawings. He set down his drink and clamped his mouth shut.

Raisa's eyes widened. Her mouth opened as well, but she blurted out, "Cousin Haddy!" and turned to Captain Troyem. "Did you give Bill her picture?"

The captain shook his head with a twinkle in his eye. "Think again," he said.

Raisa turned to Wolf and gushed, "You saw Haddy on the mountain?"

"So, you know her?" Wolf said.

Raisa clasped her hands together and said excitedly, "*YES!*" and froze. She blanched and covered her mouth. "I mean *NO*," and burst into tears. Raisa rushed into the bathroom, saying, "I'm going to be sick," and slammed the door behind her.

Stefan had gone white and lay down on the floor. He massaged his chest and dropped two nitros under his tongue. He said weakly, "We can't."

"Can't what?" said the captain and Wolf.

"Six days ago, my granddaughter, the woman you saw on the mountain, died from head injuries from a suicide bomber in Tel Aviv."

STEFAN'S ANGINA RESOLVED. Raisa came to his side quietly. She looked at Wolf and said, "I'm so sorry, but we were sworn to secrecy."

After silence returned to his suite, Wolf lay still, his dream gone. In a foul mixture of hatred and anger, Wolf threw his tumbler at the Desis and wept.

38

Day 20
Elektrostal, Moscow
Saturday, October 7
Zero-seven-hundred hours

As the sun melted the morning frost, Ivan Juric sat in the airport lounge and glanced out the window. His knees jittered like tiny jackhammers as he sipped coffee and chain-smoked. True to his word, Professor François LeCompte had made the necessary conversions to the X3 missile, and with Helmut Gott's software, it packed an enormous warhead, able to level fifteen city blocks. As of Monday, five X3s were finished. The first went to Iranian Major General Xerxes Garshasp, who was willing to pay 10 percent over the agreed $100 million, with 50 percent now and the balance upon successful detonation. Tuesday evening, he had flown to a secret base in southern Lebanon with the second missile, making Lebanese Hezbollah commander Imad Mughniyeh happy. Wednesday and Thursday, they delivered two rockets to Hamas in the Gaza Strip. Last night, the fifth missile went to Spetsnaz Colonel Konstinovich. The next four would find their way to Jerusalem, controlled by X, and afterwards, the bulk to Assad's Syria and his terrorist organizations. This coming Friday at 4 p.m. precisely, X would flip the switch, and the missiles would arm. He would fire his four first; then the other owners could fire at will.

Ivan waited for Karpov's boarding call and smiled. After he assassinated X and buyers saw the destructive power of LeCompte's missile, Ivan would demand not $100 but $200 million for each rocket. He would also have Stanislov send LeCompte, Brianna, and her imp, Ulyana, to the bottom of the sea. Yet, not all was perfect on this sunny day. Ivan could not find Professor Danilenko or his daughter Raisa. Their phones were dead. No answer or GPS enabled his team to find them. So Ivan had an insider at HEAF pass the word to the Odessa university president to call the professor home.

Anatoly Karpov entered the lounge and gave the signal to leave, when Ivan's phone buzzed. In high spirits, he saw *"Professor François LeCompte"* flash on the screen. He answered, "Professor, I have a joke."

"Gott is dead," the Frenchman belted out. "He entered the elevator on floor seven. When the doors opened on the first floor, Helmut lay in a pool of blood."

Ivan's lip wrenched back in a painful tic. He demanded, "Where's Major Lebed?"

François's words tripped over themselves. "At the plant," he said. "He had four guards escort me home."

"And the missiles?" said Ivan.

"Helmut installed the triggers, but not the software," answered François. "They won't fire."

"I'll call Major Lebed," replied Ivan. "Stay home until I know more."

Ivan raged. Finding François LeCompte had been a coup. "Now what?" he fumed. "Time for plan B." He speed-dialed Major Nicolai Lebed.

"I reviewed the film," said Nicolai. "Gott entered the elevator on floor seven. An assassin disguised as a cleaning lady got on at floor two. She put the barrel behind his ear and spoke with him. Gott described the current state of the project; then she pulled the trigger."

"Who do you suspect?" asked Ivan.

"The Iranians or the Israelis, or possibly the CIA," said Nicolai.

"I know the Iranians want their wonder boy back," said Ivan. "I snatched Professor LeCompte from under their noses, but the Mossad might be responsible. Find the cleaning lady."

Ivan instructed Karpov to fly to the Fortress via the Mineralnye Vody Airport. He gnawed on his knuckles and thought, "All was going so well, but this is a disaster. People with Gott's qualifications are astronomically rare. Professor Danilenko could do it, but where is he?" Ivan phoned X with the news.

X seethed. "You are wasting time," he said. "Get Danilenko at once." In the background, Kitten the parrot squawked, "Bombs away. Lower the lifeboats. We're dead in the water." X continued, "Fusako, get this damned parrot off my lap." Kitten squawked displeasure, "She's got big tits."

"Danilenko went off the grid," said Ivan. "Should we postpone the date?"

"You defy my authority, Mr. Juric. Perhaps you want my skull on your shelf?"

The line went dead, and Ivan's heart thumped wildly. "Does he know? Does he suspect?" he wondered. Ivan called Rat. "Someone murdered Gott," he said. "Where the fuck are the Danilenkos?"

"They left for Israel and disappeared," said Rat. "Danilenko came back for the trustee meeting accompanied by a bodyguard and disappeared out a back door. Their phones are off. We've checked the city, but no luck. They must have an alias."

"What happened in Israel?"

"No idea, but we have a contact in Professor Danilenko's cardiology clinic. She says the professor's doctor upped his medicines last night and urged him to come in and be examined. We have someone watching the clinic. This Raisa is the star striker for their volleyball team and wasn't at the big game last night. She went online last night for one minute and posted 'Congrats' to her team, and said she would meet with her friends on Sunday, 'at the usual place.'"

"Where?"

"My place. Club Ibiza."

"How did you find out?"

"Tapped our star hacker and cracked her account."

"Get Pavlos Doukas."

"He's at his villa."

"He has a jet. Have him meet me and X at the Fortress tonight, and make it quick."

39

Day 20
Penthouse Suite One
Saturday, October 7
Zero-seven-thirty hours

A chill hung over Wolf's heart. Inside his suite, the black satin sheets were a tangled heap. At 4 a.m., a broken lover went to an all-night store and purchased a pack of Camels. He went to a cafe, drank coffee, and smoked on the sidewalk as dawn peeked over Odessa. The words of Marcus Aurelius came to mind, *"The first rule is to keep an untroubled spirit."* Yet Wolf's stomach lay in knots. He crushed the cigarette and dragged himself to the Decameron fitness center, often empty at this hour.

Inside, Wolf rehearsed the Friday evening scene with Raisa Danilenko. If Haddy was dead, why respond as if she lived? Raisa was ready to joyfully throw her arms around him and froze. Wolf had gone online and confirmed the staff sergeant's death, but maybe she was in witness protection? He looked at the Lacoste Bar and Grill, what was left of it, and read every report of the number of dead and injured. If Haddy was alive, she couldn't be more than a vegetable.

Wolf climbed aboard the running machine mad, his anger a potent fuel for a vicious workout. He tossed the sweatshirt aside and thought, "When in doubt, blow something up." On his biceps, at the edge of his black T-shirt, lay a tattoo. A redheaded pinup girl rode a banner, "75th Ranger Regiment." On her naked thigh sat a weapons holster. Wolf saw it and was ready to shoot anything. He fumed, "Damn you, St. Joshua, I thought you had my six."

The gym door opened, and Wolf sank further. He picked up the pace to shut out the distraction. The Playboy Bunny or *Vogue* model who lived across the hall in Suite Two pushed inside. Wolf suspected she was a very high-class prostitute. Her curves were endless. She moved with seductive ease without trying. The cinnamon eyes killed with a single glance. The woman got on the running machine next to his, her Lycra exercise clothing revealing almost all. Wolf had to tear his gaze from her body. He heard a clunk as she set her purse on the treadmill. Having been a target of the Sakharov syndicate, Wolf tightened. Was she an assassin? He kept an eye on the handbag. She appeared Slavic, perhaps Russian, and definitely no nonsense.

Brianna had closed François's Beirut apartment and office with Stanislov always lurking in the background. Angry and frightened, she wanted nothing more than bodyguards for herself and François. Upon returning to Odessa, she stayed in the suite with the slim Ruger semiautomatic by her side, but exercised in the morning. When Brianna saw the hardened man running easily on the treadmill, she recalled Captain Troyem's cousin Oksana gushing about the man in Suite One, who worked with her police chief uncle. She observed the tattoo. "He's an Army Ranger," she thought. "Maybe he can help?"

Brianna flashed Wolf a brilliant smile. "Suite One?" she said. "I'm your neighbor. Brianna Ivanova in Suite Two."

"Pleased to meet you," replied Wolf warily.

"My fiancé's a nuclear physicist at the Army Munitions Group, south of the city," said Brianna. "Oksana mentioned you're here assisting her uncle with police work?"

"A nuclear physicist?" said Wolf with sudden interest. "Your husband must know Professor Stefan Danilenko?"

"I don't know him," said Brianna. "But won't you join us for drinks tomorrow, Mr.—?"

"Thanks," replied Wolf. "But this is not a good time." Wolf noticed her easy confidence faltering. Tears welled up, and her upper lip trembled slightly. He noticed her cheeks bordering on gaunt, and recognized fear. "You always carry a gun?" he asked. Brianna instinctively touched the purse and turned off the machine.

She gathered her things with trembling hands. "I'm frightened for myself and my husband," said Brianna. "We need protection."

"My name is McKinney. Bill McKinney," said Wolf. "I'll talk with the captain. He knows everyone."

Brianna opened her purse, found paper and pen, and said, "Here's my number."

Wolf gave her his and said, "If you need immediate assistance, call or knock on the door."

Brianna had tears in her eyes when she kissed Wolf on both cheeks. "Thank you," she said and left.

"Wolf, what now?" said the Ranger.

40

Day 20
The Fortress
Saturday, October 7
Eighteen-hundred hours

Jaca Juric took the urgent call from her brother Ivan. Snow flurries whipped around the outside window-panes, while the thermostat kept the Control Room at a precise 72 degrees Fahrenheit. The computers hummed, and the wall-sized plasma screen displayed the Earth with military-grade satellite optics. Ivan had filled her in on the disaster, "We don't know where Danilenko is, but the daughter will be at Club Ibiza tomorrow. Pavlos Doukas is our best chance to take her."

"You don't know where she is?" asked Jaca.

"Do I need to repeat myself?" replied Ivan. "Her phone is off. We can't locate her signal. If she shows tomorrow, we'll grab her. Have you met Pavlos before?"

"I've heard the stories," said Jaca.

"Find out what passes for Adonis these days," said Ivan. "But take care; he gets crazy if he doesn't have a woman. If you give him the eye, you'll get your cup filled." Taking on an ominous tone, Ivan continued, "And get all you can. He's marked for the skull."

"I'll make sure he feels welcome, brother dear," said Jaca.

Ivan asked, "How are the plans for the party?"

"'Do I need to repeat myself?'" said Jaca mockingly. "The French jazz ensemble arrives Wednesday. Iran's General Garshasp, Spetsnaz Colonel Konstinovich, and Lebanese Hezbollah commander Imad Mughniyeh are confirmed. The Nigerian minister of defense and ten others have followed with aides and bodyguards. Kiev International modeling will supply the women. The Music Room will be the bar, and the Baroque Room for drugs with five tables: pink joints on one with a sign, MDMA on—"

Ivan cut her short. "Move on."

"Each guest has a private room; their aides are next door. Escorts occupy the Beauty Salon and Renaissance Room and the bodyguards the Hunting Hall. What's Pavlos done?"

"He's double-dipping; working for another crime boss in Dnieper."

Jaca showered and applied a light cream rinse to her hair with chocolate colorant. She trimmed and clipped and shaved, brushed her hair and teeth, and applied a light red lipstick and spritz of perfume. She slipped into casual slacks and low-heeled pumps with a fetching light gray silk blouse, which complemented her eyes and chest. She got the call from Ivan that he and Pavlos Doukas had arrived on separate jets at Mineralnye Vody Airport.

"We're on the helicopter," said Ivan. "We'll arrive at the Fortress in five minutes. I'll drop Pavlos off in the kitchen and take a rest stop."

Pavlos sat at the kitchen table, sipping strong Russian tea. The aromas of fresh baked bread and borscht filled the room. A bevy of female staff had gathered around him, mesmerized by his appearance and charm, which radiated from his person like heat waves. Galina, a buxom red-faced teen, hired to care for Ulyana, glowed, chest out. The old chef, Viktoria, found it difficult to concentrate on dinner preparations. She pulled up a chair, sipped on her tea, and stole glances at the god. Pavlos, clothed in a tailored French blue jacket, light blue shirt, tan slacks, and hand-tooled Italian shoes, held Ulyana on his knee. He had dark chocolate liquid eyes, and a strong masculine nose ending in full Greek lips. Defined cheeks and cleft chin gave him an enchanted look, as he told a story of his life on the Greek island of Mykonos. In a rich baritone, he wagged a finger in Ulyana's face and said, "I was a bad, bad boy. I threw temper tantrums and fought with my older brother and parents all the time."

"Did you have to clean your room?" asked Ulyana.

Pavlos's fine black curls shook. "Never," he declared solemnly. "I disobeyed every day. When I turned five—"

"That's my age," interrupted Ulyana.

"—my parents put a collar around my neck and chained me to the back fence. They took me to the orphanage. I held my breath and blacked out. My mother came and got me. I flunked first grade. I tell you my village thanked God when I left. What should Pavlos do?"

Jaca entered. The staff didn't recognize her at first, but the compliments began at once. She hadn't blushed in years, but her face went red as Pavlos broke into a gleaming smile of perfect teeth. He stood, connecting eye to eye with Jaca. Smiling, he took her hand, bowed, and kissed it. Leading Jaca away, he breathed. "You want me. I see it. Don't deny me."

Ivan came down the stairs and said, "You ready to discuss business, Mr. Doukas?"

Jaca whispered to Pavlos as he turned toward the elevator, "I'll be in the Control Room. Second floor. Next to Dining."

THE STAINLESS-STEEL DOOR WHISKED OPEN, and Ivan and Pavlos entered the Palace Room. The vista of flickering candlelight and mirrors, gold-inlaid walnut floor, and Louis XIV furniture, with the Caucasus Mountains so close one could touch them, took Pavlos's breath away. Fusako approached in a shimmering orange silk kimono. Her emerald eyes held him as she patted him down. She removed Pavlos's knife from his ankle holster in a blink. Pavlos flashed to that scene in the movie *Jurassic Park* when the hunter confronts the Velociraptor. In this Japanese aide, he saw the same ruthless reptile look him over like she was observing a blood sport. He walked up to the dais and ignored the mastiff.

Kitten the parrot sat perched on Smert's head and squawked, "FUCKKKK. She's got big tits."

Pavlos addressed the bird, "Thank you, bird." He noticed the gold skull, brimming with meat, and took stock of the silvered head and aquiline nose of the sharkskin-clad patrician.

"This is my personal assistant, Fusako," said X. "The bird is Kitten. Ignore it. Now to business, Mr. Doukas. You know our predicament. I need Professor Stefan Danilenko immediately." Fusako opened the plasma screen filled with Raisa Danilenko's Facebook page. "Raisa will be at Club Ibiza in Odessa tomorrow afternoon. Get her, put her on our jet, and bring her here. The job is $500,000. We deposited $100,000 to your account. You'll receive the balance upon delivery, with a $100,000 bonus if you can deliver by Monday or Tuesday. Later than Thursday midnight, and your life is forfeit."

Pavlos bowed. "I understand," he said, and left shaken.

Pavlos exited the elevator and found the Fortress cloaked in an eerie silence, save for muffled voices from the kitchen. Huge rooms and fireplaces and stuffed game animals were lit by flickering lights, each encased by soft gold sconces on black wrought-iron wall supports. It felt ancient, as if a medieval knight might clank down the hall. Pavlos knocked on the Control door.

Jaca opened. "My room's upstairs." After two hours of steamy passion, she said, "Now let me rest, until tomorrow morning." As he left, Jaca sighed to herself, "I want him alive."

Pavlos climbed the curved staircase to his room, released, if only for twenty-four hours, from his ever-ready sexual tension. He found a surprise.

Ulyana played with a toy in the hallway. "Tell me a story," she said. "I'll show you my secret playhouse if you do." With a shake of his head, Pavlos sat down under a flickering light and spun a magical tale of eagles and dragons and bears with a shining prince and beautiful princess. When he stopped, Ulyana smiled, took his hand, and tugged him down two flights of stairs to the library. She flicked on the light and threaded her way to a darkened alcove against the back wall. Ulyana ran her tiny fingers along the third row of books. She found the bright red and forest green Folio edition of Tacitus's *Wars* and pulled. The lower half of the bookcase swiveled outwards. "We can play here. Don't tell anyone I took the flashlight or matches."

Pavlos's eyes widened in wonder. He wiped off his amused expression and watched the child disappear into an inky darkness. A few seconds later, a flashlight shone, which threw her face into bold relief. Next, a match was struck, and a candle was lit. Pavlos peered inside and crouched forward. A narrow tunnel T-boned into another. Pavlos bumped his head and scraped his shoulders as he joined the five-year-old. Dolls and toys lay scattered about. He whispered, "Ulyana, how many others know about your playroom?"

"Only me and Galina," she said. The child pointed. "The tunnel goes up and ends," and pinched her nose. "If you go down the tunnel, it stinks."

Pavlos ran his hands over the granite walls and observed, "They chiseled the stone." The cobwebs were dense, and rootlets penetrated from above. "Ulyana, thank you for showing me your secret playroom," he said. "Don't tell anyone I was here, okay?" The child nodded, and soon Pavlos tucked her into bed.

Pavlos returned to the tunnel. He went forward and noted the passage followed the curving contours of the castle wall. It ascended on a gentle incline, and every so often, a side tunnel appeared. When he worked the levers at the end of the side tunnels, hidden panels opened into different rooms. At the top, he put his ear to the wall and heard the Japanese girl talking to herself. Pavlos turned around and descended, went past his entry point, and continued down. The tunnel came to a wooden landing, which split into two. A set of ancient wooden stairs angled up, while the other went down a set of steps to a putrid odor. Pavlos went up. After twenty minutes, it ended with a lever. He pushed down and stepped out into the cold night. The door was a large block of stone, concealed in the back of a cave. An overhanging rock ledge formed a roof. The moon shone through light snow flurries and revealed a field of massive boulders. Pavlos followed a snow-laden trail, which wound back and forth among the large rocks, crossed a frozen stream, and ended above the trees on a ridge. The Fortress lay on the opposite ridge farther below. Though early in the ski season, Pavlos could see bright arc lamps lighting up ski slopes for night skiing across the valley, at least two miles distant. The lights of the tiny sports village of Dombay filled the valley five miles to the west.

Pavlos whistled at the discovery. The five-year-old had stumbled upon a hidden tunnel system, carved centuries earlier. "Should I alert X or Jaca?" he asked himself, while returning to his room. Perhaps this knowledge might come in handy? He didn't like threats from anyone, especially the aging giant in the Palace Room.

Pavlos turned his thoughts to the next day. In hours, he would bed the lovely Jaca. Then the helicopter would take him to the airport and back to Odessa. He would call ahead and have his red Porsche Spyder waiting and check into the MI Hotel fronting the Black Sea. He pored over Raisa's Facebook page and noted her friends, high school, and volleyball activities. She earned straight As, and the Odessa National Medical University featured in her plans next year. Raisa posted about Logan Tom, her volleyball hero, numerous boyfriends, and Tae Kwon Do activities. Yana Balanchuk was her best friend. Normally, the girls studied all day and returned late after practice. Pavlos sighed. "I will take you tomorrow, my dear lamb. You will look into my eyes and want me."

41

Day 21
Mitzpe Ramon Special Operations Base, Sinai Desert, Israel
Sunday, October 8
Sixteen-hundred hours

Haddy had sent a blazing hand through the paper bag Friday. She slipped and fell trying to cut through the paper with her foot, but with dogged persistence succeeded. Operators had gathered around her in a circle and cheered when the bag tore. She continued sparring with Yosef on Saturday, taking his blows with a steadfast determination to win.

By early Sunday, Haddy, like a chess player, was planning her next move. On paper, she knew Mitzpe Ramon was safe. She was protected, but Shin Bet told her the same thing at Sourasky Hospital. If someone could get to her that quickly, they knew her location. They would find a way to kill her. Neither could she ignore her own inner sense of where the threat of danger was real and not. She learned early on she had a sense for survival, an early-warning system of wordless red flags. Time and again, Haddy's intuition said, "Go left." When others followed orders and went right, they died. She felt that way now. Her inner voice said, *"Leave."*

Finally, Haddy couldn't ignore the vision, no more than August Kekule had in his groundbreaking discovery in 1861. Haddy remembered from her studies the chemist had fallen into a deep daydream in front of his fireplace. He saw a vision of the unique chemical structure of the benzene ring, which ushered in a new era of scientific discovery. She had that same sense now. What she saw in the ICU had proved right, when she found the exact box in Rome. Though Haddy did not divine its meaning, it glowed as if lit by an inner fire. *"The Shema. Original one-of-a-kind Louis XIV 1786. Gift for a Jewish courtesan. Mozart's Requiem."*

At breakfast, Haddy joined Yosef and said, "Have you given any thought to what we talked about Friday?"

"Passport, cash, and a ride?" replied Yosef.

"To Ashdod," said Haddy.

"Normally? Absolutely not, but something's in the wind," replied Yosef. "We are getting hard intel of an upcoming op. For some reason, I think you are part of it. But let's be clear: I'm doing this for one reason. Ori."

Late afternoon, after a five-mile run and practice, Haddy looked at herself in the mirror. She carefully trimmed away the fraying butterfly strips and admired Dr. Adina's artistry. Thirteen days after the blast, the numerous cuts and gashes were closing into thin red threads. The swelling and colorful rainbow of splotchy bruises had faded.

At dinner, Yosef slid the passport to her under a napkin and gave her a roll of cash wound tightly in a rubber band. "The men chipped in," he said. "$2,500."

"That hurt," gasped Haddy. She peeked at her new identity,

"Leah Berenson" and commented, "Good work, thanks. Now let's walk a bit." Outside, Haddy continued, "I should tell you, I'm heading to Rome." Haddy tapped the roll of cash. "For lots of reasons, but the biggest is fear. My finger froze on the trigger back at the Sourasky. I lost my courage."

"Blast trauma can shake any soul into hell," said Yosef. "But, if I may butcher Shakespeare, *'when you hear the blast of war, imitate the tiger; stiffen the sinews, summon your blood, and disguise your nature with rage.'"* Yosef pressed a phone into her hand. "A burner with my number. I'll stall the major if he asks where you are, but you won't have much time." He leaned over and kissed her lightly on the lips and continued, "Ori had uncommonly good judgment in many things; women were one. Maybe when this is over ... Anyway, good luck."

42

Day 21
The Roman Catholic Church of St. Peter the Apostle,
Odessa, Ukraine
Sunday, October 8
Sixteen-hundred hours

After meeting Brianna Ivanova, Wolf nursed a fifth of Maker's at Arcadia Beach. With a ball cap pulled low, he slumped back in a beach chair, watched the surf, and chain-smoked. How quickly he forgot Kathryn when Haddy appeared like a genie. Now, broken, the sounds of the ocean lay distant. Kathryn had captured Wolf's heart fair and square. He did love her, at least until now. Should he call off the engagement? Postpone the wedding? How long must he grieve over this ghost?

Wolf returned to the suite, showered, and dressed. He went to the Roman church for the English Liturgy. Wolf took a seat in the back pew and pored over Jesus' question of Peter, "Simon, do you love me?" Wolf asked himself, "Do I love Kathryn or not?" He closed his eyes through much of the service, fighting the conflicting gales of shame and anger. He wanted to fight, hit something, yet his anger concerned God and a dead woman. Wolf thought of Jacob wrestling with the nighttime angel. The patriarch persevered and earned a new name and a dislocated hip. Wolf imagined facing the same angel and beating him to death, tearing him in two and pulling his joints apart. But he was the one ripped in half and would limp the rest of his life.

Letting the sacred atmosphere percolate through his black despair, when the Mass was offered, Wolf went forward for the blessing, but not the sacrament. He returned to his seat, crossed himself, and prayed bitterly, "Holy Saint Joshua, my warrior prince. Pray I forgive you and God and heal from this untimely grief. Though my arms never held Haddy, she was closer than my heart. Help me love Kathryn as promised. Dearest Haddy, may you rest in peace."

Wolf walked back to the Decameron, called Katy. "Hi," he said.

"Hi, yourself," she replied.

"I have something to tell you."

"You've met another woman."

"Yes and no," said Wolf and confessed the entire story, beginning with Captain Troyem and ending with the Danilenkos' dark truths about Haddy's death.

Kathryn gasped. "My God, Wolf. The Snow Queen? The one you buried; she's alive?"

"She died," said Wolf.

Kathryn repeated, "But you met her?"

"Kathryn," said Wolf impatiently. "Back up and listen. Remember the terrorist bombing in Tel Aviv at the Lacoste Bar thirteen days ago? She was there and died from massive head injuries. Check out Staff Sergeant Haddy Abrams, if you don't believe me."

"That's horrible," said Kathryn. "I feel terrible. How do you feel?"

"Like I've been kicked in the head by a mule."

"Grief. All over again," said Kathryn and changed subjects, "Do you want to postpone the wedding?"

"I love you, Katy," Wolf replied. "God willing, I'll be there this Friday. We'll marry, get drunk, and fuck like rabbits on the Bosporus."

"And bury this ghost?"

"Once and for all."

Wolf heard the relief in Kathryn's voice. "I love you so much."

"And I you," said Wolf, but thought, "Do I really?"

43

Day 21
Club Ibiza, Odessa, Ukraine
Sunday, October 8
Seventeen-hundred hours

P avlos lounged at Club Ibiza, waiting for Raisa. So much depended on getting the teen alone and adding Rohypnol, his reliable "date rape" drug, to her drink. From there, he would "help" her into his car. Her Facebook post said, "With Friends," and Rat could provide good-looking staff to dance and split them apart.

Pavlos saw the commotion at the entrance in the bar mirror. Raisa and three friends came in laughing. Leaning against the bar, he turned and let the girls see him. Raisa stared as the others giggled and tugged her to a backseat table. She had left the back of their hotel as Yana pulled up in her father's Mercedes. Raisa piled into the front seat, hugged her friends, and tried to answer their questions about her disappearance. She wisely shifted the conversation to the game and boys.

Pavlos signaled to the waiter. The man approached the foursome and let them know the man at the bar would cover their drinks. He watched them view him with excited eyes. He gazed at Raisa, who in turn drilled him with her sparkling blues and tossed her hair back.

The waiter served vodka tonics with twice the usual amount of alcohol. As he passed by Pavlos, he said, "They say you're a model. And one is daring the blonde to come over and bump you with her breast."

Raisa got up and walked straight towards him, asking smartly, "What's with the drinks?"

Pavlos said, "To help you celebrate. I saw Transportna Seventy-Seven won Friday night."

"I wasn't there," said Raisa with a pout.

"Still, it is special and deserves a gentleman's gift," replied Pavlos and extended his hand, introducing himself, "I'm Alexis Alexander."

Raisa's face went red. "I'm Raisa."

"I'm honored to meet such a beauty," said Pavlos and glanced at his Rolex. He leaned towards Raisa and let her smell his cologne, a dark enchanting woody spice with floral high notes. He poked his head up, glanced at the crowd, and said, "I've been stood up."

"Why don't you join us?" replied the smitten teen.

"Thank you, but don't bother," said Pavlos. "Your boyfriends will arrive any moment." Raisa laughed. She took Pavlos's hand and introduced him to her friends.

"Alexis" regaled them with stories of world travels as a male model. He strictly forbade pictures. Rat happened by and greeted Pavlos as a lost friend. He snapped his fingers, and the group were escorted to a secluded back section. In the midst of the gaiety, Pavlos swung Raisa to the dance floor as Rat brought partners for the others. Pavlos wrapped his arms around Raisa's waist. "You are exciting, full of zest," he said. "I must watch myself or I could drown in those eyes." He squeezed her butt and saw her gasp. Pavlos leaned in and opened his lips. Raisa kissed him and lingered. They came up for air, and Pavlos said, "Let's go somewhere private."

Raisa nearly swooned, when Yana tapped her shoulder. "Long-lost sister?" she said. "We need to freshen up."

In the restroom, Yana, with two other girls, said, "Raisa, those drinks are strong. And any closer with that Greek god and you'll lose your virginity," which brought titters of laughter from her friends.

"With him? I'd do it in a second," replied Raisa. "He wants to take me somewhere private. I'm going and you can't stop me."

"Dream on, Wild One," said Yana. "I have strict instructions to return you to the Londonskaya Hotel by eight o'clock tonight."

"I know," said Raisa. "But Alexis is so hot. I've never been kissed like that."

"Ask Captain Troyem to check him out if you want him so bad," replied Yana.

Raisa said, "I hate you."

"Hate me now, thank me later, but you're not getting out of here without me," said Yana. "I hope I can drive. Those drinks were spiked."

Giddy and drunk, the teens dismissed Rat's boyfriends and started gathering their things. Raisa put her head on Pavlos's shoulder. "I have commitments," she said. "I really want to go out with you. Rain check?"

"Tomorrow?"

"I play against Kiev this Friday," she said. "Come, and we can go out Saturday."

"You won't let me drive you home?" asked Pavlos.

"I'm sorry, I can't."

"We can dine in the Ibiza VIP room any time, day or night," said Pavlos. "But I leave for Paris early Friday morning."

"Stay ... right here," Raisa said and took Yana aside. "Best friend?" she asked coyly.

Yana's eyebrows narrowed. "What?"

"What if I could get out Thursday evening? Would you pick me up?"

"What for?" asked Yana.

"For a dinner with Alexis here," replied Raisa. "He's leaving Friday morning."

"Not without your father's approval," said Yana.

"He said I can join the team against Kiev. He's wrapped up in his software and wouldn't miss me for a few hours. Pick me up at the Londonskaya kitchen at seven thirty and drop me here. Pick me up at ten and take me back. This whole charade ends Friday anyway."

Yana's eyes tightened in concern. She said slowly, "I don't know, Raisa."

"Please," said Raisa, pleading with her hands held in prayer. *"Please."*

Before Yana could say, "Okay," Raisa jumped in her arms and squealed gratefully, "Thank you," and went back to Pavlos. "This Thursday from seven thirty to ten p.m."

"We'll have a wonderful time," said Pavlos.

Pavlos escorted the girls outside. He and Rat watched Yana drive off. Pavlos jumped in his Porsche and followed from a safe distance. The sedan let Raisa off at the Londonskaya Hotel, and Pavlos parked a block away. No need to wait. He would arrange a kidnapping immediately. He walked up to the receptionist, inquired as to where the tall blonde stayed, and produced a purse. "Miss Danilenko left it at the club."

The receptionist searched the registry. "I'm sorry. We don't have anyone here by that name."

"I saw her come in," said Pavlos. "Is she under a different name?" He showed the receptionist Raisa's photo and slipped her one hundred dollars.

The woman took the money and smiled. "She took the elevator to the second floor; that's all I know." Pavlos phoned Rat, who came over with four associates. Flashing police badges, they examined every room in the famed hotel from top to bottom.

No one had seen or knew Miss Danilenko, until a kitchen staff member identified her photograph, saying, "She walked out an hour ago."

44

Day 22
Mitzpe Ramon Special Operations Base, Sinai Desert,
Israel
Monday, October 9
Zero-four-hundred hours

At 4 a.m., Yosef rapped quietly on the wooden door. Haddy got up from her bunk, cloaked in a sea-green hoodie with strands of blonde hair covering her face. She took the leather satchel with her belongings and followed. Haddy curled up in the trunk of the military vehicle. They left the base, and minutes later, Yosef pulled off Route 40. She came up front, and he glanced at the stylish tourist and said, "Can't recognize you."

Haddy pulled back the hood. "Hair color and sunglasses," she said. "Let's go to the marina. I'm looking for a private ride." Yosef took the 41 and two hours later parked in a fast-food parking lot, which overlooked the bustling port of Ashdod. He looked at Haddy. *"Who dares, wins'* is our motto. Don't doubt yourself, and use the phone."

"How long before the major asks questions?" said Haddy.

"Depends," he replied. "Give yourself an hour, but Ashdod is a favorite port for stowaways."

Haddy kissed Yosef on the cheeks and stepped out into the Mediterranean salt sea air. Hidden behind the aviators and inhaling the bracing early morning breeze, she strolled down the walkway. Haddy walked to the end of each pier, examining a four-masted clipper ship, schooners, and yachts. As sunlight flickered off the polished hulls, she noticed a shiny white cruiser at the end of the last pier. The gulls were calling and diving when she heard noise behind her. An Army vehicle had scrunched to a halt. Soldiers hopped out, intent on a search. "Dammit, that was fast," she said. Haddy hastened to the low-slung, sleek cruiser. Gold letters on the stern announced, *"Astrea, Roma, Italy."* Fifty feet long, trimmed in blue, gold, and teak, the boat bobbled in the waves, with a tied-down mast.

The rig looked like a modified Cigarette racer. A rigid inflatable raft with a 60 horsepower Yamaha outboard lay lashed to the back with a small winch. No bikini-clad women or men in wide-brimmed hats and bright Hawaiian shirts lounged on the roof. Two roughnecks manhandled small wooden crates into the hold. They worked noiselessly, focused on the job at hand.

Haddy glanced over her shoulder at two soldiers talking to a yacht owner, two piers away. She stopped at the *Astrea*'s gangplank and addressed a swarthy, fortyish barrel-chested man with a tangle of eyebrows. A cigarette dangled from his lower lip. Haddy adjusted her voice and asked innocently, "Are you going to Rome?"

He gave her a quick glance. "No tourists here," he replied brusquely.

His partner, a young, muscled seaman, pushed past him. "We port in Civitavecchia on the coast," he said with eager eyes.

"Rome's inland." Haddy watched him stare at her figure greedily, as he continued, "Where's your family?"

"In Florence, but I want to spend time in Rome," she said.

The seaman's teeth flashed. He said quickly, "Talk to Captain Dymus. He's in the wheelhouse," and stepped aside to let her by.

As she ducked into the wheelhouse, she overheard the older man growl, "Get your head out of your pants and get back to work."

Haddy glanced back and saw the young seaman making curves in the air. She stood inside a roomy walnut-trimmed pilot house, reeking of tobacco. Empty brews and a stack of dog-eared porn magazines lay on an instrument panel. She addressed a weathered crag of a man. "I need a ride to Rome." The captain looked outside, and Haddy followed his gaze. Two soldiers on the next pier showed deckhands a picture. They shrugged and shook their heads.

The captain looked at her suspiciously. "Friends of yours?"

"No," said Haddy.

The captain lit a cigarette and blew the smoke at her. "Seven hundred and fifty dollars a day in cash. We stop in Cyprus and Crete, unload cargo and overnight in Legrena, outside Athens. From Legrena, we have a long voyage to Sicily on Tuesday, about thirteen hours. We port in Civitavecchia on Wednesday."

"Superfast," replied Haddy.

"Big engines for big business," said Captain Dymus. "We have a stateroom in the bow with its own bath. You met the deckhands; the younger one has a big brother named Xuthus. What's your name?"

"Mercedes," said Haddy and peeled off $2,200. "And no questions," she added.

The captain snorted. "You're no tourist. The younger one serves breakfast, lunch, and dinner. There's always fish stew and coffee on the stove, and lemons, limes, and oranges on the counter." He gave her a set of keys and pointed. "Your room's at the end of the hallway."

Haddy picked up her satchel. As she walked down the hall, she heard the tiny click of a camera. Haddy said to herself, "Watch it, baby girl. Captain is up to no good."

Above deck, the seamen released the ropes amid a blue sky, with prevailing winds from the east and warm shirt-sleeve temperatures. The skipper engaged the engines. The ship shuddered. Haddy had a passing knowledge of Cigarette racers, and they sounded like twin Mercs. She recalled each engine churned out between 1,350 to 1,550 horsepower, depending on the racing fuel. The captain swung the *Astrea* to open sea and opened the throttles. The propellers responded like thorough-breds at the starting gate. The gleaming hull skimmed off the one-foot swells. Haddy locked the cabin door and tossed the satchel on the floor. "Big business, my ass," said Haddy to herself. "Drug runners, more like it." She heard Shira in the back of her mind say, "You're on the run, thumbing a ride with scum. Be careful, Sis, I'm not there to watch your six."

"Don't I know it," replied Haddy. She lit a Lucky Strike, inhaled deeply, and watched the thick smoke twirl into the air. "Why didn't I listen to Yosef? Stay on base? This is so fucked, and fuck the music box thing."

The *Astrea* arrived in Larnaca, Cyprus, a few hours later. Haddy estimated the ship's speed at a blinding 70 knots. She peered from her port window, followed the two seamen, and observed a giant, who must be Xuthus, carry wooden crates off the ship to black SUVs on the wharf. After forty minutes, they departed for Crete. The ocean smoothed out to glass, and Haddy knew the captain must have changed the fuel. The boat leaped to 80 knots and ran over the sea like a sprinter.

They made Paleochora in six and a half hours. The transfer of crates to SUVs went smoothly, and Haddy judged the big man a bit taller than six and a half feet, weighing 265 pounds. She watched Xuthus manhandle the hoses and listened to the high-octane fuel rush through the hose, as though in a wind tunnel. Haddy jammed a chair under the door handle and continued to smoke. In the back of her mind, she wrestled with the main issue of who wanted her dead. Yet other fears intensified. "I hate to disappoint my family and especially Yosef, but there's no tiger inside this carcass. You're not the woman you used to be."

45

Day 23
Legrena, Greece
Tuesday, October 10
Zero-three-hundred hours

The *Astrea* floated quietly in Legrena while Haddy slept with one eye open. At 3 a.m., the engines gurgled, and the lights of the port city faded from her window. Hungry, she stole into the galley. The wheelhouse door lay ajar, and she overheard the captain say, "The syndicate won the bid."

The seamen replied in tandem, "How much?"

"Forty-eight thousand dollars, but when Piaro sees her, I think more," replied Captain Dymus. "We'll take her tonight in Marsala. Warn Xuthus. No touching."

A cold wave of fear spiraled down Haddy's spine, and she crept back to the stateroom. She practiced breathing and calmed down, but her stomach continued to growl for food. An hour passed, and Haddy opened the door. The engines roared and the waves splashed as the boat sliced through the water. She steadied her movements against the bouncing by keeping her hands on the wall. Cool air met her face. The odors of food and carnauba wax mixed together. Haddy touched her Glock and the knife tucked in her waistband.

A single light cast a dim glow over the stove in the narrow, deserted galley. Balancing herself, Haddy planted her feet on the tiled floor as the vessel bounced and swayed. She filled a bowl with stew and tossed in a loaf of bread. Haddy heard a rustling behind her and whipped around. Xuthus had the same idea of an early morning snack, and in the soft light, Haddy's silhouette stood out. The big man downshifted to first gear. His motion slowed as two small eyes fixed themselves on the woman like lasers. He put down his plate, the size of a tea saucer in his hand, and stepped towards her, mesmerized by this shiny toy. Xuthus reached out, his fingers inches from Haddy's face, and speaking in a high-pitched catlike meow said, "Let me pet your hair."

Haddy instinctively stepped back and bumped against the stove. Her right hand went to the pistol, while the other pushed the lion's paw aside. "Not today, big fella, or ever," she said and glanced left and right for a way out.

Xuthus's eyes hardened and voice darkened, "I want to pet it." With surprising quickness, the giant stretched out his arms like albatross wings and boxed her in. He towered over her. "The captain won't hear. Don't scream like the others." Haddy's chest seized in panic. Her body became mush as her worst fear materialized like a ghost ship from the fog. The Glock had no legs. The knife had no hands. Xuthus squealed in delight and put his palm on her head; then he grabbed one breast. Like a magician's fire, Haddy's rape flashed up. She was falling under blows from long ago, tied up and spread open for this giant. The claustrophobia clamped down on her throat. Xuthus touched her pelvis. Suddenly, in her chest, Haddy felt the fiery lightsaber come alive and an inner voice say, *"When you hear the blast of war, summon your rage and strike like a tiger."* Like an explosion from a cannon, Haddy's hand shot out. Aiming for the back of Xuthus's throat, her fingers sliced through his skin like the paper bag. They stopped at the spinal cord. On their way out, the fingers snapped shut like a bear trap and ripped out the windpipe, arteries, veins, and all. Blood sprayed like water from fire hydrants, over the ceiling and walls of the galley. Xuthus turned pale. His eyes glazed over. The giant toppled like a redwood and landed on the floor with a loud crash. A pool of dark blood spread out beneath the Leviathan as the skipper rushed in and yelled for his mates. The younger seaman ran in and saw his brother. He fell on the mountain of flesh and let out a bloodcurdling scream. The skipper and the barrel-chested seaman stared openmouthed at the terrible blonde, who held an enormous chicken neck in her hand. As her blood boiled, Haddy snarled, "Fresh meat for your fucking fish stew."

"You fucking bitch!" yelled the raging captain. "You cunt!" Xuthus's brother launched himself at Haddy. She pivoted and slammed her foot into the side of his head. He hit the counter like a soccer ball, but bounced back and grabbed her wig. He unknowingly pressed on the burr hole, and dizziness and nausea kicked Haddy in the stomach. Yet, filled with her own reserves of fury, Haddy loosed a high-pitched scream and raked the young seaman's face with a claw hand. He twisted away with an agonizing scream, clutching the wig, as the older mate entered the fray. Haddy slammed an elbow uppercut into his chin, kneed him in the groin, and, as he bent over, kneed him in the face. She heard the cracking of facial bones. He vomited blood and dropped like a sack of groceries. The captain's eyes widened in shock as he saw a bareheaded Haddy, with fresh scalp wound and a face of zigzagging sutures.

His hand flew to an iron skillet when Haddy put the gun under his chin. "Try it, motherfucker," she seethed. "Give me one reason not to add your brains to that pile of shit on the floor." The pan dropped. Haddy picked up the stew and bread and tucked the wig under her arm. "Fucking bad hair day. I'll be getting off in Sicily for a stylist."

Shaking like a leaf, Haddy jammed the chair under the cabin handle. She plunged her head into the washbasin, rinsed her mouth, and toweled off. Haddy put the wig and blood-soaked clothes into the bathtub. The medicine cabinet contained a bottle of hydrogen peroxide, and she poured that on the clothing and hair as well. As the adrenaline drained away, Haddy opened a fresh pack of Lucky Strikes and opened the small cabin window. The fresh air and rising sun, shining red against the cirrus clouds, did not bode well for the weather. Haddy had to get off the cruiser, which meant the raft.

The thrum of the deep-throated Mercs and the unchanging bounce of the bow through the waves assured Haddy the skipper had stayed on course for Sicily. When she saw the island emerge off the port bow, she knew it meant docking in Marsala in three hours. But drastic events required drastic plans. Haddy decided to commandeer the raft and steer to Portopalo di Capo Passero, ten miles distant.

Haddy readied the satchel. She tugged on the black watch cap and latched the Glock and knife to her waist. She made ready to dash out to the inflatable, when the cruiser suddenly changed direction and closed on Portopalo di Capo Passero. They docked quickly, and Haddy watched Captain Dymus lash the vessel to the cleats in time for a wealthy-looking Italian and three roughnecks to walk aboard. Realizing she would be trapped in the stateroom, Haddy slipped into the hallway bath.

"Where? Where is she?" bellowed a loud voice.

"Locked in the stateroom," Haddy overheard the captain

say. He added, "Mr. Piaro, we brought up the footlocker with weapons."

"You tossed the cretin?" Piaro said derisively.

"In chains," said Captain Dymus. "I see you brought help from the syndicate. The woman's a witch."

Piaro asked the young seaman, "Can you see?"

"She scratched my eyes, but yes, Mr. Piaro. I've got a submachine gun, enough to fill her fucking body with lead."

"I don't want her dead, you moron," said the mob boss. "Captain, you and this hothead stay here." Piaro addressed his henchmen. "Stun the hell out of her; I want this bitch alive. She's worth a lot of money, and the price just went up." Three men passed the bathroom and trod softly to the stateroom door, guns and Tasers out. Haddy watched a short stocky man knock, backed up by a tall roughneck. A man with a wide cruel face turned to check the hall bath.

The short man rasped, "Miss Mercedes, open the door slowly. Throw your weapons out. You won't be harmed." Haddy retreated behind the shower curtain with her suppressed Glock at the ready. The short man continued, "Don't make this harder than it has to be. Come out at once." The wide cruel face slid back the shower curtain. The 9mm round coughed into his eye. The other two prepared to break down the stateroom door.

Piaro shouted from the wheelhouse, "Shoot the lock off." Haddy stepped over the dead man and aimed her pistol through the partially opened door. As they fired, she sent a bullet into the tall man's head. As his partner turned, Haddy's semiautomatic spoke again, and the round hit center forehead. Piaro yelled, "She's in the bathroom!" and shouted at Xuthus's brother, "Go, go, go!"

Enraged beyond reason, the youth sprayed the hallway with bullets. Haddy dove into the tub. When he kicked down the door, she kept her head down, but raised her pistol and shot three times. The submachine gun clattered to the floor.

Piaro dashed to the doorway, brandishing a large bore stainless-steel revolver, and fired. Haddy waited, popped her head out, and aimed. Three rounds caught him in the chest. Then she heard a splash from the starboard side. Taking the seaman's submachine gun in hand, Haddy dashed forward. Captain Dymus had thrown himself overboard, and like an aging windmill, churned the waters towards the dock. Armed gunmen had emptied the SUVs, but Haddy opened fire. She raced forward, cut the lines, pushed the gangplank into the water, and dashed to the wheelhouse. Haddy jumped into the skipper's chair when a round grazed the top of her shoulder. Though she ignored the pain, a familiar wave of cold ice washed through Haddy's veins with deadly calm. Her fingers roved over the knobs and buttons, until they fell on a red letter "S" inscribed on a white button. With blood oozing from the shoulder wound, Haddy pressed. The twin Mercs exploded into deep gargles. Haddy slammed into "reverse," and the cruiser leaped back. She whipped the bow around in an arc and jammed the throttles forward. Haddy flipped on the *racing fuel* fob, and the sleek ship lifted off the waters like a Saturn rocket. It left Haddy's stomach back at the dock as 3,100 horsepower launched the *Astrea* to 100 knots. Its new captain threw back her head and let out a piercing war scream.

46

Day 23
Penthouse Suite Two, Decameron Apartments
Tuesday, October 10
Zero-four-hundred hours

Brianna tossed and turned. François had informed her of Gott's murder, which caused her more alarm. She got out of bed and paced. "Should I call Bill McKinney?" she asked. Brianna found François's corduroy sport coat thrown over the couch. Without thinking, she checked the pockets and became alarmed when she found a phone she didn't recognize. Brianna turned it on and saw calls made while she and François had been in Beirut. She checked the area code. New Mexico? Who was in New Mexico? As a light rain fell upon the skylights, Brianna dialed and got the Los Alamos National Laboratory. Frightened, she searched the coat and found a paper napkin with François's distinctive scribblings. She glanced at it and paled.

Brianna put her hair up and dressed in yoga pants, a loose cotton shirt, and slippers. She adjusted the thermostat higher to take off the chill. She made coffee and waited for François. When he stepped from the shower, Brianna handed him his robe, served him coffee, and said, "Join me?"

"What is so important?" François replied. "You're trembling."

"I have some questions," she said. "Can you explain this phone and calls to New Mexico?" Brianna opened the napkin. "And this?" François had drawn two circles; one was labeled "Jerusalem," surrounded by little rockets under which he had written, "X3s." In the second circle, Jerusalem lay in flames with "4 p.m. 10/13," "ON," and "OFF" underneath. Brianna burst into tears. "What are you planning?" She watched François's eyes glaze over. "François? Say something, please."

François took her hands in his own and said, "Ignore the burner phone and the Los Alamos calls. As to my doodling, I work things out on paper. You mustn't take them seriously."

"But Jerusalem at four p.m.?" she said pleadingly. "To murder those people?"

"Things are very complex," he said.

"You're planning on blowing up Jerusalem?" Brianna said, aghast.

François raised a calming hand. "Patience, let me speak," he said. "With Helmut dead, Ivan is beside himself. We have missiles but no triggers, and without triggers, they will not fire, so the doodles are meaningless." Brianna reeled inside, asking herself, "Who am I marrying?" as François continued, "But darling, what if Ivan finds someone like Helmut, like a magician's rabbit out of a hat? Someone whose software makes them work? Then I face a dilemma: How do I make the rockets work for us and against them? To protect Jerusalem and our fledgling family, and kill Ivan Juric and destroy the mighty Eastern

Machine Systems simultaneously? It's an enigma, but I may have found a solution. That's all I can say. You must trust me."

After François left, Brianna's tears soaked the pillow. She did trust François, barely, but if someone killed Helmut Gott, someone could kill him and her and Ulyana. Brianna opened her purse and found Bill McKinney's phone number. "Call him," said her inner voice, "or knock on his door."

47

The *Astrea* plunged through the dark wine waters of the Mediterranean Sea, bouncing from swell to swell. Haddy reduced the speed to 30 knots, but the steady beat of the hull hammered her brain. She had survived the melee, but barely. Though her anger had subsided some, she yelled, "Fucking flesh traders." Haddy set the glistening craft on autopilot, as her shoulder throbbed. She weaved down the hallway, muttering, "I hate the ocean," and stepped over the dead bodies back to the elegant stateroom. Haddy pawed through the spec-ops medic satchel and gave her herself painkiller injections. And though the wound wasn't deep, the bleeding must be stopped. Along with emergency narcotics, morphine, and antibiotics, she found a suture set. Haddy went back to the hall bath, wondering if the swells had worsened.

Cursing the waves, she tossed the blood-spattered shirt on the floor. Haddy took the forceps, clamped down on the curved needle with attached thread, and drove it through the edges of the gash. The crude closure worked. Haddy squeezed on triple-antibiotic ointment, dressed the wound with gauze, and tugged on a fresh shirt.

The painkiller injections helped. Haddy lit a Lucky Strike, and the nicotine sharpened her thinking. She chambered a round in the pistol and found the barrel-chested seaman moaning in his bunk, carried there by his shipmates, with a swollen black-and-blue jaw and temple. Haddy filled a bowl with water and splashed it on his face. The man opened his eyes, which grew wider when he saw the pistol. "Stand up, you piece of shit," she said. The seaman hesitated, and Haddy forced the gun in his mouth. "I said get up, we're going for a walk." The seaman wobbled forward as she steered him to the deck. Fresh winds were blowing as the *Astrea* roared through the waves. "What's in the crates?" she asked.

"Heroin," said the seaman. "There are millions stowed away in the hold, but the boat has location finders. Piaro's men will hunt you down."

"Who is Piaro?"

"You killed the head of the Sicilian Sakharov syndicate, Giovanni Piaro," he replied. "You need me. There's a big storm coming."

"Yeah?" said Haddy. "Then get off now." The seaman shouted in fear. Haddy continued, "I thought you liked the sea, you motherfucker. Take a bullet or take your chances with the fish." Haddy backed him overboard. The seaman hit the water. The sea swallowed up the splash, and Haddy returned to the bloodied bodies of Giovanni Piaro and Xuthus's brother. Her face flushed red as the anger rose. Haddy dragged the two men to the stern but searched the fine Italian suit of Giovanni Piaro. She found the price of her flesh: $50,000 in ten $5,000 rolls of cash. "Time to throw out the fucking trash," she said, manhandling the mob boss and the young seaman over the railing without looking back.

Her anger cooled but left in its wake a disastrous position. If the *Astrea* malfunctioned, Haddy would be stranded in the middle of the ocean. She entered the wheelhouse. Haddy didn't know the sea like the windswept barren plains of the Middle East, but understood maps, compass headings, and directions. She checked the compass. Her heading lay 300 degrees west by northwest with the island of Sicily to her right. As she sped along its southern coast, Haddy glanced outside at the high clouds, like those in Yemen. The sun filtered through them like gauze, but to the north, clouds were gathered in round, darkening cotton-ball-like masses, which presaged storms. Eight hours ago, the barometer read "30.2" with a smiling sun next to it. Now it had fallen to "29.8," indicated by an unhappy face.

Haddy cleared away the porn and beer cans and noticed a pint of rum tucked into a corner. "*Sunset Rum*, 84.5% alcohol." "Damn," she said, and took a swig and gasped. Her hand clasped her chest as the fire flowed into her tummy. She danced a tiny jig. "Wow!" Haddy found the ocean charts, spread them out, and examined her predicament. She could have raced up through the straits of Messina, but the boat was well away to the west. She could swing around Marsala and steer north between the islands of Isola di Marettimo and Levanzo, taking her into the Tyrrhenian Sea and Rome's ancient port town of Civitavecchia. Yet, if they were tracking her, where could she escape?

Opening the footlocker placed in the wheelhouse by Captain Dymus, Haddy observed a cache of weapons, ammunition, and grenades. With the cruiser on autopilot, she ducked into the hold and found bags of white powder behind panels running the length of the boat on each side. Haddy ransacked the cabins and found foul-weather gear and another $8,455 in rolls, packets, and single notes. She hit the galley for food and returned to the wheelhouse in time to head north. Should she go to Civitavecchia? They would be waiting. She could head to the Amalfi Coast and run the ship aground, but they'd know in advance. The thought of using the raft crossed her mind, but she rejected it as unwise with a storm coming.

As the clouds gathered, Haddy considered turning around and returning to Ashdod. She could turn herself in to Major Rudin and wait for the Shin Bet's scolding. Maybe there hadn't been a vision? If she hadn't "leaped" none of this would have happened, and Ori Daniels would be alive. Her family would grieve her suicide and move on. "Maybe I've been wrong about all of this?" she asked herself. "Should I turn around?" The rum burned in her belly, and then Haddy looked astern and saw Xuthus looming in her mind's eye. "I was dead, until he touched me. The blast of war crashed into my ears like cymbals. I took his life with deadly speed and power." Haddy's face grew grim. "And found my purpose." She set her chin. Her eyebrows knit together into a dread resolve. Haddy gripped her knife and made the course correction. Civitavecchia lay three hundred miles north. "There is a time in every race, where one risks it all," she said. "I must go forward ... to Rome."

48

Day 24
On the Ocean Foaming
Wednesday, October II
Zero-three-hundred hours

As the storm mounted in fury, the seas rose to mountains and darkening ravines. Rain pelted the *Astrea*. Gales pushed the sleek craft like a leaf in the wind. Haddy feared a rogue wave might capsize the craft. She held on for dear life and made a slight course correction. If the boat stayed on its present course, the *Astrea* would smash into the docks of Civitavecchia. Cutting the engines would let her enemies know she had run for it. "I'll keep the boat at thirty knots and gamble on the raft. *'He who dares wins.'*"

Haddy plastered her face with a thick layer of ointment and tugged on the watch cap. With weapons secured, she put on the young seaman's waterproof pants, anorak, gloves, and life vest. Clutching her satchel, she opened the wheelhouse door. The gales caught it and flung it against the outside wall in a loud crash. Haddy gripped the railing on the gunwale and stepped out. The wind and rain lashed her face like cat-o'-nine tails. She raised the satchel to protect herself, as the elements shoved her to the cruiser's stern. Haddy steered herself back and stowed her supplies in the rigid inflatable. She released the winch and spooled out the cable. Her gloves were sopping wet, and the rain drenched her face. Haddy watched the raft with its outboard engine hit the raging waters and bounce, dip, and tip wildly like a cork, a roller coaster on steroids. When she turned to check the winch, the unthinkable happened. She lost her footing. The wind picked Haddy up and sent her in a cartwheel up and over the raft. At the last moment, she caught the rope that wound around the craft. The *Astrea* and the inflatable, bound together by the winch, dived and lurched through the tumultuous black waters.

Haddy held on, trying to avoid the outboard propeller, which popped up and dived into the water. Haddy threw her other hand to the rope. When the raft rose on a wave, she leaped into the raft. Haddy crashed inside and bounced up and down before she hit the cable disconnect. The *Astrea* vanished into the stormy darkness, a white horse into a black night. Not giving herself a chance to rest, Haddy pulled the cord, and the outboard coughed, sputtered, and came alive. With her hand on the tiller, she took a bearing at 60 degrees and buzzed up and over the raging waters like a tiny gnat on the back of a galloping steed, towards Santa Severa. With luck, she wouldn't drown.

~

MATEO PIARO VERGED ON SEASICKNESS, but the Rome Sakharov syndicate head had been notified of his brother's death in Portopalo di Capo Passero. Ivan went cold when he learned of the disaster. He ordered Mateo to launch a fast boat to intercept the stolen cruiser, which was traveling with over $6 million in heroin in the holds. "Capture this woman," he had ordered. "The moment you see the *Astrea*, call me."

The *Sea Ray* and six crew were dispatched into the storm from Civitavecchia. Mateo and its captain had tracked the *Astrea* along the southern coast of Sicily, around Marsala and north through the Tyrrhenian Sea. It maintained 30 knots and never varied course, save for a 5-degree correction minutes ago. Mateo gripped his semiautomatic for comfort, anxious to board the *Astrea*, but the skipper cautioned patience. "The waves, wind, and rain work in her favor. Patience, Mr. Piaro."

"Turn on the lights," ordered Mateo. A bank of ten halogens flashed into the storm like midday suns. They caught the *Astrea* crashing over the waves like a frothy stallion. Mateo reached Ivan on the phone and said, "We've got her."

"The *Astrea* has a motorized raft," said Ivan. "Is it there?" The skipper had gunned the engines, caught up with the *Astrea*, and swung alongside, ready to board in the stormy waters.

Mateo reported, "No."

"Could she have gotten off?" asked Ivan.

"The seas are ten feet at least," said Mateo. "I doubt it."

"Get word to the police and contacts in Rome," ordered Ivan. "Have men cover every inch of the coast: roads, trains, and buses. Check hotels and hostels. What's happening now?"

"We're boarding." Moments elapsed. Ivan heard, "We've cut the engines. No one's aboard. We're checking the hold. There's gas below and *grenades* ..." An enormous boom followed, which pierced Ivan's ear. The phone fell to the floor.

∾

WITH TREMBLING HANDS, Haddy piloted the raft over the wind-tossed waves towards the ruined fort of Santa Severa. In the far distance, she heard an explosion. The booby trap worked. "God damn motherfuckers," she said as her teeth chattered. "Go to hell." She must make landfall or succumb to hypothermia. Haddy heard the surf thundering in the distance and glimpsed the ragged ruins of the fort and beach. An outcropping of rocks jutted forth, covered in a lather of bursting surf.

As she drew closer, Haddy tried to time the waves and keep away from the merciless rocks. The storm made an omelet of the normal orderly procession of sets, but she discerned a few stretches of smooth water. Hoping to stay *ahead* of the next breaker, Haddy gunned the engine. When it caught up to her, she cut the engine to avoid becoming a surfboard. She was successful with this maneuver for two waves, but with the third, when she looked back, her mouth fell open in shock. The wave loomed like a wall behind her. She was going too fast to cut the engine. To her horror, the water crested higher and higher, until Haddy saw the raft's propeller spinning out of the water. The craft was nearly standing up, vertical. The bow lay buried in the trough below. The wave crested and flipped the craft over and flung Haddy out, like a rock from a sling.

She flew headfirst into the sand, the microscopic shards of silica tearing into her skin. They stung like fire ants as the wave rolled past her. Then the undercurrent pulled her back into the froth. Shivering, stunned, and freezing, Haddy tried to hold on as another wave hit and pushed her down. Strength drained from her body, which was fast becoming an icicle. Haddy summoned the last shreds of her will. Fighting against leaden cold, she placed five fingers on the sand and dragged the other hand forward. She gripped the wet sand and pushed up, as another wave slammed into her body. Haddy pulled her knees beneath her and finally stood. Swaying in the winds, she saw the satchel bobbing in the surf. Haddy waded out step by step and dragged the soggy luggage to shore under a copse of trees. She tried to pull off her clothes but couldn't make her fingers work. Haddy grasped her knife and cut the anorak's buttons and the rain pants. She slit her shirt and bra, panties and tights top to bottom. Haddy tore off a piece of cloth and placed it between her teeth to prevent her tongue from lacerating from the uncontrollable chattering. In this temporary shelter under the trees, Haddy got into the wig and dry clothes from the sealed bags prepared earlier while aboard the *Astrea*.

Placing one foot in front of the other, she began jogging to the Via del Castello, the main highway to Rome. Haddy hugged the walls of the town to avoid the light cast from streetlamps and arrived at the Maestrale Ristorante Pizzeria. A light shone from a rain-streaked window out back. Next to the trash bin sat a small rusty pickup truck. Haddy crept up and looked inside the restaurant. The owner worked at a table.

Haddy's fingers fumbled at the hot-wire. The engine sputtered to life, and she clambered in the front seat and hit the accelerator. The vehicle spun out in a shower of gravel. She looked in the mirror and ducked as the owner ran out with a shotgun. Haddy raced ahead, ramped up the heater, and stayed south on the SS1 Via Aurelia to Rome, expecting police flashers, but seeing none, drove to the Antica Locanda hotel.

The sleepy clerk arose from the back room with a startled face, shocked by the sudden appearance of the bedraggled woman, but Haddy mumbled about the storm and checked into a room. She stumbled into the shower, turned on the hot water, and let the heat soak in. Haddy walked like a zombie back to the bed. She flopped down and pulled the covers over her and mumbled Churchill's refrain, *"Never, never, never give up."*

49

Day 24
Antica Laconda Hotel, Rome, Italy
Wednesday, October 11

At zero nine hundred hours, the alarm jolted Haddy awake, filling the room with an annoying buzz. Her eyelids opened to a spartan dresser, lamp, and wall-mounted TV. The Triconnia Gallery opened in an hour. Haddy reached up and knocked the clock on the floor, but it continued to rattle away. She fell out of bed with a thump, cursing at the shoulder wound. Haddy got up, took aim, and kicked the clock across the room. It caromed off the wall into the bathroom. "Score one for me," she said. Haddy badly wanted to fall back to bed and sleep but continued, "Get your ass in gear." She limbered up, stretched, and saw herself in the mirror. The stormy night in the deep, coupled with the thrashing at Santa Severa, had torn up some of Dr. Adina's artistry. The sand had scraped off small areas of fresh healing tissue. Removing Dr.

Adina's lotions from the satchel, Haddy brushed on the healing ointments. She examined the red and swollen shoulder and applied fresh gauze. In the bottom of the satchel lay her Winnie-the-Pooh bear, sealed in a plastic bag. Her father's gift, given to her by Sasha, winked at her. "What awaits us, Pooh?" she said, and wondered how to get past her fears. She had survived in spite of the *Astrea*, the crew, and Piaro. Haddy admitted she wanted to return to see Shira or her Manhattan apartment and Sasha and David Abrams. She took a deep breath; the more she stayed on this course, the lonelier it became.

Haddy donned a forest-green compression shirt, black fitness tights and black hoodie, and wig. She performed a few jumping jacks, crunches, and push-ups. She reached for the ceiling and then ran her hands over her washboard stomach, steely thighs, and calves for reassurance. She needed coffee and food. Haddy holstered the Glock and hefted the knife. She threw it across the room into the door frame. It stuck with a resounding deadly *thud*. Haddy checked her passports, put "Leah Berenson" in her pocket, and went downstairs.

The storm had continued unabated outside, and the ancient city lay under wind and rain-soaked clouds. Haddy went to the hotel restaurant and took a seat along the bar. She ordered a four-quad breve, bagels and cream cheese, smoked salmon and eclairs drenched in dark chocolate. She watched the TV, which broadcast a local soccer game, and checked the train schedule. After going to the art gallery, she would catch the ferry from Genoa to Morocco into Arabia.

A sudden news flash came on. A helicopter news camera hovered over police boats and divers and a crane amid floating debris in Civitavecchia's harbor. The announcer breathlessly went on about bodies, heroin, a racing boat, and a cruiser called the *Sea Ray*. "Have you seen this woman?" the newsperson said. "Her name is Jael Benjamin, twenty-seven, slender, five-feet-nine inches tall, black eyes and black hair, and may be wearing a blonde wig. She's wanted for questioning." Haddy restrained herself from putting down the coffee. The photo was from when she was in training years ago. Where in the hell had it come from? Who could see her military files? Evidently, Giovanni Piaro had spoken to someone in this Sakarovkh syndicate about her appearance and blonde hair. The syndicate had an inside person within the Israeli military. Haddy pulled the hood over her face but caught movement in her peripheral vision. A patron watching the broadcast had seen her and was picking up his phone. She threw money on the bar and fast-walked through the gales along the cobblestoned Via Panisperna to the gallery.

The RB Triconnia Art Gallery lay on the first floor of a five-story aged honey-colored limestone apartment building. The entry lay under a trellis of brightly colored begonias dripping with rainwater. The Via Panisperna was wide. Across from the entrance were parked bicycles, scooters, and motorcycles. The clerk unlocked the door at 10 a.m. sharp. Haddy elbowed in and asked for the manager. The clerk said dismissively, "We're not hiring, but you can leave an application."

"Good, I'm not applying," said Haddy. The clerk shrugged and pointed to the back of the store. The air had a delightful rose scent. The floors were polished oak with fine rugs. The walls were white as befitted an art gallery. Haddy walked past high-priced paintings, and postmodern sculptures of a lamppost, a rusty bicycle, and a metallic woman with three heads. She noticed a bevy of rare clocks behind locked glass cabinets. The sign over the door read, "Domenico Biachi, Esq., Owner." Haddy gave a knock and entered. A precise older man in a crisp white shirt, gold silk tie, and beige slacks looked up from his paper, croissant, and coffee. The desk was mid-century modern Scandinavian teak. A screensaver of tropical fish swam back and forth on a large desktop screen. A thin laptop lay at his right hand, and irritation crossed his face. "If you're here for a job," he said, "leave your application with Niccollo outside."

Haddy pulled back the cowl. She let the satchel hit the floor and removed her sunglasses. "I was searching your website and found a music box you sold," she replied, and removed the folded piece of notepaper, *"The Shema. Original one-of-a-kind Louis XIV 1786. Gift for a Jewish courtesan. Mozart's Requiem."* "I'm tracing ownership. Can you help me?"

The owner set down his coffee, leaned back in his leather chair, and lit a cigarette. "You have credentials?"

"Do I need any?"

"It's an unusual request," said the owner. Keeping the screen private, the owner typed the description into the computer. His eyebrows lifted, and he examined Haddy closer. "Leave your name and contact information with Niccollo."

Haddy's chest tightened, her nerves on edge. She zipped open the satchel, removed $5,000, and peeled off twenty-five one-hundred-dollar bills. "A finder's fee would be in order," she announced.

The owner straightened his tie, smoothed back his hair, and glanced once more at the screen, saying, "Most unusual." Haddy plunked down the remainder of the roll, like putting down four aces in a poker game. The owner blanched, coughed, and affected a bruised embarrassed reluctance. He held up his hand. "Enough," he said, and hit "enter." The fish aquarium disappeared. The man stood abruptly, tucked the cash in his pocket, and motioned with his hand to his chair. "Be my guest. Take all the time you need. Would you like some coffee?"

"No," said Haddy as the door closed. Haddy's heart pounded erratically. The pulse thrummed behind her eyes. For fourteen days, the silver porcelain music box had hovered on the edges of her consciousness. It infiltrated her dreams and seemed to glow with increasing brightness as she walked through Rome. Haddy bit her lip. Her tongue flicked through the gap in her teeth as she looked at the music box, *her* music box. What she saw was an exact replica of her vision. Underneath in bold letters lay inscribed: *"Purchased by Joseph Abrams PhD for $473,500. July 7, 1989. 55 Linden Lane, Southampton, New York."* Haddy reread the statement, "Purchased by Joseph Abrams, PhD," and felt a ball of lightning roll out of the desert and slam into her. She clasped her chest and shouted, "It can't be!" Haddy put her head on the desk. Her father had sent a priceless heirloom to his home in Southampton. Her grandfather David must have it. She must find the box.

Weak and dizzy, Haddy wove her way past the paintings and sculptures. She threw open the gallery door and collapsed on her hands and knees, retching. The fall saved her as a bullet shattered the glass behind her. Haddy flattened and rolled instinctively. She saw a leather-clad motorcyclist across the street take aim. She whipped out her Glock and fired in one smooth motion. The motorcycle helmet shattered into a burst of blood. Haddy sensed movement to her right and saw a young mother pushing a baby carriage on the sidewalk. The woman bent over and pulled out a gun. Haddy held the pistol with both hands and fired through the carriage, but felt a sting in her thigh. The assassin staggered into the wall. Haddy knew then that the phone call from the Laconda restaurant patron had been intercepted. No doubt the man was told to follow her and report on her movements.

Haddy heard a roar to her left. A small car screeched to a halt on the curb, and two assailants jumped out. The driver, a man with a scarred face, bounded out while the passenger-side assailant raised his pistol. Haddy fired through the door. The man went down with bullets to his chest. The driver had come around the front. He viciously kicked her in the ribs and knocked her pistol down. Haddy cried as bones cracked like dry twigs, but like a tiger, she grabbed the driver's foot, twisted violently, and heard the ankle snap. As he staggered back, she leaped to her feet and took her blade. The knife flew into the assailant's throat.

Holding her ribs and thigh, Haddy loped to the motorcycle, gasping for breath. She shoved off the dead assassin and hopped on. The four-cylinder Ducati 1098 roared in power, and she sped away. Haddy coughed up blood as she turned corner after corner, through the narrow streets, until she passed an alleyway. Haddy slammed on the brakes and skidded on the wet pavement. She backed in and behind a trash bin coughed up more blood. Haddy gasped from the razor-sharp rib pain. She opened the medic's kit from the satchel and gave herself an injection of a broad-spectrum antibiotic and a painkiller. Haddy's hoodie and tights were blood-soaked. She tossed them in the trash and placed a roll of gauze around the leg. She tugged on fresh pants and a burgundy mountaineering parka. Checking her app, she saw the Roma Termini lay close.

The Ducati roared again. Haddy wove in and out of traffic, came around a corner, and ditched the bike. She joined the travelers within the Termini, splinting her ribs with her left hand, while muffling her coughs and trying not to limp. Haddy moved through the throngs to the schedule board and searched frantically for the fastest way to Frankfurt. She found the FC 9626 Express to Milan, departing within the hour. Using the Leah Berenson passport, and aware that the police as well as the nefarious Sakharov syndicate were searching for her, Haddy purchased the Executive pass at the ticket booth. Clenching her jaws against the pain, she limped across the street to the Farmacia Farmacrimi. Haddy loaded up on first aid supplies. At the Coin Dress Store nearby, she grabbed a shopping cart and wheeled down the aisles, throwing together a new wardrobe, accessories, cosmetics, and carry-on luggage.

Haddy locked herself in the changing room. She removed the forest-green compression shirt and sports bra. The entire left side of her chest was swollen red with purple blotches. The underlying fractures were exquisitely painful. When she touched her back below the last rib, she winced, knowing the attacker had injured the kidney. Haddy removed the tights and hastily applied a dressing. The bullet had passed through the outer portion of her thigh. "Fuck, fuck, fuck," she said, as it throbbed. "God dammit, that hurts." She wanted to apply the camphor liniment to the ribs, but time was of the essence. Haddy wrapped her chest with two 6-inch elastic bandages and a fresh bra. She reapplied a 6-inch roll of gauze around the thigh. Haddy donned a pair of hose, a gray cashmere dress, a wide black fashion belt, and a hat over her blonde wig. She slipped her feet in low-slung black pumps, wrapped a muted Hermes scarf around her neck, and touched herself with some Decadence perfume. Adding lipstick and a new pair of sunglasses, she walked out with her new luggage, forced a deep breath, and squared her shoulders.

Walking to the Strega Stazione Termini liquor store, Haddy purchased a carton of Lucky Strikes and a fifth of tequila. She wasted no time after boarding the bullet train. Haddy entered the restroom, removed the cashmere, bra, and elastic bandages, and applied a thick layer of camphor-infused liniment on her ribs. She redressed the shoulder, examined the scalp, and was relieved the gauze around her thigh hadn't bled through. Haddy returned to her seat, swallowed two shots of tequila, and kept her hand on the Glock inside the purse. She switched trains in Milan to the EC 20 train to Switzerland, and would catch the Austrian Nightjet sleeper to Mannheim, Germany.

FOURTEEN HUNDRED MILES EAST, X sat in the Fortress Palace Room, nervously fingering his cigar. His eyelids and cheeks were swollen, and his face sagged from lack of sleep. He had spoken with the Manhattan titan again over the missing Ming dynasty music box and learned nothing. More upsetting was the *Astrea* fiasco, and the "tourist" who turned out to be the Israeli sniper, Haddy Abrams, and daughter of his dead nemesis, Joseph Abrams. His own informants told him of the RB Triconnia debacle. Four associates dead. Then, Pavlos told him the worst: Professor Stefan Danilenko and Raisa remained incognito.

Fusako's phone rang. "It's the Enforcer," she said.

X replied coldly, "Have him come up."

Ivan hadn't slept either, but decided on giving X the good news first. "Colonel Yevhim backtracked the staff sergeant's family," he said. "In addition to David and Sasha Abrams on her father's side, there are two others. Stefan Danilenko and his daughter Raisa."

X's mouth opened in shock. He sat back flabbergasted, the wheels of his great genius processing this revelation. *"The Danilenkos are her family?"* he declared.

"There's more," said Ivan. "The colonel informed me the Shin Bet placed everyone associated with the staff sergeant under protection; new identities and bodyguards, which is why we haven't been able to locate them. When he found out, the colonel sent Danilenko's agent a message to return to Tel Aviv. Danilenko is now without protection."

X grabbed his cane and got up. He walked over and clapped Ivan on the back, something done only once before, when Ivan blew up Joseph Abrams's jet. Kitten squawked, "Let's go on the merry-go-round."

Ivan said, "Do you want a debrief on the *Astrea* and RB Triconnia gallery mishaps?"

"Mishaps?" said X. "Disasters, more like it."

"Then get ready for the best," said Ivan. "We located the staff sergeant. She's in a first-class cabin on the EC 20 train to Switzerland."

Fusako had remained silent as a stone, but now spoke up. "Ivan," she asked, "did you ask the owner why?"

"Why what?"

"Why was the staff sergeant at the gallery?" said Fusako.

"Our informant at the scene questioned the owner closely," said Ivan. "The staff sergeant wanted information on a music box sold at the store."

X whipped his head around and said, "When was it sold?"

"July 7, 1989."

"Superb work, my son," said X. "Your best work. Go below and await my instructions." As the elevator doors closed, X said to Fusako, "Eliminate him."

"I spoke with Rat," said Fusako. "He hates Ivan and wants his head. Major Lebed could step into Ivan's shoes."

"Clever girl," replied X. "Always one step ahead. Now, bring up this music box on our screen." In seconds, he and Fusako were examining the photos in detail. *"The Shema. Original one-of-a-kind Louis XIV 1786. Gift for a Jewish courtesan. Mozart's Requiem. Purchased by Joseph Abrams PhD for $473,500. July 7, 1989. 55 Linden Lane, Southampton, New York."* X positively drooled as he pointed out the details of the box, the prominent star and Scripture. "Notice, my sweet yakuza, the Scripture citation is wrong. It should be five-six-four for Deuteronomy, the fifth book of the Pentateuch, the sixth chapter and fourth verse. This is five-four-six, and notice the Requiem? The box was made in 1786, but the score wasn't finished at the time of the composer's death in 1791. That tells me the box contains my secrets, in microfiche form. Tell Ivan to pull his men off the staff sergeant. She is going to Southampton for the box. Who do we have in New York?"

"Juanita and Carlo Rodriguez on the mother, Sasha, and the Kliment twins in Southampton on the grandfather."

"Should we get more?" wondered X.

"In the West, they say, 'Too many chefs spoil the broth.' Yes?

In Japan, we say, 'With too many captains, the ship could end up on the mountain.'"

X clenched his fists in glee. "And they won't have bodyguards," he said. "Pour me some vodka, Fusako; this deserves a toast." X downed three shots, and holding his Kali mask crowed, "I am the goddess of death! My entreaties have been answered!"

50

Raisa studied her guts out Wednesday; her head couldn't hold any more biology, chemistry, math, and physics. Early Thursday morning, she brewed strong tea for herself and sniffed the fragrant aromas of the leaves before opening her laptop for her first online exam. Then, both she and her grandfather Stefan were astounded when the bodyguard bid them a sudden goodbye. As their questions piled on top of one another, the man begged off with "a sudden emergency," of "national importance."

"So we are safe?" asked Stefan.

"And I can get rid of this stupid black phone?" said Raisa.

"And return to our apartment tomorrow?" inquired Stefan. "What about Haddy?"

"You will never be absolutely safe until you hear from her," he said. "But as each day goes by, things improve. If you go out," the agent turned towards Raisa, "surround yourself with friends, especially at the big game tomorrow. For you, Professor, I advise you do the same if you go to the university."

After he left, Raisa said, "Weird, but after my exams today, I'm going out with Yana for a few hours."

Stefan shrugged. "I'll be in my office, finishing the software."

Yana picked up Raisa at 7 p.m. and dropped her off at the club. She sighed with longing when Pavlos opened the door. "I want to hear every detail," she told Raisa.

Pavlos escorted the teenager to the private VIP dining room. Raisa came alive to the music and thick burgundy carpet. She drank in the sweetness and the white linen with silverware and porcelain plates set to perfection. A vase with roses sat in the center under a crystal chandelier. Doctored champagne had been poured, along with water. Pavlos suggested a main course and let the teenager choose the appetizers. "I gobbled up your Facebook page," Pavlos gushed. "But first, a toast." He watched her sip and touched the glass with his lips, before urging her to enjoy more. Pavlos ignored his cell phone buzzing and let the girl talk and drink. He listened avidly and observed Raisa flush and her eyes dilate. He saw her arousal, induced by the Rohypnol, and then her eyes glaze over. The blonde teen moaned and passed out. The waiter appeared, and in minutes, Raisa lay inside a rug in the back of a white panel van. Pavlos placed her pink phone in his pocket. He called Fusako and reported the news, then placed a call to the Enforcer.

"Good work," said Ivan. "Give the phone to Captain Dimitri 'Loverboy.' He'll be at the jet waiting for you."

Pavlos Doukas relaxed, his job nearly done. He anticipated accompanying Loverboy on the jet with Raisa. They would drop her off at the Fortress, and he would spend time with Jaca after collecting the balance on the job, $400,000. Pavlos called Jaca. "I saw your text. What can't wait until we meet tonight?"

"You carry a weapon?" asked Jaca.

"In my ankle holster," replied Pavlos.

"Loverboy has instructions to kill you," said Jaca. "They know you work for another gang."

Pavlos arrived at the jet and was met by the former FSB officer. "All went well?" Loverboy asked.

Pavlos nodded with a smile and opened the van doors, saying, "You take the ankles and pull." Loverboy leaned inside the van, and Pavlos promptly shot him behind the ear. Pavlos placed Raisa on the tarmac and rolled Loverboy inside the carpet. He hefted Raisa over his shoulder, came aboard the aircraft, and handed the pink phone to Karpov. "This is for Ivan," he said.

The stewardess directed him to put the teenager in a chair. "Where's Loverboy?" she asked.

Pavlos shrugged. "Change of plans; Ivan's orders," he said. "He wants Loverboy at the Army Munitions Group and left in a cab. Call Ivan if you dare." Both Karpov and the stewardess turned away. Pavlos shrugged again and left. He put the van in long-term parking with a dead Loverboy in the back. With a different passport, he purchased a one-way ticket to Amritsar International Airport in Northern India, as far away from the Sakarovkh as he could get. The $400,000? "Bad debt," he said to himself.

51

Day 25
The Southampton Inn, Southampton, New York
Thursday, October 12
Fifteen-thirty hours

addy had arrived in Frankfurt, Germany, Thursday morning at 1 a.m. She checked into the Airport Hilton and dialed her mother before collapsing. "This is Horizon Vacation Resorts," she said.

"I'm listening," said Sasha.

"Your reservation will arrive at the 'Restaurant' at fifteen hundred hours tomorrow, your time. Can you meet them?" said Haddy.

"Yes. I'll be there," replied Sasha.

Using her Leah Berenson identity, Haddy passed through German customs, doing her best to stifle the pain. Though it took nine hours, she rested as best she could and arrived at JFK International Airport at noon. Haddy hailed a private limousine to the Southampton Inn, the "Restaurant," and watched the familiar scenes sweep past along the Long Island Expressway. Trying to make sense of the darkening forces gathered against her, Haddy wondered if those who tried to assassinate her at the Lacoste Bar and Grill were of the same Sakharov syndicate. Using her laptop, she googled the name and found a worldwide network of ruthless Ukrainian mobsters, who had their enemy skulls dipped in gold.

Haddy arrived at the inn two and a half hours later. A light mist fell on the windows as clouds rolled in from the gray Atlantic. The stretch limo emptied her out at the Southampton Inn, a home of happy memories. The salty fresh air was familiar, and ponderous waves thumped nearby. Haddy scanned the area. She asked the receptionist for a corner booth. She took a seat after freshening up in the restroom and teased strands of blonde hair across her face. Haddy smoothed out the cashmere dress and adjusted the Hermes scarf around her neck. In the booth, she glanced at the tables full of diners through the sunglasses. A soft Vivaldi concerto filled the room, and sweet lemon scented the air. Subdued conversations rose amid clinking glasses and porcelain dinnerware. Waitresses bustled about with quiet professionalism.

Recognizing Sasha's stylish blonde bouncy ponytail, fitted black Milano knit poplin jacket, and white silk blouse, Haddy lifted her hand.

Sasha approached cautiously, sensing danger, and said, "Can I hug you?"

Haddy stayed rooted against the leather cushion, stiff beyond measure and full of pain, and replied, "Not a good time."

Sasha took the hint and sat down. "That's a terrific disguise," she said. "I didn't recognize you as a *Vogue* model. The hat, the scarf, and the cashmere are gorgeous." She reached over and teased away a few strands of the blonde hair from under the brim.

Haddy pushed the hand away. "I'm a mess. Stop."

"I've been worried sick about you," said Sasha, "but Dr. Adina did a fabulous job, though your skin is red and scratched." Leaning closer, Sasha continued, "My bodyguard left this morning. I talked with David, and the same thing happened to him. Is that good?"

"David has the music box?" asked Haddy.

Sasha nodded as the waitress bustled up with menus and water. Comparing the two women, she said, "Mom and daughter day?"

"We're working on it," said Sasha. "Tomorrow's her birthday."

"You deserve cake," the waitress replied. "Free for all our birthday girls."

Haddy took a short breath to avoid the rib pain and winced. "Just what I need."

"Two servings of lox and bagels, with extra cream cheese," said Sasha.

"Double my order, with a big black coffee," added Haddy.

The waitress left with the order. Sasha said, "I know the timing is bad, but it can't be avoided." She reached in her purse and produced a card and gift-wrapped present. Looking at Haddy, she said, "I believe in you."

"Yeah, bad timing, Mom, but that's okay; things are tense."

The waitress arrived with the order and addressed Haddy. "We serve lemon meringue pie," she said. "And Bavarian triple-layer chocolate or strawberry shortcake."

"Chocolate with chocolate sauce, and hold the cake," said Haddy. After the waitress left, Haddy continued. "I found the music box online. It was purchased by Father in 1989. He sent it to David before he died. I've got to get it."

The waitress served their food. After she left, an astonished

Sasha leaned closer and said, "You ready for something freakier? The boy? The one in flames? I think I found him. I mean, I don't know what he looks like, but two weeks ago, the *New York Times* carried a story about an NYPD detective on loan to the police in Odessa, Ukraine. There's a photo of him when he was a boy. He's getting married to Miss Kathryn Brock Saturday in Odessa."

"My 'burning boy' will get married this Saturday? Good to know," said Haddy sarcastically. "Now get real, focus on the box."

Sasha lowered her voice and said urgently, "You've got to read the article and see the picture. It's in my purse, but ..." Haddy recognized her mother's telltale "I've got a dream" look. Sasha gripped Haddy's wrist and continued, "Don't be cross. Hear me out, but after you called last night, I had a dream about Raisa."

"I want to hear every word," said Haddy. "Promise, but I've got to pee."

52

Haddy rinsed her hands in the bathroom. She turned past the receptionist into the dining room to see a beefy brunette behind her mother. The woman had a Glock in her hand. Instinctively reaching for her own pistol, Haddy remembered tossing it and the knife into the trash at the Frankfurt Hilton restroom to pass through customs. Haddy erupted. She launched herself into a human javelin. With leg extended and right foot cocked, Haddy kicked the side of the assassin's head. The woman smashed into the table and hit the floor. Haddy grabbed her pistol and shot her. She reached for Sasha's hand, but her mother's eyes were wide with terror. Pandemonium fell upon patrons and staff alike. They stormed out of the restaurant.

Pulling her mother up and away, Haddy crashed through the exit at the rear of the restaurant. By now, the Atlantic winds had pushed low-lying clouds inland, bringing a cold rain. Before the door closed, Haddy saw a Hispanic male run into the dining room and fire a shot. Running with her mother in tow, Haddy stopped around the corner of the building and waited. In seconds, the man ran full tilt into the barrel of his dead partner's pistol. Haddy fired and fired again, until the gun clicked. She yelled at Sasha to open the Beemer, get in the passenger seat, and strap in.

Haddy squealed out of the parking lot and took a hard right on South Main as the sports sedan lost its grip and spun. She let the car right itself and swerved into Linden Lane, and from there headed for the familiar crushed oyster shell driveway of her grandfather's estate. They coasted to the entry as Haddy scanned the area. Strong breezes swayed the landscaped trees and bushes, and she studied them all, looking for hidden assailants.

Sasha sat next to her like a stone. "Watching you; it's the bloody dagger I birthed. I had a terrible nightmare about Raisa. Promise you'll call her or Stefan as soon as possible." Haddy ignored her and opened the car, but Sasha shouted, "Oh God! Hear me! Help me! Haddy, promise me!"

"Mom. I promise. Do you feel better?"

"Yes," said Sasha.

"Let's get inside," replied Haddy, "and get the music box, okay?"

The two-hundred-year-old brick mansion was dark as Haddy opened the front door. A chandelier responded to the light switch, while an ancient German clock gonged. The familiar smells of polish and household cleaners met her nostrils. The house was bathed in silence, though windows rattled in the wind. "David?" said Haddy and trod forward quietly on the slick oak planks.

Sasha whispered, "I'm sure he's in the library. You can smell the cigar," and called out, "David!?" Haddy rolled her eyes, ready to strangle her mother.

An aged male voice said, "I'm here!" and coughed.

Haddy and Sasha entered the soft white room. White subway tiles surrounded a fireplace in which two oak logs burned. Walls were lined with books. David sat in a worn leather burgundy chair with a Churchill-size cigar. A loveseat of the same make and model lay across from it. Between them sat an aged oak coffee table with a glass ashtray. "You okay?" asked Haddy.

"Oh my God, Haddy, you're safe!" exclaimed David. He got up and took her hands and went to hug her.

"It's good to see you, Grandpa, but not time for hugs," said Haddy.

"But you're hurt!" replied her grandfather. "Should I call my doctor? Can I get you anything?"

"Grandpa, I've been better, and as soon as I can, I'll see the doctor, but they tried to kill Mom."

"Sasha?" David exclaimed and helped Sasha to the couch. "Are you okay?"

"She's fine for now, but I can't stay long," said Haddy. "You need to get to safety too. There are assassins after me. Let's get away from the window. We'll all have to go into hiding until this situation resolves. Listen, I keep having visions of my father's music box. I left Israel to come here and find it."

"It's in the keepsakes room closet, in a shoebox. I'll get it," said David.

"No, you stay with Mom. I'll be right back."

Haddy entered the eerie antiquities room, filled with her grandfather's memorabilia. A pair of Norse throwing axes, three African spears, and an Amazonian blowgun hung on dust-filled walls along with an assortment of other keepsakes.

She opened the closet and pulled down the shoebox. As Haddy lifted the lid, the sound of shattering glass erupted.

Haddy grabbed one of the axes. She slipped off her black pumps and tiptoed down the hallway in stockings and cashmere. She wiped aside strands of blonde hair off her face and peeked into the white library. Sasha lay on her back, gasping for air as pink froth spilled from her lips. The door clattered back and forth as gales and rain swept in. A crew-cut attacker held a barrel on David's knee and said, "I have instructions to find the film. Talk, or lose the knee."

David quickly looked at Haddy, who nodded. "It's in the other room," he said. The man turned straight into Haddy's ax, which split his head in two. At the same moment, she heard the front door open.

Haddy dragged Sasha behind the curtains, while in the distance a man called, "Niki?" and continued coming closer. "Whoever you are, throw out your weapons." Haddy heard the faint creak of footfalls on the floor outside the library. She saw a faint outline from the overhead light in the hallway, a shadow of an attacker holding a pistol. Haddy removed the hand ax and chopped off Niki's head with a few swift strokes. She threw it through the open door and watched it bank off the opposite wall into the feet of the hidden assassin. There was no scream, but a quiet voice that said, "Niki, I'll kill the son of a bitch." Now certain of the assassin's position, Haddy fired three rounds from Niki's .45-caliber semiautomatic through the library wall. She heard a thump and poked her head around the door jam. A twin lay on the ground, gasping for breath.

"Fucking pile of shit," said Haddy, and put the barrel in his eye and fired twice.

Haddy took her phone and hit 911 and rushed to her mother. "Mom, don't move," she said. "The ambulance is coming."

But Sasha gripped Haddy's arm. "Call ... Stefan and take the article; it's in the white envelope in my purse."

Haddy nodded. She pulled out her phone and placed the call, "This is Horizon Vacation Resorts," and heard the strained and fevered voice of Stefan answer.

"Haddy? Can it be you?"

53

I t was getting late as Stefan put the finishing touches on his latest software system, which increased blast efficiency by 20 percent. After the bodyguard had left that morning, he remained in the hotel and then took a cab to his home-away-from-home, a coveted upper-story corner office at the university. He locked the door, but not before alerting the guards to patrol the halls, elevators, and stairwells around his office. Stefan turned on his favorite violin concerto, opened a bottle of vodka, and lit a cigarette. He toyed with his white iPhone, wondering if it was safe enough to at least check business-related emails, and decided it was "Time to get back to business." Stefan turned on the phone, locked down since Haddy's surgery. He groaned as he saw hundreds of emails in his box, something his secretary would handle. He closed it and made a hard copy of the plutonium detonation software. His phone rang. "It has to be Raisa," he said. "I hope she had fun."

"Hello?" There was no answer, but a text, which dinged. "That's strange." Stefan opened the message, which had an attachment. His heart stopped. Raisa sat blindfolded, strapped to a chair with a sign in her lap that read,

"Do not contact the police. Go to your apartment. Take a copy of your software. Await further instructions, and she will not be harmed."

The icy fingers of angina tightened on Stefan's heart. The elephant stepped on his chest. Sharp, needlelike pain radiated up the left side of his neck and down his left arm. Stefan fell on the floor, pale and sweaty. He underwent cardiac surgery six years earlier, and his doctors said the vessels would reclog if he didn't stop smoking, change his diet, and exercise. Stefan's hand shot into his pants pocket and withdrew the glass vial of nitroglycerin. Trembling and fumbling, he tipped four tablets beneath his tongue and collapsed. For the longest time, Stefan could only stare at the ceiling, before the medicine allowed oxygen to enter his heart. His breathing returned, and the pressure and pain receded. Stefan called his cardiologist. The answering service patched him through immediately. The doctor told him to stay where he was. He would send an ambulance for the hospital.

Stefan's mind sharpened. He wasn't dead yet, and now his chest tightened, not from fear, but cold rage. He spit out, "Motherfucking mob. Well, I haven't forgotten Afghanistan. Two can play this game. Raisa's captors wanted me for my software. When they get it, they will kill her and me. I'll fuck them bad."

Stefan shut off the iPhone. He pulled out the Boeing Black and called Captain Troyem. He got his voice mail, which meant the captain was on a big assignment. Stefan sent a text: *"911, 911, 911. Call back ASAP. Stefan D."* He dearly wanted to call Haddy, but didn't have her number. Stefan crawled up on the chair and opened his computer. With the sirens in the distance, he slowly but efficiently wrote in some new code in the software. Stefan heard the ambulance attendants come out the elevator when his phone rang. Caller ID: "Haddy Abrams."

54

Day 25
David Abrams Estate, Southampton, New York
Thursday, October 12
Sixteen-zero-five hours

"What's happening?" asked Haddy.

"Raisa's been kidnapped," replied Stefan. "They sent a text with a video attachment." Haddy swallowed her fury and waited as the file came through. She saw her cousin Raisa blindfolded in a dark room, with duct tape over her mouth, and taped to a chair.

Haddy read the message and said, "Call Captain Troyem."

"I tried. He didn't answer. It means he's on an assignment."

"What's your situation?"

"I'm going to the hospital," said Stefan. "I had a minor heart attack when I saw this."

"I'll call you back," replied Haddy.

In the distance, police and emergency response units fractured the cold rain and winds like the flight of the Valkyries. Haddy figured neighbors had reported the gunshots, but said to Sasha about her dream, "Damn, you're good. Like a crystal ball."

Sasha fell back and said, "Get the box."

Haddy raced down the hall, locked the door, and pulled off the lid. She picked up the ornate platinum and porcelain heirloom, on whose top lay a gold Star of David, while the Shema Israel in gold Hebrew letters proclaimed, *"Hear O Israel: the LORD our God, the LORD is one,'"* with a citation, *"Deuteronomy five-four-six."*

A ferocious pounding on the door broke her concentration. "Police!" someone shouted. When no one answered, they said, "Come out with your hands up!"

"Don't shoot!" Haddy yelled. "I'm coming out!" Haddy covered the heirloom and slid her phone beneath the shoebox.

She opened the door, and a female police officer held the pistol in her face. "On your knees." Firm hands cuffed Haddy's hands, patted her down, and rolled her over. "Honey, you're a mess. You're more blood than body."

"What's your name?" asked Haddy.

"Officer Barbara Cochran."

"How's the lady in the library?"

"EMTs have her out on the lawn. Life Flight's coming," said Officer Cochran and

led Haddy down the hall towards the dining room. As David passed her, Haddy whispered, "Get my cell under the shoebox. Read Stefan's text."

David Abrams found the phone and watched the video. Horrified, he entered his bedroom and locked the door. He took the tiny key from his top dresser drawer and unlocked his bookcase of rare first editions. He opened *The Letters of Vincent van Gogh* and removed a black leather notebook inside a hidden compartment. He found the "T's" and dialed. "Tamir?" he said.

A voice with the softness of a terrible lion, colored by years of smoke, replied, "Who is this?"

"David Abrams."

"Why are you calling me?"

"We're under attack," said David. "I'm sending you a text with an attachment. Watch the video."

The seconds dragged on until Tamir came back on the phone. "This just happen?" he asked.

"Within the hour," said David. He explained the assassins sent to kill Haddy and his family.

"Who's the girl's father?" said Tamir.

"Professor Stefan Danilenko of the Odessa National Polytechnic University. He collaborates with the Americans at the Lawrence Livermore HEAF on nuclear technology."

"*The* Stefan Danilenko?" gasped Tamir. "I'll call you right back." David locked the cabinet and headed for the dining room, past aging photos of David Ben-Gurion, and pictures of the 1967 Six-Day War and the 1973 Yom Kippur War. He ignored his blood-splattered library and the bodies of a headless assassin and his dead twin. David stepped carefully around the head and joined the others in the dining room.

Officer Cochran had cuffed Haddy to the dining room chair. Haddy's cashmere was sticky and stiff with dried blood. The gales battered the bay windows as Detective Jefferson, with hands like a catcher's mitt, leaned across the glass-topped table. He had Haddy's passport open and said, "Leah Berenson? My name is Detective Jefferson. We're short on time. Witnesses put you at the Southampton Inn with two dead, plus these two. Help me, so I can help you."

Haddy didn't hear a word. She was riveted by Chagall's *White Crucifixion*, which hung like a dead man on the wall behind the detective. Haddy remembered her rage-fueled rant at this spot after her rape where she "killed" God. "What have I done? You can't kill God," she groaned within. Detective Jefferson had stopped talking. The woman cuffed to the chair wasn't responding, but crying softly. He turned to David and said, "You acquainted with this killing machine?" and answered his phone. He listened intently for a few seconds and announced, "That's the Federal Bureau of Prisons in Brooklyn. The prison van's twenty minutes out."

"There's a mistake," said David. "She's my granddaughter and was helping me. Her name is Haddy Abrams. My name is David Abrams. We were viciously attacked."

Officer Cochran opened Haddy's luggage. "Detective Jefferson. We found this in the Beemer. This black purse belongs to the prisoner." The detective poured out the contents of Haddy's carry-on luggage. Rolls of cash, packets of one-hundred-dollar bills, and loose change scattered on the thick glass table. Haddy's additional passports fell out as well. Officer Cochran lined up the money and said, "Detective, want to take a guess?"

"At least $60,000," he replied. "And two more passports?" The detective opened them up and looked at Haddy. "Jael Benjamin and Abilene Kirsch." He turned to David Abrams. "You say she's your granddaughter named Haddy Abrams? Any ID to prove that, or any way to explain this money?" Detective Jefferson looked at Haddy. "For the moment," he said, "you are Leah Berenson, and the DEA will want a word."

Officer Cochran had opened Haddy's purse. She removed the *New York Times* clipping from the white envelope and showed it to Detective Jefferson, who raised an eyebrow. "Leah, what are you doing with an article about Detective Wolf James? I can understand the interest. If I was a woman of the manly man's persuasion, who wouldn't?"

Haddy lifted up her head and wiped her tears away. Detective Jefferson spread out the article. Under the headline, the photo of NYPD Detective Liam James showed him clad in dress blues for the Police Academy graduation, gazing out. His amber eyes were gold beacons in a stormy sea; his face, granite. Time's arrow stopped for Haddy, and the earth moved. Lava flowed from the steamy ocean of her belly into her loins. She recognized the eyes: Mr. Mt. Rainier. The detective put the clippings in the envelope. "Leah, or whatever your name is, he's not called 'Wolf' for nothing."

Haddy looked at Officer Cochran. "Barbara," she said weakly, "there were two pages. Can I see the other one?"

"Sure, honey." Haddy saw a second photo. Detective Wolf James as a boy, restrained by firemen as he tried to run across the street. On the other side, his family's shop and apartment, with his parents and sisters trapped inside, ablaze. Wolf James stood backlit by the inferno and appeared to be on fire.

Haddy threw her head back and wailed. "It can't be," she cried. "It's impossible."

"Detective James called earlier this week," said Detective Jefferson. "He asked if I'd stop by and check this place out. He's looking for Staff Sergeant Hadassah Abrams. Is that you?"

Haddy whipped her head in a race with her heart. She cried, *"He called about me?"*

"Maybe you are Haddy Abrams," replied the detective.

"What did he want?"

"To find out if you were alive." The prison van arrived. "Too late now. You can straighten things out in lockup. I'll forward your address to Detective James."

Officers helped Haddy up and escorted her to the van.

David's phone rang. He listened and gave it to Detective Jefferson. "It's for you," he said.

The detective narrowed his eyebrows in annoyance. He snatched the phone from David Abrams's hand. "This is Detective Jefferson of the Southampton Police," he barked. His eyes opened wide as he stiffened like a flagpole. "Yes, Captain. At once." Stunned, he turned to Officer Cochran. "Barbara, bring the prisoner—I mean the staff sergeant—back. Take off the cuffs and round everyone up. Our captain got a call from the police commissioner. We are officially out of here." The officers filed out as the gong sounded five. Outside, Detective Jefferson placed a call to Wolf James and left a voice mail, "Detective James, I have information on that Staff Sergeant Abrams you asked about."

55

Day 25
David Abrams Estate
Thursday, October 12
Seventeen-hundred hours

As the last vehicle spun down the driveway, a cloak of silence fell on the aged Southampton estate. Deep clouds and driving rain beat against the brick but didn't shake the old mansion, as Haddy examined the photograph of Detective James. With effort, she tore her eyes away and called Stefan. "How are you?"

"Exhausted. They've got me wired up to the heart monitor with an IV and oxygen, but I can talk a little."

Haddy refrained from telling Stefan of Sasha's condition. "Turkish air leaves JFK at one a.m. Friday. The earliest I can arrive in Odessa would be nine a.m. Saturday morning."

"You've been through too much already. Come only if you must; the captain will handle it."

"Get better," said Haddy. "Please, don't push yourself. I'll find Raisa." Haddy returned to page 14 in the *New York Times* article. *"Eight-year-old emigre from Odessa, Ukraine, Liam James looks at his family's funeral pyre. Grieving with tiny arms stretched out to a mother and father and sister caught in the upstairs bedroom in a dry goods store at 216 East 6th Street. Arson is suspected."* Turning back to page 3, she read, *"NYPD's Fighting Ninth, Odessa, Ukraine Join Forces. Odessa, Ukraine's Police Chief Artem Troyem found what he needed and more when he went to Captain Vincent Greening of Manhattan's Ninth Precinct."*

David joined Haddy for coffee and peeked over her shoulder, "The detective is not ugly," he said.

"Thanks," said Haddy sarcastically. "He's the burning boy I've seen holding dad's music box since the hospital. I've got to find him."

Haddy went to the bathroom. She redressed her wounds, washed her face carefully, and applied Dr. Adina's oil. The battle had reignited her headaches. Haddy gave herself more of the painkillers and antibiotics, when a fresh wave of fear hit her. Examining her face and torn-up body, she asked, "How can I think of meeting Wolf James? He doesn't know me at all. I look terrible. What would I say? We were meant for each other? How awkward. He'd take one look at this wreck of a body and turn away. What a fool." Haddy slipped into her running shoes, as her doubts continued. She had never been that concerned about her appearance, at least before the blast. Yosef and the Sayeret Matkal welcomed her as one of them, but Wolf James ignited a different set of passions.

Haddy took the music box to the kitchen, made espresso, and ate bagels and cream cheese. She examined the gem-encrusted box and remembered the killer saying, "Where's the film?" The music box might contain such microfiche, but where? The only man who might know was the boy on fire. He must know how to open it; otherwise, what was the point? Her mission was to find Raisa, but she would ask Captain Troyem to find Wolf. The papers said he and his bride were due in Istanbul after the ceremony. "Dammit!" Haddy shouted. "I need to find this man in so many ways."

David came into the kitchen. "You're wanted on the phone."

"Is it Stefan?" asked Haddy.

"No."

"Then not now," said Haddy.

David shuffled towards her with his cell phone in hand. "Take it."

Haddy grabbed the cell impatiently. "Who is this?"

The tone carried the icy coldness of command authority, which brooked no opposition. "Staff Sergeant Abrams, I'm Tamir Mizrahi." Haddy recognized the name immediately. The feared Mossad director continued, "What I'm about to say is classified. You understand?"

"Yes, sir."

"Your grandfather David and I worked at the Mossad for years on a secret mission code-named *Eichmann*. I handled your father Joseph in London when he worked for the London *Guardian*."

Haddy's jaw dropped. The coffee cup froze in her hand. "You knew my father? And my grandfather's an agent?"

"Both superb," replied Tamir. "When we have time, I'll share stories. That's not why I called. Israel faces an existential threat. You are the answer. The man who murdered your father twenty-seven years ago knows you. We think we know his identity. Now, while the trials of your family represent a detestable vendetta, until Raisa was kidnapped, this remained a sordid private affair. But things have changed drastically. This man *is* the Sakharov crime syndicate. He engineered Raisa's kidnapping to force Professor Danilenko to give him his latest nuclear detonation software. This fiend has built an arsenal of tactical nuclear weapons for use against Israel, starting in Jerusalem."

"When?" asked Haddy.

"Possibly as early as this Saturday." Haddy couldn't see the logic. How could she be an "answer"? Mossad, Israeli military intelligence, Unit 8200, and Shin Bet with American CIA assets would find and kill him.

"I don't understand," she said.

"We want you to find him," stated the Mossad director.

Haddy stared at the phone, her irritation boiling over. "Mr. Mizrahi, that's stupid. I'm wounded, deep-bone tired. I'm played out. If you can't find him, send in a kill squad, and kill the scientist making these things. You're an expert at that."

"We know the scientist and where he lives and works. We were close to killing him, but the Iranians poisoned the well and assassinated his lead software engineer. Army Munitions Group doubled the protection around this benighted genius. That is why this Eichmann must have Stefan Danilenko, to arm the missiles."

"How do you propose I find him?"

"He will find you, and when he does, we will take him."

"I'm a goat," said Haddy angrily, "tied to your stake?"

Tamir's voice tightened. "I have your file, Staff Sergeant. You are not called the Queen of Hearts for nothing. You possess beauty and a genius for weapons. You are superbly trained and disciplined, an elite warrior, the best of the best. But there was another Queen of Hearts, an ancient Persian queen named Hadassah, your namesake." Haddy groaned inwardly. The story of the Persian queen of the Emperor Xerxes was a part of her heritage. "He's going to hold this over my head like a stick," she thought, as Tamir Mizrahi continued, "That queen risked her life to stop the genocide of our race. As her uncle Mordecai said to her, I say to you, *'Maybe you were born for such a time as this.'"*

"You've signed my death warrant," declared Haddy.

"There are worse things." The line went dead, leaving Haddy stunned.

She turned to David. "Tamir wants me to go up in flames of glory. I'm not going to do it. My job is finding Raisa." Haddy inhaled the cigarette and continued. "You were Mossad? You're a sneaky bastard. With your intelligence network, you could have found my rapists."

"There were four and now there's one. But he remains hidden. I have clues, but my time has gone. When this is over, you will find him."

"You killed three?" said Haddy and fell into her grandfather's arms. "Oh my God, why didn't you tell me?"

"It wasn't a thing to tell."

"Amazing, but I need to rest. I fly out at one a.m." She caught the faint sounds of a helicopter and recognized the distinctive Boeing AH-6 "Little Bird" cutting through the winds and rain. Haddy ran to the window. The six propellers beat the air and set down on the lawn at the edge of Agawam Lake. She watched a man in a blue windbreaker with "FBI" emblazoned in white letters, run up and open the front door. "Staff Sergeant Haddy Abrams?" he asked. "I'm Agent Mohsin, FBI, escorting you to JFK." Haddy watched David place her luggage at her feet.

"Why am I surprised?" asked Haddy. "Why can't you or Tamir take 'no' for an answer? Who will look in on Mom?"

"I'll watch her," said David and pulled a letter from his pocket.

"What's that?"

"Your suicide note." David tore it up. "Like your cousin Raisa said, 'It's not you.' I put the other ax in your luggage with the music box." David kissed her cheeks and continued, "Thank you for saving our lives. I know you're beyond tired, but you can do this. Tamir would not have asked otherwise." David paused and then put his hands on Haddy's shoulders. The eighty-one-year-old veteran looked her in the eyes. "As for Detective Wolf James? I've seen the look. Watch yourself, young lady." David raised his eyebrow with a wry smile. "Don't get eaten up."

～

THE LITTLE BIRD sped like a falcon to the John F. Kennedy International Airport. It came to rest in front of a crème twin-engine *International Trading Partners*' jet. Agent Mohsin helped Haddy to the staircase and gave her suitcase to one of two male attendants who helped her inside. One adjusted her seat and said, "Welcome aboard, Staff Sergeant Abrams. I'm Roger, that's Yaseen. I'm a trained medic. We'll make your flight more comfortable. It's a seven-hour flight, and we gain seven hours. We're scheduled to arrive at Odessa International Airport at zero seven fifty hours tomorrow. We've been briefed and will help you find this madman."

The Gulfstream 650ER taxied and blasted aloft. It hurtled through the air, and thirty minutes later, Haddy pulled out her phone and sent a text, *"Stefan: am arriving Odessa International Airport, 0750 hrs., Flight 224 International Trading Partners, Gate III Executive Terminal. Haddy."*

Roger asked about her injuries and her pain. He touched her thigh, shoulder, and ribs and saw her wince. "Like I said, we have seven hours. Let me administer morphine. It'll help you rest." Roger injected the drug. The drowsy calm hit Haddy's system.

In the spreading dull haze, Haddy thought of Tamir and Israel. "Tamir will throw Raisa, Stefan, and myself overboard to stop this man. But I'm not planning on dying. And Mom? I saw the pink froth on her mouth. She's lung shot; not good. Will I find Raisa in time? I'm so angry … so angry … so very angry."

The morphine wafted in like a pleasing floral fragrance, and Haddy fell asleep.

Out of curiosity, Roger examined the ax in Haddy's luggage after hearing the story from Agent Mohsin. He picked up the birthday card from Haddy's lap. "Birthday's the thirteenth of October?" he said. "Well, Staff Sergeant, you are the ax, and you have one more head to chop off. I'll call you 'Lucky Norse Thirteen.'"

56

Day 26
The *Novarsk* Freighter, Pier Fourteen, Odessa Wharf, Odessa, Ukraine
Friday, October 13
Zero-three-forty-five hours

Captain Troyem's handpicked seven infiltrated Odessa's Pier 14 Thursday evening. They vanished into their assigned hideouts to lay a trap for the Rat. $60 million in Afghan heroin lay aboard the *Novarsk*, a large freighter, bathed in arc lamps and filled with cargo containers. Two snipers, clad in cold-weather military gear, had entered gantry crane cabs high above the wharf. Two others hid in a darkened tugboat, which like a sleepy toad floated next to the wharf. The final pair took positions at the end of the wharf on metal ladders. The steel rungs were affixed to the wooden, creosote-soaked timbers and disappeared into the murky waters below. Wolf and the captain entered a cargo container next to the *Novarsk*. They became comfortable and discussed the operation. "There won't be any negotiation," said the captain. "Rat will have a chance to stand down, but won't take it."

"Did the professor say anything else after I left?" asked Wolf, changing the subject.

The captain wasn't sanguine on the subject of Haddy Abrams; his sixth sense told him Stefan had lied to him about her death. "The Danilenkos are running from something. I called Raisa's high school. She hasn't been seen, but she's playing in the Odessa/Kiev tournament tonight. It's strange."

Wolf gripped his H&K G28, and checked his Kevlar, KA-BAR knife, and pistol. "I can't get Raisa's initial surprise out of my head. Maybe Haddy's in protective custody?" The captain rested against the rusting steel, while the moaning of harbor buoys punctuated the darkness. A cold drizzle had chilled the air since they arrived. The timbers were slick with water. "The wedding's on," said Wolf.

"Maybe you should postpone it?" said the captain.

"I love Kathryn, and without proof Haddy's alive, there's no reason not to. I suggested to Kathryn we marry in the US, but she refused. In the end, Haddy was a dream. Admittedly, a cayenne pepper dream, but I've been thinking. If we did meet, I might not like her. Hell, she might not like me, or say something like, 'I have someone already.' My worst fear is that Haddy will appear again, like at the wedding. When the minister asks if anyone has a problem with this match, she'll stand and shout, 'Yeah! I do!'"

Captain Troyem laughed quietly. "Yes, that's something she would do. Your phone's off?"

"The buzzer is on. I'll check my messages at zero seven hundred hours, and you?"

"The same."

Wolf glanced at his watch. "It's zero three forty-five hours.

Your informant said zero four hundred? In three hours, I'll be gone. It's hard to believe. By tomorrow afternoon, I'll be on the sandy beaches of the Bosporus."

"You said Kathryn's a stickler for cleanliness," said the captain. "Did you get Oksana to clean the place up after we left?" Wolf shook his head, worried over the glitch in planning. The use of his penthouse by eight men, who left ashtrays full of cigarette butts, urine and shit around the toilet, and dirty towels and garbage plus gun-cleaning supplies and bullets hadn't been addressed. The kitchen counter and sink were strewn with coffee cups, coffee supplies, beer cans, and empty bottles of vodka, which piled up fast. Strung out with nervous exhaustion over Haddy and Kathryn, Wolf hadn't the energy to clean the place up. If Oksana had shown up, everything would have been fine, but she had called in sick.

"The place is a pigsty," announced Wolf. "If Kathryn touches the door, she'll stick to it. If she walks into the suite, she'll either leave or make gin martinis. But her flight arrives at zero eight zero four hours on the money. I'll be gone at seven, clean up, and meet her and steer her away from the penthouse until other cleaners arrive."

"They're here," reported the lookouts on the tug to the captain. "Three stretch limousines full of men. The guard's letting them through. One went to the end of the wharf, one stayed at the gate, and the second is coming towards you."

Wolf checked in with each officer and said, "Wait for the captain's signal," and left the door of their cargo container slightly ajar. He heard the second limousine stop. An armed man got out and signaled the *Novarsk* wheelhouse with a powerful Maglite. A few moments elapsed until a burly man, bundled up against the elements with a thick woolen peacoat, trundled down the stairs alongside the freighter. No words were spoken, but he shone a light on a container stenciled with "*ISO 6346 Agripul Agricultural Machinery.*"

The limo emptied, and two men with bolt cutters opened the metal box. From their position, Wolf and the captain watched them tear apart a large wooden crate. Inside were tractor parts. Rat's men attacked them with power tools. As the screws came out, sheet metal fell away from the farm equipment, revealing large white packages wrapped in plastic. Wolf watched Rat get out and slip a knife inside one. He licked the powder and grunted with a smile. He nodded to an aide, who produced a suitcase. The *Novarsk* skipper opened it. Even from fifteen feet away Wolf could see bundles of cash. The skipper walked up the iron staircase, $60 million richer.

"Ready?" asked the captain. Wolf nodded, and the captain walked out, holding a Mossberg pump action shotgun at Rat. "Good morning," he said calmly. "Rat, you are surrounded. Put down your weapons." Wolf joined him. Like a fox, Rat sprang inside the Agripul cargo container. Wolf gave the command through his comm-link, "Go. Go. Go," as the captain let go three blasts with the shotgun. In rehearsed synchrony, the tugboat wheelhouse window opened, and a M249 automatic weapon opened up. One officer fed two hundred round- disintegrating belts to the machine gun, as it shot seven hundred fifty rounds per minute. The bullets shredded the limousine and Sakharov associates at the gate and warehouse wall. The two officers, underneath the pier, popped up like jack-in-the-boxes with Israeli Micro-Uzi submachine guns, equipped with fifty-round box magazines firing twelve hundred rounds per minute. They chewed up the first limousine, but a few Sakharov associates were able to return fire. Snipers in the cranes zeroed in on the men around Rat's limousine.

Wolf grabbed his sidearm and ran up to the cargo container. "Come out and drop your weapons, or don't. I'll fucking kill you here." Rat stayed hidden when Wolf heard the distinctive eggbeater whir of an attack helicopter. It burst through the fog over the warehouse roof, and like a dragon from its lair, shot a bright beam of light followed by a hail of lead from a side-mounted mini-gun. Wolf and the captain dived behind the cargo container as thousands of rounds churned up the dock. Wolf caught a slug in the arm as the helicopter pilot aimed at the tugboat. The toady boat burst into flames. The helicopter pilot turned the mini-guns on the gantry cranes and decimated the snipers before aiming at the end of the wharf. The two officers dived in the water.

Rat and a Sakharov associate piled into the limousine, leaving the heroin behind. The tires smoked and rubber burned as the car fishtailed away. The mini-gun paused for any prey to show itself. Wolf took the challenge. He stepped into the brilliant halogen spotlight of the helicopter and emptied the H&K magazine into the copter's window, then pulled out his M17 sidearm and continued firing. The whap-whaps of the whirling blades wavered. The helicopter pitched, yawed, and climbed high above the wharf and suddenly nose-dived into Rat's limousine. Shielding his face from the explosion, Wolf dashed towards the inferno and collided into a Sakharov thug, who flung massive fists into him. Full of fire and fury, Wolf grappled the mobster down. His hand found his KA-BAR and struck with all his might, sending 10 inches of steel into his attacker's belly. He pushed off and joined the captain at Rat's side.

The Sakharov king lay a few feet away from the burning wreckage. Wolf took one look and set his jaw to harden himself against the ghastly sight. Years of war hadn't made it any easier to see someone horribly burned. Most victims died instantly, but a few hung on. The flames of the explosion melted Rat's face and hands away. His ears, nose, and mouth were gone, leaving two tiny eyeballs glittering in the dawn sky. The skin about his forehead and cheeks was fried to a crisp. His teeth remained, but it was a horrific death mask. Rat's eyes focused on Wolf. Barely able to breathe, he said, "Your father disrespected us. I sent the Enforcer. He'll find you and dip your head in gold. We have nuclear weapons."

Wolf stared in shock but didn't reply. Rat choked on his fluids and died. Wolf looked at the captain and said, "Did he say 'nuclear weapons'?"

"Yes."

The sun poked through the low-lying clouds and illuminated the carnage. A breeze cleared the fumes as fire personnel arrived and showered the wharf with water. Wolf checked his phone: zero six fifty-five hours and no messages, a good sign, but nuclear weapons would override any wedding plans. Oblivious to his bleeding arm, beat-up face, and cut chin, Wolf entered his cruiser restless.

Captain Troyem raised a cautionary finger to Wolf and said, "Let me check messages first." He immediately heard Stefan's frantic midnight voice message and saw the accompanying video of Raisa. The captain groaned and called Stefan immediately. He motioned for Wolf to wait and said to Stefan, "I'm here."

A tired voice replied, "I knew you were on an operation, but you saw the video? My friend, I had a minor heart attack when I saw this. I'm in the hospital ICU with extra protection. I tried to delay responding to these motherfuckers. I sent them a message early this morning and told them where I was, and that I couldn't move. I haven't heard anything back, but knowing these fuckers, they'll mount an attack and take me away. I have one more thing to say, and don't be angry. I got a call from Haddy last night."

Captain Troyem rubbed his face a few times. "My God, I knew it," he said.

"We swore an oath of silence to the Shin Bet," said Stefan. "Haddy's arriving at Odessa International Airport, Executive Terminal Gate Three, at zero seven fifty-three hours. It's a private flight registered to International Trading Partners."

The captain checked his watch. "You talked to her?" he asked.

"No. It was a text," replied Stefan.

"A text? Stefan, you know the ways of espionage," replied the captain. "Let's hope it's Haddy, but I won't know for sure until I see her. I'll send detectives to the hospital. Await my call." Captain Troyem hung up, thinking, "That jet arrives in less than fifty minutes. Mossad, no doubt." The captain returned to Wolf with a strange hope that Haddy would step off that plane, but the captain had been fooled before. He said, "Wolf, I'm sorry, but ..."

"What?" barked a wary Wolf.

"Raisa Danilenko has been kidnapped, engineered no doubt by the Sakarovkh to get to Professor Danilenko."

"Who's an expert in nuclear weapons," replied Wolf.

"I just learned the Mossad is sending in an agent to find Raisa and by extension Stefan. We are talking nuclear war. I can't compel you. We had an agreement, but assisting this agent would be invaluable."

"Murphy's Laws of Combat, 'No PLAN ever survives initial contact,' and *'A five-second fuse burns in three seconds,'"* flashed through Wolf's mind. "I'll take care of it, Captain," he said. "Kathryn will just have to understand."

57

**Executive Terminal Gate Three, Odessa International
Airport, Odessa, Ukraine
Zero-seven-fifty hours**

Roger jostled Haddy awake at zero seven hundred hours, fifty-three minutes from Odessa. While the Gulfstream's twin turbofans hummed, Haddy asked Roger about Sasha. "We got an update an hour ago. She's out of surgery and in the ICU, condition still critical. We prepared you food." Haddy checked her messages and found one from Captain Troyem. "Haddy, sending an officer to pick you up," it said.

Haddy washed her face. She put on the hoodie over the blonde wig, black shirt, and compression pants. She ate her fill, and afterwards, Yaseen said, "I put a fifty-thousand-volt black Taser, a Glock, and a Navy Seal MK-Three blade in your belt, and resupplied your migraine and non-narcotic injectables."

The wheels touched down on the grimy cement runway, as

Haddy chewed on her finger and lower lip. At the last second, she applied some bloodred lipstick, not knowing exactly why. Out the windows, sunny shafts of light broke through the light gray overcast. Yaseen opened the door and lowered the staircase. The sounds of jets and electric luggage and mechanic carts were familiar, but she lowered her sunglasses and covered her eyes with her hand, expecting to see a police officer. "Yaseen, I don't see anyone," she said, and then caught movement. A man had swung through the gate doors, bearing an uncanny resemblance to Detective Wolf James. Not clean and neat and dressed in NYPD blues, but clad in fatigues, his arm bandaged and face bruised and bloodied. He wore a cognac bomber jacket. Haddy's breath caught. Her stomach dropped. With sunglasses perched on her nose, she stared at the man with amber eyes, who saw her and stopped mid-stride.

The stutter-step saved Wolf, as a bullet singed his scalp. He hit the pavement when a second round slammed into his chest. Galvanized into action, Haddy scanned the runway and yelled, "Roger, Yaseen, sniper at the fence line!" and emptied her Glock at the assailant. The Mossad agents opened the weapons locker, ran out, and engaged the assassin with Tavor 7 assault weapons. Haddy slammed home a fresh magazine into the pistol. Roger ran out to Wolf, but Haddy's fingers, like the claws of a tiger, grabbed his shoulder and pulled him away. "He's mine! Get the shooter!"

Haddy pushed over the lifeless body. She ripped off the jacket and saw the Kevlar vest. It had stopped the bullet, but the force stopped Wolf's heart like a sledgehammer. "No fucking way you're dying on my watch," Haddy said. She wiped the blood off his face, tipped his head back, and listened for a breath. Nothing. She jammed two fingers against his neck. *No pulse.* Haddy pinched his nose, covered his mouth with her own, and blew twice. She locked her elbows and gave the flaccid figure five powerful chest compressions, shouting,

"Wake up, you son of a bitch!" Haddy gave more mouth-to-mouth and yelled louder, "Breathe, you big bastard, breathe!" On the fifth round, frantic and on the edge of panic, Haddy saw Wolf turning blue. She raised a fist and slammed it into his chest with Krav Maga fury and cried, *"Live, you fucking pussy Ranger!"*

The big chest gasped, coughed, and moaned. Wolf gave his bushy head a shake, and his eyelids opened. All the volcanic tension inside Haddy, lying dormant for years, erupted. She took Wolf in her arms and cradled him with a passionate embrace. "Thank God, you're alive," she said. She took off her hoodie and made a pillow for Wolf's head. Haddy lowered her face within inches of his and waited for a reaction.

Wolf's eyes were glazed. He tried to shake off the confusion while kneading his sternum. "Dammit, did you have to hit me like Mike Tyson?" he said. Wolf rubbed his chest where the bullet hit. "And did you call me a fucking pussy Ranger?"

Haddy's lips hovered over Wolf's. Like a powerful magnet, she felt him pull her in. She wanted desperately to kiss him and release her steamy waters, but said, "Are you fucking complaining? I save your pussy ass and you're complaining?"

Wolf became aware of a woman staring at him. Her mysterious black eyes glowed with desire, and he refused to believe what they told him. "Have we met?" he asked.

Mesmerized by Wolf's golden gaze, Haddy lowered her voice to a sultry growl. Her lips quivered. "I'm Staff Sergeant Haddy Abrams. Pleased to save your raggedy Ranger ass."

Wolf's blood drained from his face. "No," he said. "That can't be. You're dead." Haddy's lips fell on Wolf's, and he responded like a starving beast. His hands took Haddy's face and pulled her down. The lightning they shared shocked them, head to toe.

Haddy's loins clenched in climax. She gasped, "That was freaking-ass unbelievable. So, am I alive or dead?"

Wolf had stiffened in orgasm, and warm fluid ran down his legs. He said, *"Resurrected,"* but thought, *"Kathryn's waiting, and I am so fucked."*

THE SOUNDS of police and ambulance vehicles rushing to the scene halted further intimacy. Squad cars raced to the fence, and officers cordoned off a dead assassin and questioned Roger and Yaseen. Captain Troyem screeched to a stop in front of Haddy and Wolf and gave them a quick once-over.

"I'm okay," said Wolf. The captain glanced out to the fence line. Shaking his head, he announced, "You two are open game. I'm sure Sakarovkh informants within the FBI, or Southampton Police, talked to Ivan. He followed Haddy from JFK here. Wolf, you heard Rat. Sakharov wants you as well."

"Raisa's my concern," said Haddy.

"That will wait," replied Captain Troyem. "Stefan is our immediate concern." The captain marched over to the EMTs and barked out orders; they returned with stretchers. "I'll issue a press release saying you're in surgery from gunshot wounds, and post guards. An unmarked cruiser will take you both to Wolf's suite out of the hospital rear loading dock."

Within a fast and furious twenty minutes, Haddy and Wolf were wheeled into the hospital and out back, and placed next to each other in the back seat. Haddy still had her purse and retouched her lips, brushed her hair, and freshened her fragrance. Her heart pounded as red-hot chilies of desire reignited. She yearned for more and had to get it, needed it more than air itself. Her rich pheromones and perfume flooded the space between them. Haddy felt the heat radiating off Wolf's body. She watched Wolf wipe the sweat from his fore-head, lean forward, and ask the driver to put on the air condi-tioner. He rubbed his palms on his fatigues. Suddenly, he placed rock-hard fingers on Haddy's thigh and squeezed. "You're under my skin and in my blood, and I don't know what the fuck to do. What the hell is that perfume?"

Haddy leaned towards Wolf and breathed, "Sexy, isn't it? Mr. Pirate," and thought, *"One more moment with that hand on my leg, and I would have gone again. If we were alone, I'd take him right here like a mare in heat."* "You're pretty banged up," she said. "Tell me about it."

"Soon enough," replied Wolf. Haddy watched as he lowered his head and moved his mouth silently, hearing a faint "Saint Joshua."

"Are you praying?" she asked.

"Yes," said Wolf. "Thanks again for the Maga CPR."

"You're welcome."

Haddy didn't know Kathryn Brock but saw Wolf between the proverbial rock (her) and hard place (Kathryn). In his eyes, she had risen from the dead, but she still must find Raisa, check on her mother, and have Wolf tackle the music box. The sedan pulled into the underground lot, and Haddy and Wolf went to the elevator. An accompanying officer punched the button. Haddy stole another glance at Wolf and saw her lipstick smeared across his mouth. She turned away with a smile.

"What's funny?" he asked.

"Nothing," she replied.

The elevator doors opened, and Wolf had the officers wait in the hallway, while he approached the penthouse door with Haddy. Wolf said, "This is a huge clusterfuck. If Kathryn's inside, she's royally pissed. It's a mess in there, and she's got a thing about germs. She probably looked inside and went to a hotel. If not, she's on her third martini." Haddy watched Wolf as he prattled on, delighted to watch the big man squirm. Wolf's bushy eyebrows narrowed, and he fixed Haddy with his best master sergeant scowl. "Stay behind me," he growled.

"Miss whatever-you-are. If she's inside, do you think for an eenie-weenie tiny moment, you could help me out?"

"Absolutely not," declared Haddy. "Why did you phone Detective Jefferson about me?"

Wolf ran his hands through his hair, and glared. "Dammit to hell. What a thing to ask at a time like this."

Haddy lowered her sunglasses and licked her lips. "You may hate me," she purred, "but oh, how you want me."

Wolf ran his hands over his hair one more time and said with exasperation, "Just stay behind me. And don't say anything." He toed the door open and put his mouth to the opening, saying sweetly, "Katy? Honey? I'm home."

58

Wolf's Penthouse
Zero-eight-thirty hours

Wolf pushed the door open a bit further. Haddy heard him say quietly, "Oh damn." She peeked over his shoulder. The drapes were closed, and the room was dark, lit only by candlelight. The sexy French singer Alizée was singing her hit song, "J'en Ai Marre!," while dancing on the television. A rich bergamot incense suffused the room. In the dim light, the curvaceous Kathryn Brock sat with one knee over the other, relaxing on the couch. She wore a black satin cape revealing a crotchless ebony lace teddy. A whip dangled from one hand, and with the other, she sipped a martini. A red box of sex toys and a glass dildo lay on the coffee table. A sultry voice read Anaïs Nin erotica from an iPad nearby.

Kathryn's head turned with expectation. When she saw Wolf's silhouette, she got up. "Wolfie?" she said. "I knew you'd be late. So I arranged for a cleaning crew. I am ready for you, darling, but what's that odor, and why are you standing at the door? Why is it open?"

"Katy, there was a situation at the airport," stammered Wolf. "I met an agent ... The captain ordered ... Oh hell, Staff Sergeant, come inside."

Kathryn turned on a lamp, saw the bloodied face of her husband-to-be, and shrieked. She wrapped the cloak around her as Haddy walked in and came face to face with the shocked woman. "Who the fuck," Kathryn stammered, "are ... you?"

Haddy removed the sunglasses. "Staff Sergeant Abilene Kirsch with Israeli military intelligence."

Kathryn stared, unbelieving. She blew out the candles, shut off Anaïs Nin and Alizée, and turned on the lights. She set down the martini and hurriedly closed the red box. "Wolf, please explain what's happening." Then she noticed Haddy's lipstick on Wolf's face. Anger rose like a tidal wave. Kathryn approached Wolf and wiped the lipstick from his mouth. "You dumb brute," she exploded. "You kissed this woman?" She wheeled and slapped Wolf.

Haddy stepped between them. "Miss Brock," she said. "There's a misunderstanding. At the airport, Detective James caught a sniper round in the chest meant for me. It knocked his heart out. I gave him CPR and got him back."

Kathryn tottered backwards. Turning frightened eyes at the man she loved, she said, "You died? Like dead, dead?"

"Shit happens," said Wolf, "but earlier this morning, I took out the man who killed my family."

Kathryn stumbled to find the right words, slurring through the gin, "Miss Kirsch, thank you for saving my fiancé, but you can't stay here." She turned to Wolf. "You've *ruined* the wedding. You're a mess. March into the shower. I need to call Daddy and have him postpone his arrival, maybe until next week. Don't you understand how important this is?"

"Katy, I apologize, but terrorists are after me and Miss Kirsch. Captain Troyem ordered us here for protection."

Kathryn's face went slack. She steadied herself and said, "Sit down, Miss Kirsch; make yourself comfortable. Can I get you something?"

"Water's fine," said Haddy. "Sorry to crash your party."

Kathryn went to the kitchen, dazed. "Yeah, shit happens. I need another martini. I can't fix you one?"

Haddy peeked out the windows to examine her surroundings, saying, "No thanks," and heard Wolf in the shower. She forced away the thought of joining him. "I'm really sorry this happened," she said.

Kathryn gave her an ice-cold glass of water and poured herself another drink. She raised the glass and said, "Thanks again for saving Wolfie," and fell back on the couch in a slump.

Haddy took in the glistening décor. The room felt cozy, while the views of the city and ocean were breathtaking. She glanced at the big black bed and thought of Wolf again, but stared at the Saint Joshua icon. "What is this? It looks original?"

Kathryn looked over. "It's a Russian icon from the thirteenth century. I can't understand Wolf's fascination with this stuff. I'm not spiritual at all."

Haddy noted the bookshelf chock-full of books. "Dante, Shakespeare, and Chekhov? Quite the literature buff."

"Wolf is in pre-law and is joining my dad's firm, Brock Investments. I just have to get him off the force and away from … guns." Kathryn looked at Haddy's holstered sidearm. "You wouldn't mind taking that belt off, would you?"

"Can't do, Miss Brock," said Haddy and stepped into the dining area. She saw a single artist's portfolio leaning against the wall. Untying the strings, she looked inside, saw three sketches, and placed them on the table.

Kathryn glanced over. "My God. You can't look at those," she said.

Haddy spread them out and marveled at their genius. The pencils and charcoals captured the model exquisitely while lifting out inner qualities of strength and beauty. "These are magnificent. Detective James drew these?"

"He exhibits on Bleecker Street, in ..."

"Manhattan, I know." Haddy was transfixed. At first, she thought the model was a doppelgänger, and thought how interesting it would be to meet someone who looked just like her. But on closer inspection, she saw the woman had a gap in her front teeth. Without thinking, Haddy's tongue flicked through her own, and the blood drained from her face. Her hand went to her throat, and she collapsed into the chair.

"Miss Kirsch," said Kathryn, "what's the matter?" Haddy went numb. Wolf James had captured her soul, like a perfumer who had distilled her essence. She saw white Antarctic wastes, prowling Amazon panthers, and Icelandic lava flows dripping liquid fire into the sea. Kathryn stood up. "Miss Kirsch, is everything okay?"

Haddy's mind flashed back to the ICU and the horror when she saw herself in the bedside mirror as Frankenstein, without a face or persona. The shame and disgust of that dark moment came back. But Wolf had found an indomitable, courageous woman of fire and ice, one full of beauty. In the drawings, Haddy saw herself not as a trauma victim, but as she used to be and could be. "I am the way Wolf sees me," she thought. Unable to control herself, Haddy sobbed.

Kathryn weaved over and stared at the etchings and Haddy. She traced the face and lips on the drawings and then, suddenly, grabbed Haddy's chin and sobered instantly. "Wolf's *first love*," she gasped. "You're *that* woman. Staff Sergeant Haddy fucking," and gathering her rage shouted, "fucking Abrams! It's all been one fat fucking lie! Wolf said he threw your ashes in the grave a year ago, but hey, no problem, you were alive. Then you 'died' again in some fabricated 'disaster.' You two have been in bed together, and I believed it all." Kathryn wheeled back to slap the tear-streaked woman.

Haddy's hand caught the wrist midair. An urge to strike back, to unleash her killer speed and destroy the woman standing between her and Wolf James rose. But Haddy dropped Kathryn's hand. She took off her wig. Kathryn's mouth opened in shock. Haddy peeled off her shirt and unwrapped the elastic bandages. She took off her tights, showing the bandaged thigh. After days in the dark waters of the Tyrrhenian Sea, fighting the *Astrea* crew and assassins in Rome and Southampton, Haddy's body was a mass of bruises and welts. The shoulder and scalp wounds and tiny hole in her head shouted, "Pain." Kathryn gasped and fell on the floor.

"I was blown up," said Haddy. "Detective James thought I had died, along with the rest of the world. It's on the Internet, and it's called witness protection, Miss Brock. For your information, I read about Detective James and your wedding in the *New York Times*. I'm scared to death by these drawings. They seem impossible. You have every right to Wolf. I get it, except I saw him in a vision. I was three days in a coma, and when I regained consciousness, I saw Wolf as an eight-year-old boy in flames, holding a music box. I thought I was hallucinating and so did everyone else, but the vision remained. It took me to Rome, where I learned about my murdered father, and then to Southampton, where I saw the *Times* article. I read about Detective James as a graduate of the New York Police Academy and saw him as a boy standing in front of his family's burning house."

Kathryn trembled. She stood up and touched the sketches again. "I'm a psychologist," she said. "I don't 'see' things. I'm terrified like you about these drawings. Wolf described the moment he saw you on the mountain, but he can't stop thinking about you. Jesus, we're supposed to get married, and here you show up with your lipstick on his face. CPR my ass.

Fuck you. You're a nightmare come to life. I'm fucking done with this shit. He could have been rich as fuck, and now he has you. Good luck with that."

Bursting into tears, Kathryn gathered her things together. Pausing at the entryway, she tugged off her engagement ring, a Tiffany solitaire. "Eighteen thousand dollars for this, and that dumb fuck threw the Brock fortune away." Kathryn placed the ring in Haddy's hand. "He's a hell of a person, but you know that. I never want to see or hear from you again." The penthouse shook as she slammed the door on her way out.

59

Wolf's Penthouse

Hazy steam billowed around Wolf as he stepped into the shower, unaware of the drama outside. As the water soothed his body, he didn't know what to do. He prayed for wisdom. Wolf had made a commitment to Kathryn and loved her, yet here was Haddy, and he didn't know her. He shook his head with dismay, still agitated after the earthshaking kiss at the airport. In the ride from the hospital, he knew had it not been for the other officers, he would have eaten Haddy alive. Wolf grew a lustful erection and turned the water on cold.

Wolf looked for fresh clothes. He'd been so preoccupied, he'd left them in the bedroom closet. He wrapped the bath towel around his waist and stepped into the apartment. Yellow sun poked its way into the suite through the skylights. It was deathly quiet. He saw Haddy standing at the entrance, staring at her palm, holding something he couldn't see. Her head was bare, with a healing wound. A sports bra showed a dressed shoulder wound and black-and-blue bruises over the ribs. She had on a pair of panties. Gauze covered a thigh wound. "Where's Kathryn?" he asked.

Haddy felt terrible. Kathryn was all a man could want and more: looks, brains, and money; and she loved Wolf. Yet other fears assailed her. The kiss said Wolf was real, but he had no idea who she was. Her course was set: to find Raisa and a madman bent on destroying her country. She risked death; the chances of surviving were slim to none. What kind of woman would woo him, knowing she might die? Haddy saw her future open to Wolf. She desired nothing more than to throw away her terrible call and go wherever Wolf bade her. She could lose herself in his arms, yet had no idea what Wolf would do and wondered about his love beyond the erotic. Would he have married Kathryn? Kept his word to her? Haddy needed a partner and protector as much as a hot body in bed. She saw Wolf and said, "Kathryn left," and showed him the ring.

Wolf beheld a ravaged face. His towel fell away. He went to her. "You're lovely," he said.

Haddy's eyes welled up. *"This is not the time for this,"* she thought, but threw her arms around his neck and gave her hips a shake. "Maybe it is the right time," she said to herself and announced, "I'm twenty-seven today," and kissed him.

Wolf kissed her back. He took the solitaire and held Haddy's ring finger. "Want a birthday present?"

Haddy's eyes tightened with resolve. She got control of herself and pushed it away. "I have a question. I want an answer. Would you have married Kathryn?"

Wolf looked Haddy in the eye and then pointed at Saint Joshua. "Yes. I am a man who makes commitments, and I stick by them."

Haddy melted and composed herself. "Then there are a few things you should know," she said. "I've danced with the devil all my life. I'm moody. I get angry and bite like a tiger. I like space. I can retreat into silence for hours. I hate mess. Sometimes I snore. I hate pineapple on pizza, and I want kids; do you?" Haddy exposed her neck and traced the fresh scar from the *tanto* knife. "I tried to kill myself a few weeks ago," and held Wolf at arm's length. "I've got a brain that tracks with Nietzsche, and I own all of Anaïs Nin. I'm desperately passionate, but if we do this, I want all of you, every part of you, and my greatest fear is I'll lose you, or worse, I'll lose you and watch you die. Is that what you want in a woman, a virtuoso?"

"I have you. I won't lose you again, ever," said Wolf. "And *you're* a pain in the ass? You haven't seen anything yet."

The hush deepened. Haddy laid her hands on Wolf's chest and felt a magnetic power pulling her in. She shivered against the granite physique, yet thrilled to a commander leading, shouting orders, obeying orders, and never backing down. Haddy bowed her head, overcome by his force, yet rising to the challenge. She extended her finger. Wolf slipped on the ring and kissed her again and attacked Haddy like a ravenous dog. Haddy peeled off her clothes and let Wolf roam and feed at will. She led him to the couch and gave in to the fierce honey of realized desire.

The lovers lay in each other's arms, drinking in the moment. Haddy's turmoil melted before his warmth, and her pelvis stirred again. She wanted more and led Wolf to the bed. Though her body ached, she ignored the pain. Haddy mounted her mountain man. With her hands on his shoulders, she settled down again in an easy back-and-forth rhythm. Gliders born aloft on great drafts of boiling air, Wolf and Haddy climaxed like firecrackers. They screamed together before crashing to Earth.

Wolf stroked Haddy's belly and said, "I met Kathryn and ended in Odessa. Captain Troyem saw the drawings and told me about you. I tried desperately to find you. Then he introduced me to your grandfather and Raisa. You can't imagine my joy: you were so close, until they spun some god-awful tale about the blast at the Lacoste Bar and Grill. It's been the worst week of my life; I started smoking—your fault, by the way." Haddy rolled off. She lit a Lucky Strike and gave one to Wolf. The postcoital pleasure of inhaling the sweet tangy smoke would cement this electric moment. He continued, "What's the matter, birthday girl?"

"You've no idea," she replied.

"I have a little," said Wolf. "Raisa's been kidnapped to force your grandfather to give some evil genius the ability to destroy Israel with nuclear weapons."

60

After showering, Haddy called Stony Brook Surgical ICU and learned Sasha remained in critical condition. She looped the solitaire through her mother's gold necklace birthday gift and let it dangle from her neck. Wolf had gotten dressed and came back with the throwing ax.

"It's a long story," said Haddy. She fixed coffee for herself and Wolf. "There's much I need to tell you." Haddy began with her vision of the music box and her belief it contained something hidden by her father, most likely film, which might hold a clue to finding the madman. She showed him the Raisa kidnap video and discussed Tamir's revelations. "Israel may be attacked tomorrow. Tamir assumes this maniac will come after me, and the Mossad will be waiting."

"You're the bait," said Wolf. Haddy nodded and set the

shoebox on the kitchen table. She removed the lid. "Here's what you were holding."

"Damn," said Wolf.

"My dad owned this box. He was a reporter and must have hidden evidence inside, like microfiche. Here's the Star of David with the gems on top and the Shema in gold letters on the front, but the citation's wrong. It should be five-six-four but cites five-four-six. I've thought long and hard about how to open it, but nothing comes to mind."

"The key is the citation," said Wolf. He picked up the music box and examined it closely. He remarked, "What do you think this is worth?"

Haddy shrugged. "With those gems? Five million?" Wolf pushed and probed along each surface and edge, but nothing would budge. He shook it.

"Don't break it," said Haddy. "It's a family heirloom." Wolf pulled out an extremely sharp utility knife and worked the joints.

"Don't scratch it," said Haddy.

"It's as tight as a drum, but the king's jeweler didn't make a mistake," said Wolf. "Five-four-six is a code. Did your father send David a special Bible? Maybe what we are looking for is in a Bible at this address?"

"Just the box," replied Haddy.

"'Hear O Israel: the LORD our God, the LORD is one,'" said Wolf.

"Why are you saying that?" said Haddy, irritated. Wolf went to his desk drawer and returned with a pencil. "What now?" she continued.

"Are you always so impatient?" said Wolf and kissed her. "Relax. Do you want another?"

Haddy pushed him away. "I am relaxed, you big brute. Get on with it."

Wolf flipped the pencil around and pressed each gold letter

of the Shema. They didn't budge. He counted from left to right and pressed the fifth word, then the fourth, and finally the sixth, and nothing happened. He reversed the process from right to left with no results. Wolf studied the top. The Star of David had six points, and at each lay a gem. He pressed on each. Wolf exclaimed, "*Did you see that?* The diamonds don't budge, but the others did a little. Let's try something." He pressed the eraser on the fifth gem, a ruby, then the fourth, an emerald, and finally the sixth one, a sapphire. A click was heard, and a concealed compartment under the Star of David opened.

"Fucking A," said Haddy in awe.

On a maroon silk bed underneath the Star lay six rolls of microfiche. "There's your clue," said Wolf. "Want to bet your father took pictures of his killer, the same one bent on destroying Israel? Tamir Mizrahi's jet comes equipped with a film developer. I'll call the captain."

Captain Troyem answered at once. On speaker, he said, "The kidnappers have Stefan. We placed locator beacons in his shoe, belt buckle, watch, and briefcase. They put him in an ambulance and tossed his stuff on the road. We followed them to a warehouse. Three white vans came out separate exits, each one going to another warehouse and splitting into three other vans. We lost him." Wolf described the discovery of the microfiche. "At the moment," replied the captain, "that's our only lead. Call me from Mizrahi's jet."

61

Wolf's Penthouse
Ten-hundred hours

Wolf dressed Haddy's wounds as she worried over Stefan. "They'll kill him and Raisa once they have his software." They armored up, and Haddy tucked the ring under the tight-fitting T-shirt.

Wolf gave it a pat and said, "Ready, partner?"

"Hold me one more time, and don't squeeze the ribs," said Haddy. She closed her eyes and soaked in the strength of his embrace. "Now I'm ready."

Wolf turned the doorknob just as the doorbell rang. He peeped through the hole. "Unbelievable. It's Miss Ivanova from across the hall. She asked me last week if I'd talk to the captain about a bodyguard. Miss Ivanova couldn't have timed it worse. She's engaged to a famous nuclear physicist."

"I thought the officers were out there?" remarked Haddy.

"Watching the elevator."

"A nuclear physicist?" Haddy asked suspiciously and touched her Glock. "Perhaps the man responsible for these missiles is a few steps away? Should I kill him?" she asked herself. "Crack the door and see what she wants," said Haddy.

Wolf opened the door an inch. Haddy watched the pointed toe of a gleaming black shoe wedge itself in the door.

"You said we could talk," said Brianna. "If I needed help. And—" a tight-fitting expensive outfit followed the shoe "—I do." The woman squeezed in, and Haddy observed the gazelle-like form of Brianna Ivanova. Haddy stiffened, caught off guard by the glamorous appearance, but couldn't deny the fierce look of determination from the most seductive pair of cinnamon eyes she had ever seen. The green snake of jealousy bit Haddy, and she instinctively moved in front of the vixen.

Brianna saw the fierce black gaze block her way. She arched her eyebrow, poked her tongue inside her cheek, and tapped Haddy's ring. "Stand down, tiger," she said coolly. "I'm not your enemy."

"What do you want?" said Haddy. "You've got thirty seconds."

Brianna addressed Wolf. "We spoke earlier about Professor Stefan Danilenko. Both he and my fiancé are in trouble. Thirty minutes ago, François got a call from Ivan Juric to join Dr. Danilenko at the Army Munitions Group medical clinic. Ivan spun some lie that Dr. Danilenko can help François complete his project."

"Who are you again?" said Haddy.

"My name is Brianna Ivanova. My fiancé is Professor François LeCompte, a nuclear physicist."

"Professor Danilenko is my grandfather," declared Haddy. "I know about the missiles. Come inside and explain this."

Brianna went to the coffee table. "I will show you something," she said. "François assured me he had everything in control, but I'm not convinced." She spread out François's paper-napkin doodles.

Wolf and Haddy paled as they zeroed in on *"Jerusalem in flames from X3s"* and *"4 p.m. 10/13."* "Sixteen hundred? That's six hours," said Haddy. She jammed her finger on the paper in rage. "And you love this man? When I notify the Mossad, they'll kill him; if they don't, I will."

"That's nonsense," said Brianna coldly. "Ivan Juric is behind this." She explained Ulyana's kidnapping and her forced seduction of François to join AMG. "If Ivan knew I was here, he'd kill my daughter, but François is a genius. He does not want to destroy Jerusalem or lose Ulyana."

"Then what's the meaning of these drawings?" demanded Haddy angrily.

Wolf placed a hand on Haddy's arm and said, "Brianna, tell us about this Ivan."

"He's the Enforcer of the Sakharov crime syndicate," said Brianna with undisguised hatred.

Wolf shuddered. "Rat said the Enforcer killed my family."

"The same man," said Brianna.

Haddy's chest tightened. Her knees gave way, and she sat down. She saw another piece of her jigsaw appear. Through clenched jaws, she spit, "He murdered my father and has Raisa." She pulled out her phone and called Tamir Mizrahi. "We have terrible news. The attack? It's not tomorrow, but today at sixteen hundred. Professor François LeCompte is the nuclear physicist who designed the rockets, but if you can believe his fiancée, he's helping us. We also found six rolls of microfiche hidden by my father in his music box."

"Take them to Roger immediately and report," said Tamir.

Brianna's phone rang. "It's François," she announced. "Darling, I'm with the Ranger I told you about and a staff sergeant in the Israeli Defense Force. She's Stefan's granddaughter. I'm putting you on speaker."

"Professor LeCompte?" said Wolf. "Have you seen Professor Danilenko?"

"Ivan Juric called me," said François. "They took the professor to the Army Munitions Group medical clinic. I'm to meet him and get his software. The rockets are scheduled to launch at four p.m., but I can't let that happen. Ivan has Brianna's daughter."

"I'll coordinate with Captain Troyem to get you and Professor Danilenko out," replied Wolf. "And for God's sake, disarm the missiles."

Haddy addressed Brianna with softer eyes. "Miss Ivanova, thank you. Now go back to your apartment. Wolf and I will handle things from here."

Brianna blockaded the door and exclaimed, "Ivan has my daughter! Find him and you'll find your Raisa." She took out the Ruger LC-9 from her purse. "I can use this and help you."

"We're soldiers, Brianna," said Haddy. "You've done your share. I'll find your daughter."

With an iron voice of fierce pride, Brianna said, "Maybe you think I'm weak, because of my looks? I'm a stupid ditz who only can swing her hips?" Brianna flicked ten razor-sharp fingernails inches from Haddy's face and continued, "But I won't hesitate to scratch your eyes out if it means finding my daughter. This is my fight as much as it is yours. I know Ivan Juric and how he thinks. I have sworn to kill him, protect my fiancé, and get back my daughter. Now, stop wasting time. The officers in the hallway can take Wolf to Captain Troyem. I'll escort you to the airport in my husband's car."

Haddy took Wolf aside. "I don't like it," she said. "I don't work with amateurs."

"Lay down the law," Wolf replied. "You are in charge: use her."

"Okay, but keep your eyes off those tits."

Wolf kissed her. "Jealous?" he replied. "Hmm, I like that, but you've got nothing to worry about, firecracker."

Haddy cooled and thought, "Will my love for Wolf tear us apart?"

62

After a tortuous herky-jerky escape along bumpy city streets, into dark warehouses and being hustled from one van to another, the last few miles were paved and quiet. Stefan heard the driver say, "Building Thirteen," and knew he was being ferried to Army Munitions Group, a manufacturer of small arms south of Odessa.

In poor condition already, the ride drained Stefan. He lay blindfolded in a stretcher with an attached IV and oxygen and medications. When he was allowed to see, Stefan found himself in a spotless medical clinic. A nurse busied about the bedside as three men left the room and a young surfer joined him.

"Professor Danilenko?" announced the surfer. "I'm Professor François LeCompte. We met in Beirut."

Stefan glanced around and said, "Are they gone?"

"The guards went out back. I know why you're here," replied François.

"About my daughter?" said Stefan.

"Yes, it's extortion pure and simple for your software," answered François. "They also kidnapped my fiancée's daughter to force me to help them."

"I loathe them, but if I don't give you my software, Raisa dies," said Stefan.

François leaned closer and whispered, "We are not without our wiles. I have a plan."

"And so do I," said Stefan with a sudden gleam from his gray eyes. "My software is on this thumb drive; you have a fast computer?"

François nodded and opened the Getac X500. He strung out an Internet cord and plugged in the thumb drive. He texted Wolf that he and Stefan were in the AMG medical clinic.

Stefan observed, "I'm sure they're tapped into your computer."

"I know their tricks, Professor," said François. "Let's hope they don't discover ours."

63

Brianna gripped the steering wheel tight as she sped to the airport. She said, "Let me tell you about myself."

"You're a fashion model," said Haddy, "or a prostitute."

"I'm the highest-paid escort in Moscow, with a degree in Russian literature from Lomonosov University. I met Ivan Juric at Moscow's Platinum Girls Gentlemen's Club. He offered me $100,000 for one night of work. I accepted and never escaped."

"François knows?" replied Haddy.

"Yes, but he has a contact, I think with the American CIA. They told him everything. Haddy, escorts long for love like any woman. I found it six years ago with a Spanish prince and gave birth to Ulyana, but his family rejected me. François is different. In spite of my betrayal, he loves me and proposed marriage. Did you ever model? You have the look. Intense, muscled, and lithe. Swimwear, I bet."

"This woman is sharp," Haddy said to herself. "Anything else?"

"You've suffered, and I'm not talking about your injuries."

"That obvious?" replied Haddy.

"We speak the same language," said Brianna. "What's your sign?"

"Libra. I'm twenty-seven today."

"Auspicious," said Brianna.

"Brianna, I appreciate what you are doing. You know how to use that gun, but this is war." Haddy patted her pocket. "This film may lead to nothing, and you've wasted your time taking me to the airport. So, let's get a few things straight. You support me. You give me intelligence to find Raisa and Ulyana. Say yes."

"Yes," replied Brianna.

"If I say, 'Stand down,' that means, 'Stop what you're doing.' If you don't do what I say, someone could die. If you get in my way, I'll drop you. Questions?"

"And François?"

"If ordered, I'd kill him."

Brianna's shivers traveled down her back. "I hope that won't be necessary."

They parked, and as they walked among the throngs of travelers to the Executive Terminal, Haddy noticed the crowd part for Brianna. The escort swung her legs easily, turning heads left and right. Haddy thought, "Use the woman; don't fight her."

The women came out Gate III. As Haddy neared Tamir Mizrahi's ITP Gulfstream, her thoughts focused. She cradled the music box and microfiche and said to herself, "This must be valuable, but how? So much has changed in thirty years. What my father recorded is likely history and nothing else." The women stepped aboard, and Yaseen and Roger greeted them, cool towards Haddy's guest. Yaseen gave Brianna water, and she took a seat. Haddy gave the Mossad operative the six tiny spools. Yaseen entered a small room where he enlarged the photos and sliced the negatives. He put them in a scanner and placed them on a ROM disc. Haddy gave the music box to Roger, who placed it in the onboard safe. She sipped on espresso. Yaseen came out a few minutes later and said, "Staff Sergeant, there are forty-one prints. The prime minister and Tamir need to see this."

"Important?" said Haddy.

"You have no idea."

Haddy sat in front of the computer screen and clicked on the first photo, which read,

"For My Precious Hadassah. I opened a Royal Bank of Scotland account, #10-10235448 under, 'Hadassah Abigail Abrams,' on August 1, 1991. The Trustee is Avery Galinsky of the London firm of Akin, Gump & Strauss LLP. I purchased 10,000 shares of each of the following stocks in your name: Apple, Inc., ($92,610.23), IBM ($187,810.65), Chevron ($112,300.19), Nike ($65,800), and Microsoft ($56,320.82). This can be accessed with suitable identification. The account will close if not claimed by 2030 and sent to next of kin."

Haddy stiffened and set down her coffee. She thought little of money, only training and obeying orders. Roger examined the document. He pulled up the share price of each stock. "Staff Sergeant," he said. "If these figures are accurate and you sold at the fifty-two-week high, you'd be $23,890,000, minus the initial investments, richer. Should I contact Avery Galinsky, or his firm?" Haddy stared mutely at the screen. "Staff Sergeant?" said Roger, nudging her shoulder gently, "do you have a will?" Haddy shook her head, numbed by her father's gift. Roger placed a piece of paper and a pen before her. "Keep it simple. Tell your survivors who gets this money, sign it, and I'll notarize."

Brianna overheard the conversation and said playfully. "As I said, 'auspicious.' It's your birthday, lucky thirteen. Congratulations."

A world of possibilities opened up, but if she died, the funds would go to David, Sasha, Wolf, and Shira. Haddy became dizzy as a new world beckoned. She wrote down directions and signed the paper. Roger procured his notary stamp. He placed the document in an envelope inside the safe. Tremulous, Haddy clicked on the second photo.

"OCTOBER 12, 1991. In London, I'm known as Aaron BenMenashe and write for the London *Guardian* on weapons manufacturing and trade. Contained therein are the stories of Jewish families defrauded of savings, belongings, and children. An unmarked package arrived on my desk, the summer of 1989. A phone with a video file showed a handheld rocket manufactured by the Army Munitions Group in Odessa, Ukraine. Eastern Machine Systems (EMS) owns the company. After much digging, I discovered the CEO of EMS is Daroghah Vulkan, referred to simply as 'X.' I pegged him the *Ukrainian Eichmann*.

"X creates layers of CEOs and board members to remain hidden. In the course of my research, I learned he *is* the Sakharov crime syndicate. In 1976, Daroghah Vulkan formed the Ukrainian Israel Travel Agency (UITA) to 'aid' Jews in their exodus. On Saturday, October 5, 1991, I witnessed the following aboard Vulkan's yacht, *The American Dream*.

"Above decks, Daroghah and his brother Rat were celebrating their Ugandan Defense Ministry arms deal. I had received an invitation to the party, which included a hundred guests, prostitutes, live music, and drugs. I stole into the engine compartment and searched for contraband and evidence. I had pried off the top of a wooden crate. A bill of lading, *421 New London House*, lay underneath. I had purchased a Minox B spy camera and took pictures, when syndicate thugs dragged a hooded figure down the steel staircase. Daroghah descended, took off his jacket, and rolled up his sleeves. He took a swig of vodka as his men ripped off the hood of a badly beaten and bloodied man. Daroghah nodded to his lieutenant, a man named Ivan Juric who stood by holding a human skull dipped in gold. Ivan handed Daroghah a pistol.

"'Do you recognize me, Vlasta Korovich?' asked Daroghah. The wretch begged for mercy. 'You know the penalty for traitors? We've taken your family.' The man started to vomit, but Daroghah jammed the barrel against his chest and pulled the trigger three times. He turned to his lieutenant and ordered, 'Take his head and throw the body overboard.' I captured everything on my camera.

"I feigned illness the next day and took a boat ashore. I flew to England and through Tamir met a locksmith at the New London House complex on 6 London Street. We entered Suite #421 and passed through a receptionist's room to a back room containing UITA travel brochures and file cabinets. I found hundreds of Jewish emigre documents and snapped photos with the camera. Outside, the knob rattled. I hid under the desk as a guard threw a flashlight beam across the room before leaving. I dashed home and put the microfilm inside a secret compartment in a Louis XIV music box I purchased in Rome. The dealer showed me the clever '5-4-6' code for depressing the ruby, the emerald, and the sapphire in the Star of David. I put the music box in my closet and hurried to the train station. I had to get to Odessa in time for Hadassah's birth.

"I took the Gatwick Express South to Gatwick International Airport. As I boarded Ukrainian International Airlines PS114 for Odessa, the airline announced the flight had been canceled. I returned to my apartment, called Tamir, and expressed my concerns. Why had the flight been canceled? Had I been discovered? The next day, I took the music box to the Royal Bank of Scotland and instructed the manager to send it to my father, David Abrams, in Southampton, New York, if I didn't contact him within one week. I informed Tamir of what I had done. He advised me to check into a hotel and wait a week.

"I'm going back to the airport. Tamir has no children. I must be by Sasha's side.

"Joseph Abrams."

Haddy thrust her head into her hands, struck by the enormity of this revelation. She had said to the voice at the pool, "To know ... why ... you killed my father when I was born." Haddy had her answer. Tamir counseled him to wait, but Joseph ignored it. She closed her eyes and heard her father say, "I love you." He had acted with courage and uncovered a secret worthy of the Pulitzer Prize. Haddy wanted to weep, to catch a plane with Wolf and go away and grieve, but now was not the time. She bowed her head in gratitude and respect for the man she never met and whispered, "Father, rest in peace, and thank you."

Haddy phoned Tamir. The Mossad director said, "Joseph was a superb agent. Israel will always be in his debt."

"Now we know the 'who,'" said Haddy, "but not the 'where.' Time is running out."

"The game's just started," replied Tamir. "I have an ace up my sleeve named 'White Vampire,' a white hat/black hacker in Unit Eighty-Two Hundred. Expect a call."

64

Haddy went outside to smoke. A light rain blew off the sea, and she wrapped herself in the windbreaker. She thought of Wolf with their lovemaking fresh in her mind. "Wolf, I command you to not die. Do ... you ... hear ... me?" Using the plane as a shield, she lit a cigarette.

Roger poked his head outside. "Staff Sergeant, Tamir's in touch with Captain Troyem. Detective James will need me and Yaseen."

"Detective James is coming here?" asked Haddy.

"Another officer will pick us up."

"Where's my backup?"

"Tamir's making calls. He alerted the Sayeret Matkal at Mitzpe Ramon, but until we know more, he can't make firm plans."

Haddy touched the throwing ax, hanging at the belt for

reassurance. She knew any full-scale assault would risk the lives of Raisa and Ulyana, while the surprise and stealth of a small team often triumphed.

The Executive Terminal catered to private jets. Tamir's beige Gulfstream was parked at Gate III. Haddy puffed on the cigarette while, without thinking, she walked towards Gate I. Her cell phone buzzed.

A prepubescent boyish voice, that of someone who sounded all of ten years old, spoke rapidly. "Staff Sergeant Haddy Abrams?" he said. "The sniper who shot herself into the record books, late on the *Astrea* with travels to Rome and Southampton, I'm Vampire. How can I help?"

Haddy was astounded. "How can you possibly know that?" she said. "Don't bother, I'm impressed. I'm sending you a video of my cousin Raisa. I received it last night at twenty-three hundred hours. Find her, and we find my father's Ukrainian Eichmann."

"On it," declared White Vampire.

Haddy retreated behind a luggage cart as a gust of wind swept across the tarmac. Suddenly, a gleaming black jet taxied past her to Gate I. On the tailfin in gold letters read, *"EMS, Eastern Machine Systems, Inc."* Haddy walked closer. She observed a pilot come down the stairway and walk to the terminal followed by a flight attendant, who met her replacement. Haddy called White Vampire and said, "I need an airline registration for R-R Three Five Two E."

"Hold it." There was a pause before the hacker said, "Here it is: *Eastern Machine Systems, Inc.* The flight manifest says the plane left Odessa International Airport last night at twenty-two hundred hours and traveled to Mineralnye Vody Airport in Southcentral Russia. It left seventy minutes ago and just arrived."

"I have a plan," said Haddy. "Upload the photos of Daroghah Vulkan and Ivan Juric killing that man. Make it gruesome. I want eye-popping headlines. Put it on the World Wide Web. How long would that take?"

"Fifteen, twenty minutes."

"Good," replied Haddy. "Follow with the Jewish émigré files. Can you hack into his bank account?"

"Already started."

"I want to return the money to those families," she said.

The staircase into the black Citation X remained open. Haddy crept closer, and seeing no one, mounted the stairs and stepped inside the cabin. An attractive stewardess was reading a women's magazine. Haddy tapped her on her shoulder. She whipped her head around, startled, and went for her knife, but Haddy placed the Glock's barrel on her forehead. "Put down the knife." Haddy read her nameplate. "Irena."

"What do you want?" said the frightened woman.

"Where's the pilot?" said Haddy.

"In the Gold Star Lounge. What do you want?"

"Why are you here?"

"We have orders to pick up two scientists," said Irena.

"Who?"

Irena opened her purse and checked a paper. "Professors François LeCompte and Stefan Danilenko. They're arriving within the hour."

Haddy crumpled the paper and declared, "This plane flew from Gate One to Mineralnye Vody Airport last night with a cute blonde girl named Raisa Danilenko, my cousin. She was kidnapped. I'm rescuing her, with or without your help."

"You won't hurt me?"

"I've got a short fuse, and I'm not in the mood for tricks."

The stewardess opened her purse. "See? No gun," and reached inside. She removed her phone and hit speed dial. "Natalia, where did Karpov take the teenager last night? Okay. Thanks," and disconnected. "Your cousin's at Dombay, a tiny resort village in the Caucasus Mountains, one hundred miles northwest from Sochi and ..." The stewardess stopped talking and stared over Haddy's shoulder. Haddy spun around, thinking "attack," but heard Irena cry, "Brianna, thank God!"

"You should have called me, Haddy," said Brianna. "I know this plane and I know this attendant. We're friends." They exchanged greetings and Brianna continued, "Irena, Ivan has my daughter. Where is he keeping the girls?"

"An ancient castle called the Fortress. Hidden in the forest five miles north of Dombay. You travel to Mineralnye Vody Airport by jet and take a helicopter from there."

"We'll need this plane," said Brianna firmly.

"I hate Ivan Juric," Irena said. "But you'll need a pilot, and today it's Karpov." Haddy observed the effect that name had on Brianna. The escort stiffened.

"Does the name 'X' mean anything to you?" said Haddy to Irena.

Visibly shaken, Irena replied, "I've worked a few times when he flies to Mineralnye and Odessa. He owns Eastern Machine Systems. He's a billionaire. He's a super paranoid savant and has some pretty sick tastes. And he's a sadist. His personal assistant is a young Japanese lady, gorgeous, but scary. I still don't see how she stands it."

"He's in the Fortress?" said Haddy.

"I talk with the kitchen staff when I assist on the helicopters. He lives on the top floor by himself with the Japanese lady."

"I'll get the pilot," said Haddy to Irena and continued, "Should I handcuff you to the chair?"

"If you want," replied Irena. "But I won't run. These people are criminals, and I want to see Karpov sweat."

Haddy spoke to Tamir as she and Brianna walked into the terminal. "We know who and we know where. Daroghah Vulkan is in a castle north of a ski resort in Dombay, Russia. I'm hijacking their jet. Find out if we have assets in Dombay."

Brianna and Haddy approached the Gold Star Lounge. "I have a score to settle with Karpov," Brianna said and described being dangled from the black jet by her ankles over the Black Sea. She placed the Ruger LC9 in the front pocket of her black leather motorcycle jacket.

"Keep your anger in check," said Haddy. As they entered the lounge, Haddy faced Brianna and said sternly, "Stay behind me. Follow my lead."

65

Army Munitions Group Campus Medical Clinic
Eleven-fifteen hours

Major Nicolai Lebed, Senior Sergeant Grigor, and First Sergeant Talgat watched Professor LeCompte enter the rear entrance of the medical clinic to meet their prisoner. They smoked and rehashed the kidnapping. Grigor flicked his butt on the ground and said, "Haven't heard from our Captain Loverboy since yesterday. You think he's dead?"

"Killing Pavlos Doukas and delivering the Danilenko girl was the plan," said Nicolai. "But I checked. Karpov said Doukas brought the girl to the plane alone. Pavlos said Ivan Juric called Loverboy to return to the AMG quarters. Lies, all lies. Either Doukas or Ivan Juric took him out."

"If Loverboy is dead," said Talgat, "we split twelve bars of plutonium three ways; that's $3.2 million each inside the coffee thermos, with my family in Uralsk."

"Plutonium is nice, but I want Ivan Juric," said Grigor.

"Once Professor LeCompte has Danilenko's software," said Nicolai, "our orders are to escort them both to the jet and the Fortress; then we'll get our chance." Nicolai's phone rang. "Hold it," he said. "It's Irena."

His partners put their hands over their hearts and said mockingly, "Ire ... nah. Oooo."

"Irena darling," said Lebed. "You shouldn't call me during work."

"Niki!" Irena exclaimed. "Pull up your browser! Go to BBC News!"

The mercenaries opened their Internet browsers. Their jaws dropped and mouths opened as they read, *"Ukrainian Billionaire and Oligarch Daroghah Vulkan, Owner of Shadowy Eastern Machine Systems, Inc. and the Sakharov Crime Syndicate, Has Murdered Many, Sources Say."* In photo after photo, short- and long-range, a young Daroghah Vulkan pulled the trigger three times. The body of a bloodied and beaten man shook as the rounds took him in the chest. Next to him stood Ivan Juric holding a gold skull. Several photos zoomed in on the skull, caught in a frozen scream. Next came, *"Vulkan: Called by Many the 'Ukrainian Eichmann.' Identified by Joseph Abrams, London Guardian Investigative Reporter Before His Fiery Death on UIA Flight PS114, October 13, 1991."* Dozens of pictures of Jewish families flashed on the screen. Nicolai spoke urgently, "Irena, where are you?"

"In the jet, waiting for you. But Niki, listen." Irena told him about the black-clad warrior and Brianna. "They're kidnapping Karpov and hijacking the jet."

"To where?"

"To Mineralnye Vody. I think they're going after X." Irena stopped and continued, alarmed, "Oh, Niki, EMS stock just plummeted."

"You still want to run away with me?" asked Nicolai.

"Don't say such a stupid thing, of course I do," said Irena.

"Then listen, go with them. I'll take care of everything." Nicolai disconnected and motioned with his head. "Comrades, follow me. There's been a change of plans."

66

The Fortress
Eleven-fifteen hours

X donned his leopard coat and grabbed his cane, as Fusako helped him totter outside to the Palace garden for fresh air. The snow swirled, making talk difficult, but he needed a tonic, a break from the full-blown orgy inside the Fortress to calm his nerves while assessing the latest intelligence plus something far worse. "I am the messiah," he muttered and inhaled great draughts of icy air. X paused and repeated, "I am the messiah." He looked over the ancient ramparts into the white forest and shivered, not from the cold, but the dark forces tearing him apart. He stood poised to unleash his rage on Israel, but the goddess Kali had seemingly turned her malevolent energy on him. "You know the staff sergeant killed Juanita and Carlos Rodriguez," he said to Fusako. "And the Kliment twins. Then she boarded a Mossad jet to Odessa. Rat is dead, killed by the chief of the Odessa police, and assisted by an NYPD detective. Rat was burned alive and the heroin vanished."

"I know our assassin shot the staff sergeant and detective at the airport," replied Fusako. "They are in emergency surgery. Ivan has Danilenko at the Army Munitions Group." The discussion was rudely interrupted by a drunk general who opened the French doors and shouted, "X, you should see this!" X and Fusako went inside. On the monitor, they watched the worldwide news flash of X's murder of Vlasta Korovich, plus picture after picture of bereaved Jewish families.

X grabbed his cane before falling into his leather chair. He said, "Turn off the monitors throughout the Fortress. Get everyone out of here." Fusako herded the jazz ensemble along with the naked, drug-crazed, and drunken twosomes and threesomes into the elevator and punched the down button. "How did this happen?" said X as he wiped perspiration from his brow.

"The staff sergeant found the film," said Fusako, as EMS stock plunged from \$183.56/share on the NYSE to \$23.47/share.

"Find the Enforcer," he seethed. "Fusako, against all odds, the staff sergeant may come to the Fortress. I need your protection."

67

International Trading Partners **Gulfstream 650ER**
Eleven-thirty to twelve-fifteen hours

Brianna ignored Haddy. She marched up to Karpov, who was hunched over his laptop in the lounge, and pressed the barrel of her Ruger against his temple. With barely controllable fury, she said, "Come with us, you pig."

Brianna kept the pistol on Karpov's ribs as the trio boarded Tamir's Gulfstream. Haddy's nerves were on edge. Without support, a one-person rescue mission was suicide. The spy plane had a large well-equipped weapons cache, but Haddy saw a scoped Barrett .50-caliber rifle with ammunition on a seat. Tamir's pilot said, "Captain Troyem grabbed it from your grandfather's office. Said it would come in handy."

"It might indeed," said Haddy and told the pilot, "Call Tamir. We need to talk." Then she addressed Anatoly Karpov. "I need intel, and fast."

Brianna placed the pistol barrel on his temple, cocked the hammer, and said, "Talk, you pig."

"Ask your questions," replied Karpov fearfully.

"How long from here to the Fortress?" asked Haddy.

"Seventy minutes. Then, thirty minutes to the castle by helicopter."

"Tell me about the castle and the guards."

"You're insane," said Karpov, shaking his head. "You can't do this. X is throwing a gigantic celebration, which started Wednesday. He beefed up the place with extra mercenaries and dogs. The castle walls are fifty feet high with a minefield to the south. A seventy-five-foot-tall watchtower stands in the center with two guards twenty-four seven. The trees are loaded with cameras and motion sensors, with a three-hundred-foot clear-cut on the north and east sides. There's no cover."

"How many are inside?" asked Haddy.

"Minimum two hundred," spilled Karpov. "Officers and terrorists with bodyguards and aides, plus musicians, chefs, and prostitutes, plus it's snowing; you'll freeze to death."

"How do you get in?"

"You are crazy, I hope you know that, but there's only one front and no rear entrance," replied the pilot. "There is also a kitchen door. An abandoned church sits on the southeast ridge. It's twenty minutes from the Fortress through the forest."

"This compound comes with generators?" asked Haddy.

"Two big ones," said Karpov, shaking his head in disbelief.

Haddy fretted about backup. Did Tamir not understand?

"Is there a shiny Jewish ass in this piece of trash?" announced Sergeant Shira Alian. The buffed soldier hopped into the jet.

"Shira!" shouted Haddy.

"Yeah, it's me, dammit," said Shira. "I was chilling on the Bosporus, boobs and butt lathered in suntan oil and driving the faithful mad with envy. Then the battalion CO called. Told me to put my clothes on and get down here. I've been wondering how long you'd stay quiet. When I got the call, I knew you were back in town."

Shira saw Brianna, who extended a hand. "I'm Brianna Ivanova. I'm mother to a little girl captured with the staff sergeant's cousin Raisa."

"The motherfucker," said Haddy, "is located in an impregnable mountain fortress poised to fire nuclear weapons at Jerusalem in four hours, and it takes a hundred and ten minutes to get there."

"That gives us two hundred and eighty minutes," said Shira and set her timer. "Storm the castle, rescue the girls, save Israel, and relax for a brew. We can do this. Hand me a rucksack."

The soldiers opened the onboard weapons locker and grabbed two Tavor 7 Israeli assault rifles equipped with Mepro MOR sights and an integrated laser and infrared pointer. Haddy threw twenty-five-round Magpul clips into the pack.

Shira tossed in four M26 fragmentation grenades. "Damn. Look what we have here," she said and grabbed two sticks of high explosive C-4, packaged as the M112 demolition block. Haddy added eight clips of 9mm for the Glock 19s, containing the standard fifteen-round magazines. She threw in wire cutters, flashlights, and two spec-ops first aid kits containing morphine ampoules, aspirin, amphetamines, energy bars, and injectable migraine medicine. Shira found winter coats, thermal underwear, and gloves.

Tamir Mizrahi called. "Thanks for Sergeant Alian," said Haddy, "but two more like her would help; too bad you had to pull Roger and Yaseen."

"Here's what we know," said Tamir. "Mossad and Shin Bet were pulled back to Tel Aviv yesterday on high alert, leaving us skeleton crews at best. Captain Troyem, along with Roger and Yaseen, is helping Detective James disguise themselves as an ambulance crew to enter Army Munitions Group and get the scientists out."

"This is what I've learned," said Haddy, and filled Tamir in on Karpov's details of the Vulkan compound.

"Sayeret Matkal can get to Mineralnye Vody in three hours," replied Tamir. "We looked at satellite photos of the Fortress taken a year ago, for a HELO drop, but there's a snow-storm. We're blind. As a last resort, we bomb it."

"You'd do it?"

"Millions for two?" Tamir replied. "Yes."

"According to the pilot," said Haddy, "if we left now, we would get to the Fortress close to fourteen fifteen hours. If the Matkal leaves Tel Aviv by C-One Thirty, that puts them into Mineralnye at fourteen forty-five hours. The C-One Thirty transports a helicopter. They would hit the fortress at fifteen fifteen hours."

"And be seen immediately," said Tamir. "The hostages would die, and no telling if this madman wouldn't set off the rockets."

"I'm not sure he can before sixteen hundred hours," said Haddy.

"And you believe that?" replied Tamir. "Staff Sergeant, prepare for the worst and make your plans."

Haddy replied, "The best approach is stealth, but Shira and I need help, and you're asking us to sit on our butts for an hour waiting for the Matkal unit."

"I think it's our only option, except for one thing," said Tamir. "Captain Troyem called. The man who kidnapped your cousin is out for revenge, claiming a double cross by Ivan Juric. He told the captain there's a hidden tunnel inside the Fortress. It exits from a cave on the northwest ridge in a large boulder field. Above the tree line, there's a path that crosses a stream. A hidden door lies in the cave, opened by a lever under a smooth rock."

"And you believe that?" said Haddy, not wanting to trust Raisa's kidnapper.

"Believe it or not, it may be our only hope," said Tamir. "I also located an asset in Dombay, the owner of the Alan-Ash restaurant."

"You think this asset could shut down the power plant to Dombay at fourteen thirty?" asked Haddy.

"It's a tiny village," replied the spymaster. "She not only knows everyone, but can open any door with a case of vodka. She could make that happen."

Haddy, Shira, Brianna, and Anatoly Karpov headed to the black jet. Haddy left Wolf a voice message: "Hey, big boy. Sergeant Alian and I are hijacking the EMS jet. Captain Troyem has our location. I can't tell you how much I want to hold you. Come and get me, Ranger. I'll be waiting in the castle." She gave him the coordinates and hung up.

The Army Munitions Group Campus Medical Clinic
Eleven-forty-five to twelve-seventeen hours

S tefan's detonation software downloaded to François's computer. François sent the program to the onboard computer system of the X3 missiles. Stefan observed François's Three Stooges T-shirt, *"As Private Eyes, They're a Public Menace,"* and said, "How can you wear such idiotic stuff at a time like this?"

"Laughter is the best revenge," said François solemnly. "Time to phone Ivan?"

"Now or never," replied Stefan.

François called Ivan, who answered angrily, "Professor LeCompte? Are the missiles armed?"

"X may fire at four o'clock, sixteen hundred hours, exactly. However, Professor Danilenko must return to the hospital. I've called an ambulance."

"And the men who brought him, where are they?" demanded Ivan.

"Out back, smoking," said François. "But Ivan, I've made a few modifications. I installed an off switch in Professor Danilenko's software, and the rockets will not fire until I give the word. I know Ulyana Ivanova and Raisa Danilenko are in the Fortress. I'll release the missiles when the girls are out of harm's way."

Ivan exploded, "A threat!? You think you can blackmail me with a bluff!? You've just signed their death warrants."

"Risk punishment if they're not in Dombay in twenty minutes, Mr. Juric. And keep your eyes on your satellite monitor," replied François.

"You are a blind man, Professor LeCompte," seethed Ivan. "My men will bring both you and Professor Danilenko here. You can't escape." The phone clicked off, and François started his stopwatch.

In moments, the clinic receptionist rushed into the exam room. "The guards out back, where are they?" she asked nervously. François shrugged. She rushed to her desk. François overheard her say, "I'm sorry, Mr. Juric," breathlessly. "The guards aren't in or out of the building. Yes, we have two nurses on duty. Search again? ... Hold on." The woman shouted. A scurry of steps was heard throughout the clinic. Doors opened and slammed shut. She returned a few minutes later, huffing and puffing. Panicked, she said, "We went everywhere, Mr. Juric. They are not here." François had gone into the receptionist area. The secretary told the nurses to lock all the doors. "Do not let anyone in or out," she said. "Mr. Juric is sending guards to take the professors and computers into custody."

Suddenly, François heard the screech of tires outside and grabbed Stefan. "Get up," he said. The professors looked out the window and saw Wolf, disguised as an EMT, pull up in an AMG ambulance.

Wolf approached the entrance. Finding the doors closed, he shouted, "Open up! We've orders to take Professor Danilenko to the hospital."

"The clinic is closed. Go away!" said the receptionist. The door blasted open with shots of gunfire, with screams from the clinic staff.

In moments, Wolf entered the room. "You okay, Professor Danilenko?" he said.

Roger ran in from the back and announced, "Detective James. There's a squad of guards coming our way."

"And from the front," said Yaseen.

François wasn't listening. His stopwatch struck the twenty-minute mark. He put up his hand and said, "Silence." He called Ivan. "Are they free?"

"Fuck you!" yelled Ivan.

François placed his finger over a preprogrammed number as Yaseen put his pistol on François's temple.

"Professor LeCompte," said Wolf. "Hold it. What are you planning?" Wolf turned to Professor Danilenko. "We have orders to kill him."

"Professor LeCompte and I are in this together," said Stefan. "Kill him and kill me as well."

Yaseen looked from one to the other, paused, and made his decision. He put down the pistol. François pressed the button. A few seconds elapsed before the ground shook violently, as a muffled explosion emanated from the campus center, followed by five more bellowing blasts. Vials and medical instruments crashed to the floor, tables tipped, and glass shattered.

"What the hell was that!?" exclaimed Wolf.

François phoned the campus security chief. "This is Professor LeCompte," he declared. "There's been an explosion in Building Thirteen with toxic nuclear gas released into the vents. Sound the alarms. Call President Sokolov. Evacuate the campus immediately."

Wolf, Roger, and Yaseen, along with the two professors, stole to the windows. The campus erupted into pandemonium and panic. Sirens wailed and screamed over the twenty-odd factory buildings. People streamed through doors and windows, pushing and shoving their way north to the campus entrance. Cars, buses, and trucks came to a halt in the melee. Guards ordered to take the scientists into custody retreated. "Get in the ambulance, pronto," ordered Wolf.

François phoned Ivan, who yelled, "Did you just sabotage Building Thirteen?"

"Release the girls, Mr. Juric," said François.

"Or what?" asked Ivan.

"Risk further reprisal."

"Fuck you. FUCK YOU! Go to hell. You're bluffing and out of tricks," shouted Ivan.

François ran out to the ambulance. He hopped in the front seat and told Wolf, "The front gate is jammed with traffic, but there's another way out."

The men assisted Stefan into the back, and Wolf hit the gas. François shouted, "Take a left." Wolf sped across the AMG campus, filled with Soviet-era brick factories. Wolf found his going easy since the traffic went in the opposite direction. After a mile, François barked, "Take a left onto that dirt track. You'll see a forest across the open field." François marked the time. "Twelve seventeen hours. Be prepared for a nuclear demonstration."

"What!?" shouted Wolf and slammed on the brakes. "I thought they were disarmed!"

"We control them," said Stefan from the back.

"They're armed?" said Wolf.

"Steer for the trees," said François. "They will be disarmed after my demonstration. Now, witness LeCompte's wrath." François pressed a second preprogrammed number. There was a slight pause. Then a sudden pressure blast swept across the campus like an exploding ball of fire. The ambulance's electronics burned up as the vehicle coasted into the trees. "EMP burst!" shouted François. "Next, the wave!" All the men looked at the campus. Their blood drained to their toes as they beheld a ten-foot wave of earth rolling towards them. As if a giant had snapped a carpet, a tsunami of soil and earth rippled through the ground. Buildings and windows shattered. Smokestacks toppled, and gas lines ruptured into massive fireballs. Then, a giant cloud of flame, dust, and debris shot up from where Building 13 had stood moments ago. As the wave of earth shot towards them, François uttered, "*Mon dieu!* I wired four together, but Danilenko's software boosted the blast; much more than I calculated!" The ambulance bounced off the ground like a gymnast on a trampoline and crashed to the earth with a loud thump. Wolf opened his eyes. His ears rang, and he couldn't hear a thing. He was covered in glass and saw François lying unconscious. Yaseen and Roger groaned, and Stefan appeared dead. Wolf picked up François's phone, now shattered on the floor, and groaned, "A royal clusterfuck. The missiles are still armed."

69

Gate One, OIA Executive Terminal
Twelve-seventeen to thirteen-thirty hours

The women had fastened their seat belts, and the Citation soared aloft like a falcon. Their flight path took it south over the Army Munitions Group campus before turning west over the Black Sea. Suddenly, a blinding flash filled the skies, followed by an invisible pressure blast, which spanked the aircraft like a newborn infant. The electronics failed. The jet stopped midair and plummeted. Haddy heard Karpov trying to restart the engines as they spun out of control. Her body tightened like a coiled rope, and she heard Shira scream, "Oh Lord, not again!" The plane hurtled downwards towards a grassy field as Karpov's third try worked. The jets ignited, and with seconds remaining, he curved away from the ground. Haddy heard the underbelly of the plane scrape the field. As it gained altitude, the wingtip clipped a smokestack tumbling down in the midst of chaos.

Haddy sat on the starboard side of the jet and witnessed firsthand the effects of a nuclear blast. She screamed, "Wolf!" She ordered Karpov to go back. The plane banked, and the women looked down on a campus reduced to rubble.

"Jesus," said Shira breathlessly.

Brianna stared out the window, dumbfounded. "François," she cried. "Oh God, no."

Haddy wrapped her arms around her belly to squeeze away the gut-wrenching pain. She closed her eyes in terror. "I can't take it anymore. *Wolf, Wolf, Wolf. Why?*"

Irena turned on the news, but the screen remained blank. Shira rushed over and held Haddy, who sobbed bitterly, "I lost myself and Wolf gave it back, and now he's gone." Haddy looked at the Barrett .50 caliber rifle, which seemed out of place and useless. "Why would God do this to me, to Wolf, to all of us?"

"He's not done anything," said Shira. "Until we know for sure, Wolf is not dead. Let it go and get your game face on. We've got a job to do." Haddy kissed the diamond solitaire with a fierce resolve, which deadened the pain she felt. She would rescue the girls and take Ivan and X apart. Haddy felt the throwing ax and gained fresh courage. "Wolf," she said to herself. "I own you. Now hear this. Crawl out of those fucking ashes and come get me."

Within the hour, Karpov landed at the Mineralnye Vody Airport amid light snow. He taxied inside the hangar next to a twin-engine jet helicopter, whose blades hung limp at its sides like a dead locust's wings. Haddy and Shira gathered their rucks and gear and waited until Brianna, Irena, and the pilot deplaned. "Irena," said Haddy. "Send the mechanic home after he gets the helicopter ready. Karpov, take us to the Fortress."

Just then, she heard voices and looked up to see three men. "Halt," announced Nicolai, supported by two others holding Kalashnikovs. "Drop your belts. Kick them over." Haddy said to herself, "This cannot be happening." Senior Sergeant Grigor took Haddy's ax and examined it with admiration. Nicolai said to Brianna, "I know about your pistol and ankle knife. Hand them over."

Irena joined Nicolai and said, "I wasn't sure what you had planned. Did you see the explosion?" Nicolai shook his head and Irena described the nuclear disaster to the Army Munitions Group.

Haddy raised her voice. "What the fucking hell do you want!? We're wasting time."

Nicolai appraised the group quietly and nodded at the Barrett. "You any good with that?"

"Try two thousand, six hundred, and sixty-four yards," said Shira.

"X plans to nuke Israel in two and half hours," said Haddy. "Cut these ties and let us do our job."

Nicolai made his decision. He turned to First Sergeant Talgat and said, "Help the mechanic take the helicopter out, then shut down the airport." He let a tiny smile cross his face and said to Grigor, "Senior Sergeant, cut their ties, let the Ladies from Hell do their job. Take Irena and fire up the Cessna; we have hot coffee awaiting us in Uralsk." Nicolai's eyebrows narrowed as he addressed Haddy, "We have a score to settle with Ivan. If you fail, we won't."

70

The Fortress

Twelve-seventeen to thirteen-thirty hours

Jaca Juric sat openmouthed and dumbfounded, watching her private monitor in the Control Room. The smoke boiled up in thick clouds from the Army Munitions Group. Ivan collapsed and said, "What in the fucking, fucking, fucking hell did that Frenchman do?"

"We won't know it all, until the area-wide communications return," said Jaca.

Fusako opened the door and drilled Ivan. "Come upstairs," she said solemnly.

In the castle's atrium, a salsa band played while dozens danced nude. Ivan stumbled forward to the top of the stairs in an angry haze. His facial tics were stronger, more painful, and coming faster. His nerves on edge, Ivan held back from strangling anyone who lay in his path as he tried to descend the marble steps.

The television screens were blank throughout the Fortress. The partiers were happily unaware of the destruction of the Army Munitions Group campus and tumbling stock of Eastern Machine Systems. After a mid-morning pause, powders and pills refueled fresh orgiastic activities. The close environment, the storm outside, spice-laden French and Chinese cuisines, perfumed escorts, naked-body sweat, and semen had mixed together to create a hot sauna of wild unhinged ecstasy, which enraged Ivan further. Halfway down the staircase, he stepped on a discarded prophylactic, slipped, and fell. He caught himself expertly, but kicked the nearest man and woman as he entered the elevator. Ivan swallowed his gall and entered the Palace Room into Fusako's pistol.

The Ukrainian oligarch tossed meat to Smert as Kitten ruffled his feathers and squawked, "She's a killer. She's got big tits." Bartok's eerie violin concerto played, and X held his finger aloft, moving it like a conductor. His coiffured hair matched his silver sharkskin suit. He looked at the plasma screen, filled with the scenes of total destruction at the munitions factory.

"Ivan," he said heavily. "My son, what the hell happened?"

Ivan described the heated conversation with LeCompte. "He altered Danilenko's code and said there would be retribution if I didn't release the captives. When I refused, he blew up Building Thirteen and then the campus. I've tried calling him to stop, saying that I'll give him the girls, but he doesn't answer."

X petted Smert and mused, "Professor LeCompte blows up Building Thirteen to force the workers off site. Then he detonates the plutonium, but like a fool dies in the explosion with Danilenko." X laughed and turned to Fusako. "You have Yuri Kharitov, from the Institute of Chemical Physics Explosion Laboratory on the line?" Fusako nodded. X said to Ivan, "You remember I told you Yuri is an expert both in nuclear bombs and detonation software, and a coding genius?" X put the phone on speaker. "Yuri," he said. "So good to talk. Your debts, all paid off?"

"Thank you beyond my wildest dreams, Mr. X," came the reply.

"Good. Professor LeCompte began downloading Professor Danilenko's software at eleven forty-three hours exactly. You've had time to examine it, I assume?"

"I focused on the ignition protocol and found a destruct sequence, which activates at sixteen hundred hours."

"So I push the button and ... ?"

"Nothing. The software dissolves."

"How deliciously clever."

"I removed it," said the professor.

"You earned a big bonus, Yuri," replied X. "Thank you." The line disconnected. "I didn't trust either LeCompte or Danilenko. I sent Yuri a copy of Danilenko's software when it downloaded." X pointed at a map of the Middle East on the monitor. Small ruby-red lights represented X3 missiles. Four ringed Jerusalem, while five others stood ready in the Gaza Strip, the southern border of Lebanon, Tehran, Damascus, and Moscow. "So, the missiles are armed. At sixteen hundred hours, I'll fire my four and release controls to the others. Is the staff sergeant dead?"

"Not yet," said Ivan.

"Where's our jet?" asked X.

"Parked at Gate One, but with area-wide communications down, we can't contact either Karpov or the airport controller," replied Ivan.

In a tone laced with venom, X said, "Destroy the staff sergeant, Mr. Juric. I want her head on a platter. Now, get the fuck out of my sight."

After Ivan left, X said to Fusako, "Find those who

purchased X3s. If they ask about Army Munitions Group, tell them it demonstrates the destructive force of my missile. Star-Comm will release a worldwide ad campaign for Eastern Machine Systems any moment now. The stock will bounce back in a month. Now, collect our guests for the four o'clock extravaganza."

Abandoned Cemetery Southeast of the Fortress, Dombay, Russia
Fourteen-zero-eight hours

The twin-engine jet helicopter snaked through the snowy Teberda valley in Karpov's capable hands, urged on by Brianna's pistol. The steep, forested Caucasus Mountains lay in a fresh blanket of snow. Their mighty peaks couldn't be seen, covered as they were by windy clouds. Haddy and Shira checked their gear as Karpov slowed the helicopter in a wide circle over the ruins of a church. He landed on the edge of an Orthodox cemetery dotted with tiny stone houses bearing lavish crosses.

Haddy turned to Brianna. "This is where we part. You've been a big help, but any further and you'd get us all killed. Don't worry, we'll find your daughter." Brianna exchanged hugs and kisses with both soldiers and watched the sniper and spotter jump out. Haddy grabbed the Barrett while the helicopter spun away.

Shira turned to Haddy. "You okay?" she said quietly.

"No use worrying about Wolf. If he's dead, he's in God's hands; if he's alive, I'll fucking kill him for being an idiot. Let's get the girls and take out X."

Haddy's and Shira's boots sunk into the thick carpet of leaves and pine needles deep in snow. The soldiers jogged west, threading their way through the trees, hopping over brambles and ducking under low-lying branches. They reached the ridgetop in half the time mentioned by Karpov and peered below at an aged limestone structure. They got out their binoculars.

"Never seen a castle up close and personal," said Shira. "That's a big sucker. That wall is high. I see two guards in the tower with scoped rifles, and two-man patrols and dogs spaced five minutes apart. They did the clear-cut, but left stumps."

"The generators are surrounded by a ten-foot-high cement wall," said Haddy, "topped by concertina wire. Damn, it's freezing." Haddy's and Shira's breath coalesced into tiny puffs of steam. They negotiated a zigzagging descent through forest. The snow muffled the sound while the trees and fog cloaked their presence. They came to an abrupt stop at the edge of a cliff and traversed south before trying another chute. This worked, and the soldiers crept down to the clear-cut and knelt down. Haddy scoped the area with her assault rifle. "We've got a two-man dog patrol at two hundred eighty-five yards. The dog has his nose in the air. Dammit, he's catching our scent. I'll take the dog and handler. You take his partner."

Flakes of snow swirled as Haddy watched the animal sniff the air. She pulled the trigger and sent a .308 round into its head. Before it dropped, Haddy put a second round into the handler's forehead. His partner wheeled in surprise when Shira's bullet blew off his cheekbone. Staying low-crouched, the soldiers dashed through dozens of stumps towards their quarry. Ten yards out, they low-crawled through the snow, using their elbows and knees to get to their victims. Ragged breathing erupted from Shira's target. The man lifted his rifle in a last attempt to fire. Shira shot him with her suppressed pistol.

Terribly exposed, the soldiers ran the remaining distance to the generators. Two guards were stamping their feet and clapping their gloves when suddenly, a dog barked. The handler let the leash go, and the beast charged straight at Haddy. Raising her suppressed Glock, she drilled a round through its chest in its midair leap towards her. Alerted, the guards raised their submachine guns to fire, but Shira hit them with the Tavor 7 rifle. Haddy said, "We've lost our surprise. Let's get the generators." Shira removed the wire cutters and two sticks of C-4 and ran to the cement wall. Haddy made a stirrup with her hands. She braced herself against the rib, shoulder, and leg pain, as Shira's boot hit her hands. Shira caught the edge of the wall above. Haddy grabbed the soles of her boots and heaved.

Shira snipped the wire and disappeared. When she jumped back down, Haddy asked, "You set the C-4?"

"And there's fifty-gallon drums of diesel next to them; there's going to be some big fireworks."

"Let's move," Haddy said, grabbing the Barrett. "Place will be crawling with guards. I thought when the place goes dark, we could slip inside the kitchen entrance, but ..."

"I vote for that northwest ridge and hidden cave," said Shira. The sounds of barking and men shouting galvanized the warriors, and a bank of tungsten arc lamps burst open.

"Stay low. We've got a hundred-yard dash to the trees and some fog," shouted Haddy. They dodged stumps, jumped over fallen limbs, and crashed through the bramble as sporadic automatic weapons sought them out. Sniper and spotter dove behind the root ball of an upturned tree. "What's our time?" said Haddy.

"Fourteen thirty hours," replied Shira.

"Let's hope the vodka worked," said Haddy. The soldiers saw a soft glow emanating from the resort town of Dombay. Suddenly, the castle lights blinked out, and the valley below descended into darkness. The bullets stopped momentarily. Then the generators sprang to life, tripped by the loss of city power. Housed inside steel cages, the generators started humming like diesel earthmovers, spewing exhaust into the air. The arc lamps came back to life, and the guards released the dogs to find the intruders.

"The detonator ready?" asked Haddy.

"All set. Those Generac liquid-cooled generators are huge," replied Shira. She snuggled against the upturned tree and flipped the switch to green. "Partner, hunker down next to me and cover your ears." Shira pressed the button. Two massive fireballs erupted. Enormous balloons of fire and smoke shot into the sky before collapsing into a furious cloud of black smoke and flames. A tremendous blast of searing gas swept over the upturned roots and tore them away. "Damn!" shouted Shira and peeked out. Fifty-gallon drums of fuel exploded and spewed burning oil in a wide circle upon the walls and surrounding forest. Guards lay dead, while a few survivors put out their flaming clothes.

The C-4 boom, like the aftershocks of the F-35 fighter jets, triggered a Lacoste Bar and Grill flashback in Haddy. Terrified, she got up to flee. *"Get out, get out!"*

Shira wrestled her down until it faded. "Hold it together, partner, we've got to run. Follow me." The soldiers powered up the steep ridge in a gut-wrenching, gasping sprint. Rocks skittered, and bramble cracked and fell away, until the soldiers clambered like bears on hands and feet in their mad dash to safety. The incline steepened further, forcing them to crawl through the ice and snow on their bellies, elbows, and knees. Haddy slipped and slid backwards before catching herself on a limb, heaving with exhaustion. It was no use. She couldn't go any further. The days of running, fighting, unending stress, and mounting injuries had taken their toll. Then she heard Shira command, *"Staff Sergeant Abrams! Come to attention!"*

"Help me," said Haddy weakly. "I can't do this."

"Help you?!" shouted Shira. "Get your fucking ass up and move, soldier. Get up and move! Do you hear me? You can and you will *move!*"

Shira grabbed the big Barrett and Haddy's belt. With her boots, she punched into the dirt to make steps. Two big thighs churned up the hill like a D-9 Caterpillar. "Fuck me," she panted. "You owe me big time for humping your tiny ass up this hill and back to that idiot Ranger. You two deserve each other. I hope he got his pussy shit together and is on the way to save your silly ass."

The forest finally thinned, and giant boulders appeared. The snow had let up, and a depression indicated a trail. The soldiers followed along carefully, squeezing between slabs of granite. They came to a cave. "Give points to the kidnapper," said Haddy. "He's been right so far." Haddy flicked on her flashlight and went inside. In the back on a ledge lay a flat rock, and she pulled it away. In a hollowed-out depression below sat a lever. Haddy gave it a pull and heard a click. A cleverly hidden wall of stone opened.

Shira went inside. "Fuck me, it's going to be tight. But we have a real, bona fide tunnel."

Haddy's claustrophobia clamped down on her chest. "Oh God," she cried to herself. "This is worse than the rest."

"Let's drop our gear and get out there," said Shira.

"Drugs first," said Haddy, and pulled out the first aid kit and syringes. She gave herself the injectable migraine and non-narcotic pain medicines, swallowed aspirin and amphetamines, and passed two of each to Shira. Haddy's mind cleared. "It's time for Stefan's Barrett."

The soldiers left the cave and glanced upwards at the boulders. Shira pointed to a large one, and they clambered up to a level perch. Haddy zipped open the gun case, while Shira swept off the snow and cleared the area. Haddy opened the bipod and screwed on the suppressor. She slammed in a ten-round magazine and stretched out behind the rifle. Shira readied her Tavor 7 and peered through her binoculars, equipped with laser and infrared detection, wind speed, and direction finders. "Take a look," said Shira. "Those explosions shook that place up. We have a lot of activity in the parking lot. I count twenty-seven ... twenty-eight ... twenty-nine vehicles. Guests and guards are running about; there's an armored troop carrier in the center. You see the helicopters?"

Haddy stuffed her ears with plugs and put her eye to the power scope. She saw a panicked rush of people in military uniforms, business suits, white robes, and kaffiyehs running across the icy cobblestone lot, fighting each other to get in the commercial helicopters. The jets had ignited, and the blades were winding up. Haddy's spine tingled. "Shira, you see that guy with the generals at the helicopter? He fits Brianna's description of Ivan Juric, the man who killed my father."

72

The Fortress

I van returned to his third-floor stateroom, counting the minutes before he returned to the Palace. According to their previous arrangement, he would use Fusako's gun and kill the maniac. He imagined throwing X's body over the wall and calmly telling the dignitaries, "Meet the new CEO of Eastern Machine Systems."

Suddenly, his table lamp went out. Ivan got up, irritated. "What now?" he said and glanced outside the window. Snowy, blustery winds beat against the glass, and he noticed the lights of Dombay were out. "What the fuck?" Then the diesel engines roared to life, and the castle walls vibrated. The lights flickered on, and Ivan breathed a sigh of relief while dashing down the stairs to the Control Room. Ivan lost his footing as two enormous booms echoed throughout the Fortress. The castle shook and windows shattered. Ivan crashed into partiers, dazed and bleeding.

The Control Room door swung open. Jaca came rushing out with a flashlight in hand and yelled, "Get up! Come inside and look! We're being attacked!" She tossed him a flashlight, and brother and sister peered at the security monitors. They saw two infrared images dash up the northwest ridge. Cries and screams were heard from rooms. Guests and consorts cowered, screamed, and cursed, while others looked for flashlights. Jaca had turned on the elevator camera, which showed dignitaries trying to get away.

Ivan shoved his way through the partiers, opened the kitchen door, and ducked back inside. The generators had grown hotter as dense plastic components melted into fiery cauldrons. They exploded and sent chunks of molten metal and plastic down on the lot. He covered his face and ran towards the guard house, but rested behind a sedan. Suddenly, the front doors of the Fortress opened, and a flood of frightened terrorists raced across the icy lot to the helicopters. Ivan ran over and shot his pistol to get their attention and to guide them inside. Pilots staggered out, put on their jackets, and started the engines, and the blades churned.

73

The Fortress
Fifteen-zero-seven hours

"Payback time," said Haddy.

"Spotter up!" said Shira. "Range is four hundred forty-five yards. Snow flurries, intermittent, from the west at twelve to fifteen miles per hour. Click two right and one up."

Haddy calmed down, at home behind the cannon. She wanted to lay waste this mountain of darkness and this one particular pile of shit. The migraine had receded, and though she was freezing, the drugs and amphetamines helped her energy. Her mother's words flashed in front of her, "You will kill your father's killer." "Shooter up!" Haddy said and saw the Enforcer leaning inside the helicopter's bay doors. He was assisting a man dressed in an Iranian military uniform with three stars on the shoulder boards.

"Send it," said Shira. Haddy squeezed off the round, but the helicopter skid lifted off the ground. *Ka-boom!* Even with a suppressor, the monster gun shocked Haddy's head. "Fucking helicopter moved," said Shira. "The round grazed his arm; he's crawling away."

"Dammit!" Haddy set the crosshairs on the helicopter's rotor. The bird had risen twenty feet. She fired just as the pilot tipped the blades to soar down the mountain. The round tore up the shaft housing. The copter twisted and turned on its side and slid towards the second helicopter, packed with guests. Two fireballs ignited and spewed out men in flames. Haddy shouted, "Where's Ivan!?"

"Behind the troop transport, like a fucking cockroach," said Shira. Haddy zoomed in on the diesel fuel tanks, which were hanging like swollen fruit, and fired. Like a fountain, diesel fuel poured out, flowing towards the inferno. Suddenly, the diesel ignited from the helicopter explosions. The flames showered on the surrounding vehicles. Haddy emptied the ten-round magazine into limousines and flashy sedans and rammed home another.

Shira aimed her assault rifle and fired on guards in the open, catching them like clay pigeons. "I see him!" shouted Shira. "He ran behind a wall! He's in the guard house! Dammit, he's got a mortar!"

The soldiers watched Ivan command guards to set up the tube behind a wall. In no time, they heard the whine.

"Incoming!" shouted Haddy. The round fell short, but rocks fell on them like hail.

"Leave the Barrett and the field jackets," said Shira, and they jumped down to the cave opening. Another shell whistled overhead and exploded with a loud boom. The soldiers dived inside, as a third shell fell on the cave roof. Haddy and Shira watched the stones crash into the opening and snuff out the light. Both started coughing from the dirt and dust and turned on their lights. It was deathly quiet.

"The place is full of decay," said Haddy. "But God dammit, sis, when I'm normal, my claustrophobia is bad. This thing is less than three feet wide and five feet tall." Dozens of cobwebs clung to the rock, while rootlets from cracks in the granite roof hung down. Mouse droppings, animal carcasses, and a fresh set of footprints were present. A thick air, noxious from mold, dirt, and decay, filled the tight space.

"Calm down, baby girl," said Shira. "You and I are crawling down this tunnel. Fast. Keep your eyes off the walls and on my butt. Haddy?" Haddy held her head in her hands between her knees, frozen by fear. "I know you're ticklish," said Shira playfully. Shira touched Haddy's right armpit.

Haddy burst out of her claustrophobic cave and shouted, "What the fuck? Don't you dare touch me!"

"Wolf knows you're ticklish?"

"Damn you, Shira. I'll kill you."

"You'll have to catch me first," said Shira, and slipped on her ruck and crawled into the tunnel.

Haddy's nerve returned, the spell of fear broken. "Can I touch your ass?" she asked.

"Don't you dare," replied Shira. "That's man's territory."

"A little?"

"In your dreams. You touch me, I swear to God I'll really tear you apart."

Shira and Haddy kept up the back-and-forth banter, as they crawled and took tiny fast steps hunched over. Soon, the passage steepened. The soldiers came to a staircase of ancient timbers and stepped down carefully. At the bottom of three flights, they arrived at a landing, and the tunnel split into a "Y." A stench came from the right.

"Rock, paper, or scissors?" asked Haddy.

"If I win, you go to the shit," said Shira. Making fists, they counted. Haddy made a "rock," while Shira "paper." Shira laughed quietly. "I win. I'll join you or you join me, whichever first."

"Be safe, baby girl," said Haddy.

"Hah. Always," Shira replied.

Haddy's passage rounded a corner and ended in a tiny chiseled-out room filled with a foul stink. Her flashlight illuminated a lever similar to the one at the cave entrance. She covered her mouth with a handkerchief to ward off the smell, flicked off her flashlight, and pushed the lever. A panel clicked. A sliver of light shone into the cave, followed by an overpowering stench of rotten flesh and formaldehyde. Haddy backed away to catch her breath. She gathered her wits and nudged the door open with her pistol.

A circular table lay in the center of a small room. In its center stood a 6-inch-diameter candle with a tall willowy flame. Next to it was a bowl of partially eaten soup and a severed head. Haddy edged farther in. Suddenly, fingers like steel cables latched onto her wrist. Haddy was wrenched off balance with a vicious twist that sent her gun to the floor. She instinctively rolled and turned with the pull, not fighting but moving with the hand. Haddy came up and kicked. Her foot connected with a thud, and the shadow groaned. She whipped a punch into the face, but in a flash, her attacker caught her arm, raised it, and spun behind her. Like a slippery eel, he put his hands under her arms and locked them behind her skull, forcing her head down in a full nelson choke hold. Furiously, Haddy butted the back of her head into the shadow's face and heard a scream. She stomped down with her heels on his feet and heard bones crunch with a garbled cry. The shadow screamed again as Haddy pounded her knuckles into his eyes. As she felt his grip loosen, Haddy relaxed her shoulders and slipped through the hold. She turned on a dime and delivered an elbow uppercut, but in a desperate weakening grab, the bony fingers fell on her scalp, found the mesh plug, and struck home.

74

The Dungeon
Fifteen-thirty-eight hours

As her eyelids fluttered open, an ice pick-like pain pierced Haddy's head. Her eyes grew wider and wider, terrified, as she saw her wrists cuffed. She hung from a meat hook in the ceiling. She bent her head down and saw her ankles in cuffs as well, linked to a steel ring in the floor. Haddy screamed, but a gag swallowed the noise. Then, she realized she was stripped naked. A small man was bent over a stainless-steel countertop, arranging a set of syringes and vials of medicines. Haddy scarcely noticed the green tile or headless corpse on the autopsy table. She gave no thought to the surgical instruments, but with mounting horror, saw him remove an electric instrument from the wall, turn it on, and listen to it whir. He placed a few drops of oil on the blades. He turned it off and picked up the syringes.

Black, bottomless fear gripped Haddy. Her mind and lungs

and heart, her guts and toes, all stopped, as a fathomless fear crept closer. Suddenly, Haddy remembered Wolf and his drawings. The man who had loved and divined her glory, a glory and light infinitely stronger than fear. Like an alchemist transmuting lead into gold, Wolf saw in her a strength that changed her tears into fierce joy. He had captured her indomitable will to live. Haddy found her courage, and raging like a lioness shouted, "If you touch me, I will shove that machine up your ass and rip it out your throat!"

SHIRA HAD INCHED FORWARD along the left-sided tunnel. It ascended, and she found a side passage, which she explored. She pulled down on the lever at its terminus, heard a click, and saw a shaft of light. Shira pushed it open carefully and stepped into a darkened room of knight's armor. At the door stood two guards under a torch. Shira shot them before they reacted. She backed out and repeated this tactic in a second room stuffed with game animals. Shira kept going, when she saw a flickering light from the third side passage. Stealthily, she entered. A maid and young child screamed. Shira lowered her weapon and put a finger to her lips. "English?" she whispered.

"Who are you?" gasped the maid.

"You first," said Shira. Galina introduced herself, and the child as Ulyana Ivanova.

"We're trying to escape this madhouse," Galina said.

"Where's the blonde teenager?" asked Shira.

"In the dungeon below, in the second cell," replied Galina. Shira relaxed. Haddy was there. "I want you and Ulyana to go down below and join my partner." Shira gave Ulyana a penlight and instructed Galina to bear left at the wood landing.

Ulyana thought this a fun game. She squealed in delight and skipped ahead of Galina, ignoring her fading calls to wait.

Like a mouse in a maze, the five-year-old dashed below with the bright light in hand. She stayed left and entered the small carved-out alcove. Ulyana saw the opened panel and pinched her nose against the stench. She passed inside, and because of her size, went beneath the table, head, and candle. Ulyana saw a flashlight lying on its side near the door. It illuminated a green belt with two pineapples, an ax, a knife, and a black toy gun. The child ran into the hall and stopped. In the next room, a woman hung from a hook. She twisted and writhed back and forth like a big marlin fish Ulyana had seen on TV. A man with wispy gray hair held a syringe with a long needle. He had steadied the woman's arm and was preparing to inject it. Galvanized, Ulyana ran back and grabbed the toy gun. She raised the plastic pistol at the man, aimed, and pulled the trigger. Two tiny prongs flew out like angry hornets and stuck in his neck. He collapsed to the floor in a Saint Vitus's dance of violent paroxysms and contortions. Galina ran into the room, took one look, and lifted the woman off the hook. She released the cuffs, grabbed the rucksack, and helped the woman revive.

Haddy guzzled water and scarfed down an energy bar. She got her clothes on and said a silent "thank you" to heaven and checked the time: fifteen thirty-eight, twenty-two minutes left. Haddy stood up shakily, pushed her shoulders back, cracked her neck, and said to herself, "Dammit, I'm still alive. Weak but alive. Let's kick ass." She told the woman who identified herself as Galina to bind the man. Turning to the child, she kissed her and said, "You have a protector for the rest of your life. Thanks." Haddy ran to the steel door that guarded the dungeons and wondered if Raisa was being tortured. "Israel is first," she reminded herself, but said, "Raisa, I'll give you five minutes."

Haddy started her timer and stared at the iris scanner. "Galina, distract Ulyana, please. I'm going to have to do something disgusting to get us through this door." When Haddy saw

Ulyana could no longer see what was about to happen, she went to work. She pushed the headless corpse off the autopsy table and hefted the man onboard. Haddy had never enucleated an eye but heard tales from the Sayeret Matkal. She lashed him to the table and injected his body with the medicines prepared for her. *Ninety seconds.* Though dumb with drugs, his eyes opened in crazy fear. He tried to shake his head, but the head strap didn't budge. Haddy reached for the scalpel and his exertions doubled, becoming maniacal. She noticed "midazolam" on the shelf and remembered anesthesiologists used it before surgery. Haddy injected a vial of the medicine into the man's veins and watched his eyes close quietly. *Sixty seconds.* She made two sharp incisions through the upper and lower eyelids of the right eye and peeled them away with the forceps. The eyeball stared at the ceiling like a sightless Ping-Pong ball. Haddy inserted a tremulous fingertip, fueled by amphetamines, between the globe and rim of bone surrounding the orbit. Taking extreme care not to puncture the firm gelatinous globe, she popped it out. *Forty-five seconds.* The eyeball lay on his cheek, tethered by a thick bundle of nerves and vessels. Haddy took the mosquito forceps and put two threads of suture, one high and the other low, around the bundle. She cut between them, and the organ fell into her hand, like a hard-boiled egg yolk. *Sixty seconds.*

Haddy ran to the scanner. She placed the gelatinous orb against it and waited. When the lock didn't open, she tried again with the same result. Desperate, Haddy spit and wiped off the scanners and tried one last time. Four bolts snapped back, and the door swung open. Total time: *Five minutes.*

Raisa lay inside the second cell on a wooden plank, emaciated and shivering. Her hands were tied behind her. She burst into tears as Haddy ran in and cut the ropes. "Get your clothes. We're leaving," said Haddy. Holding Raisa's hand, Haddy led her past the man on the stretcher and through his den. They joined Galina and Ulyana in the small antechamber around a flickering candle.

"Is that horrible creature dead?" asked Raisa.

"Not yet," said Haddy.

"If you don't kill it, I will," announced Raisa.

"Stay here," said Haddy. The anesthetic drug had worn off. The man struggled against the leather ties. As his remaining eye roved back and forth, his chest arched up, nearly breaking his back. He uttered loud garbled cries for help. Haddy placed her pistol against his temple. "You're not worth the bullet," she said, "but you've got an appointment with the Judge. I guarantee you'll get there on time," and fired.

75

Fifteen-forty-nine hours

The thick forest lay under snow and ice as Ivan found his way back to the parking lot from the mountaintop ridge. The big bullet had hit his arm. The force had knocked him to the ground, and he applied a hasty field dressing to staunch the bleeding. His scalp and face were burned from the helicopter explosions and troop carrier's diesel fuel. Ivan caught the muzzle flash from atop the northwest ridge. Spurred on by blinding rage, he got the mortar up and firing. After three rounds, the firing ceased.

Ivan grabbed an automatic weapon and scrambled up the slope, trailed by the cadre of remaining soldiers. On the exposed ridge, a former sergeant motioned to him from the top of a giant slab of stone in the boulder field. He held up the remnants of the Barrett and shredded field jackets. Ivan relaxed. It was done. The staff sergeant and spotter were dead.

Making his way past the smoking cars and burning tires,

Ivan went to his security chief, who stood next to the shattered kitchen door. He commented on Ivan's burns and suggested he go inside and rest. "You've earned it," he said.

"Those two will have backup," said Ivan. "They'll come over the bridge below. Take our remaining men, mortars, and automatic weapons down to the river. I'll send everyone else in the castle out."

Ivan stalked through the kitchen, which lay in disarray as chefs, staff, and prostitutes alike begged him for ways to get to Dombay. He ignored them and went to the atrium. Unlike thirty minutes earlier, when it lay packed with naked party-goers dancing to the salsa music, his flashlight found the great room empty. "I need guards," he seethed and opened the Library door and stumbled over two dead men. "What the hell?" he said aloud. "Did you kill each other in a panic?" He stormed to the Hall of Knights and found other dead and more bodies in the Hunting Hall. Frightened and angry, Ivan climbed up the steps. He found two more in the Dining Room. In the Renaissance Room, a gaggle of models cowered as he walked in. "There should be two guards in here," he said. "Where are they?" A model lifted a bedspread, pointed at the bodies, and described the soldier, who appeared and vanished. Pounding his fist into his palm, Ivan said, "Jaca knows."

Ivan burst into the Control Room and found his sister in her chair, head back, open-eyed, and lifeless. A small hole lay in the center of her forehead. Trembling, he examined the monitors of each room in the Fortress. *There!* In the Baroque Room, filled with drugs and liquor, were two guards dead, plus a soldier lying lifeless on her back. "I'll make sure you're dead in a moment," he said to himself. More dead and many cowering guests were seen throughout the thirty-one-room castle. But what about Galina and Ulyana? Ivan rechecked the tapes. After the generator exploded and the lights went out, he saw Galina break down the bedroom door. With Ulyana in tow, she went downstairs and entered the Library Room. Ivan flipped the monitor back and saw nothing. Child and nurse had entered and disappeared.

Ivan ran down the steps into the Library, which contained ten thousand volumes of rare collector editions catalogued in stacks. With a flashlight in hand, he searched the room until he stood in a rear corner alcove. Ivan flashed the light on the plush rug and saw footprints. He ran his light over the books, pounded on the wall, and sensed a faint echo. Furiously, he tore the volumes off the shelves, starting at the top. Ivan stopped when he saw Tacticus's *Wars* sticking out a bit. He pulled on the book, heard a click, and watched a small panel swivel out. "Fucking tunnels. Should have known," he said. Ivan opened the panel. Pointing the flashlight beam ahead, he crawled into the passage. The light bounced back, and he recognized a main tunnel. Then he heard a faint scuffling and switched off the light.

Haddy had scrambled past the first two passages, hunched over with flashlight and pistol in hand, asking herself, "Where in the hell is Shira?" Her knife and grenade were on her belt, while she placed the throwing ax between the back of her pants and her skin. Haddy moved forward, and bumped her head and scraped her shoulders against the rough-hewn walls. She tried to restrain her coughing, but the dust, mold, and mildew made it difficult. She hurried forward, glancing at her fluorescent dial: eight minutes before rocket launch. Haddy inched forward and came to a third side passage. Like a turtle, she poked her head around cautiously.

A pistol jammed against her cheek. A flashlight beam stung her eyes. "Put down your weapon, Staff Sergeant," said a steely voice. "Slowly, where I can see it. Slide it over here." Haddy did as she was told. The gun scraped along the rock floor. "Drop your belt. Slide it over and come out." Haddy entered the side passage with the SIG Sauer barrel pressed against her forehead. "Come out slowly. No tricks. I know them all." As they backed out into the Library, Ivan continued, "Open your mouth. Swallow the gun."

Haddy stepped into a room faintly lit from two torches on the wall at the door. The Enforcer took out his knife with the other hand, placed the point under her eyelid, and pressed. "I'm Ivan Juric. I killed your father. Your partner is dead, and ..."

The image of Bruce Lee striking so fast his hand couldn't be seen flashed in Haddy's mind. In that instant, she struck faster than any cobra. The fingers of her left hand exploded up into Ivan's eye, while her right forearm knocked the gun from her mouth, snapped the blade aside, and smashed into Ivan's nose. Her knee came up and struck a vicious smash into his testicles. Ivan bent double and Haddy grabbed his shoulder. She ground her forearm into his jaw, grabbed his bicep with her other hand, and kneed him in the face. Blood and vomit poured to the ground. Haddy slipped backwards and broke her fall, lifting her head, but as soon as she landed, Ivan was between her legs like a crazed boar. Haddy felt his hands on her throat. She grabbed them and pulled them towards her waist. Ivan's grip loosened a little, and Haddy put one knee on his sternum, pushed herself backwards, and kicked his face repeatedly. She leaped to her feet and kicked him beneath the chin. As Ivan lay unconscious, she took the ax and split his forehead in two down to the brain, and then chopped off his head.

Haddy rolled off, panting, when a beam of light from the hidden passage flashed on her. A tattooed arm, draped in a green translucent garment, pointed a pistol. An icy voice said, "Jerusalem will burn, but you won't live to see it." Haddy heard the gun cock.

76

Fifteen-fifty-seven hours

Wolf James had staggered out from the ambulance three hours earlier. He directed Yaseen and Roger to care for the professors and jogged along the dirt road through the trees. He climbed over the back gate and ran to the highway. Wolf knew that Army-mobilized emergency response units contained their own communication hubs. He flagged down a military jeep and directed the driver to the closest one. From there, Wolf called Captain Troyem.

"Thank God you're alive, Wolf," said the captain. "No word from Haddy. Their plane went off the radar at twelve seventeen. Everything went off the radar, but they were heading for Mineralnye Vody Airport and on to Dombay, Russia."

"Just get me there," said Wolf.

"Stay where you are," replied the captain. "I'll have a helicopter pick you up and take you to Tamir's jet at Gate Three."

"What's Tamir planning?" asked Wolf.

"A Sayeret Matkal insertion," said the captain.

Wolf found Tamir waiting for him at his Gulfstream. "Get aboard. You're late," he said. Once aloft, the spymaster showed Wolf maps of South Central Russia and the Caucasus Mountains. He discussed an entry point for the Mitzpe Ramon unit. "Trying to insert the Matkal at Mineralnye Vody won't work," he said, exasperated. "Too much radar and risk of attack, but if the unit can skirt the Caucasus Mountains along its northern edge, they could land south of the city of Karachayevsk on the A-155 highway. At this point," Tamir placed his finger on the map, "the road is wide enough for a C-130. There's a stretch of highway right here, straight and over thirteen hundred yards long; plenty for the plane. The unit can then drive to the Fortress in two IDF Hummers. Ten minutes, tops."

"Risky, but a good plan," said Wolf. "What are you and I doing?"

"Get to Mineralnye Vody and provide backup from the plane."

Wolf clenched both fists. "Dammit, I've got to get to that Fortress and help Haddy and Shira."

Tamir and Wolf arrived at Mineralnye Vody Airport, which was awash with snowflakes. It was quiet; no controller stood in the tower. Wolf looked outside the International Trading Partners jet and saw *Eastern Machine Systems, Inc.* stenciled above the hanger doors. A twin-engine jet helicopter sat parked out front, frosty with snow.

Wolf stepped down the jet stairway and crossed to the helicopter. He entered the hangar. In the corner was an office, and inside, Brianna Ivanova wept loudly. "Brianna?" said Wolf.

"Wolf!" Brianna ran into his arms and exclaimed, "Karpov took off. I've got to find Ulyana."

"Wait here." Wolf ran back to the Mossad jet. He and Tamir returned to the helicopter with assault rifles, grenades, and ammo. With Tamir and Brianna aboard, Wolf fired up the helicopter engines. In seconds, he steered the helicopter along the A-155, following the Teberda river.

Tamir said, "The Matkal have landed. The C-130 left." Wolf piloted the helicopter over the bridge. The Sayeret had mounted a full-scale attack on armed guards sent by Ivan. Tamir got off the phone. "They're breaking through and will be at the Fortress in two minutes."

Wolf roared past, and in seconds, the threesome saw the ancient castle surrounded by destruction. Two helicopters and numerous cars, limousines, and trucks burned while rubber tires smoked. Where once two electric generators stood, only a smoking pit remained. The north wall of the castle was stained black. Wolf estimated over a hundred dead. Guards and guests were scattered over the parking lot with men trapped inside the vehicles. Not a soul moved.

"Good God," said Brianna.

"For such a time as this," said Tamir, "let's hope our warriors made it."

Wolf set the craft down where the road adjoined the parking lot. "It'll be ugly, Brianna. You sure?" he said.

"Ulyana's in there. Give me a rifle," replied Brianna.

Tamir, Wolf, and Brianna picked their way past burned bodies and burning cars. Tamir approached the kitchen door, while Wolf and Brianna peeked inside the front. The large Atrium Room lay bathed in quiet. Wolf palmed his M17 sidearm and heard voices from the kitchen area, accompanied by delightful culinary smells. Suddenly, a commotion was heard as Tamir entered. Shouts of joy and relief echoed along the corridors. Wolf had walked into the Hall of Knights and Hunting Hall and saw the dead guards, and recognized Haddy and Shira's work.

Brianna tapped Wolf on the shoulder and whispered, "I heard a commotion from the Library," she said. The door lay ajar, and two torches cast a flickering light among the stacks.

Wolf moved to the rear on the plush carpet. He heard a voice around an alcove just feet away, "But you won't live to see it," and a hammer cock. Wolf leaped forward like a goalie preventing the winning soccer kick. He twisted sideways and took in the scene. A gun-wielding hand protruded from a small passageway from the bookshelf. The pistol pointed at Haddy, lying on her back on the floor. Wolf fired. A voice screamed and the pistol dropped.

Haddy's head fell back next to a severed head. In her hand lay the Norse throwing ax.

Brianna joined the duo. Haddy looked from Brianna to Wolf and said, "What took you so fucking long ... pussy man?" but didn't wait for an answer. Addressing Brianna, she said, "You are a fucking warrior. Take a flashlight. Go into the tunnel and take a left. When it forks, stay to the left towards the shit smell. You'll find Ulyana with Raisa." Wolf and Haddy watched Brianna scurry into the passage on hands and knees.

"We have only a few minutes," said Wolf.

Haddy looked at her watch. "*Three*, to be exact. Let's go."

The soldiers entered the tunnel on hands and knees. Suddenly, they heard in the distance an echo. A small shrill girl cry of delight,

"Mama! They told me you were dead!"

Followed by a loud enthusiastic "Baby! I'm here. Mama's here."

77

The Palace Room
Sixteen-hundred hours

Fusako had hastened back up the tunnel, holding her wounded hand. She stepped into her room through a similar secret passageway. She and X had discovered the tunnels, just like Ivan Juric, when they reviewed the monitors from the Palace Room. Fusako wound a tight gauze wrap around her bleeding hand and grabbed a roll of duct tape. She opened her drawer, removed her own dermatome, and strode into the Palace. Smert sensed something amiss, growled, and came to attention. Fusako kicked the beast unconscious. She hit Daroghah with a blow to the temple. As he regained consciousness, X found his arms and feet lashed to the chair. "Traitor!" he shouted.

"I want username and passcode," said Fusako calmly. "To your EMS account, before the Israelis find it. I also need the name of the man who can find the Ming dynasty music box."

X's face contorted into a mask of derision. Trying to spit on Fusako, he shouted, "Fuck you!"

Fusako removed a knitting needle from her hair and slid the steel point under the fingernail of his index finger. X let loose a bloodcurdling scream. Fusako shoved it to the bone, waited a moment, and then scraped it back and forth. The yakuza assassin remained coldly passive as X's screams rose higher. She pulled it out and started on his middle finger. All blood drained from X's face. He became stark white, vomited, shit, and peed. "We haven't much time," Fusako said, and opened the computer and repeated, "The passcodes." The whites of X's eyes turned red as tiny arteries burst inside. His head fell over.

"No," he muttered. Unperturbed, Fusako left the needle in place and removed a second. Holding his big toe, she shoved it in.

"The codes," Fusako repeated. X stopped breathing, and she splashed water on his face. Fusako flicked open her stiletto. "Next, your eyes." X lay gasping for breath, panting, delirious in pain, as Fusako held his head and placed the knife a hair's breadth from his cornea. "Username."

"AuschBirk nineteen forty."

"Password?"

"Eighty-eight FlashingSwordDeut three two four one"

"Name."

"No, I can't." Fusako yanked Daroghah's head back and held his eye open. The blade sliced.

X gurgled a deep-throated cry. "The virus ... by Changchang Liu Yang. The man ... Lawrence Brock." X's head fell on his chest as Fusako turned on the dermatome. She had never endured such humiliation from this filthy beast and knew X would have fed her to Trang. Fusako opened X's shirt. The black, red, and gold skull gaped at her. In neat 2-inch rows, she mowed off five 10-inch strips. Fusako rolled them up like sushi and dropped them in a plastic bag with iced saline. Next, she placed the handheld firing button in X's hand. The global map of the world with red lights marking the location of nine X3 missiles burned brightly. "The missiles arm in sixty seconds, thanks to Kharitov removing Danilenko and LeCompte's booby traps. If you are alive," she said, "launch your rockets and watch Jerusalem burn."

Fusako donned a tailored wingsuit. Once inside, she resembled a flying squirrel. She sprinted out the French doors and leaped over the garden ramparts. Fusako spread her wings and sailed to the A-155 highway.

X's eyes rolled back as his tongue hung out. His chest bled freely into a pool that dripped on his lap and the floor. His breath became agonal, something reserved for the comatose elderly in their last remaining moments of life. He made a series of tiny, short breaths, followed by a long pause and then a heave. Though delirious, X gathered his remaining strength. He pressed the button down to make sure he could and prayed one last prayer. "Oh Kali, great goddess of death, grant me strength to unleash your terrible chaos on this filthy city."

In the distance of his mind, X heard a grenade explode, followed by the touch of a hand on his chin. He opened his eyes to see Staff Sergeant Haddy Abrams. He couldn't smile but tried. "Too late," he said, and out of the corner of his eye saw the plasma screen and its large, red digital clock beating out the seconds, "1559:57," "1559:58," "1559:59." X felt the barrel of a suppressed semiautomatic on his forehead and heard the final cough.

EPILOGUE

Wolf and Haddy lay against each other under the black satin sheets. Eight days had passed since Daroghah Vulkan's demise. Chief Sergeant Yosef Adelman found Shira in the Baroque Room, hanging on by a thread. Tamir, Haddy and Wolf, Raisa, Brianna and Ulyana, and the Mitzpe Ramon Sayeret got into the Hummers. They drove aboard the C-130 and roared aloft. Shira underwent emergency surgery in Odessa and remained in critical condition.

Wolf straddled Haddy's back and massaged her neck and shoulders. "You can't keep your hands off me, can you?" she said. "Watch the ribs, pussy man. Apart from visiting Shira, I'm supposed to rest. With you, that's impossible." Everything ached, and Haddy got up slowly. She had slept, smoked, and sipped on tequila, and let Wolf hold her. "You like the new ring?" she asked.

Wolf had sold the solitaire and purchased a gold band. "I love it; definitely more practical. Don't get up. You need more massage," said Wolf with a twinkle in his eye.

"I'm deliciously sore. I need a break from you."

"I'll go to the market. We're out of coffee, cigarettes, and liquor. Later, we can check on Shira."

"And Sasha is out of the ICU."

"And David wants us back in Southampton."

"You talked with him?"

Wolf laughed. "I think he likes me. At least I'm not ugly."

"It was nice to get a call from the prime minister."

"He wants you in the officer corps, bad."

"I told him about Fusako and the Ming music box. He and Tamir are on it." Wolf gave Haddy's rump a squeeze and left.

Haddy made coffee and lit a Lucky Strike. The Black Sea lay calm in the distance. She opened a window, refreshed herself in the cool breezes, and returned to the kitchen table. A nagging inside to set the record straight settled on her. Looking above, she said, "I am *a pain in the ass*, but after all this, proud to be *your pain in the ass*." Haddy became still. "On that day back in the Ben Shemen Forest, I said, 'What do *you* want?' and you asked me, 'What do *you* want?' I wanted to know why you killed my father on the day of my birth, and you told me to '*leap.*' After reading my father's letter, you didn't murder him. Tamir warned him, but he went ahead. He made his choice. I blamed you for everything, even my rape, but Sasha had warned me. I 'knew best' and went to that party. Vicious dogs attacked me. I don't think you were happy with my stubbornness, but you were furious with those jackals. All but one has paid dearly, and *I will find the fourth man*, if it's the last thing I do. Wolf will help me. I've got money. We'll get married, and raise the kids Jewish." Haddy continued to plumb her depths and saw the storms on the Tyrrhenian Sea. She laughed ironically. "I can still feel Xuthus's throat in my hand and hear the throwing ax strike Niki's skull. I was so bitter, sitting handcuffed before Chagall's *White Crucifixion*, convinced you were my enemy. Then you gave me Wolf." Haddy wanted to leave her deep meditations, but the nagging continued. Something was there. An answer, which lay on the edge, a mist in her mind ready to vanish. It came in a flash. "I think I've had this wrong all along," she said. "I could have died fifteen times, but you saved me a thousand. My dad's death on the day of my birth? It tied me to the Ukrainian Eichmann. I was the Stinger you fired, with one homing beacon: Daroghah Vulkan and Ivan Juric. It took twenty-seven years, but with your help, I brought it home. We saved Israel. I'm thankful for my namesake, Hadassah, and I confess with all my heart, *'Hear O Israel: the LORD our God, the LORD is one.'*"

ACKNOWLEDGMENTS

I wish to acknowledge Karin Cather of Karin Cather Editorial Services, who helped bring Blood Sapphire's Revenge to its present form. While at first her suggestions struck me as severe, her editorial skill trimmed away the excess and made for a fine manuscript. Karin divined and brilliantly brought to life Haddy Abrams's ferocious, steely-eyed determination to overcome her demons and rescue her country. Supported by her direction, the manuscript took shape and came alive. Thank you, Karin.

I also wish to acknowledge and thank Antonia Maguire, Melissa from The Writer's Ally, and Kimberly Gilmore for their gifted editorial work.

I have had many friends, family, and professional colleagues support me as I wrote this book. To name a few: Martha Blake, MBA, NCPSYA, Jungian analyst. Dipl. Analytical Psychology, Zurich.

My children, John, Amanda, and James, who stood by their father over the years and with bemused expressions encouraged, and wondered, about his efforts to write Blood Sapphire's Revenge. In the end, their faithful love helped bring this book to life.

Additional thanks to my son, John Farmer for help with promotions and publicity. Thanks also to audio engineer and voice talent extraordinaire Josh Millman, for both voice coaching and technical production of the audiobook. Special thanks also to photographer Sheldon Sabbatini for capturing both a resonant "Haddy" for the cover and excellent work on the author portrait. Finally, special thanks to Tom Briggs and the publishing team at epigraph for assistance with the cover artwork, final manuscript review, and overall stewardship of the last-mile publishing process.

ABOUT THE AUTHOR

Dr. Bruce Farmer

A far-ranging and adventurous life has taken Dr. Bruce Farmer to multiple countries and across multiple careers. From practicing emergency room medicine to teaching Science and Theology at a small liberal arts college, Dr. Farmer's diverse and far-ranging life inspires his writing.

A father and grandfather, Bruce has three children and five grandchildren. A lifelong hiker, mountaineer and skier, Bruce appreciates the character that the outdoors can uncover. Dr. Farmer has summited numerous mountains throughout the Cascades Range in both Oregon and Washington. He lives in Portland, Oregon. *Blood Sapphire's Revenge* is his first novel.

Also Available on Audiobook.

BLOODSAPPHIRESREVENGE.COM

- Interviews

- News & Announcements

- Special Offers

- Bonus Material

- Alternate Artwork

Printed in Great Britain
by Amazon